Century in Scarlet

Lajos Zilahy

with a new introduction by
HUGH MACPHERSON

PRION

Published in 2001 in Great Britain by
Prion Books Limited
Imperial Works, Perren Street,
London NW5 3ED
www.prionbooks.com

First published in 1965

British Library Cataloguing in Publication Data
A catalogue record for this book is available from the
British Library

ISBN 1-85375-387-4

Cover design by Bob Eames
Cover image courtesy of AKG London

Printed and bound in Great Britain
by Creative Print & Design, Wales

'Government is the conspiracy of the Few against the Many.'

François Noël Babeuf
Guillotined in 1797

To the memory of
my great uncle PETER

whose name appears on the endpaper of my grandmother's Bible: *cous. Peter 19, ct II NH reg died at S-vár
while fleeing*

The bare words 'while fleeing' deprive my great uncle of
the slightest suggestion of heroism. The abbreviation *ct*
means cornet, the lowest commissioned cavalry officer, and
II NH reg stands for the Second National Hussar Regiment.
The stingy word cous. for cousin leaves Peter's surname in
darkness. In our very large clan he could have been a member
of many families; and if he was a second or third cousin, the
possibilities multiply in geometrical ratio, spreading the
shame of his cowardly death to almost the whole Hungarian
nation. As a nineteen-year-old pennant-carrier cornet, instead
of carrying the regiment's flag to victory, my great uncle
desperately tried to save his and his horse's lives when the
bald hills of Segesvár suddenly donned a dark forest of
spears and the Cossack cavalry, pouring in torrents down the
hillsides in three directions to the plain, dealt the death blow
to the last cohorts of the Hungarian War for Liberty in the
year 1849, on that hot day of July 31, around three o'clock in
the afternoon.

Contents

INTRODUCTION

Century in Scarlet is the first in a trilogy of books about an aristocratic Hungarian family, and is one of Zilahy's best achievements. The three books follow the Dukays from 1814 until the Second World War and, through the story of the family's fortunes, tell of the decline of the aristocracy and the way their fate was intertwined with Hungarian and European history.

This first book sets out the dramatic events of the 19th century through to the declaration of the First World War — the event which, in Zilahy's eyes, truly brought the regimes and way of life of the previous century to a close. In Zilahy's account, history is told through the stories of twin brothers — Antal and Dali — whose separate educations reflect the Austrian and the Hungarian aspects of the Empire they have been born into. The year of their birth, 1814, is also that of the Congress of Vienna, designed to restore order in Europe after the Napoleonic wars. In this story the statesman Metternich speaks at their christening and presents the opening of the Congress in that October as the real beginning of the century. Thus, Zilahy regards the declaration of war (by Germany on Russia) on 1 August 1914 as an end that comes '60 days, 9 hours and 23 minutes' short of the due passage of the century.

Zilahy sees history as sometimes deeply influenced by the characters of those who live it, and at other moments as utterly, often tragically, beyond their control. So, at the very end of this book, when the German ambassador delivers the declaration of war to the Minister of Foreign Affairs of Imperial Russia, the two men are fully alive to the real meaning of the formal messages they carry on behalf of their countries, and there is an emotional scene before they part (as there was in reality).

Zilahy is strongly interested in the convolutions of history, but what gives his books their true quality is that he is even more fascinated by every aspect of human behaviour and by the detail and texture of the lives we lead. Whether ultimately in control of their fate or not, all his characters share an immense zest for life, and all the colour and scent and taste and physical business of being in the world.

This is Zilahy's strength: that people always interest him, whether he admires or is appalled by them. Because of this, he is never dull. In any situation there is always something vital that catches his eye, something about which he wants to tell us with his usual enthusiasm.

He himself experienced the 20th century with a vengeance. He was born in 1891 in Nagyszalonta in Transylvania, then part of Hungary but incorporated into Romania under the 1920 Treaty of Trianon. He studied law at the University of Budapest, but became a journalist, and editor of a daily newspaper. He served in a regiment of chasseurs in the First World War, and was badly injured on the Russian front. While recovering he published a volume of poems and wrote his first play. He published his first novel in 1922. His plays and novels were internationally successful throughout the inter-war years, with the novel

INTRODUCTION

Two Prisoners (*Két fogoly*) — partly based on his war experiences — being particularly well-received. He became the Secretary General of Hungarian PEN, and was awarded the Hungarian Academy Vojnits Prize on four occasions. He supported social reform, and in 1942 gave much of his money to the nation to establish a new college.

He was opposed to both the Nazis and the Communists. He began the trilogy in 1944 while hiding in a cellar in which he survived the fighting in Budapest. In 1947 his disagreements with the regime led him to leave Hungary with his wife and son. He went to the US, lived in New York, and continued to write. His plays were produced on Broadway and some filmed in Hollywood. He died in 1974.

Because of his exile, the books of the trilogy were first published in English (though a first draft appeared in Hungary in 1947 without his consent). *Century in Scarlet*, though chronologically first in the series, was the last to be written and published. It came out in 1965 (with an edition in Hungarian published in Novi Sad, Yugoslavia: *Bíbor évszázad* in 1969). *The Dukays* (second chronologically) came out in English in 1949 (full edition in Hungarian *Rézmetszet alkonyat* in 1967) and the third volume *The Angry Angel* in 1953 (*A dühödt angyal*, 1968).

HUGH MACPHERSON

Century in Scarlet

PART ONE

THE
BENEVOLENT
DESPOTS
1814–1837

CHAPTER ONE

"MY HAIR!" COMMANDED THE young officer as he sat before the dressing table in the small, vaulted room of the Hotel Fontenoy.

The old hussar, his private servant, jumped for the paraphernalia. He knew all the tricks of barbering the manes and tails of horses, and was no less adroit at cutting, trimming and perfuming his master's foot-long pigtail, ending in a small goat-skin bag, with a five-inch black silk bow above it; and the soft brown locks with the frivolous shape of a wild duck's tail on his master's temples.

The air under the low ceiling was rich in odors; aromatic vapors of Eau de Cologne mingled with the peel of the famous *fromage de Brie*, left on a greasy table, and the distinguished smell of mouse urine from under the bed. But the reigning smell was the fine, strong fragrance of a brand-new saddle on the floor by the wall. The silver plate on the pigskin saddlebag bore the monogram E.D. with a nine-pointed crown, and stood for Count Endre Dukay, Captain in the Pálffy Hussar Regiment in Vienna.

It was the dark, early morning of March 31, 1814. The candle-clock pointed to four. These candle-clocks dated back to the time of Christ. Around the thick tallow candle were rings of equal width in alternate black and white; and each ring represented an hour. The silver backing of the oval mirror was as ragged as curling smoke. It looked as if it had been recently saved from a great fire. The whole of Europe, fired by the torch of the French Revolution, had blazed for a quarter of a century. But now Napoleon's great empire had collapsed, and France itself was invaded by the allied armies. Yesterday evening, as the siege of the outlying fortresses of Paris ended, the allied officers returned to their headquarters at the Hotel Fontenoy in Meaux, on the right bank of the Marne, some twenty miles northeast of Paris.

While the old hussar worked on his barbering masterpiece, Captain Endre could hardly keep his eyes open. He had slept only an hour after the celebration the night before, when regiments of champagne bottles fired their corks, speakers tortured their comrades one after another, and at the end of every toast the officers of the victorious allied armies jumped to their feet, their arms jerking up with the glasses as they shouted in French, English, German and Russian: *"Vive!"* "Long live Czar Alexander!" *"Hoch!"* *"Dazdravstvuyet Tzar Aleksandre!"* Fragments of the revel chased each other in chaotic order in Endre's sleepy memory. He was twenty-three. With a dark, thin mustache, piercing brown eyes under bushy brows, and a slightly saber nose, his face was orientally aristocratic and consciously intelligent, which he was not.

When his barber had finished, Endre sat at the small desk to write a long lettter to his eighteen-year-old wife, the former Jadwiga Radowski, a Polish countess whom he had married four months before. The style of his letter was that of a cavalry officer when he wanted to be amorous, witty and poetic. ". . . and I hope," he wrote among other things, "that the stove in your room no longer smokes. Did Herr Schild repair it? If not, I will cut off his fat pig head with my sword when I return. Vienna is still cold, but here in France . . . ah, *le printemps Français* is already most beautiful. Every thought of mine kisses you the way the velvet zephyrs kissed the freshly opened hyacinths in the French villages I rode through."

Alone in the room, he read this sentence aloud to himself. He liked it. "Whenever I am alone with my thoughts of you, I still

4

see the bashful pride in your eyes when . . . do you remember, dear? . . . you told me of the mysterious little life—hardly more than that of a young silkworm now. My son! Our little son! In six months he will be with us! Yes, he will be a boy. God will answer my daily prayer. He will not allow the most ancient Dukay family to become extinct."

After assuring his "sweetest and dearest dear little Jadi" of his utmost and eternal matrimonial fidelity, he finished his letter with a million kisses.

Endre was not a veteran of any battles. As one of the secretaries of Prince Clemens Metternich, omnipotent state minister of the great Habsburg monarch, he had been sent to Paris to ride in triumphal procession along with other brilliantly uniformed minor diplomats representing England, Belgium, Prussia, Austria-Hungary and, above all, Russia.

At five-thirty Endre was dressed in his full hussar uniform—tight vermilion trousers, richly trimmed cornflower-blue dolman, high shako tied to his left shoulder by a thick golden cord, and lute-shaped sabretache, in which he kept a number of items indispensable for a young cavalry captain travelling in dangerous France: a dozen balls and gunpowder for the oversized pistol hanging on his right hip, an ivory-bound prayer book, crested writing paper, a violet wax stick for seals, mostly for poetic love letters to petty *mon amour*-s, and a small bottle containing a less poetic specific against gonorrhea.

As he walked in his bright uniform toward the breakfast room, he resembled something between a figure in a gothic stained-glass window and a male bird of paradise. His dignified steps were accompanied by the soft music of his silver spurs and the complaining creak of his citrine boots.

After the Napoleonic wars, coffee and sugar were scarce in France. Breakfast at the Hotel Fontenoy consisted of herb tea, black bread and, as a special luxury, a chestnut-sized stock of brown sugar hanging at the end of a long string above each table. While drinking his tea, each guest had the right to hold the sugar in his mouth for a few seconds, then pass it on to his neighbor.

After breakfast, in the company of other officers, Endre rode toward Paris at a gentle trot. They saw several dead soldiers and horses still lying in the fields, the price of yesterday's engagements. In the distance the guilded crosses of Notre Dame caught the first arrows of the morning sun and threw them back to the pale olive sky with shafts of gold. The St. Etienne Cathedral in Meaux dwarfed to finger size behind them. Paris was hardly more than an hour away.

They arrived in Paris around nine, and joined the procession which started at ten. The crowds in the streets roared, *"Vive Alexandre! Vive le czar!"*

Czar Alexander's black Don stallion seemed to swim high above the ecstatic crowd in the waves of uniforms, flying flowers, and thunderous ovation.

It was de la Tour du Pin, one of Talleyrand's secretaries, who called the Napoleonic wars, not without justice, the Third World War. The first occurred in the fourth century B.C., when another Alexander (the Great) conquered the then-known world. The second was fought nearly a millenium later, when Attila, king of the Huns, lost the bloodiest battle of history on the wide Catalonian plain. Here the united Western armies beat the hordes of barbaric tribes from Asia.

And now, after the "third" world war, March 31, 1814, Russia appeared on the European stage for the first time in history as a great power, and, as she claimed, as the single absolute victor. The thirty-six-year-old Czar Alexander Pavlovitch Romanoff rode his stallion into Paris as the liberator of Europe. He was feted almost as a god by the French people, who knew him as a disciple of Rousseau, a great defender of human rights. His tall, ice-gray Astrakhan headpiece, ending in two sturdy horns fashioned from lambs' feet, gave him a diabolical appearance. These horns were ancient symbols of the whole of limitless Asia, worn by the mighty Khans, chieftains of nomadic tribes. Aside from the headpiece, the czar's uniform was in French fashion. The stiff collar on his pea-green redingote stood up more than half a foot and was richly embroidered in silver. Wound around his bull neck was a four-yard cravat of light, foamy silk held together by an egg-sized tiepin with a symbol etched upon it: an angry bison bull with lowered head caught in the moment of attack. The buttons of his butter-yellow moiré waistcoat were masterpieces from the hands of Turkestan

6

goldsmiths—all but the bottom button, which was a miniature Swiss watch, a birthday gift from his one-time Swiss tutor, General la Harpe, the great educator.

The czar's classic Brutus haircut had only recently snatched the heavy and airless powdered wigs from gentlemen's heads.

"*Vive Alexandre!*" screamed a girl in Montmartre, her black blouse, reviving the vogue in the days of the Directoire, revealing a meager white breast.

"*Vive Alexandre! Vive!*" shouted Anne Boutot Mars, waving her sky-blue parasol; and those in the crowd who recognized her, shouted: "*Vive Anne!*" She was the leading actress of the Comedie Française, Andromaque in Racine's play and Celimene in Moliere's; she was the walking *Carte de Tendre*, as her colleagues dubbed her, the map of the Empire of Love, representing all the love-stricken females in Paris. Princess Maligny, about fifty now but still beautiful, represented the exaggerated pomp of the great baroque from the Sun King's Versailles. She had escaped the guillotine in Robespierre's days because, wearing a dirty apron and ragged slippers, she was mistaken for her maid. All the city's pastry cooks attended the procession, along with all the candle makers and tailors, all the official rat exterminators, exhibiting on their flags a suckling-sized black rat among the white Bourbon lilies; former nabobs in rags stood alongside the former pickpockets in rich attire. Everyone of importance attended: Barras, Carnot and Abbé Gregoire from the old Guard of the Revolution, the urbane Prince Talleyrand, representing the Bourbons, and Jacques-Louis David, the master painter of "Napoleon's Coronation as Emperor in Milan with Charlemagne's Iron Crown"; on every street corner revolution and royalty embraced each other.

"I am very much afraid," Endre Dukay wrote to his wife, reporting the details of the great festive day, "Uncle Clemi will have a stroke when he learns that Monsieur Windbag has been in a great hurry to enter Paris and harvest alone all the acclaim of the allied victory."

Uncle Clemi was Prince Clemens Metternich, and Monsieur Windbag was Czar Alexander's code name in Vienna. And indeed, two weeks after Endre wrote this letter, Emperor Francis

I of Austria, accompanied by Metternich, and England's Lord Castlereagh, representing George III, arrived in Paris to find themselves faced with a *fait accompli* on the most important issues.

That month in Paris, in the first flush of victory, everyone was at everyone's throat. Some monarchs seemed to regard a whole country as a chair too small to sit on. And among these chairs was divided Poland, not large enough for the big bottoms of the Habsburg monarchy, Prussia or Russia.

2

After considerable debate and numerous postponements, the diplomats in Paris finally decided to hold a congress in Vienna, a congress of heads of nations, states and principalities, however small, accompanied by their chancellors, marshals, and military and economic experts. The Congress of Vienna was to deal with the just and peaceful reconstruction of Europe, in ruins after the Napoleonic wars.

On the morning of September 3, 1814, in the huge courtyard of the czar's Winter Palace in St. Petersburg, Prince Igor Effremovich Opatkin, marshal of the journey, lifted his silver trumpet and signaled the departure for the long trip to Vienna. At the sound of Prince Igor's silver trumpet, the procession began to move, pouring out through the palace's magnificent iron grille gates. Leading and following the string of carriages rode a contingent of Don Cossacks, dancing their mounts to the brisk rhythm of a military band. The flanks of their bays shone like chestnuts just drawn from the pod. Watchers in the crowd that had gathered waved handkerchiefs and had genuine tears in their eyes. Only two years before, Napoleon had slept in the Kremlin, and Moscow, in self-sacrifice, had become a sea of flames. Now Russia set out to Vienna to dictate the terms of the everlasting world peace.

Miles and miles of smooth roads led into Finland; on several occasions Prince Igor commanded a gallop, and the entire procession seemed to be flying.

On the second day of the journey the royal couple were served under the spreading branches of a large oak, a little apart from where the ducks, geese, turkeys, lambs and badgers were turning on spits. Farther off at the edge of a field, several members of the czar's entourage discovered an object of unusual interest.

"It's well worth seeing, Your Majesty," reported Prince Adam Czartoryski, the "reconciled Pole," the czar's former foreign minister and close friend.

Alexander approached the ring of spectators. Beyond them the skeleton of a horse lay in the high grass. Its bare ribs already bleached, it was getting a final polish from millions of ants—an undulating black veil on the naked bones. Near the horse lay the skeleton of a man. The ants, streaming from the eye-sockets, resembled a shower of black tears. If the soldier had died possessed of a musket or a pistol, it had been removed—not by foxes or ravens, but by members of the Polish underground. The dead soldier was one of the less fortunate of Napoleon's 600,000 who, two years before, had slogged dejectedly through the cruel Russian winter.

On the twenty-fourth of September, Vienna's swine pasture at the northern edge of the city, cleared of the animals, blossomed in gay garb and gilded coaches, flags and flowers. The entire aristocracy and all the outstanding citizens were there, awaiting the arrival of the czar and his entourage. The forty-six-year-old Emperor Francis was a tall, slender man, his long and narrow Habsburg face resembling that of a noble Afghan hound. On his white coat he now wore only the Great Star of the Russian Black Eagle. The 200 members of the military band tuned and retuned, the deeper instruments grunting like the swine that had been driven away. When the procession arrived, the Russian anthem sounded forth. *Bozhe Czaria Chrany!* But as the Viennese band played it, it sounded like Austria's *Gott erhalte unsern Kaiser!*

Emperor Francis hurried up to Czar Alexander with open arms. After a passionate embrace, they kissed on both cheeks. They hated each other. Alexander had never forgiven Francis for having so panicked as to give his daughter Maria Louise to Napoleon, nor had Francis forgiven Alexander for what he had done in Paris last March, when he alone had issued, in the name of the allies, the manifesto: ". . . the allied sovereigns therefore proclaim . . . they will recognize and uphold the constitution

9

which the French nation decides upon." The French nation, indeed! *That* revolutionary mob!

Endre Dukay and Countess Jadi were among those present at the great reception. Jadi rode in a sedan chair, for her physician, Dr. Samuel Kunz, had forbidden her to ride in a coach over Vienna's bumpy granite cobblestones. The padded sedan chair, tenderly carried by four lackeys, was a much less dangerous conveyance for a woman nearly at term. Jadi was seated in the chair near Frau Obergelderkämpfer, the monarchy's ranking midwife. In front of the sedan chair, Endre rode a yellow mare, to make way in the dense crowd. On the right side of the chair, Doctor Kunz, on horseback too, was at hand in case of a confinement.

There were tears in Jadi's greenish-gray eyes when she fell on the neck of her sister, Olga, who came with the czar's entourage. Twenty-year-old red-haired Olga was the wife of Prince Leon Serebraniy, captain of the guards in the Winter Palace. She had accompanied her husband to Vienna so that she could be with Jadi when Jadi gave birth to her first child. Jadi's mother, the former Princess Vyola Voronieczki, had died nine years before. Olga and Jadi were "reconciled" Poles, faithful and happy wives of the pro-Romanoff Prince Serebraniy and the pro-Habsburg Count Dukay. They never talked politics. In the library of the sisters' home in Poland, there was a book called "The Bible of Targovic," which was written by the poet Niemcevic, an aide of Kosciusco's. One line from the volume summarized the girls' attitude: "The deeper the wound in the heart, the fewer the words to tell it."

The sisters' father, the widowed Count Maurycy Radowski, had arrived from Warsaw two days before in the company of his brother-in-law, Prince Stanislaus Voronieczki and other Polish noblemen. In Poland's third partition in 1795, Russia had received nearly twice the combined shares of Austria and Prussia. What would Czar Alexander, drunk with Russia's surging prestige, demand now? How would the Congress of Vienna affect Poland? Olga, Jadi and Prince Stanislaus were very hopeful, because Czartoryski had confided to Papa Maurycy that Lord Castlereagh's instructions from the Parliament were to insist on Poland's independence.

When the czar arrived, there were only six days until October first, the opening of the congress; and as the days passed, Endre, one of the little wheels in Metternich's huge machinery organizing the receptions and quartering of the dignitaries arriving from every corner of Europe, was so busy that he found it difficult to be attentive to his "sweetest and dearest dear little Jadi."

One morning Frau Obergelderkämpfer had very bad news for Endre.

"I am extremely sorry," she said, "to report to Your Excellency that the child will be a girl."

"Are you sure, Madame?" Endre asked mournfully.

"There can be no doubt. For three days I have mixed seven drops of Her Excellency's urine in the drinking water of Pookie, my male dachshund. Each time he has refused to drink it."

Countess Jadi's greatest concern was not the sex of her child. Far more frightening questions crowded her mind: Will he have a club foot like Lord Byron? Will he be feebleminded like Crown Prince Ferdinand? Or if she's a girl, will she be a nymphomaniac like Baroness Toinette, who from the age of thirteen had love affairs with stableboys, butlers and old princes? Or will she inherit the Voronieczki vein? Jadi's mother had been most saintly—a devout Catholic, a devoted wife and mother, a generous hostess, a skillful equestrienne, and the gracious lady of her house.

On the morning of October first, Frau Obergelderkämpfer sat on the low midwife stool at the side of Countess Jadi's bed, and slid her large hands beneath the blankets. She began to massage the young mother's abdomen with a gentle but firm movement as if she were kneading "a kind of heavenly bread." Two women stood behind her: her assistant, holding a large tray upon which were a pile of soft cloths, several bottles and ointment jars, a cord and a pair of scissors. Next to the assistant midwife stood Princess Olga, her eyes filled with tears of sympathy for her very dear young sister's sufferings. The two women stood silent and immobile, watching Frau Obergelderkämpfer's every move with tense, anxious faces. Olga had been pregnant three times, but each time she had lost the baby. And the last time her doctor had confirmed her worst fears: she would never bear a child. She envied her sister for this greatest moment in human life. Frau Obergelderkämpfer slowly drew her left hand from under the blankets. When she saw her fingers and palm wet with blood, glistening in the candlelight, she stood up and threw off the blankets, exhibiting the naked abdomen of the young mother. Countess Jadi gave a sharp cry, which made Olga drop on her knees at the bedside in mute prayer. A few moments later Countess Jadi's features twisted with anguish, and then the baby's squalls filled the room. Frau Obergelderkämpfer looked at the red, wrinkled baby as if someone had insulted her. In spite of her prediction, the baby was a boy.

"A boy! A boy! A boy!" echoed the corridors and stairways down to the kitchen and to the stables, and through open windows to the neighboring palaces. "A boy! A boy!" Endre Dukay was already fully dressed, but he had to wait a few moments at the bedroom door until the blankets were put back on his wife. When the door opened, he first dashed to the bed, bent over Countess Jadi, and kissed her forehead, which was wet with cold sweat. Then he stepped to the fireplace, where the midwife held the baby for the warm bath. Endre just touched the baby's forehead with a trembling hand, and dashed out of the room, flying down the staircase four steps at a time. At the palace gate a groom held the rein of his riding horse, and Endre jumped into the saddle and galloped away toward the chancellery.

Outside the bedroom, Princess Olga grabbed a dusty bottle of Tokaj wine from the hand of the butler. The assistant midwife poured the golden wine into the steaming warm water before the baby was put into the bath. It was the tradition to pour a bottle of wine into the first bath of a newborn boy. If the baby had been a girl, a bottle of Eau de Cologne would have been correct.

At that moment Countess Jadi gave another sharp cry. The blankets were thrown off again, and she gave birth to a second boy. The maid dashed out to the corridor and shouted down to the servants:

"Hot water! Quick! And another bottle of wine! Yes! Twins!"

The second baby was bathed, too, and laid on the cloth-covered table next to his elder brother. Princess Olga bent down over Jadi and tenderly cut a six-inch length from the blue ribbon on her blond hair. Countess Jadi looked so worn out that only her light blond hair, flung in a rumpled mass about her head, and the sky-blue ribbon in it seemed still alive.

"Which one is the firstborn?" Olga asked Frau Obergelderkämpfer who, with her back to Olga, was washing her hands. The number one midwife of Vienna did not answer immediately. When she spoke, she sounded doubtful.

"The right one. Next to the fireplace."

Both tiny red babies were squalling energetically, as if competing with one another. Olga tied the blue ribbon to the right wrist of the baby next to the fireplace, marking him as the firstborn and the legal heir to the huge Dukay estate.

It was obvious that the twins would not be identical, for the light fuzz on one's head was a pale gold, while the other's remained very dark, even after it had dried.

The golden handle of the porcelain clock on the marble mantelpiece showed two minutes after seven.

3

Prince Clemens Metternich entered his office at exactly seven o'clock, as was his custom. Seated at his desk, he studied the schedule. Plainly, with the congress opening, it was to be a crowded day. When he finally looked up at his waiting secretaries to give his orders, he saw that there were only five.

"Where is Endre Dukay?" he asked.

One of the secretaries answered in some embarrassment. "He has not yet arrived."

The chancellor glanced reproachfully at the large rococo clock in the corner of the room, as if the clock were responsible for the delay of his military secretary. The clock pointed to four minutes past seven.

Rising from his desk to pace the room, Metternich dictated detailed instructions to his secretaries. After some ten minutes of this he broke off and, forgetting that he had already asked the question, repeated: "Where is Endre Dukay?"

One of the secretaries quickly disappeared, returned, and reported that the count was still not in the building.

At this very moment Endre, on a yellow mare, was galloping through the narrow streets. Before the chancellery he leaped out of the saddle, threw the reins to a porter, and hurried up the marble stairs with his shako under his arm. He clicked his large spurs and, still breathing heavily, greeted his chief with military precision. Metternich returned the greeting sourly and pointed to the clock. The five secretaries faded from the room as noiselessly and tactfully as the air. They knew the chancellor's feelings about delays. And on such a day as this! Metternich's extended finger still pointed to the clock, when Endre Dukay, his dark mustache making his face seem paler, reported: "I humbly report to Your Serenity that my wife gave birth to a child at seven this morning."

The chancellor's stony face relaxed and Endre seized the moment:

"Try to guess whether it is a boy or a girl."

Metternich, who, for all his severity was a charming man with a fine sense of humor, raised his face to the heavens as if to seek the answer. He appeared to find it:

"A girl."

Endre shook his head mutely and happily.

Metternich, after further meditation, raised his arms:

"I give up."

Then he laughed, and wrote a few sentences of congratulation on his private stationery. Summoning his private secretary, he directed that the note be delivered to Countess Jadwiga Dukay along with a dozen red roses.

"And now I shall go to the Burg," the chancellor announced, glancing at the clock.

The congress was to be opened in the Burg, the seat of the Habsburgs since the seventeenth century.

The baroque allowed the architect to steal from every style—even his own, if he had one. In the centuries when there was no freedom of thought or movement, the baroque architect enjoyed complete freedom to express the greatness of the rising dynasties. Sculptured mythological scenes decorated the façade, Roman columns were built into the walls, supporting nothing but the dying passion of the new caesars for splendor and luxury. The baroque was more lavish, more artificial, more extravagant than anything ancient Rome had ever produced. The Burg of the Habsburgs was pure baroque.

The mirrored hall awaiting the opening of the congress seemed, however luxuriously furnished, too small for the repair of such a big piece of rusty scrap as feudal Europe. The round table in the corner, its dark-green velvet cover hanging down in fat pleats to the marvel of the oriental rugs, was hardly large enough to seat a dozen persons. Above it hung the life-size portrait of Francis I dressed in a scarlet imperial robe. On a gilt table lay his bejeweled sword which never saw a battlefield, and in his right hand he held the scroll of the constitution that he denied the empire's people. Flashing mirrors, colored marbles and gilt and silver enriched the room.

Talleyrand reported to his king that in the last weeks of September ". . . not even the methodical English have done any preparatory work for the Congress, so fateful for not only every nation in Europe, but for the whole of mankind."

Talleyrand was totally mistaken. Austria, Great Britain, Russia and Prussia had already established the Quadruple Alliance. Its secret article was to maintain the settlements of the Congress intact against such unreliable minor powers as France, Spain, Turkey, the innumerable German sovereigns, the Papal States and other little fishes.

At half past seven Rudolf von Eigler, Metternich's personal secretary, in the company of the editor of the *Österreichische Beobachter*, Herr Pilat, who was Metternich's propaganda counsel, appeared in the room to supervise the lackeys who were putting the final touches to the inner sanctum of world politics. Von Eigler ordered four Louis Quinze silk armchairs arranged in a semicircle, so that the representatives of the four Great Powers, Czar Alexander, King Frederick of Prussia, Lord Castlereagh and Metternich should not mix with Suzy the prostitute, as the czar wittily called the Sous-Alles. These were to sit at the table in the corner, headed by the lame sixty-year-old Prince Talleyrand, in Napoleon's opinion the greatest genius and greatest prostitute in world politics. When Count Nesselrode, Foreign Minister of Russia, an elegant man with the hooded eyes and the long, wrinkled neck of a vulture, entered the hall, old Talleyrand jumped to his feet and embraced him so vigorously that the latter was covered from head to foot with the powder of Talleyrand's white silk wig, whose curved locks reached almost to his shoulder.

Metternich, the first to arrive, entered the hall a few minutes before ten o'clock. Then, with Prussian precision, William Frederick III arrived sharply at ten. The German king, a tall man of about forty, wore his dark hair in the same Brutus style the czar affected; he had a dense mustache and wide whiskers reaching to the middle of his bony cheeks; he was dressed in a field marshal's gala uniform.

Two minutes after William Frederick's arrival, Lord Castlereagh appeared, a slender, handsome figure, elegant in his blue tail coat. Castlereagh's monarch, King George III, was unavoidably detained in England by his strait jacket. Like Metternich, Talleyrand, Nesselrode, and King Frederick, Castlereagh was accompanied by his staff of military and civilian advisers.

At half past ten, the fourth armchair was still empty. Finally, a few minutes before eleven, Czar Alexander arrived in the company of Czartoryski and Igor Effremovich Opatkin. The czar's steps were rather uncertain and his face was almost as red as the room's heavy silk drapes. According to Metternich's secret police report, Alexander had been drinking until six o'clock in the morning in the boudoir of Princess Sagan, and only a miracle wrought by his confidential masseur, along with many buckets of ice cold water, enabled him to fill his chair without great harm to his dignity.

Through the wide-open French doors one could see in the next hall the crowd of minor diplomats and observers, among them Monsieur la Harpe, a bewhiskered gray old man, now Alexander's adviser on Swiss affairs. Among the unofficial delegations were the German Catholics and the Jews of Frankfurt, observing in the general interest of their people.

When the gong commanded silence and Metternich started to read his opening speech, Endre Dukay, still unaware of the birth of his second son, was eagerly goosenecking in the crowd to see and hear as much as he could of the great historical moment.

On the eighth day after his birth, Jesus Christ was carried to the synagogue in Jerusalem for the ceremony of circumcision. By 1814 the Christian world had abandoned the ceremony of circumcision, but it kept the Jewish tradition alive by setting the christening eight days after the birth. Therefore on the eighth day of October there was to be a great christening party in the Dukay palace.

After much negotiation it was decided that the first born was to receive the names Antal, Endre, Zsigmond, Demeter, Hypolit, Omello, Paul, Nepomuk. Each of these names commemorated a Dukay ancestor except Nepomuk, which was the fourth name of Prince Clemens Wenzel Lothar Nepomuk Metternich, who was gracious enough to become the godfather of the Dukay heir. The busy chancellor astutely accepted the honor after learning that Her Imperial and Royal Highness, the Archduchess Blanca Augusta Sophia Maria Annunziata, had accepted the role of Antal Nepomuk's godmother. Moreover the chancellor volunteered to bring Czar Alexander to the christening party. This would be a marvelous present for the vanity of Endre, and it would cost Metternich nothing.

The statutes of the feudal estates were unfavorable to second boys or female children in every way. The second boy Dukay twin was to receive a much shorter name: Adalbert Maurycy Árpád; his godfather would be a Hungarian nobleman, Baron Árpád Zeker, of no great estate or high office.

The name Maurycy commemorated the twins' Polish grandfather in Warsaw, and Árpád was the founder of the Magyar nation. The difference between the godparents and the length of the twins' names clearly indicated that the firstborn boy was to represent Austria and the second-born boy the second-rate Hungary in this personal Austro-Hungarian union.

In the week before the christening a regiment of valets were busily cleaning windows and mirrors, scrubbing floors, and polishing doorknobs and silverware. The Dukay kitchen had always been uncontested for the monarchy's blue ribbon. It was especially famous for its pike, which came from the estate's own ponds, where they were fed with live trout for six months before they went to the horse-radish sauce in sour cream. On the smoky wall of the vaulted, spacious Dukay kitchen stood a marble table, installed by Prince George in 1789, with a quotation in Latin from the first Greek cookbook 2000 years earlier, in which Archestratus sang about a slice of roasted meat fresh from the spit, hot, seasoned only with salt, and warned the world against sticky, clammy sauces.

The brush of that master of details Peter Breughel should have painted Monsier Couteaux in the Dukay kitchen, shouting his commands to the *kuktas*, squires, cupbearers, scullions, pages, peasant women plucking pheasants and peacocks, scaling the fish, washing with ashes the bowels of swine for sausages; while the brass mortars steadily rang as if in panic. The Czar of all the Russians does not come for dinner every day in the week. On the walls, as in a strange butcher shop, a deer, an ibex, and a calf hung head down, still dripping blood, and next to them a hairy wild boar cut down the center nonchalantly smoked his curved meerschaum pipe of yellowish-white tusk.

From the dwarf turtles to the pear-shaped eggs of the peewits, to the lights of swine, to the scarlet combs of turkey-cocks, to the slaty eyes of lambs, to the roes of 200-pound Danube sturgeons, to the soft fingers of cow udders, to the paws of bears awaiting the boiling peppered red wine, to the spiced dark-red bull's blood sauce, to the brains of hamsters—every kind of epicurean specialty was succulently prepared for gourmets.

Endre Dukay paced his room, deep in satisfied thought; many princes in Vienna would suffer envy when the products of the Dukay kitchen became known. Perhaps His Majesty the Czar, overeating, would get a stroke or a heart attack at the height of the ceremony. One could hope for nothing better. Not only the Dukay palace but the name of Endre Dukay would shine in the pages of history!

At Metternich's request, the party was to begin at six o'clock in the evening. At half past five the Gisellastrasse was already crowded with luxurious carriages. Endre himself, dressed in gala Hungarian uniform, with a panther skin on his shoulder, greeted the guests. Of course, young Countess Dukay was not at his side, for, like all correctly supervised mothers of the time, she would not get out of bed for another five weeks.

Aristocrats, bishops, generals and delegates to the congress of even higher rank streamed into the palace. Talleyrand and Lord Castlereagh excused themselves with polite notes and huge bouquets of flowers, but Lady Castlereagh, tempted by rumors of sublime entertainment, could not stay away. The Habsburg family was represented by Archduchess Blanca as godmother, who, with her overpowdered face, decorated the salon magnificently. She was the fourth cousin of Emperor Francis, but in several tongues her loudly pronounced title was *Kaiserliche und Königliche Hoheit,* Your Imperial and Royal Highness, *Votre Altesse,* or *Fenséges Asszony.*

The intellectual world was poorly represented. The guests mostly had German, Hungarian, Italian and Polish names and titles of duke, prince, count, marquis, and baron; they were dressed, more or less, in the still reigning French fashion, though a few wore the new, simpler and more masculine English fashions.

Until they were dispersed through the smaller salons, the costumes rubbed elbows—tight-fitting breeches and trousers of satin or elastic fabric, stockinet, buckskin or finely striped cotton, and the most popular buff or yellow nankeen. There were gaiters in bright-colored embroidered silk, piqué or percale waistcoats, dark-blue, pea-green, sunset-pink, thrush-yellow or tobacco-brown masterpieces, with borders of contrasting colors. Striking buttons were very fashionable; one set bore carved scenes from Ovid's *Metamorphoses,* another, the notorious postures of Aretine; still others showed puns and minatures under glass, or scenes from popular new plays. Among the Brutus haircuts appeared many powdered white wigs even above young faces. The festive christening of the twins was undoubtedly the last meeting between the dead eighteenth and the newborn nineteenth centuries. Bicornes and swords emphasized the full dress the men wore for the occasion.

The frilled collars and the cuffs ending in jabots did not have to be clean, so long as the material was expensive. In Vienna the October days were already chilly, and some aristocrats wore three or four dirty shirts and several pairs of silk stockings.

And the ladies! Semitransparent lingerie chemise gowns, belted under the breasts and worn over a sheer slip; the taffeta could be made so thin that on the snow-white skin of Princess Bagration, a large, dark, mysterious spot—her pubic hair—showed faintly through.

A variety of classic styles rustled through the room; a tunic of colored silk or velvet over white sheath gowns; clouds of batiste, lawn, mull, tulle, gauze, moiré, crêpe and cashmere. The very light muslin was rather rare because the contagious "muslin disease" required dozens of those laced and embroidered tiny handkerchiefs. Montaigne, two centuries before, had already called these articles the most stupid of human inventions.

La Garde Chambonnas, a thirty-year-old French count who was present at the congress only as a spectator, came to the christening with the first guests and did not move for a single moment from the side of his old friend, Prince Ozzolini, a treasure chest of dirty information. Chambonnas spoke only French and was not well informed concerning the people of the Habsburg monarchy. He had learned a few days previously that Hungarian was not just German slang, that it was not true the Slovaks ate only the leaves of trees, nor that the Rumanians still walked on all fours. Chambonnas diligently scribbled notes in his red-velvet notebook with a pencil, a bare piece of lead, thin as a toothpick. The pages of his red-velvet notebook were rapidly filling with such information as:

George, about 70. Only prince in Dukay family. Old gash on bald skull not caused by Turkish sword. Chinese vase thrown by wife, Princess Josephine of Hesse, once concubine of Leopold II, father Emperor Francis. When I asked him if he was happy when he learned of the birth of the twins which ended the fear that the ancient Dukay family would become extinct, old George stared at the floor for a long time to find a proper and elaborate answer. Then he said: "Yes."

Frédèric César la Harpe, 60, one-time Swiss tutor of Czar Alexander. Court councilor at the Winter Palace in the rank of Russian lieutenant general. Fine profile.

Edward Norige (Morike?) famous playwright, young, disheveled hair, Klopstock school playboy. On his moiré waistcoat is painted the climactic scene of his play *The Tender Aurora*. Waistcoat huge success, play a flop.

Nathan Loew and *Solomon Rothschild* rich bankers. Jews, but already accepted.

Rudolf Leibingen (or Leiningen?). A relative of the House of Hanover, now on the British throne. Very handsome, about 60. Too bad that his head too small on massive shoulders. Like the sculptor's ridiculous distortion of the figure of Atlas supporting the balcony of the Dukay palace entrance.

Count Sándor Rhédey, black hair, slender, handsome. Married Claudia Dukay, sister of Endre. Lost his left arm at Austerlitz.

Baron Rudolf Dukay-Hedwitz, husband of Endre's sister, Appolonia. Their young son Erich was in line as heir after Endre. Twins were horrible news. According to O., they are dreaming of an accident in which the twins perish.

Count Paul Leznay, a Hungarian Gengis Khan, about 80. There are stories about his cruelty in the treatment of his serfs. Has a small estate on the shore of Lake Velence, near the Dukay estate. Leznay was born a peasant boy coming from the worst barbarian stock. When a young hussar private, Maria Theresa ordered him to Schönbrunn because of rumor he could make love twenty times a night. Empress counted aloud: ". . . fifteen . . . sixteen." Leznay corrected: "Seventeen." "No, only sixteen," Empress insisted. "Let us not argue, Your Majesty, let us start again." Got title of count. (When Ozz. told story, Nesselrode, foreign minister of Russia, said angrily, "You Westerners steal every good thing from us, story happened not to M. Ther. but to Catherine the Great.)

Chambonnas' notebook understandably failed to mention that in the multitude of guests were several pretty ladies in the pay of Baron Franz Hager, chief of the Austrian secret police, or in the pay of the Russian embassy, or both.

But what had delayed the czar?

Metternich had set the christening at six because he thought that in the preceding two hours he would have effortlessly tucked the czar in his pocket on all important issues. Their secret meeting in Metternich's private hideaway needs no explanation. It was the victory of secret diplomacy over the limitless speeches of the congress, which got nowhere.

But that afternoon Metternich was too optimistic about the length of time it would take him. The entire congress already knew that Alexander was interested in nothing but the portion he would get of Poland.

The czar, who the spring before had ridden into Paris as the Liberator of all the Nations, at the second day of the congress had already told Talleyrand in a private audience that "everyone must follow the rule of *expediency!*" And, Talleyrand reported to his king: ". . . then, lifting his hands and waving them about as I have never seen him before, in a manner which reminded me of the concluding passage of Marcus Aurelius' Eulogy, the czar shouted rather than said: 'It is time for the play!' "

With these words Poland's fate was sealed again. Lord Castlereagh's closed, silent face did not give any hope to the "reconciled" Poles that Great Britain would declare war on Russia for Poland's independence.

That afternoon at four a closed carriage arrived at a modest house in Hymengasse, a dead-end street. It was deserted, except for the invisible secret policemen in all the five small houses in the street, standing behind drawn window curtains. On the door Metternich and the Czar entered was an inscribed brass plate: "Doctor Wendell Mayer, Professor of World Diplomacy's History." Metternich sometimes spent whole nights in Professor Mayer's library, but if his wife, the angelic Eleonora, granddaughter of Maria Theresa's great chancellor, Prince Kaunitz, would have appeared in Professor Mayer's house, two great surprises would have waited her. There was not a single book in the library, nor a Professor Mayer in the house, which was Metternich's secret quarters. The forty-one-year-old state minister met the important agents of a spy network here behind closed doors. They were mostly young and pretty women.

"I shall keep what I have occupied!" the czar shouted at Metternich during their secret meeting, while Endre Dukay's guests awaited them both. It was past six o'clock, but they were still drawing the frontiers of the large portion of Poland that Russia would get, each grabbing the pencil from the other because neither could find his own.

Metternich's butler, acting on his master's orders, diligently kept opening the bottles of *Liebfraumilch*—oh, what a label! —the milk of a love-stricken woman, the queen of greenish-golden Rhine wines, from Metternich's own cellar.

"Rather a war than give up what I have occupied!" repeated the czar for the tenth time. But under the influence of the Charret cognac he had consumed after lunch and now of the milk of a love-stricken woman, his left eyebrow was raised to the middle of his forehead and he could not bring it back to its normal place.

At half past seven, Metternich glanced at the wall clock and stood up.

Ten minutes later, Endre Dukay rushed in from the street and shouted to his guests:

"The carriage of His Majesty the Czar has arrived!"

He dashed back to the street. As the czar alighted, he shook the hand of the Dukays' uniformed porter, taking him for a German king. It is related in the *Staatsarchiv* that during the congress the monarchs distributed a ton and a half of decorations, not only among themselves and to the lesser members of the congress, but to thousands of government clerks, private secretaries, valets and doormen.

When the czar extended his hand toward a lackey, Metternich tactfully touched his elbow and directed the imperial handshake toward Endre Dukay, who, in his gala hussar uniform, stood at attention.

"Count Dukay, our host," he introduced Endre.

The czar offered his white-gloved hand rather to the air than to Endre, and peered at Endre's left ear with a friendly smile. Then his majesty took a cautious step forward, half closing his eyes as if in fear they would start spouting liebfraumilch. In his stomach the queen of rhine wines and the Charret cognac were having an increasingly nasty argument.

When the czar and Metternich entered the Dukay salon, followed by the black-bearded Prince Igor Effremovich, everyone stood up. Most of the ladies turned their faces to the precise angles they thought most effective, then waited in vain for the glazed, searing eyes of the czar to look their way.

It was Metternich who spoke first.

"In view of the late hour, may I postpone the introduction till after the ceremony?"

Host Endre Dukay led the czar to a thronelike brocade armchair.

The twins appeared in the arms of their godmothers; the first-born Antal Nepomuk in the robust Habsburg arms of Archduchess Blanca Annunziata, and the second-born Adalbert

23

Árpád in the thin arms of young Olga Serebraniy; standing three steps behind the archduchess.

The faces of the twins were hardly visible in the frills and laces of their swaddling clothes. The five-pound blond Antal had been a silent baby, while the dark-haired seven-pound Adalbert had wailed day and night from the moment of his birth, warning the world that he would have plenty to say in his lifetime. But now he was sleeping deeply, thanks to the opiate added to his mother's milk in order that he might not wail during the solemn ceremony.

The adjoining yellow salon had been converted into a chapel. There Cardinal Consalvi washed his hands in a golden bowl, donned the surplice and the violet stole.

In the following half hour nobody—not even Chambonnas, a secret disciple of Voltaire, not the Pasha of Vidin, in his sky-blue kaftan, not the two Protestant German princes—was immune to the beauty of the ancient Catholic ritual.

"Quid petis ab Eclesia Dei?" (What dost thou ask of the Church of God?) The old cardinal directed his questions to the sleeping newborn but the answers came from the godparents.

"Fidem!" (Faith!) chanted Metternich, Archduchess Blanca, the deep-voiced Árpád Zeker and Olga Serebraniy in unison.

"Fides, quid tibi praestat?" (What does faith bring thee to?)
"Vitam eternam!" (Eternal life!) chanted the godparents.
"Oremus!" (Let us Pray!)

Cardinal Consalvi knelt. Almost everyone followed, including Nathan Loew the banker. Only Solomon Rothschild, the *Moslem* Pasha of Vidin, and the two Protestant German princes did not kneel. The others repeated fluently and in chorus the long Latin intonations.

Then the old cardinal stood up and poured water from an ewer on the head of Antal Nepomuk.

"Deus omnipotens. . . . Pax tibi . . . et cum spiritu tuo. Amen."

When his turn came, Adalbert Árpád awoke and started to wail. He stopped only when the cardinal laid a white linen cloth on his head:

"Accipe vested . . ." (Accept this white garment which mayest thou carry without stain before the judgement seat of our Lord.)

Thereupon the cardinal gave Prince Metternich a lighted candle resting gently in a golden stick. To Baron Árpád Zeker he gave another candle in a silver stick.

"*Accipe lampadem ardentem. . . .*" he chanted. (And keep thy Baptism . . . and live forever and ever. Amen.)

This was the end of the ceremony.

Everyone now wished anxiously for the climax of the evening, Metternich's speech. The prince stepped forward and took from the hand of his personal secretary a large dark-green portfolio containing the text of his speech in the artistic script of the chancellery's best calligrapher. However, he hardly glanced at the manuscript. His handsome falcon face scanned the audience with a smile of greeting.

"*Ihre Majestät!*"

The czar still stood by a tapestry chair. The only change in his face when Metternich spoke was that his right eyebrow climbed up his forehead.

"*Kaiserliche und Königliche Hochheit!*"

This was addressed to Archduchess Blanca, who gave the prince all the attention she had left after the emotionally exhausting ceremony.

"*Ihre Reverendissime Eminence!*"

This was addressed to Cardinal Consalvi, who at that moment was being discreetly smuggled out of the salon. It was now a quarter after eight.

After booming out these illustrious titles, Metternich lowered his voice, and as if he were standing on the top of a mountain, he threw the words into the depths:

"*Meine Damen und Herren!*"

Of course he spoke a wonderful French, but by using the German tongue he emphasized that the Habsburg monarchy was a greater power at the congress than Russia. He was a wonderful and moving orator, partial to poetic phrases.

"The centuries," he began, "are like living creatures. They are born and they die. Their massive tombstones stand in ranks in the cemetery of history. However, they are not always in their exact place. For example, the fourteenth century died not in 1400 but in 1414, with the opening of the Council of Konstanza, which reconstructed Christianity.

"It seems," continued Metternich, "that the figure fourteen plays a mysterious and providential role in the counting of years. We are now in 1814, and no one can doubt that the opening of the Congress of Vienna is the birthday of the nineteenth century. If this newborn century will live its allotted span our great grandchildren will carry its tombstone into the cemetery of history in the year 1914. But we cannot see into the future. The tombstone of a century is extremely heavy and it may slip from the hands of its carriers, especially if they are drunk, as we have seen in the case of Bonaparte . . ."

Polite laughter honored this witty remark.

"The centuries also resemble human creatures, in the sense that they are all different. There are great centuries, such as those of Pericles, Marcus Aurelius or Justinianus. And remember the miserable fifteenth century, when waves of plague stormed over the world. There are heroic centuries, there are lazy centuries, there are thinking centuries. All of us in this room save the twins, were born in the love-stricken eighteenth century, set to music by the greatest composer who ever lived, whom I remember from my childhood playing his harpsichord in my father's castle—Wolfgang Amadeus Mozart, the eternal shining star of Austria."

Great applause.

"The Dukay twins just christened," said Metternich, "were born eight days ago, the very day of the opening of the congress. They themselves thus represent the newborn nineteenth century. Providence has placed as gifts in the cradle of the newborn century the most unbelievable discoveries of modern science— the steam engine, the oven that can hatch eggs, and the recently invented phosphorous stick, which by a simple stroke of the hand produces a flame. And the great wisdom of the immortal monarchs of our time," here a slight bow to the czar, "has placed in that cradle the gift of everlasting peace, the welfare and happiness of all the nations. This century will be *glücklich, das glücklichste Jahrhundert* . . . the happiest, the merriest century. . . . It will be a gala century, a century in scarlet, not only in dress and uniform, but in human thought and human effort. Human deeds will appear in full regalia, nobility will be associated not only with rank or birth, but with the honorable and generous behavior of rich and poor alike."

Great applause. Lacy handkerchiefs went to the eyes of those ladies who had lost loved ones under the guillotine or on the battlefield of the unhappy decades past. A gentleman's fingers secretly went up to squash a tear in the corner of his eye.

"This century," Metternich continued, "will be a long, long sunny Sunday, it will be a giant merry-go-round, for the cheerful children of mankind.

"Je cherche un homme!" Metternich quoted eloquently. " 'I am looking for a man!' Diderot said. Perhaps one of these twins, from a very ancient and noble family, born in *Felix Austria,* will be the man of this noble and happy century."

At these words, Adalbert, frowning, waved his tiny clenched fists as if protesting the great honor being bestowed upon him. Antal meanwhile slept quietly in the arms of his godmother, as if these robust Habsburg arms were the very arms of Happy Austria. The Archduchess' rice-powdered face remained immobile, but there were tears in the green eyes of Olga Serebraniy as she looked upon the paprika-red face of second-born Adalbert Árpád.

The tears were asking: What are these tiny fists hiding? Into how many faces will they strike? Into the face of a wife and many mistresses? What whispered, feverish love confessions, what obscene raging curses, what roaring laughter, what moans of pain will pour forth from that little mouth?

Metternich, in a moving eulogy to the dear eighteenth century, gave a brief summary of the events of the last decade and was speaking of the Treaty of Paris when the czar, from deep within him, gave a loud belch. Metternich, of course, continued his speech undisturbed. But the belch was only the beginning. The czar's mouth, between the tightly blown up cheeks, became as tiny as the twins'. The big Stroganoff boots staggered forward and the bulging brassy eyes desperately sought for the door. Endre Dukay and Prince Igor quickly went to his aid, and hardly touching his elbows, directed his steps to a door which led to a corridor. Metternich raised his voice, but it could not cover the unmistakable drawn-out howl that gushed forth with the vomit.

The Dukays' guests behaved wonderfully. No one heard or saw anything. Metternich's undisturbed sentences served as beautiful baroque motifs to that perfect discipline. The only change in Metternich's speech was that he leapt over those passages that eulogized the human and statesmanlike greatness of the czar. Soon, like a trapeze artist high in the air, he grabbed the swinging bar of the closing words of his speech:

"Long live the newborn century! Long live the newborn Dukay twins!"

Thunderous applause greeted this close, especially as the great doors of the dining room immediately flew open and the buffet, massively laden with miracles and treasures, like a huge altar, came into view, glowing in splendor under the multitude of candles in the huge chandeliers.

While the guests satisfied their appetites, Count Rudolf Leiningen entertained the party with his theories on comparitive linguistics.

"For example," he said in his thin voice, "let's take the German *genug,* which means enough. Let's trim the first *g,* remains *enug.* Put an *o* and *h* into *enug,* you get *enough.*"

"Amazing!" remarked Archduchess Blanca, who spoke English well. The pronunciation of *genug* and *enough* is as different as the . . . the . . ."

"As the Austrian and British constitution," interjected the second-born twin's godfather, Baron Árpád Zeker.

After a few seconds of embarrassed silence, Count Leiningen went on with his lecture:

"Or let's take the word *glücklich,* which means lucky, or the Latin *felix* as Emperor Joseph called his great empire: *Felix Austria.* If we trim *glücklich,* we get *lucki*—a clear proof that the word lucky . . ."

"Excuse me," said Archduchess Blanca, saving the party with her interruption from Leiningen's endless examples of philology, "too bad we didn't hear your wonderful lecture before my godson, Antal Nepomuk was christened. One of his names might have been Felix. It would have reminded him throughout his whole life that he was a true son of *Felix Austria.* Alas, however, it's too late now. But let's give him the nickname 'Flexi.' "

General applause honored Her Highness' suggestion.

"Great idea!" said Árpád Zeker. "A Hungarian count loyal to the Habsburg throne must be flexible."

Endre Dukay raised his hand discreetly. The little pleading movement meant: "Shut up, Árpád." Prince Schwarzenberg, whose son was christened Felix, threw a sharp glance at the booted, screw-mustached, "horse-smelling, barbarian Magyar."

The second-born twin, Adalbert Árpád, on the suggestion of his godfather, was nicknamed "Dali." In Hungarian *Dali* meant stalwart, chivalrous, martial.

The linguist Leiningen whispered to Schwarzenberg: "In Turkish 'dali' means crazy."

In Jadi's heavily carpeted and curtained bedroom, lit by candelabras, the ladies recounted every detail of the christening party, including the scandalously transparent tunic of Princess Bagration and the slight indisposition of the czar.

Olga was silent. In her arms, she could feel the second-born Adalbert, as she had held him during the christening ceremony. Now Jadi had two sons, while Olga must remain forever childless. Although only his godmother, Olga loved little Dali with all the passion of frustrated motherhood. St. Petersburg, she reflected, was terribly far from Buda-Pesth; she would see her godson, maybe, once a decade.

As she mused over her own tragedy and Jadi's good fortune, Olga suddenly recalled an episode from her childhood. One day, when Jadi was five and Olga seven, Olga was confined to her room by her mother as a punishment for some childish offense. Jadi had come into the room, knelt in the corner, put half a *brznig*, a kind of Polish brioche, on the floor, and disappeared, as silent as an angel. Jadi loved the brznig, made with ground nuts and strawberry jam, but she shared it with her sister, who had gotten none. Did Jadi preserve her generous heart? Would she be willing to share the twins? Would she let Olga adopt Dali? Would she allow her to take him to St. Petersburg to grow up as a Russian, as Prince Adalbert Serebraniy-Dukay, heir to the nearly one-million-acre Serebraniy Ural estate?

When her thoughts reached this point, Olga turned her eyes to Jadi's face. Tired from excitement, Jadi lay against her pillows, one twin cuddled in the curve of each arm. Feeling her sister's gaze upon her, Jadi looked up; her eyes, meeting Olga's, were radiant with a quiet joy. Olga looked away. Sadly she abandoned her daydream. Jadi would never be able to part with her own child. However rich Olga could make him, Jadi could never send him so far away, nor could she want him to grow up as a Russian, alien to her own country and his father's.

The morning after the christening, Andris Zeker, four-year-old son of Adalbert's godfather, was brought to the palace to meet the twins. Thick-necked Andris, a miniature Hercules with a charmingly-stupid face, was growing up on the remote Zeker estate, between puppies and kittens. These were the first human twins he had ever seen. He gazed at them appreciatively, then pulled at his mother's skirts and whispered:

"Which one are they going to keep?"

For the time being the answer remained the deep secret of the faraway future.

CHAPTER TWO

GIBBON, WHO TOOK AN uncommonly wide view, states that the happiest period in the history of mankind occurred during those 103 years from the death of Titus Flavius in the second century A.D. to the death of Commodus, son of Marcus Aurelius. Gibbon attributes the happiness of that century to the fact that the Romans lived under a "benevolent dictatorship."

Gibbon should have been living to appraise the years after the Congress of Vienna. Emperor Francis was a most benevolent dictator. As he strolled, or sat on a bench in Schönbrunn park, anyone could approach his majesty. The military court could not try a young infantry lieutenant, a known gambler who cashed a note of 10,000 florins with the emperor as co-maker, because the signature turned out to be genuine.

In the field of foreign affairs, Francis I left matters entirely up to Metternich, but he was his own prime minister. He was interested in each detail of home affairs—so much so that when there was a fire in Vienna, it was his majesty who directed the firemen, "standing in the orange light of flames in his white imperial coat." And whenever the monarchy was troubled by the "fire" of political unrest, or even only the scent of spiritual smoke, it was His Majesty who directed the secret "firemen." On such an occasion, he would simply summon Herr Meisler, chief hangman, for an audience. Herr Meisler had already hanged several hundred "firebugs" with his own large and expert hands. And whenever Master Meisler could inform his majesty of new improved methods of hanging, Emperor Francis I would listen to the chief hangman's lecture eagerly.

It sometimes happened during the course of history that "benevolent despotism" created prosperity. Such was the case during the long reign of Francis I.

The ten months of the congress enticed thousands of merchants to Vienna to sell their jewels, costumes, saddles, pretty snuffboxes and pretty women to the delegates and tourists. Emperor Francis complained to Metternich that the whole of Vienna became a huge brothel.

Soon after Waterloo, in the summer of 1815, the congress retired from Vienna like a giant goddess of prosperity, but it seemed that her huge, velvet train was caught by the sharp gothic edges of the Stefanskirche's tower. Vienna became the capital of Europe, the center of music with *"Herr Pedhofen, pianiste, un talente considérable,"* as Chambonnas' notebook misspelled the name of Beethoven, who in Countess Brunswick's salon refused to play Haydn's "Russian Quartet" in honor of the czar.

While Czar Alexander ranted against the Corsican adventurer and against the leniency (his own) that had allowed him sanctuary so close to France, Prince Metternich secretly entertained thoughts of allying Austria's might with Napoleon's undoubted military genius against the overbearing Russian bear. But such contemplations remained unspoken, and the courier who carried to Vienna word of Wellington's victory at Waterloo found the congress' participants proceeding on ostensibly amicable terms. Not long afterward, the congress declared its work completed and retired from Vienna. But the aura it had brought to Austria's capital remained, like the lingering scent of a great perfume. Vienna became not only the capital of Europe, the center of music, but also of the home industry, and tourism: and most of all, the center of politics. The Habsburg monarchy emerged as the greatest power in the world.

The people of Vienna enjoyed a prosperity never before experienced. The giant ferris wheel in the *Prater*, the huge park Emperor Joseph had given the city, was full of colorful folk costumes, and under the ancient chestnut trees throughout Vienna, people danced to the tunes of accordions.

In the spring of 1817, Countess Jadi gave birth to her third child, a daughter christened Carola and nicknamed Rolly. Doctor Kunz and Frau Obergelderkämpfer, mindful of the appalling risks of puerperal fever, still taking its ghastly toll of mothers around the world, strongly advised her to have no more children.

Prince George Dukay lived in Buda, on the second floor of his renaissance palace in Septemvir Utca; his constant companion was the prayer book of Thomas á Kempis, bound in mother of pearl. From the window of his room he could see over the rooftops the Danube and beyond. He had retired from his Vienna palace in Gisellastrasse before the congress, when Endre married Jadi.

In the summertime, Countess Jadi and the children lived on the huge Dukay estate in Hungary, called Ararat, which was some ten miles south of the Danube between Vienna and Buda-Pesth. The Ararat castle was always full of guests, and its 400-acre park offered every joy and sport of the summer: swimming in the pond, fishing in the brook, horseback riding, falconry, and hunting with greyhounds or with *uhu*, the great horned owl.

Endre worked at the chancellery in Vienna, but almost every weekend he returned to Ararat to be with Jadi and the children. When the gate bell signalled his arrival, Countess Jadi would snatch up her golden-black Persian kerchief and speed down the long sandy drive to meet him. Endre usually arrived on horseback, and their reunion was always warm but never theatrical. Endre, sometimes dressed in his bright hussar uniform, sometimes in a tobacco-brown frock with a wide black cravat setting off his frilled shirt, would dismount casually and toss his bridle to a groom, who always seemed to appear out of nowhere. Then he would kiss Jadi's hand and look at her mutely. His wide brown eyes revealed, to her, his joy and desire. But he never took Jadi into his arms and never kissed her in the presence of a servant.

Jadi loved him and wanted him—he was so handsomely strong and elegant, his long legs thick with saddle muscles. He was so awkwardly tender, like a real cavalry officer. Since it was the "house law" in the chancellery that everyone said exactly the contrary of what he thought, Endre's conversation with his wife, unlike his letters to her, was aloof, dull and foggy. His formality gave Jadi the impression that her husband's heart and soul had always been dressed in some sort of stiff gala uniform, but she never resented it. It was his way, and she understood his inarticulate tenderness. Moreover, it helped her to build an invisible screen around her Polish loneliness in the Austro-Hungarian atmosphere.

Although Jadi had been only seventeen when she married, and the Radowskis were not rich, her mother, a Voronieczki princess, had brought her up in the tradition of great ladies, able to shoulder the responsibilities of huge estates. After her wedding in the Stefanskirche in Vienna, Jadi was ready to manage the three Dukay households. The main headquarters, of course, was the large baroque Dukay palace in Vienna. In size, age and style it hardly differed from the other massive baroque dwellings of Vienna's nobility.

The Dukay family usually spent seven months in Vienna, from November until the end of May. June, July and August found them in Ararat castle, September and October in Buda, where they owned a small renaissance palace, with only sixteen, though beautifully vaulted, rooms.

Naturally, when official or social duties called them, a wedding or a christening party, a court ball or some other festive occasion, they travelled from one place to another. The distance between Vienna and Buda-Pesth was about 100 miles, and even with the fastest horses it took two days.

With their indispensable personal valets, nurses and miscellaneous servants, the Dukays and others of their class travelled in glassed-in coaches, loaded with foods and drinks, with medicine kits, cards for solitaire, books of poems and novels to while away the time. A covered wagon furnished with nightpots served for toilets.

The coaches were escorted by six armed and mounted guards because of the *betyárs,* the romantic bandits of the period.

Countess Jadi had great talent for handling the army of employees and servants who staffed her three households. Everyone in her employ, from the chaplain and librarian, the stable master and the major domo down to the cleaning women, as well as the French chef, the boys' tutors, and Rolly's governess, responded to her quiet, firm commands. Wherever she appeared, she brought dignity and grace. Every servant or peasant who met her discovered her kind heart within minutes. Endre's vanity would have suffered tremendously if he had realized that, despite the choleric tone in which he shouted his orders at Ararat or in Vienna, the servants obeyed only the gentle voice of Countess Jadi. In her manner, there was a suggestion of unintentional apology, some mute apology toward the servants, the serfs and the poor, because of the tremendous difference between her privileges as a wealthy aristocrat and the condition of the other classes. Even the Jewish physician, Doctor Kunz, the schoolteacher in the village and other middle-class people in her world enjoyed but little prestige compared to that of the landowners.

Countess Jadi, like so many mothers of that diary-writing period, kept a "daybook" about each of her children. Inscribed in gold letters on the green-leather book was the name: *Flexi.* The red-leather book was lettered *Dali,* and the blue-leather book was lettered *Rolly.* The weights and heights of the children were entered every Sunday, as well as dates of all new teeth and all indispositions.

As the twins grew, their characters developed in totally different directions. Flexi was the ideal boy, obedient, polite and softspoken, who went to bed at eight without a word of protest. Dali had a separate sleeping room, because it took a long time to persuade him to go to bed. Once when Countess Jadi checked his bed, past midnight, she found Dali missing, although the door was locked. The servants were awakened and the castle was searched. The five-year-old had climbed out through a high window, and was found in the stable listening to folk tales told by a blind old serf.

The blond, blue-eyed Flexi always looked as clean as shining glass. In Dali's dark hair there were usually a few chicken feathers. When Flexi's diary read: "Complained of pain in the stomach," Dali's said: "The three kreuzer-size buttons he swallowed Monday came out all right." As the months passed, Rolly's and Flexi's diaries had many empty pages, but each page of Dali's was filled with such entries as: "Emperor's birthday. Endre gave Dali sound spanking. He had pissed into Endre's brand-new crimson boot just before E. went to the Burg with the delegation."

Peasant boys went to elementary school—if they went—at the age of seven, and middle-class boys at six. But the education of aristocratic children began at five, sometimes at four, on the supposition that they were born with a greater spiritual capacity —which was not always the case. At the age of four, Flexi already played the *Einst war ich klein* kindergarden song on the harpsichord which Mozart had played many times in the Dukay palace. Flexi could read German fairly well, and could write such words as "Papi" . . . "Mami" . . . "Dali" . . . "Rolly" on the blackboard. And for Christmas he surprised his father by writing the first line of the *Gott erhälte,* the emperor hymn, set to music by Haydn.

At the same time Dali, left alone with the harpsichord after his first lesson, broke two white and two black front teeth of the keyboard with a kitchen knife. He said during the interrogation that he hated "the ugly grin" of the harpsichord.

"Une imagination très malsaine!" cried out Rolly's scandalized French governess, who loved harpsichord music.

Dali was six before he could write his name, and even then his quill moved as slowly as a "sleeping snail," as Endre put it. But godfather Baron Árpád Zeker defended Dali: "Why, when Charlemagne was already emperor, Bishop Alcuin still had to lead his fist whenever he signed a document."

Aristocratic boys rarely went to a public elementary school. They were taught reading, writing and some basic mathematics by private teachers at home. When Flexi and Dali were five,

Endre hired two teachers for them. A clean-shaven Austrian taught them German, and a mustached gentleman from Buda taught them the Magyar tongue. The two teachers accompanied their pupils to Vienna, to Buda, and to Ararat, too, for the long summer vacation. Besides full board, a pair of new boots, a used suit and hat, and two shirts and drawers (all from Endre's wardrobe, whether the clothes fitted them or not) each teacher received a monthly salary of three pounds of tobacco and one and a half silver florins. Not only that. Count Samuel Leznay, a neighbor landlord, told his boy's private teacher: ". . . and if my son happens to kill you during the lessons, don't worry, I will pay the expenses of your funeral."

One day in 1821, when Dali was seven, this entry appeared in Countess Jadi's record: "I left Dali holding Falcon in the park. When Endre dashed out to the terrace shouting the news that Napoleon had died, Dali very nearly died too. He climbed into Falcon's saddle, Falcon tried to shake him off. Dali's foot caught in the stirrup, and Falcon dashed away. Not until after a gallop of over a mile was Falcon caught, and Dali was hanging head down from the stirrup the whole time. His head must have bumped the ground many times. Even Doctor Kunz is worried about his brain having been shaken so badly. I asked if it might affect him permanently. We don't know."

The teachers of the boys belonged to two different schools of pedagogy. Herr Pick, the well-dressed, pomade-smelling Austrian, lectured to the boys as if they were on the mental level of university professors, while the mustached Hungarian treated them as hopeless idiots. Flexi listened with sincere eagerness to both teachers, and made good progress. Dali yawned and often fell asleep during the lessons. And if his eyes were open he showed more interest in catching flies than in the rules of the *der, die, das*. Once he asked Herr Pick:

"Why are German girls neuter? *DAS Fräulein! DAS Mädchen!*"

"Because . . ." Herr Pick explained, "they are not kissing with boys yet. After the marriage, they lose their neutrality and become females. *DIE Frau.*"

"But why is my sister's skirt male? *DER Rock!* And why are my trousers female? *DIE Hose!*"

Herr Pick could not explain.

A year later, when again there was no entry in Flexi's book, Countess Jadi wrote in Dali's:

"Walking in the park I nearly fainted when I saw Dali on the top of the ancient Turkish watchtower leaning out of an upper peephole, his left hand grabbing a stone, his right reaching to a hawk's nest for the eggs. At my shriek he lost his balance, fell seventy feet, and broke through the rotten reed roof of the ice cellar at the tower's base. I expected to find him dead, but he dashed out of the cellar in fear of spanking. I will not tell Endre or anyone else. Who would believe it?"

And in October, 1824:

"He is still in bed. I could not curb Endre's rage. He broke a stick on Dali's back. I am glad that Metternich could not come and was not present at the milk affair."

The "milk affair" occurred in the Dukay palace in Vienna at the twins' tenth birthday celebration, and in the presence of most of the 500 guests who had attended their christening. For the main event, it was Endre's idea that the boys should recite to Archduchess Blanca a passage from Metternich's christening speech. Flexi was dressed, just for fun, as a miniature Emperor Francis, in knee-long white imperial coat, a small "Golden Fleece" at his neck, while Dali was dressed as a miniature Attila, in sandals, moth-eaten wolf-skin tunic, a curved sword, and the leather shield of a Hun warrior. Flexi's performance was wonderful. In fluent German he faultlessly recited his portion of Metternich's tribute to the eighteenth century. Just before Dali's turn his father forced him to drink a glass of milk, in the hope that it would smooth his hoarse Hun voice. Dali stepped up to Her Highness and spat a mouthful of the milk straight into her face. He then jumped back, pulled out his curved wooden sword, and with fire in his wildly dancing dark eyes, prepared to defend himself to the death. In the painful silence after he was disarmed and led away, General von Hedwitz, Endre's brother-in-law, whispered to the screw-mustached Árpád Zeker:

"That child is not normal."

"Why not?" asked Dali's godfather.

Following this harrowing episode, Endre decided that his

sons should not only have separate bedrooms but separate countries. Flexi would continue to grow up in Austria, spending
most of his time in Vienna. Dali, the harpsichord-hater, possess-
ing an inborn loathing for the Habsburg family, was to grow up
in Hungary. This decision did not mean exile for Dali. Many
Hungarian aristocrats normally raised one son in Austria and
another in Hungary, in an effort to be faithful to the spirit of
friendship and brotherhood of the dual monarchy. Nor were
Flexi and Dali entirely separated. They spent the long summer
months together in Ararat; and during the winter season Dali
often visited Vienna, and Felxi often journeyed to Buda to see
his great-great-uncle, Prince George.

2

Endre had word of the death of Czar Alexander through his
work at the chancellery. Neither he nor his family thought to
mourn the amorous Czar, whose vulnerability to wine had so
disrupted the twins' christening party. But not long after his
death, Olga's letters to Jadi revealed that the new czar, Nicholas
I, far surpassed his predecessor in cruelty. A popular belief in
Russia held that Nicholas, impatient for the crown, had not
waited for his elder brother to die, but had murdered him.

In any case, his accession was not uncontested, for many Russians believed the throne should have gone to Grand Duke Constantine, viceroy of Poland. Constantine was also Alexander's
brother, and was older than Nicholas; but while Alexander still
lived, Constantine had made a love match, marrying a Polish
countess not of royal blood. Czar Alexander, enraged, had forced
him to resign his right to the throne. The resignation was kept a
deep secret.

After Alexander's sudden death in December 1825, when
Nicholas wanted to take the oath from the St. Petersburg regiments for himself, army officers and intellectuals regarded him
as an usurper and organized an uprising. They hated Nicholas,
who was often referred to as *Palkin* (meaning man of stick) because as Grand Duke he had disciplined his soldiers with a club,
sometimes beating a poor fellow to death.

The rioters in December gained little but a page in history as
the *Decembrists*.

The Southern School wanted a National Duma.

When the guards regiment in Moscow shouted "Long live *Constitutsiya!*", the artillery fired grapeshot at the mutineers, killing enough to quell the trouble. It turned out that these illiterate Russian soldiers had no understanding of the word "constitution" anyway. They thought *Constitutsiya* was Constantine's Polish wife.

The December uprising was poorly organized, erupting only in St. Petersburg, Moscow and Kiev. When, on December 26, thousands marched toward the Winter Palace, the canister tore gaps in the ranks of the mutinous regiments, and many civilian bystanders died on the Senate Square as well. As the crowd fled across the frozen Neva, cannon balls broke the ice and scores were drowned. Prince Sergei Trubetskoy, colonel of the rioting guards, fled to the Austrian embassy, where he sought sanctuary, knowing that even Metternich preferred Constantine to Nick the Stick.

Olga wrote to Jadi describing an execution in St. Petersburg. Early in the morning five condemned men were led to the gallows before the St. Petersburg fortress, to find that Czar Nicholas himself was presiding. When the czar gave the signal to the chief hangman, the drums began to roll and the bench was kicked from under the feet of the condemned. Three of the ropes broke. The spectators cheered with joy and gratitude, thinking that the czar, moved to compassion, had taken this means of extending clemency. But the czar gave the signal to continue the drums. The executioners fished out the three "lucky" men from the moat. One of them had had his leg broken and another his jawbone shattered. New ropes were hung, the prisoners resumed their places under the gallows, and nooses were again fastened around their necks. The doomed man with the shattered leg summoned all his strength, and cried out, so loud that his voice was heard in spite of the drums: "Unhappy land, where one does not even know how to hang!"

When Jadi read of these incidents, her gentle heart bled for the poor people of Russia, doomed to live under the harsh tyrant. But even more painful to her was the thought of her fellow Poles, who must now endure not only a foreign monarch, but an inordinately cruel one. She spoke of these feelings to no one; concealing her sorrow, she busied herself, as a good wife

39

and mother should, over her husband, her household, and her children.

The year 1826 opened uneventfully in Vienna, and when Jadi answered Olga's letters, she wrote chiefly of the children, in whom Olga preserved the liveliest interest.

Flexi is a half inch taller [one letter read], but Dali is nine pounds heavier. They will be twelve in October. Flexi's French is already fluent; his Hungarian is fading away in Vienna, while Dali's Hungarian is becoming rich in the most obscene expressions. After he hastily swallows his breakfast, he runs out to the stables; and his best friend is Pista Kerge, the son of a serf on the Leznay estate, which adjoins ours. Pista is a year older than Dali, not taller but seemingly much stronger. On a thin golden chain, Dali wears a small cross around his neck; on a thick, dirty string Pista wears a book-size piece of baked pumpkin: his daily food. This is the way serf mothers feed their children.

Flexi's friends are, besides Archduke Johann Salvator (a nephew of godmother Blanca), the young Auersperg, Eszterházy, and Lichtenstein princes, and Solly Rothschild, boys his age who certainly are fed on more than pumpkin. Flexi is very polite to his friends, but he has not a "best" friend among them. Perhaps Solly. For Flexi, friendship is a noble duty; for Dali, friendship is a passion, full of shouting and even fist fights. Last week when Dali punched Pista on the nose, Pista—the son of a serf!—threw him into the deep manure ditch and Dali, wearing his new Sunday clothes, climbed out of that horrible moat with chicken bowels around his neck. If it had happened to a Lichtenstein or Schwarzenberg boy . . . I don't dare think of the fate of a Pista. I thought that Dali's and Pista's friendship was finished forever. But the same afternoon I saw the two boys on the back of Rolly's white donkey, the rein and whip in Dali's hand, and behind him Pista, hanging onto Dali with both arms.

The elementary school opened last Monday. Dali voluntarily attends the school each day for an hour or so; he has no thirst for the lessons and discipline, but he likes to hide under the benches and laugh at the hunchbacked teacher.

Last Monday, after the school teacher lectured about the ancient Hungarians in Asia who sacrificed white stallions to their pagan gods on a huge pyre, Dali played chieftain Ordony, who was the founder of the Dukay family. With the assistance of Pista, Dali built a large pyre, mostly from the new, expensive oak benches in the park.

When the stable master chased the boys out of Endre's riding stallion's box, Dali compromised on poor Sha-sha, the white female rabbit from Rolly's zoo. Eight-year-old Rolly, when she learned the fate of Sha-sha, went for Dali's eyes with all her ten fingernails, screaming hysterically. Fortunately, Endre was in Vienna. Needless to say no one would tell him a word about the Ordony pyre. But when I told Doctor Kunz, he said that we must watch Dali to see if he is a pyromaniac.

When Endre returned from Vienna to Ararat for his usual summer vacation, all the fifty-two guest rooms of Ararat castle were filled with guests who had come to hunt. The huge Dukay estate was very rich in quails, partridges, pheasants, hares, red deer, boars, foxes and wolves. Endre rarely went hunting. His daily topic of conversation with his wife was the coming twelfth birthday of the twins. At twelve, an aristocratic boy received his first personal valet, his first riding horse, his first hunting rifle, and his introduction to sex, through the female servants of the castle. And at twelve, each boy graduated from the care of his elementary teacher and received a tutor of professorial rank.

The candidate for Flexi's tutorship was Professor Karl Loebel, a sixty-year-old scholar from Vienna, with a large beard.

Professor Loebel, recommended by Archduchess Blanca, was a highly educated pedagogue, and so refined that even in his thoughts the name of an Archduchess never appeared as "Her Highness," but always as "Her Imperial and Royal Highness." During his first lesson in history, he told Flexi:

"Your Excellency will see later during the course of world history that strong and healthy societies are held together by titles, as strong ladders are held together by long and thick nails. The ancient Greek and Roman empires collapsed because the titles they bestowed for public service were not hereditary. Early English kings were called only 'Grace' or 'Mighty Prince,' and Great Britain's greatness began with Henry VIII, the first who was called 'Majesty.' "

Between Flexi and his tutor there was a mutual reverence. Flexi addressed his tutor as "Herr Professor," and he addressed Flexi: "Your Excellency, Count Antal."

Flexi's education on a straight pro-Habsburg line had been perfectly secured.

To get a tutor for Dali was a different task.

"I would suggest the toughest drill sergeant of the Pálffy Hussars," said his father thoughtfully.

After they had debated the problem from every angle, Countess Jadi had an idea.

"I will write to my friends in Switzerland," she said.

After the French Revolution, feudal aristocratic houses in Europe, and especially in the Habsburg monarchy and Russia, were closed to French tutors, for the nobility feared that French tutors would import baneful revolutionary ideas. As a result, many of the well-to-do were now turning to Swiss tutors, whose mother tongue was French but whose political thinking was as clean as the blue air above the snow-capped Swiss Alps. So, Jadi told her husband, Dali's tutor should be Swiss.

3

In eastern Poland under Russian occupation the new "national" anthem was *Bozhe Zaria Chrany*, God Save the Czar." But the *Bozhe Zaria* was sung in Poland only by the occupying Russian troops.

One spring night in Warsaw, when the deserted streets were so silent that, from the direction of the Novosolsky barrack one could hear the soldiers singing, a human figure suddenly appeared. Within sound of the soldiers, he ran on tiptoe, hugging the walls, his large-brimmed, potlike hat pulled well down over his ears. In his long-tailed frock coat he seemed to fly like a nocturnal lapwing from tree to tree as he zigzagged from one sheltering wall to the next. He paused to catch his breath, then continued his flight. His right knee was bleeding and the tight trouser leg had been torn as he had thrown himself over a thorny fence between two gardens.

From whom did he flee?

Liberal people, liberal thoughts were fleeing everywhere—not only in Russian-Prussian-Austrian occupied Poland, but in Vienna, Buda-Pesth, Prague, and even in Paris, where, in Lafayette's words, the Bourbons forgot nothing old and learned nothing new.

The silence of that Warsaw night was so thick that when the fugitive halted he could hear, in a distant street, the sucking sound of the hooves of Cossack horses in the mud. He even heard the suppressed grunts of Russian commands.

The fugitive raced toward the end of the street. Safely arriving at a brick house, he knocked softly on the high window—two short and one long: ta-ta. . . . taaa. . . . He had to repeat the signal five times.

"Who is there?" whispered a voice from within.

"Hyron," the fugitive gasped.

The window opened noiselessly and two strong arms reached out. Hyron vaulted through the window into the dark room.

Two weeks later, in Ararat castle, the butler announced a visitor to Endre Dukay:

"Monsieur Antoine Jules la Harpe."

The young gentleman, just arrived from Switzerland, was applying for a position as Dali's tutor. A friend of Countess Jadi had recommended him.

"How old are you, Monsieur la Harpe?" Endre Dukay asked the applicant.

"Twenty-five, Your Excellency."

"Are you strong enough, spiritually and physically, to discipline a rather vicious twelve-year-old boy?"

"Yes, I am, Your Excellency."

"Are you related to General la Harpe?"

"No, Your Excellency, I am not." The young tutor added with a wry smile: "I would like it if I were." And he lightly bowed, which was his way of putting a period to every statement.

Endre Dukay nodded. If the young man had claimed to be a relative of the great Swiss educator, Frédèric César de la Harpe, onetime tutor of Czar Alexander, Endre would not have employed him. He already knew from Countess Jadi that her protégé was the talented son of a simple but honest and religious watchmaker in Bern.

Endre Dukay did not much care for the candidate. The twenty-five-year old Antoine la Harpe was a thin man of medium height, and he did not seem muscular enough to handle Dali. His short nose was rather Slavic, his high forehead suggested a thoughtful character—perhaps too thoughtful, Endre feared. He gestured too much. His dark green frock coat was acceptably cleaned and ironed and his cravat was not too dirty, but his shoes, however carefully shined, were badly worn, and the dense silky blond hair on his nape was far too long for the prevailing fashion. His grey trousers had a cleverly sewn patch on the right knee, hardly perceptible.

Endre Dukay put his questions to the candidate in both French and German, to make sure the young man spoke both languages fluently. He did, and more fluently than Endre Dukay wished, enriching his answers with quotations from Goethe and Molière.

"How many languages do you speak?"

"French, German, English. *Ego parlo latinum. Io parlo italiano poco*," he added bowing.

"Polish?"

"Not a word, Your Excellency."

Endre Dukay nodded in satisfaction.

Countess Jadi sat in an armchair during the entire interview. Her sewing basket stood on the carpet beside her, and with effort she concentrated on embroidering a Persian motif with silver thread on apple-green velvet. Endre Dukay pointed to the long piano in the corner of the room:

"Will you play something?"

While the candidate took ten steps to the piano, Endre Dukay studied him with the same look he turned on horses he was considering adding to his stable. The walk of Monsieur la Harpe was light and elegant. If he were properly barbered and newly dressed, he might well be introduced to the Archduchess Blanca. "Monsieur la Harpe, the tutor of my son." It did not sound bad. It would be unnecessary to add that he was not related to the great la Harpe.

The candidate opened the cover of the piano. His pale blue eyes ran over the yellowing keys; then, raising his arms, he shook back his cuffs in the gesture of a professional pianist. He played Beethoven's "Adelaide." While the young man played, Endre Dukay suppressed a yawn. But the countess dropped her handiwork on her lap and turned her sad, delicate profile to the window, entirely immersed in the sweetness of the music.

At the end of the piece, Endre nodded. The candidate had passed the test. Endre's voice became rather cold, as he said:

"You probably know that when Haydn was already Europe's

greatest composer, he received a salary of forty florins a month from Prince Eszterházy. I think your demand for twenty-five florins a month is ridiculously high. Will you be satisfied with twenty?"

Antoine la Harpe raised his arms toward the huge Venetian chandelier hanging from the ceiling as if he were appealing to the heavens; then he suddenly dropped his arms and made a deep bow, a gesture of acceptance. Endre Dukay rang a small silver bell, and, when the butler appeared, said:

"Call in Count Adalbert."

This was the first time he had given the title of Count to his son. The twins were no longer to be called Flexi or Dali by the servants, but Count Antal or Count Adalbert.

Dali raced into the room and came to a sudden stop, using his soft orange boots as a brake. He wore a light blue nankeen shirt with a belt, which emphasized his slender waist. His silky dark locks hung over his damp forehead, his eyes matched the color of his hair; they were not large in the narrow face, but they were deep, and his nose and mouth were delicately carved. His face bore the same slightly Oriental look as his father's, but Dali's expression was more spiritual.

Dali looked his new tutor over from head to foot with self-assured impertinence. Monsieur la Harpe raised his arm high in the air, then dropped it to the proper level to emphasize the great importance of the first handshake.

"Bon jour, Monsieur le Comte!"

Dali shifted the bow and arrow from his right arm to his left and accepted the handshake. He had been hunting, not for squirrels, but for Monsieur la Harpe. Traditionally, he hated his new tutor in advance. He had been hiding in a bush with his friend Pista Kerge. The arrowheads were covered with soft rags soaked in ink. Unfortunately, both their arrows missed the grey top hat of Monsieur la Harpe when he arrived at the castle in an open calèche. The four Dukay grays had sped by so fast that the boys could not aim properly.

The first handshake between Dali and his new tutor was, of course, a contest. Each pressed the other's hand with all his might—Dali as a challenge to Monsieur la Harpe, the other in answer to that challenge.

"Dali!" Countess Jadi cried out reproachfully. Dali withdrew his hand—not in response to her command, but in defeat. He blew on his fingers, then shook his hand as if he were shaking out the hurt. Antoine la Harpe had won the first round. Their friendship was sealed.

"Whoo!" came a distant howl from the park, the call of Pista Kerge, who, as a peasant boy, was not allowed to enter the castle. Dali dashed from the room.

Endre Dukay retired to his study. Antoine la Harpe remained alone with the Countess. He listened for a few moments to Endre's departing steps, then took the Countess' hand, as white and weightless as an empty glove, and kissed it. His eyes filled with tears and he could say only:

"Dzieki tobie."

The words were Polish and meant "Thank you."

His name was not Antoine Jules la Harpe. He had never been in Switzerland. He was Hyron, the fugitive from Warsaw.

When Countess Jadi told her husband that Dali's tutor was recommended to her by a friend in Bern, she did not tell the truth. It was her Polish cousin, Princess Voronieczki who recommended Hyron. In at least one of her sons, Countess Jadi wanted to keep alive the memory of Poland's tragedy.

From her point of view, Hyron was an ideal tutor for Dali. Hyron Tyeminiczky-Yojtkowski, alias Monsieur Antoine Jules la Harpe, was an ardent and zealous patriot, presently in hiding from the Russian general Novosolsky's military police in Warsaw.

But Hyron's origin was to remain his and Countess Jadi's secret.

Hyron was the adopted son of Igor Tyeminiczky-Vojtkowski, the stable master in the court of Stanislaus Augustus, the last Polish king. To be stable master of a king was a title of honor. Hyron's stepfather was a Polish nobleman, with a very small estate, but with a very big heart.

Poland was the fabulous country of the poorest nobles. In the middle of the eighteenth century Poland had nearly two million nobles. Their estates were so small that, according to the saying, if a count's cow was grazing in the middle of her master's farm, she was sure to have either her head or her tail on a neighbor's land.

In the year 1794, a slender, but broadshouldered Polish patriot, Thaddeus Kosciusko, who fought under George Washington, had returned to Poland and become the leader of the Polish War for Liberty. At first Kosciusco was victorious. The Poles forced the Prussians to withdraw their forces. But later, Russia crushed the uprising, Kosciusco was wounded and captured in battle, and after bitter contentions among Austria, Russia and Prussia—"howling hyenas on the zebra's corpse"—dismembered Poland was divided for the third time. The shadow-king Stanislaus was compelled to abdicate.

Six years later Poland thrilled to new hopes when the thirty-one-year-old Bonaparte defeated Austria at the battle of Marengo in 1800. Then came another Austrian defeat at Austerlitz; then the Prussian troops were scattered to the wind at Jena. With the Habsburgs and Hohenzollerns out of the way, Napoleon drove against Russia and routed her army at Friedland.

In these years, when Napoleon reached the zenith of his power, he appeared to both Polish and Hungarian patriots as their liberator. Putting up his headquarters in Hungary, on the Danube shore between Vienna and Buda-Pesth, he offered the crown of a new, independent Hungarian kingdom to Field Marshal Prince Nicholas Eszterházy, but the pro-Habsburg Eszterházy refused the "Corsican adventurer's" offer. Napoleon wanted Poland, too, to join the anti-Habsburg camp as an independent country.

It was in these years that the childless nobleman Igor adopted the eight-year-old Hyron, who was peeling potatoes and sweeping the floor in the Govno monastery's kitchen. In the year 1820, when Hyron was nineteen, both of his foster parents died of cholera. Except for a few pieces of furniture and some twenty silver florins, carefully hidden in a mattress, Hyron did not inherit anything from them but undying Polish patriotism.

Next year, when he became a student at Vilno University, he was already fluent in Latin, German, Russian and French, beside his native Polish, and he had learned to play the piano very well. Papa Igor and Mama Vyola had been generous in providing his education.

At Vilno University he excelled in philosophy, history and literature, but spent more time in the Polish underground than at the university.

4

In contrast with Flexi in Vienna, who addressed his tutor as Professor Loebel, Dali called Monsieur Antoine Jules la Harpe just Tonchi. And in contrast with Professor Karl Loebel who addressed Flexi as "Your Excellency, Count Antal," Tonchi called Dali from the very first day just Dali.

And, also in contrast with Professor Loebel, whose sixty years and 200 hundred pounds compelled him to teach from an armchair, Tonchi insisted upon the peripatetic system of Aristotle.

"*Peripatoi* means shady avenues," he lectured as they strolled under the oak trees of the Ararat park. "Your age of twelve was regarded in ancient times as the right age to marry. The purpose of these early marriages, for example Xingo and Urivardah, the Pharaohs, was to lead the awakening sexual desires into normal channels. Do you masturbate, sir?"

And without waiting for Dali's answer, he continued:

"Don't. It ruins the nerves, the brain, the character—no, I don't suggest that you should marry right away, I am just telling you that a scratch on your nose, a kick or a bite from a girl is much better. The cradle of western civilization in Assyria and Babylonia. . . ."

And he switched back to the first chapters of history.

Next day, during his lecture in literature, he said:

"Who? Grillparzer? No, no, no! Don't listen to Flexi. Byron! Lord Byron is the greatest poet of our time! He fought for the independence of Greece. Listen to the divine charm of that Byron poem: "Sublime tobacco! Glorious in pipe. When tipped with amber . . . Yet thy true lovers, More admire by far, thy naked beauties. Give me a cigar!"

Dali dashed back to the castle and returned with a big cigar from his father's drawer. Cigar-smoking was the newest fashion, imported from England. Tonchi was crazy for cigars.

"Thank you, sir. Cigar," Tonchi said, "is a Spanish word from tobacco-rich Havana. It means a kind of cicada, a long-shaped bug. Speaking about etymology, do you know why this village is called Ararat? No, you don't. Even your father did not know it, but last night I was digging in the castle's archive. The village, an old settlement, received its biblical name in the sixteenth century, during a devastating Danubian flood which drove inhabitants to seek refuge under the ancient walls of the Dukay fortress—the present Ararat park."

He pointed to a clearing:

"Look at that wonderful pall mall. Ideal for the game I taught you yesterday, very popular in English aristocratic circles."

They started to play pall mall while Tonchi continued:

"Alexander the *Great,* not the lunatic impostor from St. Petersburg, but the Great from Macedonia, the Emathian conqueror, as Milton wrote: 'Bade spare the house of Pindar' when he burnt Thebes. Who was Pindar?"

"The tutor of Alexander the Great."

"Wrong. Pindar was a great poet. Alexander's tutor was Aristotle, the greatest. You must keep in mind that a tutor stands always high, high above his pupil. Throw me back the ball."

Instead of the wooden ball Dali threw back a round fresh horse turd and Tonchi caught it in mid-air, expertly but absentmindedly. And the fun went on incessantly during the most serious lectures.

Tonchi's development in the Ural-Altayan Hungarian language was much slower than Dali's in French and English. A new kind of folklore was blossoming in Ararat, a collection of Tonchi's mispronounciations and misuse of the Magyar tongue. Dali had a hand in building up Tonchi's Magyar vocabulary. But of course—a trick centuries old—the words for eye, ear, mouth, hand, foot, glass of water were the most obscene expressions, and when Tonchi innocently used them his audience screamed with laughter.

"Next time—just wait—I will challenge you to a duel!" Tonchi threatened Dali.

Dali fought his first duel at the age of fifteen. The affair began in the Árpád Café in Pesth, while Tonchi was teaching him to play billiards. Dali was engrossed in a difficult shot when a stranger, entering in a hurry, pushed the end of his cue at the critical moment.

"Can't you watch out, you idiot!" Dali shouted in rage.

The stranger, a nineteen-year-old Hercules with a barrel chest, smiled and flicked Dali on the nose with a knockwurstsized finger. The flick plainly said: "You sprout!" It took three waiters and Tonchi to hold Dali back. Tonchi led Dali to a corner table to cool off; and, meditating on the situation, he finally declared: "I am sorry to tell you, there is no other solution. You must challenge him to a duel."

Dali nodded. Tonchi went to the stranger's table to challenge him in the name of Count Adalbert Dukay. The Hercules accepted the challenge and agreed to pistols, the duel to be fought the next Sunday morning in the Ararat park at the close range of ten paces.

When Tonchi informed Dali of the arrangements, Dali's face flushed with excitement. Whenever he blushed or became angry at something, the upper part of his ears turned as red as a red rose. He was not frightened by the severe arrangement of the duel—oh, no! He was proud to enter manhood.

"The punctilious code of duelling sets no age limits," Tonchi explained to Dali. And, as usual, he went on lecturing: "Duelling for gentlemen has always been a highly important part of life, a divine service for such gods as Honor, Gallantry and Courage. In the fifteen century in a single decade more than 6,000 French gentlemen fell in duels, and even monks carried on their controversies by champions-at-arms. One of the most famous duels in my lifetime was between the Duke of Wellington and Lord Winchelsea. Wellington missed his aim, whereupon Winchelsea fired into the air and apologized. That's what I call *gallantry!*"

"Do you think that I must report the affair to my father?" Dali asked, chewing his nails.

"As your tutor, I must report it and ask his permission for the duel. I hope he won't agree. I don't like this affair, David."

"Why do you call me David?"

"Well, this fellow is a Goliath, isn't he?"

They mounted their horses, and Tonchi lifted his grey top hat to Hercules, who stood near the café's entrance. In reply, Hercules bowed deeply.

They rode back to Buda where the family sojourned in the Septemvir Utca palace.

Endre Dukay listened carefully to Monsieur la Harpe's report, and asked:

"What is the name of the stranger?"

"Baron Andris Zeker," answered Tonchi.

"Andris Zeker? That big boy?" exclaimed Endre. Then he turned to his son:

"He is the son of your godfather."

Then he added, blowing his nose loudly:

"Of course I know him—he is famed not only as the strongest man of the younger generation, but as a champion shot."

To Dali's great surprise, Endre gave his permission for the duel. *"Noblesse oblige* comes before all for a Dukay," he said.

Sunday morning at dawn Baron Andris Zeker appeared at Ararat with a second and a doctor. Zeker was dressed in his hussar lieutenant's uniform. The second carried the leather case containing the oversize pistols.

According to the rules the opponents had to fight stripped to their waists, in order to show that they wore no hidden armor. Before the duel Tonchi, with a jar in his hand, pulled Dali behind a bush and whispered to him:

"Don't laugh at me for being superstitious; the duelling code does not object to it—let me cover your chest with honey. It is the best armor against a mortal wound. It saved Goethe's life, too, in a pistol duel."

Dali surrendered to the old superstition because, unfortunately for him, the tossed coin had given the baron first shot.

In solemn silence and at a safe distance, everyone was on hand to witness the proceedings, including all the Dukays' weekend guests. Tonchi was right; when the opponents took their places they resembled David and Goliath. Matted hair covered the baron's huge barrel chest; Dali's chest, glistening with honey, was hairless. The silence was dramatic. When, at the short distance of six paces, Tonchi cried "Fire!" the baron's pistol rang out; and the audience screamed—with laughter. The barrel had been crammed with white down, and every bit of it stuck to the honey-covered Dali, who now looked like an oversized duck.

Among the weekend guests who enjoyed witnessing the "duel" were the handsome Prince Felix Schwarzenberg, a young diplomat, and Baron Karl Rothschild, a rather corpulent man of about forty, with tufts of graying red hair bordering a bald head. Baron Karl put a heavily ringed hand on Dali's shoulder and said with great satisfaction, "You deserved it, you good for nothing!"

Baron Karl had good reason to be annoyed with Dali. Karl was the first Jew upon whom the Austrian monarchy had ever bestowed the baronetcy. The Rothschilds had never been flamboyant about money, but Karl treasured his baronetcy, and he was proud of his new signet ring. The summer before Dali's duel, after a swim in the nearby Velence Lake, Baron Karl had cried out: "Good Lord—my signet ring slipped off my finger!"

"How much will you pay me, Uncle Karl," Dali asked, "if I'll find your ring in the lake?"

"I will pay you a hundred florins," Baron Karl said, because he knew that the bottom of the lake was soft mud, and he thought there was no hope that Dali could find the ring.

Dali dived headlong into the lake and was up again in a suspiciously short time. Swimming with one hand, he held high the ring. At that moment, Baron Karl suddenly recalled that he had left the ring on a flat stone before he went into the lake. But the greatness of the Rothschilds lay in the fact that they never went back on a verbal agreement.

There were two cousins of Dali's among the guests, Erich and Claudia. Baron Erich Dukay-Hedwitz was now a young and elegant dragoon lieutenant; he was well over six feet tall, and very thin. Baron Erich had a surprisingly small head with smooth butter-yellow hair, and the expression on his handsome face resembled that of an intelligent horse—more precisely, a gelding from the Mecklenburg stables. General von Hedwitz, Erich's father, was married to Apollonia Dukay, Endre's sister.

Claudia, a bewitchingly beautiful young girl, was the only daughter of Count István Rhédey, who had married Petronella, another sister of Endre.

Claudia's large eyes were dark blue, fringed with bristly black lashes and slightly tilted at the ends. Her velvet black brows slanted upward in her pale heart-shaped face, but the crown of her beauty was her silky raven hair, a deep bluish black. One of her ancestors must have been a "black Kun" from the ancient Oguz-Turk tribe. There were golden bees embroidered on Claudia's white muslin dress, which spread its many yards of rolling waves over a framework of hoops. Her waist was the smallest in the monarchy and her tightly fitted blouse, patterned after old Hungarian folk costumes, showed well matured breasts for her thirteen years. She looked fifteen. The year before Dali's duel she had come in second in the steeplechase for ladies. When Dali jumped into the fishpond to wash off the honey and duckdown from his chest, Claudia was greatly disillusioned. She had thought the duel was serious. She knew that Dali was desperately in love with her.

The other cousin, Baron Erich Dukay-Hedwitz was disillusioned too when the duel turned out to be a practical joke. He was third in line as heir, and if one of the twins had been killed in a duel he would have stepped up to second place.

Flexi had not known that the duel was not serious either, but his reaction was quite different from Erich's. Pale with emotion, after the great laugh, he turned to Erich: "It was a very cruel joke!" He was sorry for his brother; it had been a humiliation—for a Dukay. Flexi, under the influence of Professor Loebel, saw Dali first as a Dukay *de genere* Ordony, and only after that as his twin brother.

During that eventful day, twelve-year-old Rolly was confined in her room under the care of her French governess. She was being educated in the Vienna *Sacre Coeur,* where she was very successful in preserving her innocence against the nuns' lessons; be it history, geography, mathematics or any other tortures.

If she had known of Dali's fate in the duel, she would have been as satisfied as Baron Rothschild, shouting triumphantly: "You deserved it, you . . . !" Rolly still mourned poor Sha-sha, her white rabbit, burned to ashes on the Ordony pyre.

In contrast to Flexi's reaction, Dali was more amused than hurt by the joke. Andris, with his large, laughing brown eyes, had become his idol—especially after Dali heard that, the previous year, Andris had distinguished himself in a fight with five ultranationalist German students in a Frankfurt beer-hall. The tipsy students, followers of Fichte's theory of the superiority of the German race above all others—had made some nasty remarks about Andris' richly trimmed Hungarian *dolmány.*

"I didn't have either sword or stick, but I beat all four to the ground."

"Four? You said they were five," remarked Erich Dukay-Hedwitz, who was a German ultranationalist himself.

"Five, yes. But I used the fifth one for a stick to beat the other four," the Herculean Andris said modestly.

While everybody laughed heartily, Erich blushed. Andris was the hero of the day.

5

Endre Dukay leaned over the ear trumpet and shouted: "How are you, Uncle George?"

The old man, sitting by the window in an armchair, took the horn from his ear and nodded with a faint smile. Endre arranged the cover on his uncle's knees, although his tender gesture was not at all necessary. He pulled a chair up to the old man's, a deeply thoughtful expression on his face. He was trying to decide what his next remark should be. Should he report that he had signed a ten-year lease for the water mills on the Danube with Jacob Eskeles, the Vienna entrepreneur recommended to him by Karl Rothschild? Should he report that last week he had sold 367 fattened oxen at the Vienna market, at eleven florins apiece? Should he report that in the Transylvanian Gere estate a forest fire was still raging? Should he report that sixteen horses had been stolen by armed *betyárs* from Ararat stables, with saddles, reins, silver bridles and all?

At last, he signalled Uncle George that he had something to say. Up went the trumpet.

"Frici has climbed the ladder!"

The old man looked at the window ledge, where, in a glass jar half filled with water, a green frog sat on top of his tiny ladder, his stupid face trying to look dignified. His position on top of the ladder meant sunny days.

The next topic of their conversation was the maiden voyage of the first steamship, the *Argot*, to navigate the Danube from Vienna to Buda-Pesth. Returning, she could move upstream, too. No, no! Neither sails nor oars, just steam.

The old man's lonely face stared into space after Endre's confused attempt to explain how a steam engine works. Endre felt that he had explored all possible avenues of conversation. He rose and kissed the top of his uncle's bald head, the skin of which resembled the dry crust of *gomolya,* a round sheep's cheese. He patted the old man's sunken shoulder and left the room with the good feeling that for another three months he had performed all his filial and official duties as heir and overseer-in-chief of the huge Dukay estate.

Two months later, in January 1829, Prince George Dukay passed on, taking with him the only title of prince in the family. The death of the old man brought but one change in Endre's life: he was released from the obligatory ten-minute visit to his uncle every three months to report that the weather was nice or that it was raining.

The final entry in Countess Jadi's *Flexi* diary was dated in May 1830, and described little beyond Flexi's hope for the future. Countess Jadi wrote:

Sunday night at dinner Endre turned to Flexi and said, "There is very little chance for me, in this new age of political stability and economic prosperity, to accomplish a diplomatic coup or to win a battle, and without this I will never receive the title of prince. But I have the definite feeling that the day will come when Uncle George's title will be resurrected. It does not sound bad, does it? Prince Antal Dukay. And I can somehow imagine you wearing a full marshal's uniform—perhaps even the green frock coat of the —" Endre obviously intended to say "chancellor," but he changed it to "of an ambassador."

Flexi has never been enthusiastic for either a military or a diplomatic career. I felt that Endre was rather tactless to paint a bright future for Flexi and say nothing to Dali. But Dali did not seem hurt. He covered his mouth with his hand, suppressing a laugh, when Endre said that Uncle George's title of prince one day would be resurrected as Prince Antal Dukay. "I would be unhappy," he later told me, "to wear the ugly and ridiculous title of prince."

Next day I asked Tonchi whether he had ever noticed in Dali the second-born's envy of the firstborn. "Never!" was Tonchi's answer.

Dali (under the influence of Tonchi) is dreaming of the day when he will be a liberator of both Hungary and Poland. Flexi (under the influence of Solly Rothschild) is a great reformer too— in economics. He excitedly told me the other day that the Rothschilds are already negotiating with Uncle Clemi for a concession to build railways in Hungary.

In the early thirties, Hungary's strong desire for radical alterations in modes of living was represented by Count István Széchenyi, a Lichtenstein hussar captain. Enchanted by what he saw in England, he was dreaming of a huge stone-and-steel-chain bridge across the Danube which would make Buda-Pesth Budapest, permanently connecting the western and eastern parts of the city.

While Flexi and Solly Rothschild concentrated their attention on revolutionary experiments in manufacturing artificial fertilizers, the *trio* in Buda (Dali, Tonchi and Andris) concentrated their attention on the galaxy of new, revolutionary writers.

Byron and Shelley had laughed at the arrogance and hypocrisy of the entrenched conservatism, a new word coined by Metternich. In France, under the pen name of George Sand, a lady was the first to make peasants and humble laborers the heroes of her novels. Victor Hugo, the *enfant terrible,* began a literary revolution with his anti-classical poetry.

Writers, artists, intellectuals of the young century seemed to be a powder train across most of Europe—a train that would one day demolish the last of the eighteenth century.

In the summer of 1830, the accumulated energy of the young century exploded in Paris. When, in July, French troops captured Algeria, bigger in size than France's whole territory, France suddenly regained her conscience and self-esteem; and revolution broke out in Paris. The days of 1789 came back: the French would no longer tolerate the despotism of Louis XVI's youngest brother, Charles X. When Louis XVIII had died in 1824, the Bourbon dynasty seemed triumphant over its foes. But Charles X suffered from constitution-phobia, and had frankly said he would rather chop wood than be king in a constitutional monarchy like England's. Controlled by old-fashioned ideas, he had increased the influence of the clergy and approved a law granting cash money to nobles for the estates they had lost in the Revolution. One billion francs! When a worker hardly earned two francs a day for twelve hours' work. He issued a series of ordinances narrowing the suffrage, took from the chambers the right to suggest laws, set up a severe censorship silencing his critics, and left the French people without any check on his cruel absolutism.

The details of the Paris revolution reached Vienna and Buda-Pesth in a few weeks. Destroyed by cannons, the barricades in Paris were quickly rebuilt. On the next day two regiments went over to the rebels. . . . Then Lafayette appeared on the balcony of the City Hall with the Duke of Orleans, both of them covered, not by the white-lily flag of the Bourbons, but by the tricolor of the First Republic. Louis Philippe called himself not "king by the grace of God" but "King by the will of the people." In his youth "Philippe Egalité" had spent several years travelling in the young United States.

"Our young century is now on the threshold of the Age of Revolutions," Tonchi said. "The classic building of the Congress of Vienna, full of lice and rats, will be torn down very soon."

Twenty-year-old Andris Zeker and sixteen-year-old Dali listened to Tonchi's prophecies breathlessly. Andris was a steady guest at Ararat during the summer months, and whenever he came to Buda, a room was waiting for him in the Septemvir Utca palace.

"Isn't it wonderful," Dali said, "that Montesquieu gave the spark to the American constitution, and now Philippe has brought it back to France as a huge torch!"

The July revolution in France was the signal for an outbreak in Brussels. The Congress of Vienna had united Belgium with the Dutch Netherlands, but the Dutch monopolized the most important offices in the government; and the fact that the Belgians were Catholic and the Dutch Protestant did not help a peaceful settlement.

Plutot mourir que vivre esclaves! was the slogan of the Brussels revolution a few weeks later. The *Plutot* emblems were secretly distributed throughout Europe. When Dali showed his to his friend, Andris with a broad grin turned back his lapel and revealed the same white-green emblem: "Better die than live as a slave!"

"Sit down, gentlemen," Tonchi said one night to Dali and Andris in an unusually serious tone. "I want to talk to you."

He closed the door and said:

"There are people whose slogan is 'Better to *lie* than to *die*.' I do not want to lie to you any longer.

"I don't ask your word of honor, gentlemen. I know I can trust you. Now I will tell you my secret. I am a dead man."

Dali did not like Tonchi's pale face and the forced humor in his voice.

"Before I became Antoine Jules la Harpe," Tonchi continued, "I had to bury my dangerous past. I had to forget my origin."

He gestured theatrically.

"I am a . . ." but his humor—both in the exaggerated gesture and in his voice—broke. He dropped his elbow on the table, covered his eyes with his hand, and said with a suppressed sob:

"I am a Pole."

Dali and Andris stirred. Tonchi's words went through their hearts. After a silence, it was Dali who first spoke, his voice choked with emotion:

"Are you a Polish count?"

Tonchi regained his humor when he answered in a tutorial tone, calling his pupil to order:

"When I discussed with you the Epoch of Great Aristocrats—Montesquieu, Lafayette, Czartoryski, Széchenyi, the Belgian Count de Merode, now that greenhorn Count Dali Dukay and that fathead Baron Andris Zeker, I didn't mean that *only* aristocrats could be great men."

Andris' big arm, in appreciation, embraced Tonchi's shoulders.

"You have many relatives in Poland?" asked Dali.

Tonchi shook his head.

"None. In a true sense I am the legal son of Poland, because I was born as an illegitimate child. In the thick wall of the Govno monastery, there is a hole one foot square called the Sacred Mailbox—a tender and beautiful gesture of the Catholic Church, a heritage of the Middle Ages. A girl who had sinned would come to the monastery after nightfall, put her child into the Sacred Mailbox, and run away. We grew up in the monastery. Later we were adopted by childless parents. Five years ago I was in Warsaw when Novosolsky, the Russian commander, said that no Polish patriot would be left alive. I urged a student meeting to *answer* Novosolsky."

He looked around and whispered:

"After the Paris and Brussels revolutions, the time is here to say a few nice words to Novosolsky."

Dali and Andris did not ask what he meant by the "few nice words" to the Russian general.

After a brief silence Dali said:

"I have never seen mother's parental house in Warsaw. And I was six, perhaps seven, when I saw Grandpa Maurycy for the last time in Vienna."

"I am willing to accompany you," Tonchi said. "Let's go to Warsaw."

CHAPTER THREE

COUNT MAURYCY RADOWSKI'S wife, the former Jadwiga Voronieczki, daughter of an impoverished Polish prince, had died in 1807, on the very day when Napoleon and Czar Alexander, meeting on a carpeted raft on the River Niemen in East Prussia at Tilsit, had embraced and kissed each other and vowed the everlasting friendship that was to last all of three years.

The motherless daughters, Olga and Jadi, had been brought up in the benign hands of Aunt Eca, their mother's eldest sister. Papa Maurycy called her "Eca The Invisible" because she always disappeared when the door bell rang. She was always afraid that visitors, catching sight of her, would be frightened. For a frog, Aunt Eca would have been too big, but for a human being she was too small. Lame in both legs, she walked with the movement of a boat in high waves. With her enormous hunched back she seemed a monster to strangers; but to those who knew her well she was an angel. Olga and Jadi had had a happy childhood in her devoted care.

Papa Maurycy, however busy with the thousand problems on his estate, had always time to spend a few minutes with his

daughters. Every evening, before they went to bed after pray-
ing, he took his daughters into his arms one after another, and
tickled their faces with his big reddish-blond eyebrows, while
the little girls screamed with laughter.

After the girls were married, Olga to Prince Leon Serebraniy
in 1811, and Jadi to Endre Dukay in 1813, Aunt Eca had closed
her large, gray eyes and died, fully realizing that there was no
more need for her service.

The Radowski house in a narrow, curved street, was a modest
structure with only one floor and ten rooms; but it seemed very
large for a fifty-year-old man's loneliness. Still, when a friend
suggested that Maurycy marry again, he said briefly, "Remember King Otrid."

According to an old folk tale, King Otrid proclaimed that he
would give half of his empire to anyone who could cure his
beloved wife's muteness. Eventually a Chinese surgeon succeeded in the task, and the queen started to speak. After two
months, the king called back the Chinese and said to him: "I'll
give you the other half of my empire if you make my wife mute
again."

Papa Maurycy preferred loneliness to the risks of a second
marriage.

At the end of October 1830, Dali and Tonchi, having left
Endre with the idea that the visit was simply the gesture of a
dutiful grandson, arrived in Warsaw.

Grandpapa Maurycy kissed Dali and embraced him. "Let me
look at you!" he exclaimed. He stepped back to inspect Dali,
and was immediately pleased by the boy's masculine appearance. His looks lived up to the reputation he had been building
for daring and manliness. For example, Jadi had written to her
father of an episode of the preceding winter, when the pontoon
bridge between Buda and Pesth had been dismantled because of
the floating ice, and hundreds of spectators had been amazed to
see a young man jumping from one ice cake to the next on
horseback. Dali had not meant to show off. He was simply keeping an engagement with Andris Zeker to play billiards at the
Café Árpád.

Of Dali's interest in liberal revolutions, Grandpa Maurycy
knew nothing, nor was he sharp enough to detect the Pole in

the Monsieur Antoine Jules la Harpe, his grandson's tutor. Since neither of the young men appeared to know any Polish, and Grandpapa knew no Hungarian, their communication was in French.

At the supper table in the old Radowski house, Dali, reporting news from Vienna, took up the story of Metternich's recent marriage to the twenty-year-old daughter of a clerk in the chancellery. That she was of Jewish origin astonished the old man. "A commoner? A Jewess?" he demanded.

"Neither one since her marriage," Dali replied. "Her parents were baptized long ago, and Uncle Clemi saw to it that she was given the title Countess Bleistein a week before the wedding.

"Father says that we must understand his serenity," Dali continued. "He needed relaxation and diversion, after his difficult hours at the chancellery. His great brain was aching with the uncertainties of the monarchy's future—indeed, of the future of Europe. It was known that he was going to the apartment of this Herr Leykam four or five times a week. After dining there, he would stay until midnight."

"Because of the girl?" Grandpa interjected.

"As well as his heart, he kept his 'cello there," Dali said. "I understand that his serenity is not much of a player, but is a passionate devotee who needs music as a drug addict needs his poison."

Grandpa Maurycy knew the feeling, since one of his best friends in his loneliness was his violin. "I am glad to hear something human about the man," he said.

"Another attraction of the Leykam apartment," Dali went on, "was its atmosphere. No talk of politics there, and no danger that one of the musicians would fall on his knees before Metternich's 'cello pleading for promotion, or even worse, pleading for mercy for a relative awaiting execution."

After dinner Grandpa showed Dali and Tonchi through the old house, pointing out the family portraits and mementos of a time when Poland had been a happier land. For some time Dali stood in the small vaulted room in which his mother had lived when she was a girl. The fireplace was almost as he had imagined it from her description, and the rocking chair standing before it exactly so. In his mind's eye he saw his mother when she was fifteen, sixteen, seventeen, sitting in that chair, her knees crossed under the long, white skirts, one dainty foot tilting up the hem, the tip of her black shoe dipping into the firelight as the chair swung to and fro. She held her guitar in her lap, singing *"La petite Abeille,"* the tender romantic song for children about the little bee's dangerous adventure with the giant flower: "Zing-zong . . . zou-zou-zou . . . zing-zong . . ." was the refrain. Jadi had sung it to Dali as a lullaby when he was a baby.

Now he clearly heard his mother's voice and saw her as she leaned her blonde head over the guitar, her hand jumping rapidly over the strings because the frets were so far apart for her small white fingers, "Zing-zong . . . zou-zou-zou . . . zing-zong."

Perhaps, Dali thought, his mother was herself that little bee in the symbolic song, and the Vienna court was the bewildering flower, every petal of it a lady-in-waiting.

Next morning Grandpa Maurycy took Dali and Tonchi on a tour of his stable and barns, proudly showing off his shorthorn cattle from Switzerland and his Berkshire hogs from England.

"You don't mind, my boy," he said to Dali, "if I point out that my imported cattle and swine are as unknown on the conservative Dukay estates as African giraffes. Am I right, Monsieur la Harpe?"

"Certainement, Your Excellency," Tonchi answered; and though he had never been to Switzerland, he added: "I am delighted to see my progressive compatriots represented in your stable."

Grandpapa Maurycy took himself very seriously as a progressive agronomist. "My father," he said, "in 1772, the year of the great famine, introduced a new perennial plant, a native of the Peruvian Andes. The peasants, at first hopeful, spat out its bitter purple berries. It took some time to explain to them that the roots of the plant were the edible part. Then, within two decades, Poland became the largest potato field in Europe.

As the walk continued, Grandpa observed that Poland, within the space of a century or so, had imported five valuable commodities from the Western Hemisphere: potatoes, maize, tobacco, the acacia tree, and true democracy. "Of these," he added, "the last is still available only on the black market."

Any political remark Grandpa made confirmed Dali's belief

that he was to be classed as a moderate, if only because the leader of the moderates, Prince Adam Czartoryski, was a former schoolmate and his closest friend. Grandpa was obviously not a conservative. The conservatives, as Tonchi explained it, held that the lion is not unjust in eating the zebra or gazelle, but just stronger than his victim according to the law of nature. Therefore, it would be hopeless for the Poles to revolt against the lion—the Russian, Prussian and Austrian armies. Mostly land-owners and high office holders, the conservatives expected to do nothing until the lion grew old, lost his teeth, and one day dropped dead. The moderates, Tonchi said, not to mention the extremists, regarded the conservatives as traitors. But even as a moderate, Grandpa Maurycy seemed out of things—happier listening to the buzzing of the bees in his new, airy hives than the buzzing of the old political bees in their smoky headquarters. When Tonchi asked him if he had heard Czartoryski make his recent speech, in which he referred to the tragedy of Kosciuso's costly revolution of thirty-six years before, Grandpa said that he had missed the meeting because he was helping one of his mares give birth to a colt.

The second morning of Dali's stay, when he happened to be alone in the front of the house, a visitor rang. Dali admitted a man about sixty, wearing a brick-red cloak and gray top hat. His cleanshaven face was handsome, the profile Roman. He addressed Dali in Polish and was answered by the apologetic face of one who does not understand. The old man put his question in French, and learned that he was speaking to the son of Endre Dukay.

"One of the twins?" he asked, his eyes narrowing with sudden interest.

"Yes sir."

The man smiled and put a hand on Dali's shoulder: "I was present at your christening, my boy—Czartoryski."

Grandpa Maurycy now appeared in the corridor behind Dali, greeted his visitor with a warm handshake, and led him into his study without inviting Dali to join them. Behind the closed door they conferred for an hour. Dali kept hoping that Tonchi would return to the house before the great man left, but Tonchi did not reappear until late in the afternoon. And when Dali had a chance to speak to him privately, it was plain that Tonchi's interest in the moderates, and Czartoryski, was second to his interest in the extremists.

"The hour for Poland to rise will soon be striking," Tonchi said. His tone indicated that he had been spending his time with conspirators. Dali wanted to be taken along to the secret meetings, but Tonchi declined, saying that he had promised Countess Jadi to keep him out of trouble. "Besides, you do not understand Polish, so it would be a bore," he said. But there was more to it, Dali knew. Tonchi was being too tightlipped, putting him off with: "Soon we shall be saying our words to Novosolsky."

The question of how to "say a few words" to Novosolsky, bestially cruel to "suspicious" Polish patriots, was feverishly debated every night in the Polish underground at meetings held in the small house of old Prince Voronieczki, an impoverished uncle of Countess Jadi. It was reported that a few miles from Warsaw, on a remote shore of the Vistula, in the shadow of old willow trees stood a fishing boat, its square dipping-net pulled up for drying, its cabin locked. There was nothing conspicuous about it. The Polish underground had learned that the forty-five-year-old Novosolsky sneaked out of his office in the Belvedere palace two or three times a week, dressed in civilian clothes, in the company of two husky men. He and his bodyguards then drove in a peasant cart to the remote Vistula shore, where Novosolsky disappeared in the fishing boat's cabin while his two bodyguards pretended to fish on the shore. Hiding in the nearby bushes, the underground partisans saw a veiled lady enter the cabin, and through the flimsy walls they could hear the popping corks of champagne bottles inside.

Tonchi suggested kidnapping Novosolsky, and forcing him to give written orders to the Russian troops to join the revolution when it broke out. The majority of the underground approved Tonchi's idea. They knew that the Russian soldiers hated Czar Nicholas. But a small group vehemently opposed the kidnapping. "No good! Very risky! Let's kill Novosolsky right away!"

That night, coming home late, Tonchi saw a light in Dali's room and found him deeply immersed in literary work. On his head stood a hand-lettered placard reading: HUNGAPOLE.

Blushing as if he had been caught in some embarrassing secret, Dali put down his quill and said: "That life-size portrait in Grandpa's study. Do you know who he is?"

Tonchi knew, of course. The portrait depicted a robust and majestic man with a red-whiskered face and bright eyes, dressed in the gaudy cloak and fur-trimmed cap of a Polish nobleman of the sixteenth century. He was king István Bátori—the last name meant Brave—under whose reign Poland had risen to the peak of her power and glory. Tonchi had taught Dali to regard Bátori as an idol, the greatest man in history. The bloodthirsty barbarian potentate whom Bátori had defeated and humiliated was Ivan the Terrible, the first Russian to use the title of czar. Showing Dali the portrait, Grandpapa had told Dali that he had Bátori blood in his veins: One of his ancestors, Balint Dukay, in 1615, had married Anna Bátori.

"I was alone with my ancestor's portrait this afternoon a long time," Dali said slowly, "and I gave a lot of thought to the common fate of both my countries, Poland and Hungary."

He paused, twisting his forelock furiously. "My conclusion," he resumed, "is that the two countries should unite."

"You mean personal union?" Tonchi said.

"Yes. The same person on two thrones, just as Francis is now emperor of Austria and king of Hungary."

Dali waved at his placard. "How do you like the new name?"

Tonchi smiled, his eyes feeding on Dali's face, beautiful by the candlelight. Dali was maturing now, his young and clean mind struggling with high ideals. A Hungarian and a descendant of Ordony on his father's side—the chieftain who had made the original allocation of Hungary's land nearly a millennium before—and of the Bátori line, and a Pole, on his mother's side. God knows, Tonchi thought, in a decade or so, the product of the two nations might even become the first sovereign of a new united nation.

"Hungapole . . ." he tried the word. "It's magnificent, but I don't like it. You forget that English is spoken all over the world. Hungapole, to me, means another corpse at the end of a rope." Seeing Dali's disappointment, he added quickly: "I am just joking. How about putting Poland first?—Polahung? No, that sounds Chinese. But let's talk seriously. I am not quite sure that Hungapole is the right name for a Hungarian-Polish personal union, but your basic idea is not only excellent but timely. After the successful Spanish revolts in the last decades—Mexico, Peru, Chile, Bolivia and so on—and now after the Paris and Brussels revolutions, all of Central Europe is about to be engulfed by radical revolutions. Germany! For social reforms. Northern Italy! Perhaps the Czechs, the Slovenes . . ."

Tonchi looked around and continued whispering:

". . . and perhaps the Hungarians, too . . . and one day the Austrians. Yes! Against the Habsburgs! Revolution is a very contagious disease. The next 'victim' is Poland. Our revolution, under the leadership of Czartoryski, is a question of weeks if not of days."

"But you say," Dali objected, "Czartoryski is a moderate. How can a moderate lead a revolution?"

Tonchi, still standing with hat and gloves and cane in hand, pushed his hat back from his forehead.

"Oh, Dali! Remember Mirabeau—one of those who started the French Revolution! An intimate friend of Queen Marie Antoinette, he was a moderate compared to Marat or Robespierre, wasn't he? Czartoryski is not an extremist, but as a great patriot he is a true revolutionist."

Stepping closer to Dali, he addded:

"The Congress of Vienna did not understand the irreconcilable differences in mentality, in culture and in religion between Orthodox Greek Russia and Roman Catholic Poland. Their historical evolution is completely divergent. Russia is Asia, and Poland is Europe.

"A lot of things have happened in the sixteen years since you and our century were born. This summer the downfall of Charles X, the last Bourbon king of France, as Lafayette proclaimed, greatly weakened Metternich's position. The new government in Paris is to be a constitutional monarchy, like your Hungapole. Then the success of the Belgians' mighty blow for independence is regarded with favor both by France and Britain."

"So you think," Dali asked, "that a Polish revolution would have the same reception by France and England?"

"I have no doubt of it!" Tonchi said emphatically.

The following week, as Warsaw became the storm center of living history, Dali started to write a diary, though he sat much more firmly in the saddle than at the desk of a Gibbon or a Chateaubriand.

Warsaw, Nov. 28, 1830

Tonchi home 2 A.M. Deadly pale. Collapsed in armchair. "It was horrible," he whispered. Later told me that a band of cadets broke into the Russian headquarters at Belvedere palace, and knowing nothing of his well prepared kidnapping plan, "killed" General Novosolsky. He was shot by a volley of pistols as he descended the stairway in the palace's lobby. When he rolled to their feet, they saw he was not Novosolsky but Ritter von Eigler, an innocent Austrian general, a cousin of Metternich's private secretary, a good friend of father's.

"A very bad way to start a revolution," Tonchi concluded. "At that hour Novosolsky was in the fishing boat's cabin with his whore."

November 30

Whole population Warsaw in dark about latest news.

"Stay where you are!" Grandpa shouted to me when I grabbed my hat and wanted to go down to the street. Tonchi has not come back yet; we are left without news. Grandpa went to bed after midnight.

I stood by the open window in my room. The night was dark, full of *bees* but these not Grandpa's buzzing bees—flying bullets. During dinner Grandpa told me that first the cadet school rioted because of a rumor that Nick the Stick intends to send his army to dethrone Louis Philippe. Others joined cadets. The czar also plans to put down the revolution in Brussels.

I always imagined that a revolution would be lit by flames—the roofs of office buildings, churches, palaces, set on fire. Here only the . . . zzzz . . . zzz . . . in the dark, cold rain.

At two o'clock, window panes in my room suddenly trembled, shaken by cannon shot. Russian cannon!

I leaned out of the window, saw red lights east and south. The shooting got stronger. From east it sounded pak-pak-pak . . . from the south help-help-help . . . Though it was pitch dark, I thought I saw Polish cadets with broken swords and smoking pistols in their hands, and I imagined, too, Tonchi fighting at their sides. I saw dead heroes and fallen horses, and when the cannons thundered again I felt that I could not live with the shame if I did not join them. I dashed into Grandpa's study and grabbed an old pistol and sword from the wall. Sword slipped from my hand, made frightful noise. Grandpa did not wake.

Sneaked out front door. Streets dark and deserted at first. Only the pak-pak-pak . . . which came closer as I ran. Crossing a square, a flash lit the houses. Statue of rearing horse and rider in center of square seemed to jump at me, frightened and neighing. Vision disappeared. Terrible explosion. Then silence.

Decided that must be new, much-talked-of wonder weapon, invented by Englishman, General Shrapnel, and immediately adopted by Russians.

Ran few more steps. Deafening explosion knocked me to ground. Lay near statue wondering if I was dying so soon, without seeing even one of the enemy.

All this happened two nights ago. At dawn I returned to house, not even scratched. Went to bed. Late for breakfast, but Grandpa unaware of what I had done. Tonchi absent. Grandpa, concerned for his safety and mine, ordered me into carriage and four. I am writing this en route to Vienna. I still hear the bees singing, and when I shut my eyes, the horse jumps again out of the blinding light. I shiver. Have fever.

Dali was carried into the palace of Vienna, a victim of typhus, as Doctor Kunz soon established. For two weeks he lay in his room looked after by no servant; Jadi insisted on tending him herself. Doctor Kunz attended and administered one after another his remedies of bleeding, blistering, vomiting, and purging. Repeatedly the delirious sufferer asked for Tonchi. Each time he was told that Tonchi was in the palace, but this was simply a lie to humor him.

Dali's tutor had disappeared without a trace. For Grandpa and Endre, Monsieur la Harpe had seemed to take an extraordinary interest in the Polish situation in Warsaw, and it was to be presumed that he had met his end.

During the weeks in which Dali slowly recovered his strength, a number of reports, official and otherwise, reached Vienna about the happenings in Poland. Although the insurgents had shown a heroic determination, none of the Polish officers had known quite how to evolve a victory. In the Diet, the Polish political parties had quarreled bitterly even after Adam Czartoryski had been declared the head of the new Polish state. As a moderate, Czartoryski was unable to appease either the conservatives or the extremists, and he was wholly unsuccessful in making the Western powers, chiefly France and Great Britain, understand that the menace Russia presented endangered not only Poland, but the rest of Europe as well.

While the Western powers kept hands off, Russian troops under Marshal Pashkevich crushed the revolution, following the military action with such tooth-drawing measures as the confiscation of the insurgents' estates, the closing of the universities of Vilno and Warsaw and the secularization of the property of the Catholic Church. Receiving the title Prince of Warsaw from the grateful Czar Nicholas, Pashkevich built a citadel at the gates of the city and filled its dungeons with Poles. Thus was another revolution converted into a tragedy.

In December, 1831, Dali received a brief letter:

"Mon cher ami, for six months I was in a hospital with an unknown disease. Now I am all right, and after the New Year I intend to continue your education."

The letter was signed Antoine Jules la Harpe.

3

Revolution blazes with a roaring flame, but the blinding light soon dies. One January day in 1832, Monsieur la Harpe knocked at the door of the Dukay palace in Vienna, wearing a new pea-green coat and looking for all the world as if he had been on a vacation in Italy. Endre Dukay was glad to see him restored in health, and expressed the opinion, after listening to the tutor's story, that his sickness had been the same as Dali's. "You are a lucky man, Monsieur. I doubt if you received the care that Doctor Kunz was able to give my son."

Tonchi agreed that he was indeed lucky. "But for the grace of God," he said, "I should not have returned."

Later Tonchi told Dali the truth. He had not had even a day of illness. He had volunteered and fought in the Polish army, and after the disastrous defeat in June, he had had to flee with many of his comrades. Leaving all hopes behind, he had swum the Vistula while the Russian guards rained lead upon him.

In Western Poland, under Austrian occupation, he had hidden in a village, counting on one day being able to return to Grandpa Maurycy's house as Monsieur la Harpe. In October hundreds of Polish patriots had been tried and condemned to death, among them Hyron Tyeminiczky-Yojtkowski. "On November 13 I was hanged in the Novosolsky Barracks," Tonchi said, adding with a grin, "in absentia. I hear that I was dressed in a ragged gray coat, black hat, fancy trousers, and muddy boots, but I had no face." The clothes and boots had been stuffed with straw. From the thin neck, made of a broom handle, hung a poster bearing the letters of his Polish name. More than fifty effigies of absentees had been hanged in the same ceremony, Tonchi reported, including two of Countess Jadi's cousins, a Count Radowski and a Prince Voronieczki.

In the early spring of 1832, the fires were all out in Europe, and the political ground was momentarily frozen solid, like the Danube. The winter was unusually long. Heavy carts crossed from Buda to Pesth on the ice, and there was peace in the world.

As Endre Dukay said:

"France has her new 'citizen king,' and Belgium has made herself separate from Holland—all right, no further disorders."

Endre was greatly pleased that his heir, Flexi, expressed himself in the same manner. There were those who might call Emperor Francis a despot, but in Endre's view, this sort of name-calling was wide of the point. Who, after all, had to fear Metternich's secret police? Let him fear them who conspired against the established order. Smoking prohibited in the streets of Vienna? Fine! At least those noisy Hungarian "patriots" would no longer spit in the streets or knock out the ashes of their foul, long-stemmed pipes on the newly painted public benches. Customs officers investigate the pockets and baggage of incoming travelers? Right! To prison with everyone who would overturn this perfect social order with crazy Jacobin ideas!

Endre saw himself as "a good father, loving my sons equally." He was sometimes troubled by Dali's lack of positive attitudes. He regarded Flexi as a painter regards his masterpiece, but the melancholy Dali drew on his fatherly sympathy, as if this second son had been born with a club foot or some sort of spiritual abnormality. Both boys were excellent horsemen, but with a difference. Flexi sat in the saddle as if he were leading a cavalry regiment past the imperial box during a parade. Dali seemed always to be riding unwatched, alone, with no saddle. Endre could picture the mane of Dali's horse streaming out as he raced senselessly, hurdling fences and galloping through muddy village marketplaces where the ducks and geese quacked and cackled in panic—and the girls too—as they scattered before him.

Thinking of Flexi's future, Endre foresaw a great diplomatic career. That Flexi was not in any sense a genius did not matter. A great diplomat did not have to be a genius—only loyal, five feet eleven inches tall, blue-eyed, and slender and handsome, as Metternich was when he received the title of Prince. Flexi was in possession of all the requisites, and he had an additional advantage. He had been born a Dukay. Metternich? . . . well, he had been only a poor vineyard count from the Rhine, Endre reflected.

Flexi and Dali, in a certain way, continued to love each other; but they were careful in their conversations never to touch upon any political, economic or religious question that might upset the comfortable balance of their brotherhood. Whenever they met, they chatted amicably, like two gentlemen in the corner of a salon, who were sure that they had met several times but had no idea of each other's name or calling. Each of them loved something in the other that each thought missing in himself. Dali often yearned for Flexi's elegant peace of mind, and Flexi envied Dali's daredeviltry. Flexi's sense of financial responsibility sometimes led him to worry about his brother. Once, after Dali's return from Poland, he offered a loan if Dali should need one. Dali blushed; the words touched his heart and at the same time hurt his pride. He assured Flexi that he had no need for extra money—which was by no means the truth, for his meager allowance melted away, much of it in emergency loans to his friend Andris Zeker.

In the summer of 1832, Dali's cousin, Claudia Rhédey, became a "queen." Alexander, the heir to the throne of Würtemberg, decided to make a morganatic marriage with Claudia. To do it, he had to resign his rights as crown prince and take up the subsidiary title of Duke of Teck. Even so the Habsburg courtiers regarded the alliance as a great honor for Endre Dukay, a close relative of the Rhédeys. Such Hungarian patriots as Andris and Dali, took the marriage as an insult to the national pride, because before the marriage, Metternich made Claudia Rhédey a Countess Hohenstein.

"A Hohenstein!" Andris fumed. "A Hohen-Hohen-Hohenstein! It sounds almost like Hohenlohe or even Hohenzollern."

"Transylvania is twenty times the size of Würtemberg!" Dali grumbled. "Isn't it terrible that she threw away the ancient name of the Rhédey counts, *de genere* Aba? Ferenc Rhédey was the king of Transylvania!"

"For six days," remarked Andris, who had no great feeling for family lineage.

"Six days or sixty years," Dali went on, "the Rhédeys fought for freedom, and they died on the battlefields while the Würtembergs died of overeating. Mother told me that during the Congress of Vienna the table of the king of Würtemberg had to be cut in a half circle to accommodate his majesty's stomach!"

Dali's wedding gift to Claudia was the two little innocent love letters she had written to him when she was thirteen. He sent them back with no word of congratulation.

Life was gay for Flexi in Vienna where new restaurants and hotels were opening. Many people came to the "emperor's city" for shopping, for the opera and theatre performances, for concerts: money-spending and money-making people. Among them were the noble families of the Balkans, merchants of Trieste and Lombardy, the flamboyant Magyar nabobs. The streets of Vienna were crowded with colorful people from every corner of the monarchy: Tyroleans, Slovenes, Hungarians in folk costumes, Musulmans wearing the red fez, Bohemian musicians and kaftan-ed Jews mixed with French courtesans and every kind of political refugee. The *jeunesse dorée*, the "golden youth," as Flexi and his company were called in these years of romanticism, danced in the salons of the *Schwarze Bock* or Don Mayer's Casino, swirling to the measures of waltzes by Johann Strauss, holding in their arms the pretty Gretchens and Helens.

By contrast, the streets of ancient Buda were empty. Dali and Tonchi sometimes stood under an open window and listened to an invisible piano. Unlike Vienna, Buda heard concerts only rarely. Andris was often a weekend guest in Septemvir Utca.

Playing billiards with Dali, Andris set up a very severe rule: if he had won the game, Dali had to pay the one silver florin bet in cash, but if Dali won, the silver florin existed only in Dali's note book, where Andris' other debts were recorded for posterity.

Sometimes Dali and Andris went on a duck-shooting party to Lake Velence, on the estate of count Samuel Leznay—until one such party, in December of 1833, ended for Dali in a soul-shaking tragedy.

Count Samuel Leznay, grandson of the legendary lover of Maria Theresa, had inherited the Genghis Khan character from his grandfather. A widowed man over fifty, his local interests were hunting, greyhound racing and peasant girls. He enjoyed setting the girls on the wildest of his horses and hearing them scream when they were tossed in the air. When he travelled in the open coach on winter days, he would take with him two girls, one on either side to keep him warm; and as a matter of course he still demanded his right to the *jus primae noctis,* under which he would take to bed and deflower a virgin serf on her marriage night.

On idle days Count Leznay sprawled in a massive carved oak chair in the middle of the largest room in his castle, now and then brushing his stringy half-moon mustache back and shouting commands to his serfs. Coming to the end of a bottle of wine, he would smash off the neck of a new bottle against his chair and pour the contents down his throat. Around the foot of his chair were not only splinters of glass but dog turds, for he kept his four greyhounds, in which he took an inordinate pride, always with him.

Dali and Andris hated the old man, but they accepted his occasional invitations because they too enjoyed hunting, and because Dali's boyhood playmate Pista Kerge, now twenty-one and still a serf of the Leznays, was always coachman during the hunt.

The tragic hunting party in December began in the usual way. Dali and Andris arrived in the evening at the Leznay *kuria,* as the small castles were called. The date had been set soon after Pista had reported that the sheldrakes, wearing their snow-white waistcoats and tobacco-brown trousers, were migrating from the North to Lake Velence. In order to reach the shore of the lake at the best shooting hour—just before sunup—the hunting party sat up all night in the dining room. The hostess, wife of Karoly, Samuel Leznay's son, retired after midnight, and the four hunters were left alone with new bottles of wine and their most obscene anecdotes.

At four in the morning, Pista Kerge wrapped himself in the sheepskin *bunda* of a peasant coachman and drove the hunters toward the lake. There was no dog in the coach—the English retriever had not yet been introduced into Hungary.

Andris used to tease Pista. "I hear Pista," he said to him, "that you are going to marry Kotyogó, the oldest gypsy whore. My congratulations."

"That's true, sir," Pista answered goodhumoredly, cracking his whip above the horses' ears. "Our wedding will be next Sunday and I would like to ask Your Excellency to be my best man."

Dali laughed heartily at the reply but there was no sound out of old Samuel and his son. A Count Leznay would never enter into such a conversation with a serf.

They arrived at the lake in good time and set out along the reedy shore, Károly Leznay and Andris going one way, old Leznay, Dali and Pista Kerge going the other. Though the first snow had not yet fallen, the edges of the lake had begun to freeze. At the center the mirror of open water shivered in its nakedness.

After a few moments, a sheldrake flew from the reeds and old Leznay's rifle rang out. The duck fell like a stone and floated motionless on the open water, some 200 feet from shore.

"Go get it!" the old man commanded Pista Kerge.

Pista threw off his heavy *bunda* and stepped into the water. The thin ice cracked under his boots. When he reached open water, he started swimming. His boots and clothing weighed him down, and the water was numbing. After he had swum some hundred feet, the sheldrake was still far off. He realized he could not make it and started for shore.

"Go get it!" shouted the old man. His order was so harsh that Pista made another try. But after twenty feet, he turned back again to save himself before his strength ran out.

74

"Get it, you son of a bitch!" roared the count. But by now, Pista's only thought was to reach shore. Then, suddenly, Leznay's rifle rang out, and a second later Pista sank, leaving a stain of blood on the surface.

Dali dashed furiously at the old man, but before his fist reached Leznay's face, Leznay struck him on the mouth with the butt of his rifle with such force that Dali fell to the ground. As Dali staggered to his feet, Leznay jumped into the coach shouting for his son; and by the time Dali's strength began to return, the two were already speeding away.

When Andris came running up, Dali, deathly pale, was spitting out an upper front tooth. Yet Dali was the first to speak.

"Can that bastard get away with this murder?"

It was an open question in the year 1833. Pista Kerge was a serf, Leznay the feudal lord.

Dali wiped his bleeding lips with the back of his hand. Then he looked at Andris. "What can we do?"

Andris, as furious as Dali, suggested:

"We can at least tell the story to a lawyer."

They had to walk some six miles to the nearest village. There they succeeded in hiring a *forspont* with two fast horses to take them to Buda-Pesth. Night had fallen when Andris pulled the bell cord at the house of a lawyer he knew.

The man who admitted them was the lawyer himself. He looked about thirty years old, and was an exceptionally handsome man with large dark blue eyes. Beneath his cleanshaven chin he wore a beard from ear to ear. His brow was high and beautifully shaped under the rich locks of his light brown hair. His dignity impressed Dali at once, for it seemed wholly unaffected.

He shook hands warmly with Dali. "Of course, I am acquainted with the name of Dukay," he said in a deep voice. "Do have a seat and tell me what I can do for you."

The room was lit only by two candles on the lawyer's desk. Near the door by which Dali and Andris had entered, two pairs of chickens and a pair of ducks lay on the floor, their legs bound together. Next to them lay a dead hare. On a chair in an old straw hat were perhaps three dozen hen eggs. Obviously all these were legal fees paid by peasants.

When Andris and Dali had finished their story the lawyer did not comment immediately. Smoothing his beard thoughtfully, he stared into space.

"What do you think, sir," Dali asked at last. "Can the old murderer be punished?"

"You are asking a tragic question," the lawyer said. And as if it were his favorite topic, he continued:

"We still live in the dark ages. Most of the powers of government are exercised by overlords. Have you ever heard the expression *jus palladii?*"

Dali's eyes went to Andris for help.

"There are a few palladiums in the Ararat armory. That long, straight, double-edged sword," Andris explained to Dali.

"Before Doctor Guillotin gave us his great improvement," the lawyer resumed, "the palladium was the instrument of justice—a very clumsy, heavy instrument."

"My great uncle, Count Sigray," Andris said, "who participated in a republican conspiracy, required six strokes before his head fell off. By the grace of Emperor Leopold," Andris added bitterly.

"Leznay is not only a lord who wields the sword of law," the lawyer continued, "he is also 100 per cent pro-Habsburg. And a lord is a lord not only in Hungary. I was told that the father of my favorite poet, Lord Byron, in a rage, shot his coachman with no consequence to himself."

"So you think," Dali asked with a catch in his voice, "that Leznay won't be punished either?"

"I strongly hope," the lawyer said, "that all the serfs of the world will be liberated in the near future. The day cannot be far away. A half century ago even Catherine the Great flirted with the idea of liberating the Russian serfs. But presently, during the reign of Emperor Francis, there is no hope of bringing Leznay to trial."

After a few silent seconds, Dali stood up and asked:

"How much do I owe you for your advice, sir?"

The lawyer glanced at the hat on the chair, full of eggs. Obviously wanting to cheer Dali up, he said:

"You owe me two eggs, sir." Then he put a hand on Dali's shoulder, almost embracing his new young friend, and said: "I hope you will be in my camp when we fight for the liberation of the serfs."

The strong, sonorous voice, Dali felt, contained the firm determination of some one who believed in his vocation.

As they left the house, Dali asked Andris:

"What's the name of that lawyer?"

"Lajos Kossuth," Andris said. "He is a very nice fellow. I still owe him six florins card debt. He never asked for it. Now he's gambling on bigger stakes."

Dali did not hear Andris' last words. His thoughts were on the shore of Lake Velence. He could not help but see the large pool of blood on the greenish water's surface where Pista Kerge's head had disappeared.

4

In the spring of 1834, Metternich appointed Endre Dukay to represent the monarchy at the coming-of-age birthday—his sixteenth—of the Russian crown prince, Grand Duke Alexander. Endre set out for St. Petersburg early in April, accompanied by his secretary and two valets. Endre made his journey through Prussia by mail coach, and boarded the Steamer Nicholas I for the voyage to the Gulf of Finland. In a letter to his wife, sent back on the same vessel, he described the voyage as a great achievement of Russian technology.

In St. Petersburg, Endre stayed with his sister-in-law, Olga Serebraniy in her residential palace in Karamsin Street. The years had brought new tragedy to Olga, for her husband, Leon Serebraniy, Colonel of the Guards, had been killed on his estate in 1829, during one of the many peasant riots. The red-haired slender Olga was now one of the richest widows in Russia.

Following the great celebration at the Winter Palace, Endre dispatched a second letter to his wife. After some comment on the lavishness of the crown prince's birthday, he continued:

... but my most unforgettable memory of Russia will surely be my half hour talk with His Majesty during my state audience. Nicholas is taller and handsomer than his late brother, Czar Alexander. His noble head, well placed between his broad shoulders, reminds me of a portrait of Peter the Great which hangs in the chancellery. The effect the czar produced on me while we talked was enormous. I confess I was overcome by his great personality. These things were said:

The Czar: Distances are the scourge of Russia.
Me: In Europe there are no distances. The people lack space. This will never happen either to Russia or America.
The Czar: (Sorrowfully) I lack time.
Me: Sire, Your Great Majesty, you have the future.

Endre's long letter was full of enthusiasm for Czar Nicholas. He continued:

Eyewitnesses told me that during the dreadful hours of the December revolution in 1825, when the archbishop had already tried in vain to calm the rioting soldiers, the czar behaved miraculously. After making the sign of the cross, His Majesty, riding his black stallion, went out to master the rebels alone—alone!—solely by the magic force of his dignity and countenance. He had resigned himself to the possibility of dying. He pulled out his sword and cried, "Kneel!" They all obeyed. I was told by those who beheld the scene that one saw the czar grow with each step, advancing upon the mutineers.

With a sad gesture, Countess Jadi handed her husband's letter to Tonchi. He read it carefully, then said:

"I am afraid I know much more about Czar Nicholas than his excellency. After he had crushed the Decembrist uprising, a colonel who had participated was brought to him in chains. When the colonel refused to disclose the names of his accomplices, the czar started to kick the chained man in the stomach so brutally that . . ."

"Yes, I know," Countess Jadi whispered in horror. "Olga told me that the prisoners were not only chained but blindfolded. Many of them died or went mad in the Petrowski dungeons."

But Endre, faithful to his monarchist principles, managed not to hear such rumors. Upon his return from Russia, he reiterated, in even more glowing terms, his great reverence for the czar. And every time he told of his meeting with the Russian sovereign, the conversation they had had grew longer and more spirited. Jadi, as was her custom, greeted his stories respectfully, and with every appearance of sympathy.

In the spring of the following year, 1835, after a reign of forty-three years, Emperor Francis died, marking the end of the Epoch of the Benevolent Despots. However benevolent was the

78

emperor, he, not unlike his Russian counterpart, mercilessly persecuted reformers with a petty, sadistic urge. The Olmütz fortress in Moravia was a veritable hell for those who were not satisfied with the old order. The jailer was directly responsible to the emperor, and his majesty regulated the prisoners' daily routine, himself devising tricks to torture them.

There was a strong group, not only in the Habsburg family and in the court, but among potential government officials and army generals, that wanted forty-two-year-old crown prince Ferdinand to resign his right to the throne in favor of his younger brother, Archduke Karl. Ferdinand was feebleminded. The leader of the opposition was Karl's wife, the energetic Archduchess Sophie, mother of a blue-eyed angelic boy, five-year-old Franz Joseph. In her ambition to put her husband on the throne, Sophie was so energetic that Metternich dubbed her "the only male member of the Habsburg family."

After Ferdinand, as the unchallengeable legal heir, had occupied the throne, Metternich—in the interest of the monarchy, of course—grabbed all the powers for himself.

A month after Ferdinand's coronation, when Andris Zeker showed up in Buda and the trio convened, Andris said to Dali and Tonchi in a triumphant tone:

"I must tell you the *knödl*-story."

The emperor-loving people of Vienna had already given Ferdinand the name *Der Gütige,* The Benevolent. Ferdinand's pinkish face always wore a grin, especially when, rain or shine, he held his beloved umbrella in his hand.

"One morning," Andris began the story, "*Der Gütige* appeared for his daily solitary stroll in Schönbrunn Park. He did not return for dinner, and the police and two infantry regiments were alerted. Had the emperor been kidnapped? Murdered by a fanatic? Late that afternoon his majesty turned up in a neighboring village sitting at a peasant's table, devouring his third generous helping of *knödl*—a kind of dumpling boiled in sauerkraut," Andris explained to Tonchi, "among a dozen noisy children."

"A feebleminded German king on the Hungarian throne!" Dali exclaimed. "Our nation has to repeat that winter day when young Matthias, last national king of Hungary, received an ova-

79

tion from 40,000 who stood on the ice-covered Danube, and . . ."

". . . and gained the throne," Tonchi finished the sentence, "instead of Frederick III, Emperor of the Holy, the Wholly Rotten Roman Empire."

"The hereditary dynasties," Tonchi went on, "from the feebleminded Isaurian Leo on the Byzantine throne, to George III who died in a strait jacket, or the sadist Czar Palkin, just to mention a few, and now that *knödl*-crazy, benevolent Ferdinand . . ." He turned to Dali without finishing the sentence: "Are you ready with your draft?"

Dali smiled nervously. The black hole left in his smile after he had lost an upper front tooth in his fight with old Leznay had been filled by a barber who had some side skill as a dentist. Depending on the size of their purses, some people had precious stones or the teeth of corpses fitted into their gaps. In Vienna and certain other centers of enlightenment, there was a growing move toward dog teeth. Dali's restoration came from the jaw of a wolf. The brass wire that fixed it to its neighbor teeth had soon lost its color, and by now Dali's smile already showed a strange greenish tint.

But no one was thinking of this as he answered Tonchi, "Yes I am." The three were in deadly earnest now. Dali cleared his throat and read:

"Hungapole's constitution accepts the basic idea of the American constitution, that the government is *for* the people and *from* the people, but denies its third command, *by* the people. It rejects the hereditary dynasty but maintains the kingdom system which is deeply rooted in the ancient history of Poland and Hungary."

Tonchi nodded and inserted this remark:

"The poorer the people, the greater the pomp and glamor of their king, czar or maharajah. The Greeks populated Olympus with beautiful and immortal gods and goddesses to make it easier to carry on the hopeless burdens of human life on earth. Continue, please."

"Hungapole," Dali went on, "the territory of Hungary and Poland, has a greater population than England, and occupies one of the most fertile plains of Europe! Her mountains are rich in gold, silver . . ."

"It will touch the North Sea and the Adriatic!" shouted Tonchi.

Andris turned to Dali:

"You don't mind if I ask you something? You are a Hungarian *de genere* Ordony, and your mother is a Radowski, with Polish royal blood in her veins. Who will be the first king of Hungapole? Have you ever thought of . . ."

Dali silenced Andris with a gesture.

"That is of no moment now. Whoever the king is, he will share the executive power with a directorate of five."

"But no first consul," Tonchi suggested, "which could lead to a new Bonaparte."

"Who are the five consuls in your mind?" asked Andris.

"Czartoryski, Kossuth . . ." Tonchi said, while cleaning his nails with a penknife, ". . . and the three of us."

Then the conversation turned to the big issues: the liberation of the serfs, throwing the Habsburgs out of Hungary, and throwing the Prussian-Russian-Austrian tryants out of Poland, as the first steps of the realization of Hungapole.

"Everything is wonderful," Andris declared, "but I am afraid, boys, we are chewing fog."

Tonchi placed a reassuring hand on Andris' broad shoulder:

"*Mon cher ami,* every great change in history began with the whispering of two or three."

Less flamboyant but more determined were the political developments in other European countries. In the early thirties the high walls of the Urals, the Carpathians, the Alps, the Appenines and the Pyrenees echoed the word: reform! . . . reform! . . . reform!

The *Risorgimento* in Italy, the *Reichstagjugend* and other organizations in Germany openly held subversive ideas, and were ready to hurl the torch of insurrection. The battle cry of the *Jugend* had drawn momentum from the Paris, Brussels, and Warsaw revolutions and now demanded reforms, freedom and independence all over Europe.

In Hungary, as if in answer, a royal command, signed by *Der*

Gütige (decided by Metternich) dissolved the Diet, a crude imitation of the old German parliamentary assemblies, the members of which were rich landowners who alone had time to enjoy such things as politics. But conservative aristocrats did not bother to travel hundreds of miles on horseback or in shaky coaches to attend every session of the Diet, held in Presburg, a big town near the Austrian border. They sent representatives, mostly their lawyers, who were authorized to vote for them. Lajos Kossuth represented a count, and was at the same time editor of the *Parliamentary Reports*. Kossuth was a brilliant "stylist," as writers and journalists were then called.

However, printer's ink stinks in the nostrils of all police. The nostrils of Metternich's police grew larger in proportion to Kossuth's growing influence on liberal Hungarian aristocrats, like Dali and Andris, to say nothing of the *jurati,* university law students, who had declared that the best form of govenment was the republic, and whose idol was George Washington. They wanted to liberate Hungary from the Habsburgs as Washington had liberated America from George III.

Metternich dissolved the Hungarian Diet mostly because of Kossuth's influential *Parliamentary Reports*. But as a result, the brilliant stylist simply became a brilliant orator. The quill-copied *Parliamentary Reports* had influenced a few thousand patriots and *jurati.* Touring the country and making speeches in open markets, Kossuth now influenced a few hundred thousands. It was the beginning of Lajos Kossuth's fabulous political career.

And while the whole of Europe was threatened by ideological explosions, a hot July day in Paris brought a dreadful physical explosion. On July 28, 1835, when Louis Philippe was passing on parade, an infernal machine exploded 100 large kegs of gunpowder.

As reported by the Viennese papers, the explosion killed Louis Philippe and his three sons, as well as 317 persons in the king's entourage; and it critically wounded some 600 spectators in the cheering crowd. First reports in the world press about a great event have been slightly exaggerated since the time Gutenberg invented the printing press. The next day it was revealed that Louis Philippe and his three sons had escaped without even minor injuries; in the king's entourage, not 317 but 17 were killed; and in the crowd, not 600 but 60 were wounded. Still, the Corsican Fieschi's attempt against a Bourbon king was the greatest plot in history against the life of a ruler.

In the following year, 1836, István Varga, a young *juratus* and an ardent follower of Kossuth, who worked in Kossuth's law office, one evening told Dali in the Café Árpád that he had been engaged, with no salary of course, to organize Kossuth's tours in the country.

"Do you need a courier?" Dali asked.

"Uncle Lajos would be glad to have you in his camp."

The following week, a secret police report on Metternich's desk included this entry: "Count Adalbert Dukay, about 22, entered into Kossuth's service as a mounted messenger . . ."

The report was signed by Baron Erich Dukay-Hedwitz, who the previous September had entered the secret police.

Andris Zeker, who had been promoted to lieutenant of the hussar regiment, joined Dali on his rides to the country whenever his military duties permitted. Tonchi, whose horsemanship was poor ("I prefer a broken piano chair to a brand new saddle") remained at his desk in Septemvir Utca and at a corner table of the Café Árpád, collecting data from the foreign papers concerning the reform movement throughout Europe.

Neither Endre nor Flexi, nor even Countess Jadi, was informed in detail what the trio was doing; but they knew, as everyone in Europe knew, that the air was full of ideas: foul and tangled ideas to Metternich, but to Countess Jadi, Dali, Tonchi and Andris full of the sweet fragrance of new hope for a better human life in Poland, in Hungary, in the whole world.

5

On the night of May 5, 1837, an Austrian patrol surrounded the *Isten Szeme*—God's Eye—a summer hotel on the summit of Svab Mountain, near Buda. The patrol's leader, Dali's cousin, Dragoon Captain Erich Dukay-Hedwitz, accompanied by two lieutenants and six sergeants, all of them with loaded pistols in their belts, climbed the creaking wooden stairs of the hotel with care that, because of the thunder of the stormy night, was quite unnecessary.

Deploying his men before the door to a room on the second floor, Captain Erich knocked brusquely. A voice asked sleepily: "Who's that?"

"Military police."

A moment later the door was opened by a bearded man, with long, disheveled locks; he was clad only in slippers and a nightshirt.

"Sind Sie Lajos Kossuth?"

Candle in hand, the crusader for the liberation of the serfs, looked into the cleanshaven face of the dragoon captain.

"Was wollen sie von mir?"

Kossuth's arrest shocked not only the people of Hungary, but every reformer in Europe. And not only in the underground. Louis Philippe, under great pressure from the assembly, gave general amnesty for political offenses in France to show the world that France was different from despotic Austria.

"When his serenity asked my opinion," Endre Dukay said at the family table, "on what to do with Kossuth, I advised him briefly: *'utilizieren oder aufhängen!'* " It meant: exploit him or hang him.

Neither Countess Jadi nor Flexi made any comment. They knew that Metternich never asked Endre's advice on anything; and everyone around the chancellery knew that the advice Endre quoted was given by Count Széchenyi, a political adversary of Kossuth. Széchenyi's words went down in history as a norm of how a government should deal with a dangerous reformer.

"Széchenyi is a great patriot," said Andris when the trio next convened in Buda, "but he is wrong when he thinks that a war for liberty against the Habsburgs would mean the suicide of Hungary."

"Széchenyi agrees with the Polish conservatives," Tonchi observed. "He thinks that the only way for a small nation to survive is to wait, wait, and wait until the despotism grows old, looses its teeth, and one day drops dead."

"Despotism will never die," Dali said, "until it is shot through the head."

"Correct," said Andris. "Metternich calls revolution 'the creeping malady of nations,' but for me despotism is not a malady, but the coffin of a nation."

When at the end of May, Baron Erich Dukay-Hedwitz, promoted to major for his handling of Kossuth's arrest, came to spend a weekend at Ararat, Endre warmly congratulated him. Present at the meeting, Dali found his father's enthusiasm sickening, but Tonchi counseled him not be upset. "The issue is not your father, but your fatherland," he pointed out.

The following month, July 1837, news came from London that King William had died, and his successor to the throne was young Victoria, granddaughter of George III. The same month, Prince Igor Effremovich Opatkin, once aide-de-camp to Czar Alexander, arrived in Vienna on his way home from the United States of America, where he had served as military attaché at the Russian embassy. Delaying his departure for St. Petersburg, he came to Ararat for a week of hunting.

Dali, examining the prince's handsome horsewhip, discovered that it bore an inscription on it's silver handle: *For Horses Only*. Prince Igor, who was proud of the whip, told Dali that it had been presented to him by the late American President, James Monroe, himself a great horseman.

Soon after Prince Igor's visit, Endre saw the first of his children married. Carola, Rolly, became the bride of the Marquis Alphonse des Fereyolles, a young diplomat at the French embassy in Vienna.

Rolly at nineteen was a beauty. Her full lips and milk-white skin seemed ever hungry for the most passionate kisses, and her warm, greenish gray eyes were ever thirsty for laughter. To the embarrassment of her mother and brothers, Rolly sometimes revealed in public a spectacular ignorance. As plans had been made for her sixteenth birthday celebration, she had expressed disappointment that Herr Wolfgang Mozart would be unable to attend, since everyone seemed to be so fond of his music. When her governess told her tenderly that Mozart had died in the last century, Rolly said briefly: "Oh." And not until she was eighteen had Rolly learned that Paris was not, as she believed, the western capital of the Habsburg monarchy.

Alphie, as Rolly's betrothed was known, was a young man

who had been born with such a horror of exercise that he had forgotten how to grow shoulders. In his pale V-shaped face, ending in a silky black goatee, there blazed the look of French intelligence. Conversing volubly and eloquently on every topic in the world, from politics to Byzantine numismatics or the best cure for diptheria, Alphie gestured like a chorus master conducting the rich melodies of his long, undulating sentences. According to Tonchi, the Marquis' data from science and history did not always correspond with the facts. The Marquis held the same opinion about Tonchi's data. But Tonchi found Alphie's French irresistible. "I imagine the fountains of Versailles must spout like that," he told Dali.

Sometimes, talking away, Alphie would interrupt a gesture in mid-air, as if he had just noticed the surprisingly agile hand, then talk for seconds to his palm, carefully observing his fingers and nails before letting the white narrow hand fly off again into the windstorm of his eloquence. Alphie was only twenty-five, but so serious on every topic that he looked fifty. It sometimes happened that a rotten apple would fly through an open window at Ararat and hit Alphie in the face as he orated. Rolly's scream of laughter would then be heard, and a moment later one would see Alphie chasing her in the park, or the two of them twisting each other's arms, pulling each other's hair, and screaming and laughing like two young animals. Jadi enjoyed the spectacle, but Endre felt obliged to point out that it was unseemly behavior for a countess and the representative of France, a great power.

The wedding had initially been set for August, and after both Archduchess Blanca and Metternich had accepted his invitations, Endre had planned a great party at Ararat with a thousand guests. The wedding, he felt, should be patterned after the nuptials of Balint Dukay, who in 1615 had married Anna Bátori. Several oxen would be roasted in the park for the serfs and village people, and the day would go down in history. But diplomacy thwarted Endre's plan.

Alphonse des Fereyolles was unexpectedly promoted to second counselor and advised that he must occupy his position at the French embassy in St. Petersburg within a month. The young couple had to be wed in a hurry in the middle of July, with no Archduchess, no Metternich, no roasted oxen, no ancient ceremonies, only the circle of family members and a few close friends. To revive a bit of the ancient tradition, Rolly wore Anna Bátori's wedding robe, preserved in the Ararat museum among such regalia as Ilona Zrini's mouse-chewed prayer book, Borbala Dukay's rusty chastity belt, and the skull of Demeter Dukay. This last rested in a case with a child's smaller skull alongside it.

"On my first visit here," Alphie said, as he and some of the wedding guests strolled through the museum hall, "I asked Rolly whom the smaller skull had belonged to and she said, 'That was Demeter's too, when he was a boy.' "

And while Rolly screamed in laughing protest, the Marquis added: "At that moment I fell in love with her."

After a few weeks honeymooning in Salzburg, Alphie and Rolly took the mailcoach for St. Petersburg via Poland and Finland. In the bride's first letter home, she told her family that her Aunt Olga Serebraniy had invited Alphie to make his home in her palace. As a childless widow, Olga could extend this sort of hospitality to Rolly and her husband without the least inconvenience.

On October 1, 1837, Endre's sons observed their birthday in Vienna. As usual, part of the ceremony took place in the bedroom on the second floor where they had been born twenty-three years earlier. As in the past, only the twins and the parents were present in the bedroom; all of them knelt, while Countess Jadi intoned a prayer of thanksgiving, first in Hungarian, then in German and then—hardly audibly—in Polish.

In the afternoon the brothers were strolling in the palace garden. With their different physical appearance and different dress, they looked like human maps of Austria and Hungary. The slightly built Flexi, slender and elegant, had a long, clean-shaven "Emperor Francis" face; his blond hair was worn in loose locks around the temples, resembling the Metternich Brutus hairdo. He wore English pantaloons in fashionable dandelion yellow. The very tight pantaloons were prevented from slipping up by the straps under the soles of his narrow black shoes. His bell-shaped robin's-egg blue coat emphasized an outline of manly strength, which he did not have. Even his voice was soft, and his words always carefully selected. One morning, a couple of years earlier, when Flexi was walking in Gisella-strasse with Dali, a drunken chimneysweep had bumped into him and soiled his brand new fawn frock coat. Flexi had raised his walking stick, and, his neck red with anger, shouted: "You. . . . You. . . ." Dali had waited for an obscenity, but Flexi had lowered his voice and said to the drunkard: "You . . . careless."

Flexi was the very incarnation of a rich and handsome young aristocrat of that happy epoch of Vienna, highly educated and faultlessly polite. He wore a miniature cross-hilted sword, pinned into his waistcoat lapel—with no belligerent purpose. Actually it was the latest version of a gentleman's toothpick.

In contrast to Flexi, Dali wore a lavishly trimmed tobacco-brown dolman; with his hunting knife tucked in his right boot-cuff and his horse whip in the left, he looked the very image of a Magyar patriot. On his tanned face he sported a thin, dark mustache. Long whiskers ran across his throat, beneath his cleanshaven chin. This was the sort of beard Kossuth had worn at the time of his arrest.

Flexi never ventured into political problems. His main interest was economics.

"In a year," he once said to Dali, "I will reach my majority. Father is getting old, as we both know. The income from the estate could be doubled, tripled! Iron plows instead of wooden ones and thorn harrows! Steamsaws in the timber forests! A furniture factory! Why, we are living in the midst of a tremendous industrial revolution."

The word revolution had an entirely different meaning to Dali.

One night, after dinner in Buda, Endre called a family conference.

"I have already suggested to Flexi that he start a diplomatic career," he told Dali. "If someone is Metternich's godson, it would not be a handicap for him in that field. But Flexi has no ambition to be a diplomat. What about you, Dali? Are you willing to go to Berlin as a military attaché?"

"Berlin? Wonderful!" Tonchi exclaimed before Dali could answer. It was Tonchi's method in discussion and debate to say "Wonderful!" with a deep nod, after which he immediately pulled out the knife of his sharp irony to pare down the wonderful idea.

" 'Berlin is the foamy intellectual center of the world with its rapidly growing schools of Hegelism.' That statement, with its typical Prussian modesty, came from Professor Hegel."

Endre laughed. Tonchi knew that Endre shared Metternich's negative views about Prussian pan-Germanism, in which both perceived a threat to Austria. "Too bad," Tonchi went on, "that all the squares in Berlin are invaded and commanded by the worst equestrian statues of the most stupid Prussian generals. If Your Excellency will entertain my humble advice, instead of Berlin, I would suggest that Count Adalbert be appointed a military attaché in St. Petersburg."

After a moment's silence, Endre asked:

"St. Petersburg?"

"Yes, sir!" Tonchi said emphatically. "Because the Habsburgs and the Romanoffs have a mutual interest in stamping out the last sparks of revolutionary spirit in that restless, dangerous Poland."

Countess Jadi, not for the first time, was afraid that Tonchi was venturing too far. But Endre, after some moments of deep thought, said:

"I think you're right, Monsieur la Harpe."

"Count Adalbert," Tonchi said, "would be introduced to the best society by his aunt, Princess Serebraniy, and she even . . ."

"Could get a grand duchess wife for Dali," Endre quickly finished the sentence and briefly laughed at his own remark. Then he continued seriously:

"When, three years ago, I had the honor to represent the monarchy in St. Petersburg. . . ." Endre was telling the story of his audience with the czar again.

Later when Endre left them alone, Tonchi grabbed Dali's arm and whispered to him in excitement:

"We are already in St. Petersburg! It was God who helped us to Russia. The key to your Hungapole lies in St. Petersburg, not in Buda or Vienna."

"I don't understand why should I go to Russia when here at home since Kossuth had been arrested . . ."

"Listen to me, Dali. Think of that three-legged marble table in your father's study. If you want to overturn that table, you have to cut only one leg. Which one? The weakest. The eleven years since Nicholas seized the throne have produced more than 200 peasant riots, and horrible bloodshed. Eighty per cent of Russian intellectuals are in the underground. And don't forget the 40,000 Polish freedom fighters who were deported to the steppes. And the Jews! Catherine the Great prohibited—in the famous *Charta Osedlositiy*—giving passports to Jews who wanted to flee to the West from pogroms. You think the Russian Jews are 100 per cent loyal to the Winter Palace? And think of Prince Igor! He was a friend of President Monroe—in the bottom of his heart he is a true democrat. And the whole Russian army! Remember Decembrists. You think the army stands firmly behind Nick the Stick?"

Within a week, Endre brought home Dali's assignment to St. Petersburg from the chancellery, signed by Metternich, together with a passport for Countess Jadi and Monsieur Antoine Jules la Harpe, private secretary to Count Adalbert Dukay. Countess Jadi's mission in St. Petersburg was not secret. She wanted to be with Rolly, who was expecting her first child.

Tonchi bought the latest map of Russia in a bookshop and the trio spread it out on a table in Dali's room.

Until then Russia had been only a word to Dali and Andris, associated with such other words as Winter Palace, steppe, Siberia or vodka. Now they beheld Russia in her authentic, dreadful geographical reality.

"Is she *that* big?" Andris asked, not believing his own eyes. "The Habsburg monarchy looks like a dachshund compared to a bear!"

The map, recently published in Weimar, was titled: *Das Russiche Reich in Europa, Asien und Amerika.*

"Good Lord," Dali said, "is that the marble table's *one* leg we want to cut off? No other country in the world could boast spreading over three continents."

"I don't understand," Andris said, "all right, Russia in Asia and Europe. But how did she get into America?"

"Take it easy, boys," Tonchi said, putting his fingers on the chain of islands, about a thousand miles long, that was identified as *Catherina's oder die Aleuten Archiepelago.*

Tonchi's finger moved from continent to continent.

"Here is *Alejaska*, which is Russian for 'big field.' A Russian sailor discovered it some hundred years ago. A very big peninsula but absolutely worthless. Look at it: not a single town in that huge emptiness. Except for the salmon, sturgeon, and fur animals, lifeless as the moon."

"Look at the names," Dali's finger wandered around the shores of *Alejaska*.

"*Lissii Ostrava* . . . it means Fox Island," Tonchi explained. "*Blizniye* . . . it means Near Island. Then Pavloskaya Bay . . . Bogoslov Strait, Novoye Archangelsk . . ."

"Like the footprints of a bear in the snow . . ." Andris remarked.

Tonchi's finger went back to Europe.

"Here is Nishny Novgorod, the last town in European Russia. The yellow strips marks the border of the Kazan kingdom, already in Asia . . . which goes, goes, goes up to here . . . to Vladivostok. Emptiness. Dead emptiness through more than 10,000 miles."

In the middle of October, Dali and his mother and Tonchi left Vienna for St. Petersburg by mailcoach. Countess Jadi's baggage was bulging with gifts for Rolly and Olga. Paris hats, Milan dreses, sandals and kid slippers for the carriage, ribbed Tyrol stockings for outdoors, Pagoda parasols, small fans of carved ivory, Venetian glasses, depilatory creams, curved pedicure scissors, mahogany backscratchers, silver-handled flyswatters and, of course, Viennese cosmetics. None of these items, she had been told, was available in St. Petersburg.

On the ninth morning of the long journey, when the mailcoach changed horses in Finland, Tonchi said:

"Tomorrow we will touch the soil of the largest country on earth. Oh, yes! Nicholas the First is a very handsome man, tall both in physical and spiritual stature. He is the High Lama of 60 million people, perhaps 65. He is the greatest sovereign who ever lived."

Tonchi made this speech because they were not alone in the mailcoach. Two raven bearded Russians pretended to doze under tall fur caps, the black lambskin *shipkas*.

Next day they crossed the border. Marshes extended on both

sides to the horizon. The overcast sky appeared ten times wider than it had above tiny Finland. Cries of lapwings coming from every direction were ghostly echoes in the cold wind. Often the deep sand of the road gave way to mud, and there, whole green logs lay crosswise on the spongy terrain. The logs shifted under the wheels, splashing mud against the windows of the mailcoach and splattering the face of the coachman on his high seat.

The chaussée led straight to St. Petersburg.

Twilight, then the darkness of the starless night closed upon the rocking coach.

PART TWO | THE
WINTER
PALACE
1838

CHAPTER FOUR

IT WAS NIVOSE—THE SNOWY
month, (as the National Convention had renamed January during the French Revolution). The New Year fell on the twelfth day of January according to the Russian czarist calendar.

In 1838, the usual gala New Year's reception was held in the Winter Palace, built by Peter the Great for the "eternal residence" of all the czars. The largest building in the world, it accommodated 6,000 people.

Petrovski Square, which separated the Winter Palace from the rest of St. Petersburg, lay knee-deep in snow. On New Year's morning there was a "reception" in Petrovski Square for over 100,000 peasants, workers and soldiers—many of whom had traveled for weeks by sled to see the czar. When Nicholas appeared on a balcony with the czarina and the crown prince, his towering figure belied the pet-name *Atyushka*, "Little Father." The crowd was delirious with excitement.

Late that same evening, in the falling snow, stood the most stubborn of the spectators, those who risked frozen noses and ears rather than take their eyes off the illuminated Winter Palace, its thousand windows shining golden through the lacy curtain of snow. Among those who remained, some were exalted adorers of the czar, others simply spectacle addicts relieving the tedium of uneventful, prosaic lives. But there were a few who carried poisoned daggers, pistols or home-made bombs in the deep pockets of their heavy fur coats, waiting in the snowfall for a chance to sneak into the palace. But to get into the palace for uninvited mortals seemed impossible. All the entrances of the palace were "walled-in" by soldiers with bayonets menacingly fixed.

In the palace, some 2,000 guests milled slowly through the carpeted halls—aristocrats, church dignitaries, heads of government and army commanders, painters, writers, diplomats of friendly and not so friendly Western powers, and Oriental potentates. There were white turbans above dark faces, multicolored military and diplomatic uniforms, thousands of domestic and foreign medals (some of them phony) for the great occasion, crosses, ribbons, stars of every kind and color on the proud and generously stuffed chests. The gentlemen looked like chatting and walking Christmas trees. And the ladies! Silky and lacy clouds of Parma violet, Bunting azure or Bagdad pink— evening dresses imported from Vienna and Paris, a kaleidoscopic milky way as they strolled underneath the multitude of giant chandeliers. Occasionally a lady would start in panic when hot wax from a candle dripped on her bare shoulder.

The most honored guests stood apart from the throng, awaiting the great moment when their wives, sons and daughters would be introduced to the royal family. One could easily recognize the Russians among the guests, not only by their costumes but by their silence. They did not chat; they greeted friends or foreign acquaintances alike with no more than a smile. Speaking publicly, even with a friend, had its dangers during the reign of Palkin.

The foreigners from the West chatted and laughed openly, lowering their voices only when making a nasty comment on the Russian system of government.

In the center of the largest room, in a circle of sycophant generals and cabinet ministers, stood Field Marshal Ivan Federovich Pashkevich, who seven years ago, when Warsaw surrendered to the Russian cannons, received the title of prince. But his greatest pride was his sword, ornamented with large diamonds, a gift from Czar Nicholas in addition to one million rubles. The czar's unprecedented bounty was due not so much to Pashkevich's success in the wars but to the fact that Nicholas, on a shaky throne, badly needed the support of the Army. And Pashkevich was the highest ranking and most popular marshal in Russia. The short-necked, stocky "Pashie's" dignity was written not so much on his round face, but on his broad chest with innumerable, huge decorations.

A 300-pound Tartar Khan, wearing a furred Mongolian hat decorated with silver coins, and dressed in a sumptuous gold-embroidered robe, supported himself against the marble wall. A typical figure of world politics in the eyes of his family and friends, he was a great statesman and benefactor of his conquered, Satellite land; but to his subjects he was a traitor who had sold them to the Winter Palace for the privilege of annually kissing the mouth of the Czar of All the Russias.

In the center of another group, Prince Igor Effremovich Opatkin, a large candle-dripping gracing his chest as a small and modest decoration for short-sighted people, listened to the chatting of some ladies. Prince Igor, after his return from his official European trip last August, had been promoted to full general and commandant of the Second Cossack Regiment in St. Petersburg.

In a group of foreign diplomats the Marquis Alphonse des Fereyolles, his young wife, Countess Rolly Dukay, and Baron Heinrich von Nordthal, the Austrian ambassador, were talking with a tall gaunt-faced English gentleman. The topic was the recent death of Russia's great poet, Alexander Pushkin.

"Poor Alex!" said the Briton. "I witnessed the duel. The tossed golden ruble gave the first shot to d'Anthes, young playboy, son of a Dutch diplomat. Pushkin collapsed, but he managed to elbow up, aim, then fire. Of course, he missed. Only then did he lose consciousness."

"Did he die on the spot?"

"Oh, no. Only after two weeks of horrible suffering in his apartment."

Rolly's shape already revealed her pregnancy, and her short merino skirt afforded too liberal a view of her shapely ankles as she leaned closer and whispered:

"Is it true the czar fathered Madame Pushkin's twin daughters?"

"No," Ambassador von Nordthal declared. "But I happen to

know from a most authentic source, from Madame Pushkin herself, who the father of her twin daughters was. . ."

His words, like a powerful magnet, drew closer all the faces around him.

Von Nordthal's square monocle revolved on its wide black ribbon as he spoke:

"The twin daughters were fathered by his majesty, the gossip. Madame Pushkin has neither twins, nor a single daughter."

"But she was a mistress of the czar, was she not?" Rolly insisted.

"There are too many versions told by too many supposed to be authoritative sources," the Englishman replied cautiously.

"I was told," Rolly said, holding to the topic, "that on the advice of the czar, Madame Puskin accepted the attentions of that young playboy d'Anthes simply to mislead the jealousy of her impassioned husband."

Alphie thought his wife's interest in the details of the tragedy excessive before his British colleague, and diplomatically led the conversation to more sophisticated channels.

"Pushkin was more than just an impassioned husband," he said, clasping his triangular black hat against his dark blue coat. "What was Russian literature before Pushkin? The *Pravda Ruskaya?* That indigestable law code? Russian literature was little more than a translation or a poor imitation of French poetry."

"And English novels," said the Briton firmly.

"But of course, sentimental, lachrymose German and English novels."

"Do you consider that Walter Scott or . . ."

Rolly left their tedious talk and went to another group in which her aunt Olga Serebraniy was the center. Here the whispering was about the czar's love affairs. Olga told the story of Captain Zorkoff, who was called to Moscow and who happened to return home some days before he was expected. Entering the bedroom of his wife, "the Venus of St. Petersburg," he found Czar Nicholas sitting by her bedside, without his tight trousers and shirt and exhibiting his broad hairy chest. The astonished captain acted with unbelievable presence of mind. Coolly addressing his wife, he said: "Hello, dear. Did anyone call?" After her breathless "No, dear," he left the room, nearly falling when he stumbled over the czar's huge Stroganoff boots. The next day, Captain Zorkoff was promoted to colonel and became the czar's aide-de-camp.

Alphie, still chatting with the Englishman, had gone on to a new topic. "What kind of girl is she?" he asked. "I was told that when she was awakened by the Archbishop of Canterbury last June and told of her succession to the throne, the poor child was frightened to death. Well, after all, a girl of fifteen."

"Eighteen!"

"All right, eighteen. But a *girl* on the throne of the great British Empire at a time such as this!"

The Briton went to the "young girl's" defense.

"Catherine was a poor German girl and she was great, wasn't she? The French Revolution broke out during her reign and Russia did not collapse."

Interrupting the Briton, Alphie leaned forward, peering through the doorway into the adjoining hall.

"Here he is!" he whispered.

Sudden silence fell on the great hall. Everyone froze, as if they were paralyzed by a magic force. Only the heads turned toward the doorway, not with the quick movement of curiosity, but slowly, almost, it seemed, reverently. No one could escape the mass hypnosis, not even Alphie, when the czar's towering figure, dressed in the scarlet uniform of the Russian hussar, entered the hall.

On his right side appeared the czarina, and behind them walked Crown Prince Alexander. The czar offered his hand to an old, white-bearded man, first in the line to be introduced. But the old man ignored the royal hand, and with trembling fingers fished a petition from his pocket. The czar stepped forward to greet another guest and the petition automatically went into the hands of his aide-de-camp.

"The poor old fellow," remarked Alphie, "is pleading for clemency. I know him. His son is behind the walls of the Petrograd prison."

The forty-one-year-old Czar Nicholas was at least two inches taller than his late brother and predecessor Czar Alexander. Though his heavy bones resembled scrap iron in a potato sack, he was handsome. His buff side whiskers were almost the width of his palm at their square ends.

The elegantly clad Czarina Charlotte was as thin as a dry reed and looked several years older than the czar. Her attitude, far from being arrogant, had the indefinable grace of resignation in a proud soul. Her coiffure was *à la grecque,* her graying ash-blonde hair falling loose and full at the temples under the large diadem of Catherine the Great. She was dressed in a cyclamen-pink frock, the bodice laced across the front like a corset.

Crown Prince Alexander was a heavy young man, almost as tall as his father, with strong German features. Although he was only nineteen, he looked like a man in his middle twenties; he was dressed as a major general of the guards.

Colonel Zorkoff, the czar's new aide-de-camp, cast glances at a list awkwardly hidden in his white-gloved hand. When Dimitri Kantemir, the actor-manager of the Lomonosoff Theatre, bowed before the czar, Zorkoff quickly peeked at the list and introduced him as:

"Grand Duke Conrad Johann of Hesse."

His majesty gave a cold hand to the man in the lavender coat. As a habitue of the Lomonosoff Theatre's royal box, the czar immediately recognized Dimitri Kantemir, but he did not want to embarrass the overworked Colonel Zorkoff for his mistake.

Next to be introduced was the widow of an Uzbek nabob, a fat, dark lady who performed such a deep curtsy before the czarina that she could hardly regain her feet. The lady started a panting but friendly conversation with Dimitri in broken German, addressing him as *Durchlaut,* the highest title for a German prince. Dimitri Kantemir politely surrendered to the fact that he was the Grand Duke of Hesse. The role was easy for the great actor, who had appeared many times on the stage as Czar Boris Godunoff, King Lear and recently even as Napoleon.

The czar stepped up to the group in which he recognized Princess Olga Serebraniy. Only the other lady had to be introduced. The aide-de-camp threw a glance at his list.

"Princess Adelaide Lichtenstein."

"I am not!" protested the lady laughingly. "I am Countess Dukay."

Colonel Zorkoff blushed and apologized. A benign smile appeared on Czar Nicholas' severe face.

"My son Adalbert," Countess Jadi introduced Dali with motherly pride. The czar did not offer Dali his hand, but he seemed to enjoy the sight of the handsome young man in his richly trimmed Pálffy Hussar uniform. Dali sported a black waxed mustache beneath the aristocratic saber nose he had inherited from his father.

"What are you doing in St. Petersburg, Lieutenant?" the czar asked. His voice was deep, strong and clear.

"I am the assistant military attaché at the Austrian embassy."

"Since when?"

"Since last October, Sire."

"Have you collected a lot of secret material for Vienna about our army?"

"Not yet, Sire!"

His quick and embarrassed answer drew a laugh from the group, and the czar shook his hand as if in congratulation for his sincere reply. He threw a parting look at Countess Jadi's jeweled diadem. The czar had the eye of an expert for unusually large diamonds.

Countess Jadi's feeling toward Czar Nicholas was entirely different from Endre's, but now that she had met the czar, she had to agree with her husband's impression of his charm.

In the largest hall a fifty-piece orchestra began to play a popular mazurka. Hundreds of the guests quickly arranged themselves into dancing pairs. The veils and trains of the ladies, the wigs of the frocks in every color flew with the sweet melody of the mazurka.

While the dancing went on, the large, winged doors opened onto a huge banquet in the neighboring hall: hundreds of silver candelabras lit the marvels of the buffet, French style, oriental in abundance. The golden-brown crispy skins of whole roasted calves, goats, ewes, lambs and sucklings glittered in the candlelight on a thirty-foot-long table, together with turkeys, geese, ducks, chickens and pigeons. The second table exhibited game of the steppes: young colts, gazelles, aristocrats of birds: peacocks and pheasants, preserving the feathery pomp of their tails. On the third table were dozens of varieties of fish, with several hundred pounds of sturgeons, multitudes of sterlets, pikes, and caviar. The fourth table was filled by architectural models of famous fortresses and palaces, all of them snowed over, of course, with sugar. The air around the tables was infested with divers odors, the mixture of the bitter smoke of the burnt wicks of numberless candles, the rich smell of the hot *borshch*, the famous Russian beet soup, the ladies' perfumes, the sour beer, the fermented cabbage, the oil of the officers' boots and the musk and amber of the nobles.

Meanwhile the musicians played old Russian folksongs and a group of Cossack dancers kicked up their rousing *Kozachok*.

At midnight the *zhonka* was served, hundreds of bowls of cognac, red wine and sugar burst into blue flames and everybody toasted *S Novim Godom!* Happy New Year!

Exactly at one o'clock, while thousands of rolling eyes and paddling elbows were still very busy around the huge buffet tables, the trumpets of the heralds, rather tactlessly, signalled the end of the reception.

The four black Serebraniy horses swiftly drew the large, gilded sleigh to Ogla's home on Karasmin Street.

After leaving his mother, Aunt Olga, Rolly and Alphie in the care of the two armed doormen of the Serebraniy palace, Dali went on in the sleigh to the Hotel Doulon on Godunoff Square. He had been invited, of course, to live in Olga's palace but he preferred to be independent. Besides his confidential talks with political friends, he also had pretty female visitors in The Hotel Doulon.

2

When Dali entered his poorly heated room, he found Tonchi waiting for his report of the great reception. Tonchi was warming himself with a bottle of vodka.

Dali threw his wolf-fur coat, his shako, and his wide hussar saber on the bed without a greeting, in the manner of a man who returns to his friend with important news.

"Well?" Tonchi said.

Dali began a vivid and detailed description of the reception.

"What was your impression of Palkin?" Tonchi asked. He always called Czar Nicholas "Palkin."

"He looks like a cross between a great sovereign and a Thracian peasant," Dali said. "His face is very noble in the animal kingdom, and very bestial in a human society."

He reported his conversation with the czar, not omitting his answer "Not yet, Sire!" about his spying on the Russian army.

"He tried to be charming, but severity is his dominant characteristic," Dali added.

"Did you talk to Prince Igor?" Tonchi asked.

"Not too much. He was always surrounded by a lot of people. When he left he said to me 'I hope I will see you next Sunday.' Olga invited him, too, for her next *spinnerale*."

"What is a *spinnerale*?"

"That's what Olga calls her tea parties. Her lady friends bring along their spinning wheels, to show their great willingness to work for some charity purpose. They have contests to see who can spin the most thread . . ."

". . . while they contest to see who can spin the most gossip," Tonchi finished the sentence, and said: "The time has come for Number Two."

"Number Two" in their conversation meant the second paragraph in the unwritten program for their mission in Russia. The program had to remain unwritten because to write it down would have been very dangerous. In St. Petersburg, raids were made not only in hotel rooms but in private apartments, too. And, if Dali's quarters should be searched, a written program might be found, with horrible consequences.

When they had left Buda in October, they had been in such haste that they had had no time to elaborate a program, and they had agreed with Andris when he said:

"You have to be there, look around, and see what you can do; only after that can you make your program."

After their arrival in St. Petersburg in November, many pounds of candle were burned in Dali's room before the program was complete.

Its first paragraph read: "Contact the Russian underground."

Tonchi had lost little time in finding Russian and Polish opponents of the czar's regime. By January, he had learned quite a lot about their secret aims and past activities. Before the Decembrist uprising in 1825, there had been two main groups in the underground.

The first group, the so-called Southern School, was led by Colonel Pestel; they wanted a national duma, modelled after the British Parliament. And through a radical land reform, they would have given each of Russia's 20 million serfs 5 acres of land. But they did not mean to give the serfs political status. Further, they planned to outlaw Mohammedanism, and deport Jews to Palestine—not out of anti-Semitism, but in the interest of the Jews, in fear of savage pogroms. The final aim of the Southern School was a republic; and to eliminate all claimants to the throne, they planned to assassinate all members of the Romanoff family.

The Northern School was more liberal. They wanted serfdom to disappear entirely. They demanded absolute freedom of speech, press and religion, and trial by jury. The constitution of the young United States influenced them greatly, but they kept the system of a hereditary emperor.

Tonchi's friends were the successors of the Northern School.

The mission in Russia program had only seven brief paragraphs; it was easy to learn them by heart. "Number one: After arrival in St. Petersburg, contact the underground. Number two: Investigate Prince Igor as the possible leader of a Russian revolution and a future liberal czar. Number three: Organize a military revolt, capture Czar Nicholas and all of his entourage. Number four: Simultaneously incite peasant riots all over Russia. Number five: Install Prince Igor on the throne by acclamation. Number six: Draft Russia's new constitution: no hereditary dynasty; czars to be elected by popular votes for a lifetime. Number seven: Have democratic Russia remove its troops from Poland and form a strong alliance with the new independent personal union of Hungary and Poland, which would come into existence after the inevitable collapse of the Habsburg and Hohenzollern dynasties.

Now that Tonchi had come to know the underground, he considered the time ripe for step number two. "Next Sunday," he told Dali, "in the Serebraniy palace, you will talk to Prince Igor—a man who learned on the spot in America what democracy means. Let's cross our fingers."

The Sunday after the New Year's reception some forty guests assembled in the great salon of the Serebraniy palace. The interior of the fifty-room palace, in spite of the magnificence of its furnishings, reflected a deep-rooted Oriental disorder. In the Russian household the bed was the least used piece of furniture. The women servants slept on the garret floors, while the men curled up on the stairway—not only the servants, but sometimes the guests too, on pillows they threw on the floor for the night.

"Well, Peter the Great used to sleep with his soldiers on the bare ground," Olga explained to Jadi.

That Sunday, at Olga's *spinnerale,* twenty spinning wheels were buzzing, some of them antique masterpieces decorated with silver or golden designs and set with precious stones. Twenty ladies contested—not too seriously—on the spinning wheels, and twenty gentlemen contested—very seriously—for the spinning ladies.

Dali stood alone by the wall waiting for an opportunity to talk with Prince Igor.

Watching him, Dali fought disillusionment. Prince Igor, his black beard shining, seemed to be enjoying a frivolous conversation with Olga. He did not look much like the one man God had ordained to save Russia and the whole of Europe. His face was permanently flushed and he sported a protruding stomach achieved through expensive feeding.

While the spinning wheels buzzed, the talk, of course, buzzed too. The conversation turned to the miracles of the Industrial Revolution. In St. Petersburg's suburbs, a few textile factories had opened in recent years. And the result? No, not a better thread than that of the good old spinning wheels; the result was the grumbling of the workers who were not satisfied with their wages, half a ruble for a whole week.

"For fourteen hours a day," Prince Igor remarked laughingly. But Dali was encouraged. Surely this was the remark of a reformer.

Prince Igor then mentioned another new device, invented only the previous year by Mr. Morse, an American gentleman: a device of small brass wheels and thin wires which was supposed to carry messages by electricity in a few seconds regardless of distance.

"Oh, yes, the *greletam*," Grand Duchess Elena remarked knowingly. No one corrected Her Highness, who should have said "telegram."

Dali finally had an opportunity to touch Prince Igor's arm:

"I have a message for you, sir."

"From a girl?" the prince asked with a twinkle.

"Well, from many girls. And from very many boys, too," Dali said mysteriously as he led the Prince out of the great salon to an anteroom where they could talk freely. Not until the door was closed and the two men were seated did Dali begin to speak.

"The message is highly confidential," he began. "I feel it my duty to deliver it to you personally. You must understand, I am not authorized to mention any names. I can only say that the message comes from Europe . . . and from Russia. It involves not only individuals, but . . ." he snapped his fingers, searching for the French phrase.

Prince Igor came to his aid. *"Un tas de gens?"*

"Yes, but more than that. Many, many people of great importance."

Prince Igor glanced at the closed door and felt himself trapped.

Then, after a moment, Dali said:

"However horrible was that night in 1801, when the Slav princes bludgeoned Czar Paul to death because they thought he was too German, I can understand their action. History teaches us that people have never liked foreign rulers. But the cruel death of Paul did not prevent the steady flow of German blood into the Romanoffs' veins. Czar Alexander married Elisabeth, Duchess of Baden, and Czar Nicholas married Charlotte, daughter of the Prussian king."

Dali's gaze searched Prince Igor's face. At last he said: "But you are different. The Opatkins are pure Slavs."

Prince Igor, his face turned toward the window, was frowning. With the tip of his tongue he was cleaning his teeth, one by one, behind his tightly closed lips, pretending that he had not heard a word of this dangerous topic.

"I have no right," Dali continued, "to criticize the domestic affairs of your great country, but my friends, looking at Russia with Western eyes, think that ever since Czar Nicholas crushed the December revolt, Russia has been living through the worst years of her history. He has converted the nation into a huge military camp where every citizen is watched day and night, and the watcher watches the watcher. My friends think . . ."

"How many friends do you have?" Prince Igor cut in with a smile.

"About 260 million, sir. Two hundred million is the population of Europe and 60 million that of Russia."

"What is your friends' message to me?" Prince Igor asked, more impatiently than curiously, folding his hands over his mandarin stomach.

"I think you will agree with my friends, Prince Igor," Dali said with great feeling, "that we live in an age when every part of the world is full of explosive materials. No one can predict what will happen next month, next week, or even tomorrow. If someone were to tell me that tomorrow revolution would break out in Germany, in Austria or even in Russia . . ."

A hearty laugh sounded from the salon and Prince Igor turned toward the door. He seemed rather more interested in the cause of the laughter than in the young man's discussion.

"In case of a general European change," Dali began, but Prince Igor placed a patient and benevolent hand on his shoulder.

"Give me the message."

"The message is this. Supposing that a great and general change occurred in the near future, affecting Russia. Would you be willing to mount the Russian throne?"

Dali's tone was as casual as if he were asking: "Would you be willing to accept the honorary presidency of the Spinning Society?"

Prince Igor did not laugh. His deep-set eyes, with their steady, inward smile, looked into Dali's with a strange intensity.

"I assume the unexpected question sounds naïve to you," Dali said. "If so I am afraid that you have no idea of who, in the eyes of not only the Russian people, but of the intellectuals of Europe, you are considered to be."

Prince Igor flicked something that was not there from his

purple-striped, dark-blue trousers. Then his gaze shifted to the large silver spurs on Dali's lemon-yellow boots. In a fatherly tone, he asked:

"How old are you, Count Dali?"

"Twenty-three last October."

Prince Igor patted Dali's shoulder gently and said:

"I wish I could be your age again."

After the *spinnerale*, Dali found Tonchi waiting for him in the Hotel Doulon.

"Well?" asked Tonchi.

Pacing the room and combing his hair with his fingers, Dali recounted his talk with Prince Igor. Dali spoke truthfully, but he did not mention his subjective feeling towards Prince Igor before their talk. He did not mention Prince Igor's flirtation with Olga, which seemed to him too frivolous for a savior; he did not mention the mandarin stomach, nor Prince Igor's wandering attention. At the end of his story, he said:

"Of course he did not give a definite yes, and he did not give any instructions on how to proceed. But I am sure I was the first to tell him that in the eyes of many many people, in and out of Russia, he is the man who has the stature of a liberator."

Tonchi nodded in satisfaction and said: "For a first talk I did not expect more. The question is so delicate—did he say that he wants to see you again?"

"Oh, yes. He said 'I hope I will see you again very soon.' At Olga's place I can continue our talk any time."

"Good," Tonchi said. "Now, I think it's time for you to meet some of my friends in the underground."

That night, after Dali had changed his hussar uniform for plain civilian clothes, he and Tonchi walked through Nevsky Prospect, entirely deserted on this dark January night. Here and there in the distance, they could see the shy yellow light of a candle, caged in a carved out pumpkin and carried as a hand lamp.

From Nevsky Prospect, they turned into a very long and narrow side street. They carried no lamp, but Tonchi knew the way. At length they entered the workshop of a carpenter, still working at his lathe. Tonchi greeted him casually, and then led

Dali to the back of the shop and entered a small room. This was one of the many secret meeting places of the St. Petersburg underground.

In the flickering light of a butter lamp, six men sat talking.

"This is my friend, Pierre," Tonchi introduced Dali; and when one of the men addressed Tonchi as Louis, Dali knew the reason for it. If one of them were unlucky enough to be arrested, no torture could get out of him the real names of his friends.

The men were almost faceless in the poor light of the butter lamp. A greasy table, several chairs, a chessboard, and a plate warmer, always threateningly sprawling its four bowed iron legs in somebody's way, were all the furniture in the small room. One of the men had an exaggerated Slavic nose like a large ivory button, and his eyes bulged so much they looked ready to jump out of their sockets. Two faces were dressed in dense beards, as if in fur coats for protection against the extreme cold. In contrast with the button-nosed face with the bulging eyes, the fourth face possessed an oversized cucumber nose and conspicuously small, shiny black eyes. In the deep shadow of the corner the fifth man seemed to have no face at all.

These five men were talking in Russian, which Dali did not understand. Behind their whispering he felt only these three words: danger, determination, death. The five seemed strange to Dali, and to some degree, frightening. They looked not like heroes of high ideals, but rather like repulsive criminals with unknown capital offences in their past and in their future.

But the sixth man was different. He was a cleanshaven, handsome youth whose code name was Serge. Serge spoke to Dali in excellent French.

While Tonchi talked to the others in rapid Russian, Dali and Serge discussed, in general terms, the present situation of Europe.

When Serge excused himself to leave and stood up, Dali suffered a horrible shock. This man's left foot hardly reached the knee of his normal right leg, and ended in a wooden stick. The miniature foot was not deformed; on the contrary, it was the shapely foot of a ten-year-old girl, and its perfect shape made it all the more horrifying.

Shaking hands with Dali in farewell Serge spoke in a tone of sincere friendship.

"*Au revoir*, Pierre!"

The next morning, Dali wrote his first long letter to Andris for delivery with a reliable courier from the embassy.

We are here for more than three months but I can hardly report anything to you of our progress, or of this city, which is more vast than beautiful, more glittering than imposing, filled more with sadness than with historical significance. Perhaps just this—that it was built, not for the Russians but against the Swedes. When Peter the Great feared a surprise attack from King Charles XII of Sweden, who had defeated the Russians in 1700, he hastily built this city—as the legend goes—on human bones, because the workers died by the thousands in the unhealthy marshes.

The *mood* of this city today? When two carriages pass each other the coachmen ceremoniously bow in their seats, kissing their fingers, their eyes twinkling. This pantomime is a comment on the czar; and it is not a friendly one. One day in the not too distant future there will be a very great change.

I do not envy the role of the czar. To play providence for 60 million unfortunate Russians is not an easy job. He has no choice but to force his disciples to conquer the world in order to prove himself to be God; otherwise he would be crushed. This is what makes a despot's life so hard, in Vienna and in Berlin, too.

We have already seen even in Russia that the steam engine will have a tremendous influence on our century. In Olga's princely kitchen a small steam engine majestically turns a whole lamb on the spit, and there are several factories and steam mills in the suburbs. I am under the impression that Russia's strange society combines the science of the West with the physical strength and fresh genius of Asia. The only explanation I can find for the great sacrifices and sufferings of the people is that Russia sees Europe as a prey which our dissensions will one day deliver to her.

I sometimes wonder what constitutes the real strength of a nation. Freedom as in France, or blind obedience as in Russia?

A third of Russia's entire population—some 20 million—are miserable serfs—serfs lower than the lowest class, and not regarded as human. They work three days a week without pay for a landlord who can flog them at will.

The status of Russia's fourteenth or lowest class is different from that of the serfs. They are free men, which means that if you kill or beat them, you are guilty of a crime and liable to a penalty. This lowest class is composed of the most menial government employees: porters, letter carriers, the like.

The class at the peak of the pyramid is composed of a single man, Marshal Pashkevich, Prince of Warsaw, who crushed the Polish revolt in 1831. The second class is of course the aristocracy, dignitaries of the government, the army and the church.

Russia's fourteen classes make up a regimented nation, with a military order applied to an entire society. Owing to this dreadful construction, all geniuses in Russia, whether in literature, the arts or the sciences, live underground.

I agree with Alphie that in France the tyranny of revolution is an evil of transition; in Russia the tyranny of despotism is a permanent revolution.

Tonchi says that a society which does not offer freedom at birth cannot expect much from the future.

On our excursions I have seen villages transformed into barracks and men leaving their poor thatched peasant houses, fully armed, in formation and good order, as if drilled to plunder from Istanbul to London. The strength of this nation is that life counts for nothing, absolutely nothing.

I have learned some details of the latest peasant riot in the Volga district. All the landowners and overseers, together with their families, were massacred. They boiled one in a cauldron, put another on a spit to be roasted alive, set entire villages on fire in a delirium of hatred and bloodshed. We remember the horrors of Attila and later of Genghis Khan's invasion of Europe. If the floodgates of Asia are again to be raised, God be merciful to our children! Asia will put up a permanent tent not only in Buda but in Vienna—Versailles, too. Alphie shares my opinion. Tonchi laughs at our pessimism. He says that the Russian colossus is weak, only its Hallowe'en mask is horrifying. The mask is the arrogance of its diplomats.

4

In his capacity as assistant military attaché, Dali earned no salary. But then, he did very little work. Once or twice a week, he would translate some unimportant reports from Hungarian into German, or vice versa. In his free time, of which there was a great deal, he enjoyed exploring the city. One of his favorite spots was in the Bolshoy Park, on the shore of the Neva in St. Petersburg, where some five acres of the park had been converted into a skating rink. Skates on the ice varied from shiny steel, rusted iron, or bone, to just plain hardwood.

Dali enjoyed testing his skill on the ice, and did so often. One day, while the brass band played popular mazurkas on the pavilion's terrace, a young girl near Dali stumbled on the ice and fell to her knees. Dali flew to her aid.

When he had helped her to her feet the girl blushed and said, "*Bolshoy spasibo.*" It was Russian for "Thank you."

"*Vous parlez Français?*"

"*Oui, je parle.*"

And she flew away. Dali flew in pursuit like a falcon after a fleeing dove.

"Nyanya!" the girl called to an onlooker on the terrace. "Time to go home."

Even her voice held Dali fascinated. Inside the heated pavilion, Nyanya knelt before the girl and tried to remove her old-fashioned skates, but the tight leather straps were too much for Nyanya's old hands.

"May I help you?"

Now it was Dali who knelt before the girl. He held the pretty ankle firmly in one hand, though it was not at all necessary, while he untied the straps.

"Are you leaving, Dushenka?" a lady asked, pausing as she passed them. The girl began to chat in Russian, which Dali did not understand. In hopes of detaining her, he dashed off to the buffet for two freshly boiled sausages, topped with grated horse-radish. But by the time he returned, the bench she had occupied was empty. He hurried to the terrace where there was a brief pause in the brassy music. The musicians were shaking the saliva from their fat trumpets; but otherwise the terrace was empty now. Meanwhile a heavy mist had fallen on the skating rink, and Dali found himself in the center of a cupola, hardly a hundred yards across. The fog wrapped the pavilion.

In which direction did they go? The fog did not tell him. Only that strange name, Dushenka, and her voice and her smile remained in the cold empty air.

The red sausages were cold, too, when Dali wolfed them, more out of anger than appetite.

Dushenka. There was no girl in Vienna or Buda-Pesth by that

name. It seemed to Dali that there was no other Dushenka in the world.

"Have you ever heard the girl's name, Dushenka?" Dali asked his Russian friends in Café Tobolsk.

"Dushenka?" Paul Tolstoy laughed. "In Russia every second girl is Dushenka. The name became popular in the last century after Hypolit Fedorovich Bogdanovich wrote a novel called *Dushenka;* it was a very bad novel, and of course, it became a hit. Even a street was so named. Dushenka Ulitza is two blocks from here."

Some days after his encounter with Dushenka, Dali passed an old lady in the street. She looked familiar but for a moment he couldn't place her. Then all at once, he turned and ran after her.

"Nyanya!" he exclaimed, as he caught up with her. "Am I glad to see you! We met at the skating rink!"

"Oh, yes," Nyanya said vaguely, narrowing her weak eyes.

"Princess Serebraniy asked me for Dushenka's address. She wants to invite her to tea."

"Oh . . . that would be a great honor for Dushy," said Nyanya in her broken French.

"What is her full name and address?"

"Dushenka Arkadievna Bobak. Dushenka Ulitza fifteen."

"Was the street named after her?" Dali asked jokingly, while he jotted down the address in his notebook.

"After her? No! *She* was named after the street," Nyanya said. "By Dimitri."

"Who's Dimitri?"

"You don't know? Dimitri Kantemir! The manager of the Lomonosoff Theater."

"Oh. Is she an actress?"

"Not *yet.* But she wants to be. She's taking singing lessons. She has a wonderful alto, you know."

"Can she spin?"

"What do you mean?" Nyanya asked, her face darkening. Around the Lomonosoff Theater, such decent expressions as "to drill," "to climb," "to knead," and so on were used as obscenities.

"There will be the usual afternoon *spinnerale* in the Serebraniy palace next Sunday," Dali explained. "Ladies spinning for charity, you know, and having tea."

"Oh," Nyanya said, visibly relieved. "Dushy can spin pretty well, of course."

"You are the mother of Dushenka, Madame, aren't you?"

"Oh, no," Nyanya said, touched by the word Madame.

"She called you Nyanya," Dali said, "I know but a few Russian words—*Nyanya* means "Mama," doesn't it?"

"More than that, Herr Captain," Nyanya replied, returning Dali's courtesy with the respectful title. "Nyanya means a lot of things. Sometimes an aunt, sometimes just an old witch like me."

And she showed her few yellow teeth in a friendly grin. "I am Dushenka's secretary, her lady companion, her maid, her cook, and her dog; but at the same time I can curse her and call her to order, you know."

Dali wanted to know more about the girl, who seemed to him the rarest of beauties.

"Where is Dushenka Ulitza?" he asked. "In the residential section?"

"Oh, no. It is a poor, narrow little street, not far from the theater. But we were lucky to find a small house for rent. We came from Novgorod last spring. There isn't a good teacher in Novgorod for stage singing, you know. Have you ever been in Novgorod, Herr Captain?"

"Never. How far is it from here?"

"About a hundred versts southwest of St. Petersburg. About three days."

"On horseback?"

"No," Nyanya answered, "on foot."

The three-day journey from Novgorod told Dali all he needed to know about Dushenka's financial and social status. Her parents, he thought, must be poor Russian peasants.

"I suppose," Dali said, "her parents do not object to her theatrical career?"

"Dushy has no parents," Nyanya said. "Her father, a gamekeeper, was mobilized and killed in the war when Prince Pashkevich—you know that great story better than I do. Dushy was sixteen then, and when her mother, a cousin of mine, died of

114

sorrow a few months later, I was lonely too—I took her into my small house; she was an only child. The schoolteacher told me for years that Dushy had the best and strongest alto in the choir, and so we sold everything in Novgorod and came to try our luck here."

Having collected more information about the "fairy of the skating rink" than he had hoped, Dali left Nyanya with a friendly handshake, and *Au revoir,* and *Mes salutations à Mademoiselle.*

There was no difficulty at all about Dushenka's invitation to the *spinnerale. "Mais certainement! Avec plaisir!"* Olga said when Dali suggested inviting her.

For the remainder of the week, the Doulon's male and female servants were kept busy cleaning Dali's boots, pressing his gala hussar's uniform, washing and ironing his frilled shirts and lacy handkerchiefs—all for his initial meeting with Dushenka in high society.

But the following Sunday, when he entered the Serebraniy palace, he was unable, at first, to recognize a single face. Then he remembered two of the ladies he had seen contesting that other Sunday, when he had talked with Prince Igor.

He felt terribly lonely. His eyes kept returning to the door, and whenever anyone entered, he turned his head hopefully. But time passed: half past six, then seven; and still she did not come. Perhaps she was with another admirer.

That night Dali was in a most disagreeable mood. He dined at the Hermitage, and went home early.

Alone in the Hotel Doulon, he lay on the couch, gazing at the ceiling. His thoughts returned to the skating rink, and the moment he had helped the unknown girl to her feet. He recalled the piquant face distinctly, as she stood there on the ice, an embarrassed smile on her lips, brushing snow from her full skirt. Her fur cap had cast its warm shadow over her pink-white face, and as she had raised her eyebrows and so charmingly half-lowered her eyelids, she had drawn the corners of her mouth to conceal a smile. He could hear the slightly singsong tone of her voice as she said: *"Bolshoy spasibo."*

Now, lying on the couch, he closed his eyes and re-examined

every detail of Dushenka's face, to its finest subtleties. Her eyebrows were delicate, their arch narrow. The left was marked by a small scar, which, though hardly visible, marred her beauty. Did it? Or was it that scar that gave her face such a curious, almost mystical expression? The large eyes, he didn't know exactly whether they were blue or deep green, were shaded by long lashes. Her nose was a Slavic nose, but not too short. The mouth was large, but the lips were delicate, and the corners of her mouth were capable of expressing every emotion. Was she a virgin? Was it possible that she was the mistress of some rich man?

It was the first time in his life that jealousy had touched Dali's heart, and it struck with an unbearable, hitherto unknown stab of pain.

5

The next morning Dali awakened with a severe headache, and a profound conviction that Mademoiselle Dushenka could not be worth so much suffering. While he dressed, he made up his mind to seek a new adventure, since the obscure little singer had been so ungrateful as to spurn his godmother's invitation. He left the Hotel Doulon determined to think no more of her.

Then, on his way through Godunoff Square, he stopped in a little flower shop, scribbled on his card: "I hope I will see you again at the skating rink," and dispatched the card, with three dozen yellow roses, to Mademoiselle Dushenka Arkadievna Bobak at Dushenka Ulitza 15.

Beginning the next morning, he haunted the skating rink in Bolshoy Park. Thursday, Friday, Saturday—nothing. But Sunday afternoon . . . there she was! The same fur cap, the same fur coat, the same Nyanya. Dali left a half-written figure eight on the ice and hurried to the pavilion. He stood before her, gave a perfect military salute, and grinned broadly. Dushenka recognized him at once, took off her glove, and offered him her hand.

"Was it you who sent me the beautiful roses?" she asked.

"Oui, Mademoiselle."

They spoke French. Her French was about as fluent as Dali's.

"Est-ce-que vous êtes Autrichien?"

"No, I am not the other dog."

Dushenka did not understand the play on the words at once. *Chien* in French means dog, and Autrichien sounds like *"autre chien"*—the other dog. The Austrians had been "the other dog" in Paris since Louis XVI had married the unpopular Marie Antoinette.

"Then what is your nationality?" Dushenka asked.

"Well, if I am an officer in the Habsburg monarchy, and I am not an Austrian, try to find out what kind of animal I am."

Dushenka laughed lightly.

"I know." Nyanya grinned. "You must be Hungarian."

As the brass band played a Strauss waltz, Dali and Dushenka flew hand in hand, over the ice, writing the graceful figure eight over and over again. The smooth bluish ice mirrored their bodies.

"Why didn't you accept the invitation to the *spinnerale?*" asked Dali.

"The same week that I received the invitation," Dushenka said, "Dimitri Kantemir at the Lomonosoff received an invitation for dinner from Prince—I've forgotten the name. Dimitri got himself a nice haircut, and, dressed in his new frock coat, presented himself at the palace. When he arrived, the butler informed him that the old prince was asleep in his bed. The invitation was just a practical joke. Actors are crazy people, you know."

But to compensate for her failure to attend Olga's *spinnerale,* Dushenka invited Dali to tea the following Sunday.

All week Dali could think of nothing but his impending visit to Dushenka. On Sunday, he dressed in his gala hussar uniform, sprinkled Eau de Cologne on his hands and hair and neck, and then walked from the Hotel Doulon to Dushenka Ulitza.

The old house Dushenka had rented was so small it could have been fitted, roof, chimney, and all, into any salon in Princess Olga's palace, but it was a beautiful house, a jewel stolen from the pocket of the sixteenth century. The inscription on the flat stone above the entrance read "Anno 1563."

Dali's speculation that Dushenka received rich admirers was entirely unfounded. The only male who had ever set foot in her small house before Dali's visit was a childhood playmate from Novgorod, Sylvie Bralin.

Sylvie was the son of a peasant baker whose house in Novgorod was separated from Dushenka's by only a small fence. Ever since their childhood, Sylvie had been hopelessly in love with Dushenka. But when they grew up, Dushenka had left Novgorod to try her fortune in St. Petersburg, and Sylvie had joined the army, where he held the rank of private.

Whenever Sylvie had a few hours leave of absence from the barracks, he rang the doorbell in Dushenka Ulitza. He rang briefly, as if with a bad conscience; for he always came on the clumsy pretext that he had seen Aunt Katya Kirin, Marya Vrishoff, Uncle Pete and God knows whom in the street, and that he brought a message, never to Dushenka, but to Nyanya. The women knew that Sylvie was lying but he was always welcome, even though he never brought flowers or bonbons.

He brought more than such small gifts. He brought to Dushenka her childhood memories. Whenever Sylvie entered her room, with his flushed face and forced, almost idiotic grin, it seemed to Dushenka that he brought the wonderful fragrance of hot, freshly baked bread, the fragrance of the Bralin bakery.

But that Sunday afternoon neither Dushenka nor Nyanya had a thought for poor Sylvie. They were too excited over the glamorous young hussar whose visit they awaited.

While Nyanya puttered about the room to see that everything was in order, Dushenka stood before her mirror, putting the last touches on her coiffeur. Her honey-blonde hair was combed up from her nape into a flat, crownlike chignon, and above her temples were two golden ringlets. This new French fashion gave her face an air of gaiety even when she was sad. And Dushenka's face now was shadowed with melancholy.

"What do you know about his background?" Nyanya asked, giving a last polishing to the waxed oak shelf above the fireplace.

"Nothing," Dushenka said without turning back from the mirror. "Nothing more than that he's a Hungarian military attaché at the Austrian embassy."

"Is he married?"

"I don't know, but I don't think so. He has no wedding ring."

"Watch out, Dushy. These nice fellows from a foreign land carry their wedding rings in their pockets. My poor niece Marina—you remember her—jumped into a deep well when, after she learned she was pregnant, her fiancé disappeared. He was an itinerant merchant from Vienna, and he was married and had four children at home."

Dushenka did not speak. She was bored by Nyanya's prattle. Her mind was filled with thoughts of Dali. For Dushenka, Dali was less than the hero of a fairy tale, but more than Sylvie or any man she had met in Novgorod or in St. Petersburg. Dali's foreign air and bright foreign uniform helped him to be, in Dushenka's eyes, somehow above reality, like the protagonist in a foreign play she had seen at the Lomonosoff theater.

Dushenka knew nothing about Dali's family or his childhood. But his warm brown eyes glowed with sincere adoration for her. And, because they were obliged to converse in French, his cautious conversation seemed far more polite than the easygoing chatter of a born Russian.

Besides that, he was a tall, handsome young man. He was the first man in Dushenka's life to whom she would say an unhesitating "yes" if he should propose to her. But Dushenka knew that this was only a dream.

Nyanya, in her thoughts, did not even dream of Dali as a future husband for Dushenka. He was the nephew of Princess Serebraniy, and in her experience, high aristocrats never married poor commoners. When Nyanya said "watch out, Dushy," she did not speak from a moral basis. She didn't want Dushy to be taken in by a false promise of marriage instead of the substantial money or valuable jewelry she should receive if she went to bed with that charming hussar. Well, a poor girl from Novgorod, dreaming of a career in St. Petersburg, has to surrender sooner or later to someone: if not a rich Russian count, perhaps a producer or director around the theater.

Nyanya never asked Dushenka if she was a virgin or not. As a voluntary midwife in Novgorod, she had helped bring many children, both legal and illegal, into the world. She had also brought about many abortions, using both chemical and physical techniques. She knew the age-old secret of the potion, boiled for seven days from seven different very bitter herbs, that caused miscarriage. And for physical treatment, she used a goose quill, well-known all over the world since the time of the creation, to scrape the womb.

In Nyanya's opinion the Novgorod girls, with a very few exceptions, lost their virginity soon after their first menstruation. Nyanya was afraid that Dushenka was one of the exceptions. She was afraid because she thought virginity a great handicap for a twenty-two-year-old girl bent on a theatrical career. The resistance of virgins, screaming and using their sharp nails, or even just sobbing during sexual intercourse, greatly disgusts every nice gentleman. Nyanya's thoughts went back to Dali.

"Is he rich?" she asked.

"I have no idea. You think it was my first question to him?"

"Well, he doesn't seem like a churchmouse," Nyanya said to herself as she went out to the kitchen to prepare the tea.

Left alone, Dushenka sat on the sofa and stared at the floor. Her face was sad. Nyanya's guess was wrong. She had lost her virginity when she was thirteen. Now, her imagination went so far that she saw herself in bed with Dali on the first night after their wedding. What would happen? What would happen if he should find out she was not a virgin? Traditions and morals are different in foreign and faraway countries. Old Marina, who had served at the Russian embassy in Vienna, had once told Dushenka that Hungarians were dangerously passionate in love. Would Dali kill her in a tempestuous rage?

A girl who loses her virginity at the age of thirteen against her will carries her grievance almost like a boy who has been castrated in childhood. Dushenka had not been raped. She had simply obeyed the rule of the feudal world. In the first part of the nineteenth century almost every European country preserved the *jus primae noctis*—the right of a feudal landlord to deflower the daughter of a serf on her wedding night. In czarist Russia, the feudal landlord enjoyed even greater rights. He could claim the daughter of any serf or peasant in his employ. It was an unwritten rule, and its practice depended on the manner and morals of the lord.

In Russia, where there still lived primitive tribes whose hospitable traditions required a host to offer his wife or daughter to any guest for the night, it was no horrible shock for Mrs. Bobak when her thirteen-year-old daughter received a discreet invitation to the castle.

Dushenka's father was a gamekeeper on a Baltic baron's estate only a few miles from Novgorod. The Baron had married a rich widow some twenty years his senior. One May afternoon, when father Bobak was away at work, Dushenka's mother told her: "Come and dress, child. I will help you. His excellency the baron saw you last week when we were looking for mushrooms. He would like your company for a night. Don't be afraid, no harm will come to you. He's a very nice gentleman."

When they arrived at the castle, an elderly woman with a heavily painted face was waiting for them.

"I am Aunt Aurelie," she said to Dushenka in a sweet tone. But when she turned to Mrs. Bobak, her manner was cool and businesslike: "I am the hostess in the absence of her excellency. The baroness, on her doctor's orders, has gone to the warm shores of the Crimea to cure her *podegra*. Now you may go. Come for your daughter tomorrow morning. Not too early. After ten."

Dushenka did not look at her mother as she left. No, she did not blame her. She knew that her mother could not do anything against the "law." She knew from Maryushka, a friend of hers, what it meant to spend a night in the baron's company. "No, it was not too painful," Maryushka said. "And his excellency gave mother 200 rubles for my dowry."

Taking Dushenka's cold hand, Aunt Aurelie led her to a spacious bathroom, where two large wooden tubs were already filled with warm water.

"We usually take a bath before dinner," Aunt Aurelie said, and she started to undress while she chattered. "His excellency is not home yet, but we never wait for him at dinner. Sometimes he does not come home until after midnight. Come on, my dear. Put your clothes on that chair. Is the water warm enough for you? Good. How do you like it? Yes, it's perfumed. Lily of the Valley, his excellency's favorite perfume. What did you say?"

Dushenka had not said anything. She just obeyed. Both questions and answers came from Aunt Aurelie. After the bath, Dushenka's small, rather muddy boots were put aside. She received a pair of blue velvet slippers but no shirt, no skirt, only a light, almost transparent silk gown which reached just above her knees and was heavily perfumed.

Dushenka was already dazed from the bath, from the perfume, from the excitement and the strange fright she felt, which did not resemble any other fright she had experienced in her life. No maid, no butler appeared during dinner. It seemed that Aunt Aurelie was the only living being in the huge castle. Dinner awaited them in a little salon. Dushenka had to drink a glass of wine to the health of his excellency. The wine was very sweet and very strong. Dushenka had the feeling that everything, the soup, the meat, the fruits, everything, was perfumed. Then she had to drink a second glass of wine to Aunt Aurelie's health. She went to bed so dazed that the next morning, she remembered hardly anything of what had happened to her during the night.

She awoke in a four-poster bed, alone. She remembered the baron vaguely. She had seen him several times in the streets of Novgorod, a tall, bearded man, jovial and generous to the beggars. People liked him. During the night, in half dream, she vaguely remembered him as he climbed into the large bed, kissing and petting her. No, it was not too painful, only strange; and so disgusting that she nearly fainted.

Hair, hair, everything was hair. The baron's bushy ticklish eyebrows on her face, neck and breast; his big waxed mustache, his beard, his chest densely covered with the mat of long hair, badly smelling of sweat; even his hands seemed to be hairy, as if the baron were not a human being but some strange beast. He licked her ears and closed eyes the way Bundie, the Bralin's big Samoyed dog, used to do sometimes.

When she awakened, she was not surprised to find herself alone in the bed. The baron and everything he had done seemed unreal. She had liked the blue velvet slippers, but they, like the baron, had disappeared. Aunt Aurelie told her to put on her own clothes and her own boots. Mother was already waiting for her outside in the corridor.

Before they left, Aunt Aurelie gave Dushenka's mother an envelope which Dushenka knew contained the money Mauryushka had spoken about. When Saturday night came and her father returned from his hut in the forest, there was no mention of her visit to the castle; nor was there ever a word thereafter. After Dushenka's parents died, her father in 1832, when she was sixteen, and her mother a few months later, she herself, the baron, and Aunt Aurelie were the only ones who knew of her night in the castle.

Dushenka glanced at the porcelain clock on the mantelpiece. It was a few minutes after five. When the doorbell rang she jumped to her feet nervously.

When Dali, admitted to the house by Nyanya, entered the room, he found Dushenka, standing in an almost theatrical pose, awaiting him.

Now she was not the "fairy of the skating rink," "the unearthly beauty" who had lived in Dali's imagination after she had disappeared in the fog at their first meeting. Without her high fur cap she seemed shorter, and here she seemed much warmer, much closer to reality. But the charm of her little smile, the greenish light in her eyes, her unconscious grace, and the warm, melodious tone of her voice was the same. She greeted Dali graciously, extending her hand.

The physical appearance of a human being depends greatly on his dress and his surroundings. As Dali entered, Dushenka saw him for the first time without his shako. He looked strange to her. Without his heavy military coat, his figure looked light and elegant.

"Why didn't you answer my letter?" Dali asked in a soulful voice. Three days before, he had composed the first love letter of his life. "Every thought of mine kisses you, Dushenka. . . . Please answer! Please!" "Don't you want to talk about it?"

Dushenka did not answer. Standing by the lukewarm clay stove, she embraced it, seeking to hide the emotion which colored her cheeks. Dali stepped closer to her.

The day was ending. The candles were not yet lit. The bluish-white February twilight pervaded the room.

Nyanya appeared with the tea. Dushenka took it from her, and patted the samovar with a pretty gesture rather like that of a woman caressing the neck of a horse.

"Chopin is fine on the balalaika, really very sweet," she remarked in a strained voice, pouring out the tea.

"Yes," Dali answered, his tone betraying his wish to be done with that subject.

123

When Nyanya had left the room, Dali took the samovar out of Dushenka's hands and set it down.

"I am in love with you!" he said abruptly.

Dushenka slowly raised her eyes to Dali's, but when their glances met she abruptly turned her head.

Dali seized her hands and imprisoned them in his. Dushenka did not seek to withdraw her hands; a fire went through her body. When Dali tried to draw her toward him, she resisted, but she lost her balance and all but fell on him. Dali embraced her so tightly that she could not move.

"Let me go!" she whispered. But she did not struggle.

That night, Tonchi entered the Café Tobolsk to find Dali sitting in a corner surrounded by gypsies, who were serenading him with old Russian folk songs. Around him, empty champagne bottles bore witness to the evening's gaiety.

"What are you celebrating, sir?" Tonchi asked, knowing nothing of the girl in Dushenka Ulitza.

Dali, rather tipsy, ignored Tonchi's question. He signalled to the gypsies to play another song, and settled back to listen.

"Bad news from Hungary," Tonchi said somberly. "A horrible flood . . . the Danube . . . 200,000 are dead in Pesth!"

"Bravo!" shouted Dali, warmly shaking Tonchi's hand in congratulations.

"Are you drunk?"

"Me? Not at all. If the news says 200,000 dead, it's a hoax, because Pesth has hardly 70,000 people. Don't worry—the greater the distance, the greater the catastrophe."

But the following week, when the first letters arrived from Vienna, Dali learned that the flood really had been devastating.

On the night of January 30, 1838, a thundering wall of water had risen from the ice-congested Danube and swept over the sleeping city. Along the shore no one escaped death. "Pesth became a pile of mud," Endre's letter reported. "Fortunately, our palace in Septemvir Utca, together with those parts of Buda which were built on the hills, were not damaged."

On April 5, in the Serebraniy Palace, Rolly gave birth to a girl. "Mother and daughter are feeling well," Jadi wrote to Endre. She did not mention Dali's infatuation—not because she feared Endre's disapproval, but because she did not think it important enough to deserve mention.

Yet, at the very hour that his sister was giving birth to her daughter, Dali was at the Lomonosoff Theater, interesting himself in Dushenka's career. In Dimitri Kantemir's artistically shabby office, Dali placed a large manuscript on the manager's desk and seated himself on the gilded chair which had served as throne to King Lear, Peter the Great, Napoleon, and other emperors of the stage. In the daytime it served the theater's distinguished guests.

"Well?" Kantemir asked. "Did you read *Cupid and Psyche?*"

"Yes, I did," Dali said.

He was not telling the truth; the manuscript was in Russian, and he could not have read it if he had tried, which he had not.

"How did you like it, sir?"

"I liked it very much."

It was enough for Dali that Dushenka liked it.

The leading part was Cupid, son of Venus, who in Roman mythology appeared as a lovely winged boy, entirely naked except for his bow and arrow. Dushenka, of course, was to play Cupid.

"Too bad," Dimitri said with a most serious face, "that I can not put Mademoiselle Dushenka on the stage in a costume consisting only of a bow and arrow—ah, what a hit that would be! Alas, we are not in Paris."

Dimitri proposed a white silk blouse and breeches for Cupid's dress, with a powdered wig for her head—the costume derived from a Watteau painting.

Dushenka loved Cupid's part and she was enchanted by the costume idea. The other part, Psyche, was to go to the aging, bosomy Zynaida Guncharovna, Psyche was but a poor *résonneur* in the play, giving Cupid frequent opportunities for long witty speeches. The play was written by Dimitri Kantemir, with music and lyrics by Dimitri Kantemir. It was to be produced and directed by Dimitri Kantemir.

"I have prepared three estimates for the production," Kantemir told Dali; "raw, medium and well done. The cost depends, as you know, on the salary of the actors, the sets, the costumes, the number of nonspeaking parts, the number of musicians and so on."

Dali glanced at the estimates.

"Rather expensive," he said.

Dimitri threw up his hands.

"Well . . . *mon cher ami* . . . *sic itur ad astra.* The road to stardom has ever been expensive."

"Let's make it medium," Dali said. "Needless to say, neither Mademoiselle Bobak nor anyone else is to know anything about my sponsoring the show."

"*Monsieur le Comte!*" Dimitri said solemnly, "the reputation of the Lomonosoff demands that the names of our friends be kept in strictest secret."

The next morning, it was Dushenka who sat in King Lear's chair.

"We are going to produce *Cupid and Psyche,* a classic play. I have you in mind for Cupid," Dimitri said to Dushenka, who was pale with emotion. "How old are you, dear?"

"Twenty-two," Dushenka said, suddenly blushing.

"Let's make it nineteen. In the theater twenty-two years suggests a girl near to thirty. I've forgotten your family name. Bobroff?"

"Bobak."

"Bobak? It means sausage, doesn't it?"

"No, sir. An animal. A ground squirrel. Its dried and powdered heart is used as an amulet against insomnia."

"Against insomnia?" Dimitri cried. "I want your performance to *cause* insomnia. What about Dushenka Insommiva?"

Tears shone in Dushenka's eyes. "You have already changed my name from Sonya to Dushenka," she said, "and now you want . . ."

"All right, all right. There are so many odd creatures about already, one ground squirrel more or less does not matter."

On Monday, when the rehearsals began, Dali was on hand to watch from the back row of the empty theater, which the candle lights on the stage left in darkness. Thereafter he appeared every day, and became very friendly with Dimitri and the players.

One night, while dining in the Hermitage after the rehearsal, Dimitri said to Dushenka:

"Show me your ring."

Dushenka pulled it off with shy pride, and Dimitri examined it with the eye of a professional jeweler.

"Did you receive it from Attila?"

He winked at Dali, who was eating his lobster with a fierce concentration.

Neither Dimitri nor anyone else around the theater regarded the splendid diamond as an engagement ring. It seemed the most fitting thing on earth for Dushenka to be the mistress of "Attila," as Dali was called around the Lomonosoff.

But in fact, Dushenka was not Dali's mistress. Whether it was the recollection of the hairy baron or the hope of marriage that deterred her Dushenka herself was not sure. But some invisible barrier stood between her and ultimate surrender. She accepted Dali's attentions and his gifts, and encouraged his visits both at the theater and, when there were no rehearsals, at her home. But she did not sleep with him.

When one afternoon, Dali appeared at his usual hour for afternoon tea, he was surprised to find a guest in Dushenka's room; for by tacit agreement she was not to receive any male visitors except himself, even for tea. The guest—a neatly dressed young Russian soldier—jumped up and stood at attention when Dali entered the room.

"Sylvester Vassilevich Bralin," Dushenka introduced him.

Dali shook hands with Private Sylvester, whose prominent ears attested to a fresh haircut, and whose shining brass buttons and boots bespoke hours of polishing.

"Sit, Sylvie," Dushenka commanded, in the motherly tone of a kind aunt. Sylvester sat, his back straight as a ramrod, his ears crimson as the hood of a turkey.

"Sylvie's father is a man of wealth—I mean, by Novgorod standards," Dushenka said. "They have a big bakery shop and a large house. We were neighbors and playmates," she added confidentially.

The short, embarrassed silence which followed this information told Dali that Sylvie was desperately in love with Dushenka, but knew already that his sweetheart loved the foreign officer.

"Nice boy," said Dali, when Sylvester left them an hour later.

Some two weeks later, Dushenka's great day finally arrived in the opening of *Cupid and Psyche*.

An hour before the curtain went up, Dushenka was ready. As a Watteau-style Cupid, she looked both boyish and feminine. She was deathly pale as she sat before the mirror in her dressing room, while Dali held her ice-cold hand. She felt as if she were facing some terrible operation upon which her life depended. The dressing room smelled like a funeral parlor from the abundant wreaths and bouquets, among them a basket of lilies-of-the-valley sent by Countess Jadi.

Eight-fifteen. The house was filled. The audience fidgeted.

Eight-twenty. The opening curtain was delayed. Everyone knew why.

Outside the theater, a line of mounted police held back the curious spectators. Dimitri Kantemir, new silk hat in hand, awaited the royal family at the main entrance stairs.

Czar Nicholas' entry was impressive. When he appeared in the royal loge, accompanied by the czarina and followed by Crown Prince Alexander, the entire audience rose. The czar, in his bright red uniform, stood at the front of his loge for a moment, acknowledging the homage of his subjects, his figure projecting a majestic air of greatness.

When the curtain went up, the stage was brilliantly lighted by a hundred thick tallow candles. Dali was anxious for Dushenka, but when she appeared for the first time, by some miracle she had regained her heart. Even in her first song her alto was strong and clear. Dushenka! The music was Dushenka, the scenery was Dushenka, a pavilion in a blossoming garden was Dushenka, the light of the hundred candles was Dushenka; the audience had eyes for nothing and no one on the stage but the sparkling beauty and natural charm of Dushenka. Thunderous applause burst out after her every song.

The four halls of the Hermitage restaurant had never been so overcrowded as they were during the festive supper after the performance. It was the greatest day in Dushenka's life.

Though his romance with Dushenka was a serious distraction, Dali never forgot his mission. And when Olga invited him to a dinner at which she was entertaining Prince Igor *en famille* he was quick to accept her invitation.

The next evening, he discussed the occasion with Tonchi.

"There are rumors," Dali said, "that Prince Igor intends to marry Olga. Until now, I have not listened to such frivolous talk; but after last night, I am not so sure." He looked dejected. "I begin to fear," he added, "that we have been mistaken, and Prince Igor is not the man Russia, and all of Europe, too, is awaiting."

"What makes you think that?" Tonchi asked.

"When Alphie asked him if he ever thought of starting a political career, he said: 'I am not good for politics. I am a damned coward whenever I have to kill a fellow who stands in my way.' Everyone laughed, but I felt that his words were an answer to the question I put to him at Olga's *spinnerale*. When he spoke them he was looking directly at me."

"Don't forget," Tonchi said, "that although someone vehemently denies his candidacy for some high position, he may just as vehemently accept the offer when it seems serious."

"But if he marries Olga . . ."

"Princess Olga is the foremost of women around the Winter Palace. Her energy, her devotion to the cause of human rights —oh, she would be an ideal czarina! Are you seeking excuses for dropping your part in our great mission?"

When Tonchi left him, Dali went to Bolshoy Park for a solitary stroll. He did not know how to convey to Tonchi his misgivings about Prince Igor, but in his heart he was convinced that Olga's beau was no deliverer. And he feared for the future of their mission, if they had no new czar to offer the country when the time came.

Deep in thought, Dali did not notice the passerby, who stopped and called after him:

"Pierre! Pierre!"

He looked back only after the second call, and recognized the handsome young cripple he had met during his first and last visit to the underground. Dali had entirely forgotten that Tonchi had introduced him as Pierre, and he did not remember the code name of the man with the deformed leg.

"I am Serge. Don't you remember me?"

"Of course, I remember," Dali said. "How are you, Serge?"

They shook hands warmly. Serge was wearing a light overcoat, and carried a thick walking stick. Only the wooden elongation of his deformed leg was visible. Serge would not have recognized Dali if he had been dressed in his bright hussar uniform, but he was wearing civilian clothes, as he had on his visit to the underground. The two men sat on a bench. Around them, the park seemed deserted.

"Do you have the *B* needle, Pierre?" Serge asked.

"What is that?"

"Oh. So you were not present when Ksandrie distributed them. Since the latest peasant riots last month in the Urals, we were informed that Palkin had decided to take 'severe measures.' You know what that means—to kill thousands of 'suspicious' people. Therefore, last Friday, Ksandrie issued us the perfect defensive weapon—the *B* needle. Incidentally, it's not a bad offensive weapon, for certain circumstances. Each of us received three tubes. There are three needles in every tube. Here, you can have this tube."

Serge reached into his inner pocket and handed Dali a small, wooden tube.

"Watch out," he said. "The tops of the needles are soaked in *Baha*, a rare and deadly snake poison from India. Try it on a dog or a horse. The slightest prick—they will drop dead.

"I have never killed either a dog or a horse."

"Neither have I," said Serge. "Even a rabid dog is a noble creature compared to a Palkin or a Pashkevich."

After a quarter hour's conversation, Serge stood up, with the slow, clumsy movement of a crippled man.

"It was good to see you, Pierre."

He shook Dali's hand warmly and, leaning on his stout walking stick, disappeared in the gray twilight of Bolshoy Park.

Late that night, after Dali had accompanied Dushenka to her home, he went for his night cap to the Café Tobolsk, where Tonchi was waiting for him. During his conversation he mentioned casually:

"I met Serge in Bolshoy Park?"

"Who's Serge?"

"That handsome fellow with a crippled left foot. Don't you remember?"

"Oh, yes. From the underground. What did he say?"

"Nothing in particular. Do you know anything about Serge?"

"Nothing."

"Is he of Polish origin?"

"I don't think so. Why do you ask?"

"There is a . . . how should I say? . . . a strange air around him."

And he dropped the topic. He did not speak of the three *B* needles. It was the first time that he had kept such a secret from Tonchi.

All night, Dali lay awake. The great mission in Russia, he thought, was in great danger. Prince Igor was not the man who would lead a Russian revolution. Then who would put an end to Czar Nicholas' horrible reign? Dali knew that Serge was right when he said the czar meant to take revenge for the latest peasant riots. Olga had said the same; horrible massacres were in the air. And the first victims would be the Poles. According to Olga, the czar had repeated the threat General Novosolsky had made after the Decembrist uprising: "No Polish patriots will remain alive in Poland."

Who would put an end to Czar Nicholas' reign? Dali thought of the *B* needle. Was it really a deadly weapon? Or was the underground deceiving itself with childish daydreams. Or, again, was Serge perhaps insane? If it should be a deadly weapon. . . . When, just before daybreak, Dali fell asleep, it was a troubled sleep, full of dark, confused dreams of torture, and massacres, twisted faces and distorted limbs and, through it all, the czar in his bood-red uniform.

CHAPTER FIVE

After her great success in *Cupid and Psyche,* Dushenka had her entire house painted and redecorated. The Bolshoy Theater offered her a three-year contract with a large salary, but Dushenka remained loyal to Dimitri Kantemir, who discovered her. Dimitri raised her salary to half of the Bolshoy's offer. She was under siege by the shops in Nevsky Prospect, all of whom offered her jewels, furs, dresses, rugs, paintings, and furniture, demanding no downpayments. Dimitri's dream came true: she caused insomnia on large scale in the upper circles, for husbands and for jealous wives as well; she had so many admirers that Dimitri dubbed her "Circe of St. Petersburg," after the goddess in the Odyssey who changed males into grunting swine.

Olga Serebraniy arranged for an afternoon musicale in the Serebraniy palace, at which Dushenka was to perform old Russian folk songs, accompanying herself on the balalaika, for a small, aristocratic audience. Colonel Zorkoff officially informed Princess Olga that her majesty the czarina and His Highness Crown Prince Alexander would graciously accept her invitation to the affair.

The afternoon of the musicale was beautiful. The blossoming plane trees in Godunoff Square in front of the Hotel Doulon filled the air with honey and the sweet fragrance of spring. May is May even in chilly St. Petersburg.

Dali opened the window of his room overlooking the square and saw an officer on horseback galloping by at furious pace, carrying an order to his commander. Such military procedures in the residential section always preceded a royal visit. The galloping officer belonged to the *tchin,* the military elite of the administration, established by Peter the Great. The responsibility of the secret police for the safety of the czar and his family had also brought out the troops, and today Karamsin Street, where the Serebraniy palace stood, was barricaded, as were several neighboring streets.

But the police barricades had no effect on Dali's high spirits as he left his hotel and set off to pick up Dushenka, whom he, of course, was to escort to the party.

He found Dushenka anxious, as she always was before a performance, and busy with the last-minute details of her toilette. When they finally left for the Serebraniy palace, they had barely time to arrive, as etiquette demanded, before the czar's family.

The Serebraniy palace was elaborately decorated in honor of the royal visitors. From its wrought iron gate to its marble steps, a red carpet was laid down for the czarina and the crown prince. The afternoon musicale, like the *spinnerales,* was to be held in the great salon. To the left of the great salon stood the buffet in the dining room, and to the right the "inner salon," which in turn opened to the "small salon."

After the introductions in the inner salon, Dushenka felt herself almost a prisoner of her own success. She was not enjoying high society, with which she had nothing in common. Her thoughts dwelt on the brevity of life, for she hated to lose the rare and beautiful spring afternoon, which she would rather have spent walking along the shores of the Neva with Dali.

There was a sudden commotion in the hall as the whisper went around: "They have arrived!" Princess Olga hurried out to greet the royal visitors. When a moment later, she returned, the guests were astonished. Instead of the czarina and the crown prince, she brought Czar Nicholas himself, accompanied by his aide-de-camp. His majesty apologized for the last minute change of plans. . . . the czarina and the crown prince had to visit a sick old lady-in-waiting whose condition had suddenly taken a turn for the worse.

Princess Olga was a lady of great experience, and she had a keen instinct for court affairs. She immediately realized that the "change" in the plans was entirely premeditated. Since the opening of *Cupid and Psyche,* the czar had gone to the Lomonosoff Theater three times. No doubt he planned to make a new Madame Pushkin of the beautiful actress. Princess Olga's face did not reveal the slightest trace of any such suspicion, but she made two changes in the program. She cut the two-hour musicale to a half hour, knowing that the czar would not stay to hear any music anyway. And she arranged to have the buffet open before the music began.

Dali harbored no suspicion concerning the czar's unexpected appearance. Instead, he was relieved that the young crown prince had not come, for the whole of his capacity for jealousy was concentrated on the popular young prince. Alexander was tall and strong, handsome and elegant; his German features were distinctive. And even among those who most hated his father, he was liked. Some of the remarks he was known to have made aroused the hope that, as Czar Alexander II, he would be more liberal than Alexander I had ever been, even in those early years when Frédèric César la Harpe was his tutor.

Czar Nicholas seemed to be in a gay mood that afternoon. His marshal's uniform was not now decorated as ridiculously as a Christmas tree. He wore only one decoration, the Grand Star of the Order of the Black Eagle. He smelled of heavy French perfume.

It was Princess Olga who introduced Dushenka to the czar.

"Allow me, Your Majesty, to introduce Mademoiselle Dushenka Arkadievna Bobak, a member of the Lomonosoff Theater."

"You say a member? I think more than a member," the czar said, as he offered Dushenka his big hand. "How do you do, Mademoiselle?"

Dushenka made a deep curtsy. There was no emotion in her face. Though Dushenka knew less about the czar's unexpected visit than Princess Olga did, her womanly instinct perceived what he had in mind. The czar smiled at her and asked:

"How much do you receive for your performance at an afternoon musicale like this?"

"Oh . . . nothing . . . I'm greatly honored by the . . ."

"Nothing! You mustn't do that! Don't let yourself be exploited by the wealthy aristocracy!"

He winked at Princess Olga, who was standing nearby with Countess Jadi. Polite laughter rewarded this sally. The czar redoubled his efforts to charm Dushenka. He looked her over from head to toe.

"You are a surprise to me, Mademoiselle," he said.

"Why, Your Majesty?"

"I know the stage is the greatest of magicians. I went one evening to the Comedie Française and saw the great Anne Boutet Mars in *Romeo and Juliet*. If I remember well, according to the play, Juliet was twenty."

He turned to his aide-de-camp:

"Am I correct?"

"Yes, Sire," answered the square-headed Colonel Zorkoff, although he well knew Juliet was only fifteen.

"Madame Boutet Mars gave the impression that she was perhaps twenty-two, at the most. Later on I learned that she was forty-nine."

Again, laughter rewarded the czar's story. Only Countess Jadi did not laugh. She understood perfectly what was going on. As she watched the scene, she was terrified for her son. Dushenka's head hardly came up to the big Black Eagle Order on the czar's chest, and in spite of the czar's studied courtesy, Dushenka seemed to Countess Jadi a sparrow caught in the talons of the huge, black eagle. What pain, what humiliation would the young actress bring into Dali's life, she thought. Covertly, she watched Dali's pale face and flaming dark eyes. Oh, yes, Dali was born to experience deadly passion.

Countess Jadi was right about the deadly hatred in Dali's dark eyes, but she was wrong about its cause. Dali was not experiencing a passion of jealousy because of Dushenka. To him, everything that was cruel, inhuman, despotic, and hateful was embodied in that German-Russian czar who stood four steps from Dali and amused himself with light royal talk to a feted young actress. Watching him, Dali's nerves tensed. His impression of the czar here, in Olga's familiar rooms, differed completely from the impressions of those few seconds at the Winter Palace's New Year's reception. Despite the regularity of his features and his forced charm, Nicholas had a very unpleasant expression—the expression of a man deeply convinced that he was born to be all powerful, the generalissimo who is looked upon as a god. While he talked to Dushenka, his gaze wandered over the faces in the group. His eyes revealed that he expected to be looked at constantly, and he did not forget for an instant that he was looked at. And he *was* looked at, and looked up to. As an

135

absolute monarch, he would have commanded adulation even if he had not wanted to. But his role was too big for him. Perhaps for every mortal. People said that Czar Alexander wished to be loved. Czar Nicholas wished to be obeyed. And he was not a good enough actor to hide his demonic character.

Strange thoughts flashed through Dali's mind. Serge had told him that the slight prick of the *B* needle was less painful than a mosquito bite, almost unnoticeable, and for a half hour the *Baha* did not cause any ill feeling. Then, suddenly, its victim dropped dead. Therefore, the wielder of the needle would have plenty of time to disappear. "But who is the man," Serge had asked, "who could brush elbows with Palkin in a crowd?" Of course, Serge had no idea who "Pierre" was. And was not "Pierre" the man?

"To tell the truth," the czar said to Dushenka, "seeing you on stage, I thought you were much older. May I guess your age?"

"Please," said Dushenka with a little smile.

The czar appraised her expertly.

"Fourteen."

Dushenka objected with a giggle.

"How wrong am I? he asked.

Dushenka showed five fingers.

"Plus or minus?"

It was a good line, and the czar delivered it with a straight face. For the first time, his audience really laughed—even Countess Jadi.

The butler's deep bow from the doorway indicated that the buffet was ready. Princess Olga turned to the czar:

"Won't Your Majesty have a bite to eat?"

"No thank you," the czar said with a slight bow. "I am not hungry and my time is short. Do you want me to sacrifice this rare opportunity to pay court to a beautiful young lady for a piece of cold sturgeon?"

"Certainly not!" Princess Olga surrendered, and her glance swept the faces of the guests like the baton of a symphony conductor. Her expression indicated that everyone should go in to the buffet. The guests strolled through the wide French doors. But Dali did not attend the buffet. Instead, he wandered into the hall, and when the cloakroom valet handed him his sword and shako, he accepted them without protest and went out into Karamsin Street.

In the great salon, Dushenka found herself alone with the czar. He looked down at her pretty legs and pointed at her slipper:

"One of your shoelaces is tied wrong."

"Oh, I didn't notice . . ." Dushenka blushed lightly.

"Well," the czar asked seriously, "how will you solve the problem? You can't sit in my presence and my rank forbids me to kneel before you."

Dushenka shrugged her beautiful, bare shoulders and, with a little laugh, said:

"There's always a solution."

Standing on one foot, she raised the other to retie the shoe lace; but of course, she lost her balance. The czar politely grabbed her—his big hand touching her breast in the process. Dushenka pulled away with a "Thank you, Sire."

"Let's sit down," the czar said. He pointed to an extremely uncomfortable Louis Quinze sofa. When they were seated, the czar said after a long silence:

"Let's converse. Ask me something."

Dushenka smiled apologetically:

"Nothing comes to mind."

"The same thing happens to me," the czar said soberly, "when I receive a delegation. Fortunately, there are some standard royal questions that help me out."

He turned to Dushenka and asked in a mighty voice:

"How was the harvest?"

Dushenka laughed. She seemed to enjoy the conversation, and, in the manner of a born actress, assumed a serious expression.

"Mediocre, Your Majesty. Especially the oats. We had very little rain."

"The cattle situation?"

"Dreadful. We had terrible hoof-and-mouth disease."

The czar fixed his eyes on Dushenka's mouth.

"Well," he said, "the hoof is all right now that you've retied the lace, but it seems to me that your mouth is too red. Did someone bite you? Who kissed you so violently?"

Dushenka tilted her head back coquettishly and looked at the czar with half-closed eyes.

"Who has been kneeling before you?" the czar went on. "Who tied your shoe lace so poorly?"

"An unknown gentleman," said Dushenka, smiling.

"Who was this ambitious gentleman? An actor?"

"No."

"An officer?"

She lowered her head slightly.

"How did you make his acquaintance?" asked the czar.

"I was skating and I fell."

"Intentionally?"

"No! Then he lifted me."

"From the front or the back?"

"From the back."

The czar nodded. "That's the right way. If you lift a lady from the front your hands get to her back, but if you lift her from the back, this way, your hands . . ."

While Dushenka conversed with the czar, Dali, walking blindly along Karamsin Street, brooded over this fresh encounter with Palkin. "Too bad the *B* needle was not with me," he thought. "He was no more than two feet from me." A slight pretended stumble . . . "Oh, excuse me, Your Majesty . . ." . . . could change the course of world history.

Dali did not know exactly why he had left the party. He felt himself frighteningly unbalanced.

Walking slowly, he passed the police cordon at the corner of Karamsin Street. Then, in a neighboring square he suddenly began to hurry. By the shortest route, the distance from Olga's palace to his hotel was less than a twenty-minute walk. If he hurried, he could be back at the party within a half hour and no one would ask him where he had been.

By the time he reached the last narrow street to the hotel, he was running. And then, a hay cart coming from the opposite direction turned into the street. The cart was driven by a black, strange looking ox, a domesticated yak from Tibet. The street was so narrow that the hay brushed the walls on both sides, and the slowly moving cart entirely blocked the way. Dali turned about and ran back the way he had come. The cart cost him a precious five or six minutes.

Panting heavily, he finally arrived in front of the hotel. As he unlocked the door to his room, his hand trembled with impatience. He grabbed the gray civilian clothes he had worn when he met Serge in the Park. Throwing them on the bed, he searched the pockets feverishly. On the first try, he did not find the needles. After a second, more careful search, he held in his hand the tiny wooden pipe Serge had given him.

He left the rumpled frock, waistcoat and trousers strewn across the bed, and glancing back into the room as he dashed out, he had the eerie feeling that his own corpse was lying there, torn into three pieces by the raging state of his mind.

Outside in the corridor, he said to himself: "Oh, excuse me, Your Majesty . . ." as if he were rehearsing his role in a great drama in which he had to appear within minutes—only as bit player, but the stage . . . yes, the stage was world history.

In the Serebraniy palace, the music started in the main salon. Colonel Zorkoff pulled out a double-cased gold watch, stepped up to the czar, and, obviously on a prearranged order, reported: "Six o'clock, Your Majesty."

Czar Nicholas stood up.

"I'm afraid I must go," he said to Dushenka. He looked deeply into her eyes and said:

"I hope to see you again, very soon."

He clicked his golden spurs and turned to the door, which opened before him. Colonel Zorkoff quickly followed him.

When Dali, still running frantically, arrived at the corner of Karamsin Street there were no police in sight. Obviously the czar had already left.

With a dead, empty feeling, Dali walked back into the palace; he felt as if he were awakening from a nightmare. Calmly he replaced his sword and shako in the cloakroom, and entering the main salon, he joined the audience's applause at the end of the last item on the program.

When Dushenka found Dali in the crowd, she whispered:

"I can't wait any longer. I'm due at the theater. The curtain goes up at eight. Let's go."

"How was your talk with the czar?" Dali asked her, as they walked toward the Lomonosoff Theater.

"Lovely," Dushenka said. "The usual silly compliments and wit . . . which Dimitri calls 'royal turd.' Sometimes there was some good dry humor in his words, but on the whole I quite disliked him."

"Why?"

"Whenever he leaned close to me, his mouth smelled so bad!"

A strong fragrance from the blossoming plane trees filled Nevsky Prospect; in the May twilight, the beauty of the afternoon had taken on a strangely melancholy quality.

At the stage door, Dali said:

"I won't come for you after the performance tonight. I have a bad headache."

"Drink a large glass of very strong hot wine with plenty of sugar and black pepper," Dushenka suggested. She laid her cool hand against his cheek tenderly, to see if he had a fever.

"No, you don't have a fever," she said. "But be a good boy and go to bed immediately."

At the Hotel Doulon, Dali sat on his bed without taking off his sword and shako; he gazed at the floor. No, he didn't have a fever. He didn't even have a headache. And yet, he was suffering—not from physical illness but from a total collapse of his self-esteem. He realized that he had, that afternoon, experienced a dangerous blackout, and the realization was frightening. More frightening was his feeling that the Russian underground, under a veneer of foggy ideals, was a basically nihilistic phenomenon, given over not to the ideal of redeeming mankind, but to a blind, revengeful lust for killing.

He remembered how Tonchi summarized his opinion of assassination: "I would not hesitate to kill a Metternich, a Czar Nicholas or any despot, if you could guarantee me that his death would mean the liberation of oppressed nations and the salvation of millions. Without that guarantee, to kill a despot is nothing but a common murder. We must always keep in mind that our aim is to kill a *system*. Therefore, our first task in Russia is to find a man, be he Prince Igor or anyone else, who would be able to step immediately into Palkin's boots. Without such a man, we cannot look for a change of the system! Without the certainty of that change, Palkin's death would mean nothing. To kill him would accomplish nothing."

Gazing at the floor, Dali tried to follow the way of his thoughts from the moment he had slipped out of the Serebraniy palace until his return after the czar had left. No matter how he tried, he could not understand his actions.

He now had the definite feeling that the *B* needle was absolutely harmless, and the *Baha*, the mysterious Indian snake poison, existed only in the sick imagination of the underground.

Sitting immobile on the side of his bed, he vividly remembered the carpenter shop where he had visited the underground with Tonchi. The bad smell of the boiled glue in the shop sifted back through his nostrils and nauseated him. Those six faces, imperfectly lit by the flickering butter lamp, appeared before him. The large, bulging eyes of the noseless face peered into his with a malicious glitter. And in the other face, the one with the cucumber nose and tiny eyes, there was an expression of diabolical cunning. Then the horrifying shock of Serge's miniature foot, a cruel deformity in an otherwise handsome figure, returned to him with revolting vividness. The whole atmosphere of that small room, the sprawling iron legs of the plate warmer, the feeling of danger and death pervading whispers unintelligible to Dali, all conveyed the most painful impression to his mind. Mentally more than physically, these men were all cripples, their deformed souls reaching out not to good, but to retaliation and hatred.

And now, he had become one of those maniacs.

He felt an unspeakable sorrow for mankind. If he himself, with his fine education, high ideals, physical and mental health and comfortable estate could sink so low, who could blame the desperate, the poor, the crippled, the outcasts?

2

Two days and two sleepless nights later, Dali received a letter from Andris, dated May, 1838. Delivered by a diplomatic courier, it had reached St. Petersburg in the exceptionally short time of eleven days.

Last week, [wrote Andris] we "celebrated" the first anniversary of Kossuth's arrest. As I wrote you in my last letter, for the time being there is no hope for any general or special amnesty. The only change, after the first year, in his prison life is that, from now on, he will be allowed to receive books and some gifts from outside. But still no visitors.

The first gift he received was a small silver cage with two canary birds. None of us know who the donor was, but one thing is sure—it is not a man.

Now I have some great news about myself. Fateful things always happen to us unexpectedly, and always in a strange way. Last Saturday night, during the intermission of Liszt's concert in the Buda Theater, there was a fantastic scene. In the crowded hall two ladies began a heated argument. The shorter and smaller of them slapped her opponent across the face. The tall lady fought back. They fell on the floor, their skirts up to their necks, screaming and pulling each other's hair, their faces bleeding from scratches. No one wanted to end the show until I arrived at the scene. I am not a weakling as you know, but it took me several minutes to separate them. I succeeded in separating the small lady from the taller one, but alas, I could not separate myself from the smaller one. I have fallen in love with her. I could carry her on the palm of my left hand—she weighs hardly a hundred pounds—but her character weighs more than my twenty stone. Her name is Irma Alacsy de Alacs, the last female member of that most ancient family. Over the centuries, the Alacsys have lost their fortune. You know the old saying: "Hungarian noblemen bleed to death on the battlefields and at the gambling tables." Irma did not inherit anything from her veterinarian father, except an adoration of horses and a passionate patriotism.

That Irma and an Austrian baroness should resort to violence over Franz Liszt is not remarkable; for women have been getting hysterical whenever he plays. The argument began when the Austrian baroness described Liszt as a German and Irma replied passionately: "He is Hungarian! There is no such German word as Liszt, which is Hungarian for 'flour'! He was born in Hungary!"

Three days after the scandal in the theater I proposed to my adorable Irma. "I am very much surprised," she said. "Why are you surprised, Mademoiselle?" I asked. "You are a Baron, a hussar officer," she said, "and I have no dowry." I laughed and wanted to kiss her but I gave up that attempt with a bleeding nose. She has sharper nails than La-La's claws (my new falcon). We are planning our wedding for the end of June. I have no money for the wedding, but I do not dare to ask any more loans of you because in the past I have been so absentminded that I always forgot to pay back the preceding ones. I am flirting with the idea of going to the Prague Humbum Circus, and under the name of Gi-Ghu, performing as a bear-wrestler as I did once when I was nineteen.

The same day Countess Jadi received a letter from Endre telling her that "... a new Great Epoch opened in the history of the Dukay family! With the help of God and godmother Archduchess Blanca, Flexi engaged Princess Maria Augusta, seventh daughter of Duke Ferdinand Wilhelm Schönheim-Altstadt and Princess Alexandra Julia Brunswick."

Andris was one of the 500 guests at the great dinner party, but his lettter to Dali gave a less solemn account of the great event.

I could get hardly into Gisellastrasse. Great excitement swept over the dense crowd when godfather Metternich's well-known glassed-in coach appeared—without His Almightiness. "Clemi is terribly sorry . . ." said his third wife, young Melanie Zichy, with an apologetic expression, but Endre knew better than anyone what the excusing words were when Metternich wished to avoid a dull gathering.

Now the guests. Just multiply the same dresses, the same silly chit-chats, the same names . . . Lichtenstein, Fürstenberg, Eszterházy, Auersperg, Obolensky, Zichy, Radziwill . . . and you have a good account of all the 500 guests—except the bride. Maria Augusta was different. As she stood in the middle of an admiring and congratulating group, she revealed a special ability of how to display her robust beauty of health and her charming stupidity. She told me with sincere sorrow:

"I am so sorry . . . terribly sorry that Dakli (sic!) is not here."

Oh, Dali, why didn't you tell me that you have become a dachshund in Russia?"

The day after Andris' letter, Dali and Tonchi had a serious talk about two other engagements.

To Dali, news of Flexi's engagement meant little. Flexi lived an untroubled life as a member in good standing of Vienna's aristocratic circles; no feverish mission troubled his mind, no nightmares of massacre and murder haunted his sleep. Why should Flexi not marry? No reason. It was natural.

143

But for Andris to marry was something else again. Andris was one of the trio, as committed to revolution as Dali himself. What would the responsibilities of a wife, and no doubt, children do to Andris? Could one be both a revolutionary and a good father? Dali had always thought not. For himself, though he had taken no vow of chastity, he had meant to remain single. But was it necessary to do so? Was it even wise?

Still shaken by his mad plot to murder Czar Nicholas only two days before, Dali asked himself whether the solitude he was protecting was helpful or hurtful. After all, if, as the gift of the canaries seemed to show, even the great Kossuth had been paying court to a lady, must Dali remain a bachelor all his days?

He had never, before now, thought of marrying Dushenka. He tried not to think of it now, for he wanted his decision to be purely intellectual and moral. But try as he might he could not keep her out of his thoughts. He felt again her cool touch on his cheek, her tender solicitude: "No, you haven't any fever," she had said.

True, she knew nothing of his mission; had she known Dali suspected, she would care nothing for it. But was that a disadvantage or an advantage? She would soothe him with her womanly tenderness. In his one fit of madness, God had sent the slowly moving haycart to obstruct his path, so that he could not attempt a pointless murder. Was it right to leave his sanity to Providence? Or should he let Dushenka help? Or had God, perhaps, sent Dushenka to ease that solitude which fostered such intensity in his feelings that he was not responsible for himself? This last, all at once, seemed quite plausible.

He did not make up his mind to marry Dushenka, but he did make up his mind that he could if he so chose. The thought made him feel so much better that he spent the afternoon celebrating, consuming several bottles of champagne in the process.

That night, after the final curtain, Dali was waiting for Dushenka at the stage entrance of the Lomonosoff Theater. The sky was clouded, there was no moon; still, a strange, faded silver light lit the whole city. It was the aurora borealis, a phenomenon not rare in St. Petersburg.

"Come on, Dali," Dushenka said, when Dali stopped and

144

gazed at the giant fan of white ostrich feathers spread across the sky.

"Let's go to the Hermitage," Dali suggested.

"No, dear. I already had my supper during the intermission. I am exhausted."

"Are there any cold cuts in the kitchen?"

"Ask Nyanya. You are a bit tipsy, Dali."

"Nonsense."

"Funny," Dali said, stopping again and gazing at the northern lights. "I wonder whether you superstitious Russians attach any significance to its appearance."

"Of course we do. In Novgorod it means a lot of rain and an extremely good harvest."

"In St. Petersburg?"

"That I don't know," Dushenka said with a hint of sadness in her voice.

At home Nyanya gave Dali a huge slice of bread and a sausage a foot long, which was all she had in the kitchen. Dali pulled his knife from his boot and with the bread and sausage in his left hand and the knife in his right, the way Pista Kerge had taught him, started to eat his supper.

"Give me a little vodka, Nyanya."

"Don't give him any vodka," Dushenka commanded.

Nyanya pretended not to hear Dushenka and brought out a bottle of vodka and two glasses. Dali was in an exceptionally good mood; by way of thanks he pinched Nyanya's backside. Like an eighteen-year-old girl, she flew off screaming. Dushenka sat next to Dali, leaned her tired head on his shoulder, closed her eyes and offered her lips with the unmistakable little smile of a woman hungry for love.

Dali took her into his arms. Then he poured the vodka and offered her one of the glasses. Dushenka took his hand.

"No. Don't drink, Dali."

"Come on, take a . . ."

"No! Did you hear what I said? No!"

"You *must*. Only this one. To us, to our happiness!"

He held the glass to Dushenka's lips.

"Drink it all, dear. No half measures about happiness."

"Go home, Dali." Dushenka exclaimed. "You are drunk."

"I am not. I have a wonderful idea." And with his free hand, he began to show her what it was.

Dushenka leaped from his lap and arranged her hair.

"Go home, Dali. It's late."

"How can you be so cruel as to chase me out into . . . into the cruel cold . . ."

"You are so drunk you don't even remember it's June."

"I am not drunk. Shall I recite the Lord's Prayer in Russian as you taught me?"

"No thank you. Go home. Be a nice boy."

"I'll tell you something. Since I first saw you at that skating rink, my imagination has always been playing around your every little, sleepy movement while you're undressing and climbing into bed. But I have only got a vague, a . . . a . . . mystical picture of the. . . ."

"What's mystical about it?" asked Dushenka as she arranged her bed, slapping the pillows. "Do you think I jump into my bed every night with a somersault?"

"Listen. I have a wonderful idea."

"Again?"

"I'll sit in that chair. I promise I won't move."

"Go home, Dali."

"My word of honor. I'll stay here only until you fall asleep. My word of honor."

Dushenka did not answer. She pulled the cord from the inside of the alcove and the curtains came together.

"Good night, Monsieur Lieutenant! It was nice seeing you," she shouted from behind the curtains.

"Good night, Mademoiselle!" Dali replied. "Sleep well," he added, as he pulled the cord and the curtains parted again. Dushenka pretended she had not noticed. While she undressed, she glanced at Dali over her white, naked shoulder with a little smile. Then she climbed into bed and pulled the covers over her head, leaving only a few stray locks of hair showing on the pillow.

Though she lay perfectly still, Dushenka was wide awake and thinking busily.

Dali was drunk. Very drunk. She had never seen him so drunk before. If she slept with him tonight, would he? . . . no, it

146

would be impossible. He could not notice that she was not a virgin. But if she slept with him, would he ever marry her? Dushenka thought not. Yet, if she did not sleep with him and he did marry her, he would be sure to realize that her wedding night was not her first experience. And would he ever marry her anyway? If she were merely to be his mistress at best, would it not be wise to let him think he was her first lover? Aristocrats never married the poor girls they made love to. But Dushenka loved him, too. Should she not make the most of the time she had him for herself? She thought she should.

While she pretended to sleep, her heart was in her throat. What would he do? What should she do?

Dali, breathless and immobile, chained to the chair by his word of honor, fixed his glazed eyes on Dushenka. Then suddenly, as if something in him had exploded, he tore off his richly trimmed dolman, and undressed frantically.

3

A week after the musicale, Dushenka received a letter signed by Colonel Zorkoff. Even with its large violet seal, it weighed hardly more than an ounce; yet it was carried by a squadron of mounted guards from the Winter Palace.

"Their Imperial Majesties, Czar Nicholas I and Czarina Charlotte . . . a piano concert by Madam . . ." read the invitation in Russian, with calligraphed Cyrillic letters under the Romanoff crest.

Dushenka put the royal invitation into her mother-of-pearl box which she kept "for my grandchildren," along with her contract with the Lomonosoff, Dali's first love lettter, and other documents deserving of the interest of posterity.

The expression on her face, as she slowly closed the box, was unutterably sad. She knew from her fellow actresses that at such concerts in the Winter Palace, there were no musicians, there was no piano, there was no audience, and there was no czarina. "What did you receive?" Dimitri had asked the pretty Mauryushka Kutzokova after such a concert. "A golden powder box and imperial gonorrhea," Maryushka replied.

Besides the feeling of physical disgust she felt toward the czar,

Dushenka knew all too well, from the fate of Madam Pushkin and others, what it meant to be the czar's mistress. Day and night under siege of petitioners—demanding patronage, promotions, cash tokens for contracts handed down by the government, and even clemency for condemned prisoners: "Only one word . . . from you would be enough . . ." and if she did not or could not comply, she would find herself the target of hatred, murderous intrigues, revengeful sadism.

Frightened by her own bravery, Dushenka dispatched a letter to Colonel Zorkoff, in which she informed him "with bleeding heart" that she had already accepted a request to appear at a charity performance . . . "but I am sure that the absence of my humble person in the multitude of guests will not be noticed," she added.

Dushenka did not say a word to Dali, or to anyone—not even to Nyanya—about this invitation or her answer. But that night she could not sleep. She knew she had been right to refuse the invitation. But she was afraid.

What Dushenka did not know was that, despite her refusal, St. Petersburg's gossips were already convinced that she was the czar's new mistress. Her conversation alone with his majesty at Olga's musicale had established her, in the eyes of the sophisticated aristocrats who had attended the event, in his majesty's bed.

On the same day Dushenka had received the invitation, Tonchi, at lunch with Dali at the Hermitage, had said casually to Dali:

"There are rumors about Dushenka."

"What are they?" Dali had asked rudely.

Tonchi was a great master of conversation and knew how to pull a word in if it had gone astray.

"Rumors. . . ." He now belittled the word. "Kantemir told me that he is spreading them himself. A great actress like Dushenka, he feels, would be finished if there were no rumors circulating about her."

But Dali was not to be put off so easily.

"The crown prince?" he demanded.

"No, no . . . Dimitri did not mention the name."

From this conversation, Tonchi was sure that Dali knew nothing at all of the rumors.

The following night, going home from the theater, Dali suggested,

"Let's go to the Hermitage for supper."

"No, my dear. There were two performances today," she replied.

In front of Dushenka's house, Dali said:

"I'll come up with you."

"No, dear. Really . . . I'm dreadfully tired."

"Only for half an hour."

"No, dear."

"Ten minutes."

"No, Dali. Look at me. I can hardly stand."

They kissed, and the entrance door closed behind her. Then clack, clack—the heavy key turned twice in the lock from inside. Dali did not move from the door. The street was silent, and through the door, he heard Dushenka's steps as she flew up the stairs. Someone who is "dreadfully tired" and "can hardly stand," Dali thought, cannot fly up those steep stairs. Since the "drunken" night when he had first slept with Dushenka, they had gone to bed almost every night. It was like a honeymoon. Dali stood outside, listening in the stillness. Was it possible, he wondered, that someone was waiting for Dushenka in her bed? Ivan Dragovich the robust actor? Dimitri Kantemir? Paul Tolstoy? Who? Tonchi? When he arrived at Tonchi's name, he turned to go, as if he were leaving his own stupid thoughts.

Next day, Dali had lunch with Dushenka and Tonchi at the Hermitage. "I must go to the rehearsal for my charity performance," Dushenka said, not even finishing the cherry soufflé she loved so much.

"She's working very hard," Tonchi remarked as he and Dali, left alone, finished their lunch.

After lunch, when Tonchi too, had left him, Dali went for a walk in Bolshoy Island. Usually on a weekday, the place was deserted. But today, it was crowded—with policemen. When two riders suddenly appeared from a side road, Dali's heart jumped into his throat. He recognized the young crown prince in civilian clothes, and as they passed at a slow gallop not fifty feet from Dali, he saw that the girl was Dushenka. Neither of the riders noticed Dali.

Paralyzed, Dali looked after them. "Must go to rehearsal,"

Dushenka had said an hour earlier. Oh! She was lying—and, so boldly, so audaciously. She was lying, that dirty little whore. Those "rumors!" Now he understood what Tonchi had meant the other day!

When he appeared in Dushenka's house at six, he found Nyanya alone.

"You look rather blue, Uncle Dali," Nyanya said jokingly. Then she added: "What a wonderful day! I took a walk here in the little park. Then I went . . . "

"I'm not interested in where you went. Where was Dushenka? You must know!"

"She was in the theater. Rehearsing. Someone is coming."

Nyanya went out hurriedly. No one was coming. It was an old trick of Nyanya's, even with Dushy, to end a conversation not to her liking by saying, "Someone is coming."

Dali paced the room, tossing a chair out of the way. He stopped, chewed at one nail, and glanced at the clock.

At last Dushenka entered, hurried to him, and with her eyes closed, offered him her lips. It was her usual greeting when they were alone. Dali did not move.

"Whatever is wrong?" Dushenka asked, looking searchingly into his dark face.

Dali walked to the door, closed it, and came back.

"How was the 'rehearsal' with Alex?"

"Alex? There's no Alex in the cast."

Dali turned to her and shouted:

"Why did you lie to me about a rehearsal this afternoon?"

"I never lied to you," Dushenka said.

"Why did you lie?" He grabbed her arm and twisted her toward him.

"Tell me the truth!"

Dushenka did not answer. She remembered old Marina's stories about the violent character of Hungarians, and she was pale with fright. Dali grabbed both her arms and shook her rudely.

"I demand the truth!"

Dushenka tried to shake free of his grasp.

"You're hurting me!" she cried. "Leave me alone!"

Dali released her arms. Breathing heavily, he asked between his teeth:

"Are you already his mistress?"

For a moment Dushenka stared at him. Then she took one step back and slapped him on the cheek with all her strength.

For a fraction of a second Dali's fist was stone-hard, ready to strike back. But then he twisted his lips into an ugly smile of contempt, turned, and left her. He did not even slam the door.

In the street he made his way with apparent calm to the Hotel Doulon. In his hotel room, he sat at the desk and wrote: *"Chère mademoiselle—je vous remercie pour tous."*

He did not sign the letter, but to be more cruel, he enclosed several hundred rubles. He gave the letter to a messenger and set out for the Serebraniy palace to spend the evening with his mother, Olga and the des Fereyolles. No, he would not say what had happened. And if in a few days, the ever curious Rolly should ask about Dushenka, he would say laughingly: "Who? I don't even remember the name."

He was so deep in thought that, on the way to the palace, he took the wrong turn and found himself on the Domski Square.

It was about seven, but the sun had not yet set. The elongated shadow of the equestrian Domski statue lay across the square, looking like a dead black giraffe with a crane in its saddle.

Suddenly two riders entered the square: Alexander, the crown prince, and Dushenka—but no, not Dushenka! The same midnight blue veil on the same black hat, the same gray houndstooth riding coat, the same profile, exactly the same girl, except that she was not Dushenka. As she turned her face toward Dali, she became Grand Duchess Marie, the younger sister of the crown prince.

And suddenly Dali realized how stupid his mistake had been. The crown prince could go to bed with any girl: but he could not appear in a public park riding with an actress, the Circe of St. Petersburg. Under no condition.

Dali dashed back to Dushenka's house. He rang desperately but there was no answer. Obviously, Nyanya was not home, and Dushenka—perhaps she had seen him from the window—would not let him in.

Dali threw his shoulder against the door and with almost superhuman force, broke it down. He flew up the stairs to Dushenka's bedroom. At first glance, he thought the room was empty. But as he looked he saw her, and the sight filled him with horror. Dushenka lay on the bed face down, her right arm outstretched, her left arm hanging down lifelessly. Then Dali's letter, *"Chère mademoiselle"* . . . and the hundred ruble notes lay on the floor. A half-filled glass of water and an empty pill-box on the table beside the bed told the whole story.

Without knowing what he said, Dali cried:

"Oh . . . she shouldn't have done it!"

He shook her shoulders and fell to his knees at the bedside, whispering:

"Listen . . . listen, dear . . . listen to me."

But Dushenka was unconscious. Taking her in his arms, Dali ran down the stairs into the street, to Doctor Shiloff's house. With each step she grew heavier. At last, he laid her on the doctor's sofa, and said:

"Clean out the stomach! Quick!"

That night, in the Lomonosoff Theater, Dimitri Kantemir announced to a full house that, because of a slight case of food poisoning, Mademoiselle Dushenka Arkadievna Bobak's role would tonight be performed by Katerina Pavlova Ugrin.

Dushenka spent the night in the "private hospital" of Doctor Shiloff. The hospital was the largest room in the doctor's apartment: it contained four beds. Only one other bed was occupied, by an old lady sleeping quietly.

Around midnight Dushenka regained consciousness, but she was so weak she did not even look around. She stared at the ceiling; she did not seem to know where she was or who was with her. She was so exhausted that she fell asleep.

At one o'clock Nyanya replaced Dali at Dushenka's bedside. She was silently weeping. They whispered, so as not to awaken Dushenka and the old lady. Their concern for the old lady was hardly necessary, since she had been dead since before Dushenka arrived. Doctor Shiloff had not told them out of sheer politeness.

When Dushenka awoke around noon and found Dali at her bedside, holding her hand, she said, hardly audibly: "Dali . . ."

Dali leaned over her, kissed her hair, and, pressing his face to hers, begged softly: "Forgive me, my dearest." When Dushenka did not answer, he pleaded again: "Oh, please my love. Forgive me. Forgive me."

Dushenka closed her eyes. Her face was pale, and so hollow she looked as if she were dead. Then her lips twisted and tears came from under her closed eyes. "Of course I forgive you, sweet," she replied. But her face looked so tragic that Dali at first could not believe her. When she insisted that she did not blame Dali for his letter, he demanded: "Then what is wrong?" But she refused to answer.

In the afternoon, Dushenka walked home on her own feet. And that same night, to the great sorrow of Mademoiselle Katerina Pavlova, she took back her leading role in *Cupid and Psyche*.

But at home after the performance, alone with Nyanya, Dushenka began to weep again.

"What is wrong, Dushy?" Nyanya asked. "Tell your old Nyanya."

At first Dushenka only shook her head and sobbed. Then, when she found her voice, she whispered:

"It did not come."

The two women looked at one another in silence for a moment. Then Dushenka hid her face in her hands, and again began to sob.

"There, there, Dushy," Nyanya soothed her, stroking her soft golden hair. "There now, poor pet, poor little Dushy."

When Dushenka's crying subsided, Nyanya took her hand.

"Do you want me to scrape it out?" she asked softly.

"No," Dushenka said. And after a few silent seconds she said it again: "No."

4

Dali knew nothing of Dushenka's pregnancy. But the morning after Dushenka left the hospital, he was in a daze of remorse and horror. How could he have been so blind, so stupid, so heartless? His insulting letter was enough to make her kill herself. The anguish he had felt when he found her lying so still, so dreadfully still, across her bed haunted him. He knew now that, come what may, he had to make up his mind, to put an end to this situation.

In the evening, while Dushenka was at the theater, Dali prepared himself for their meeting with extraordinary zeal. While his clothes were being pressed and his buttons and boots shined, he scrubbed and polished himself, brushed his hair a dozen times.

And so, when at length he was satisfied with his toilette, he left his hotel and strode to the Lomonosoff stage door. When Dushenka came out to meet him, her delicate beauty pierced him, though she still looked shaky from her ordeal in the hospital.

"Dushenka," Dali began, as they walked toward Dushenka Ulitza, "Mother wants to talk to you. She is waiting for us at Olga's place."

Dushenka remained silent. Her heart sank.

"I hope you're not too tired, are you?" Dali asked.

"Oh, no . . . not at all," she said hardly audibly, but making her voice sound normal. She felt wretched.

The countess, she thought, could only wish to inform her—very graciously—that her connection with the count, her son, amusing as he no doubt found it, was becoming an embarrassment to the family. She only hoped the countess would not be openly insulting—and, remembering Jadi's gentle face, she didn't really expect to suffer unnecessary humiliation at her hands.

Countess Jadi greeted Dushenka in the petite salon of the Serebraniy palace, in the company of Olga, Rolly and Alphie. While the family chatted happily together, Dushenka conducted herself with a poignant dignity, smiling appreciatively at every witty remark of Olga or Alphie, and following the conversation attentively, now and then, contributing an appropriate comment in her pleasant alto voice. Even Rolly was charmed with her.

After tea, following a brief, tense silence, Countess Jadi told Dushenka: "I would like to talk to you."

A great sorrow engulfed Dushenka as she stood up.

"Sit down, dear," Countess Jadi said to her. "I want to talk to you in front of the family."

She took Dushenka's hand, which lay cold and lifelessly in her lap, and held it between her own. Then she began, with mock solemnity:

"Mademoiselle Arkadievna Bobak, my son authorized me to tell you that you are the first woman in his life with whom he has fallen deeply in love, and that he wishes to know if you are willing to marry him ?"

And at that, something beautiful happened. The simple girl from Novgorod did not answer: she just looked at Jadi, without even glancing at Dali. And her large greenish-gray eyes slowly filled with the most beautiful light, and with the hardly visible tears of the utmost happiness.

It was Jadi who wrote Endre of Dali's decision, and her letter revealed such sympathy and such genuine affection for Dushenka that even Endre could not bring himelf to reply harshly.

In order to avoid "embarrassing Metternich's diplomatic corps" as he put it, Dali had arranged to resign his post at the embassy before his wedding. And, as he wryly said, "the Habsburg monarchy did not seem to be in any danger of collapsing because of his resignation."

Dali himself wrote to Andris:

I never met your Irma [he remarked], but I know the name Irma Alacsy who two years ago won the ladies' steeplechase in Transylvania. I am very much afraid my fiancée will never win such a race. Her trot is all right. But she does not dare to take a full gallop or jump. I give her lessons in Bolshoy Park; Olga has wonderful riding horses. I have found that Dushenka (she is a born Russian, a very successful and very pretty young actress) has much in common with our girls in Hungary. She is delightfully superstitious, modestly boastful, cowardly brave, poetically realistic, warm-heartedly capricious—all in all, a very sweet girl.

I have been deeply touched by the sincere affection Mother shows toward Dushenka. Rolly and Alphie are making a great effort to show that they are delighted, which they are not. Aunt Olga is wonderfully neutral, and Tonchi is openly unhappy. When I told him I had decided to marry Dushenka, he jumped to his feet and paced the floor in my hotel room. Then he stopped suddenly and said to an empty chair as if it had been occupied by an invisible person: "These three boys are the victims of the same contagious disease!"

Guess who they are. Two of the boys are you and I (he had read your letter about Irma). The third boy is our messiah, Prince Igor. His devotion for Olga looks more and more serious, Prince Igor less and less of a messiah.

"You have entirely forgotten your great vocation!" Tonchi said.

"Until you attain your firm resolve you must be unmarried, like Kossuth. Believe me, Dali, the forest is dry, from Novgorod to Valdivostok, from Kronstadt to Sevastopol—The forest is dry, and the wind is here, in the form of the Irluntz peasants' riot. We need but a single match to start the blaze, the Big Blaze." I tried to convince him that I could be married and still remain true to our convictions, but he would have none of it. He left my room without saying good-bye, but he closed the door as gently as if he were closing the eyes of our mission in Russia.

Andris was very disillusioned by Dali's letter. There was not a single word in the whole thing about his mocking threat to go to the Prague Circus as a bear wrestler. Dali did not realize his desperate financial troubles. He wanted to give Irma a diamond wedding ring. And he had to order a new uniform. Yet Dali did not offer a friendly loan.

But three days later, Dali's estate agent made a trip from Gere to inspect Andris' 300-acre estate outside the village of Zekerd, some sixty miles west of Ararat. After deciding that the property needed at least four oxen, a dozen sows, six ploughhorses, and other stock and that the "castle" and "park" needed repair urgently, the agent reached for his large purse and turned over to Andris 2,000 florins in golden coins—as a loan, of course, in order to spare Andris' pride, which was at a low ebb. The agent did not say that he was acting on Dali's instructions, but Andris knew that he was.

5

Dali and Dushenka planned to be married shortly, and very quietly. There were only seventeen names on their list of invitations. But their engagement was not kept secret, and all of Olga's friends in St. Petersburg society, as well as Dali's colleagues at the embassy and Dushenka's friends at the Lomonosoff, knew of their plans. As a concession to Dushenka's Orthodox faith, they planned to be married in St. Isaac's Cathedral.

One morning, within two weeks of Dali's engagement announcement, a clerk stepped into Dali's office at the embassy and reported:

"His Excellency, the ambassador, wishes to talk to Your Excellency."

Dali left his desk and walked up the heavily carpeted marble stairs to von Nordthal's luxurious office on the second floor.

The sixty-year-old Ambassador, Baron Heinrich von Nordthal, pointed to a Govelin chair before his desk saying:

"Have a seat, please."

When Dali was seated, von Nordthal began, very slowly, to scratch the top of his bald skull with the middle finger of his right hand.

"This is not an official matter," he said, in the tone of a doctor who knows that his patient is suffering from a very serious ailment. "I understand that you are secretly engaged to. . ."

"Not secretly!" Dali cut in. "Everyone knows our plans. Our wedding is set for next Sunday." When von Nordthal's small blue eyes grew as large as they could in a surprise, Dali went on: "The wedding will be private, but certainly not secret. Dushenka and I would be very happy if Your Excellency could find the time to attend."

Von Nordthal's face saddened.

"I am very much afraid I won't be there."

"Why not?" asked Dali, sensing trouble behind the soft voice.

Von Nordthal stood up and walked to the window. He looked out on the garden, fixing his eyes on the colorless sky. Then he turned back to Dali.

"Duty puts me in a difficult position. This morning I had a visitor from . . ."

Only a gesture indicated the great height from which the visitor descended.

"A Russian?"

Von Nordthal nodded.

"What did he want?"

"He asked me in a very cordial tone to talk to you, because he knew I was one of your father's best friends, and could talk to you as a father to his son."

Dali's face was immobile, but his thoughts raced.

157

"What did your Russian guest ask you to say to me?"

"He said that there is a great obstacle to your planned marriage to Mademoiselle Arkadievna Bobak, which you did not realize. . ."

"The church? There will be a Catholic blessing after the. . ."

"No, no, no. Not the Church. The problem is this: I was informed that the Russian government will not allow Mademoiselle Bobak to leave the country. We must understand their viewpoint. Russia is poor in talent, now, not only in literature but in every field of the arts. Dushenka Arkadievna Bobak is regarded here as a great art treasure, which means *no export.*"

"What does her talent have to do with her private life?" Dali asked, still calm.

"Not so much her private life, but *yours.* This was the point we talked over. Imagine the situation, let's say, several weeks or months after your wedding. She cannot leave Russia and you are called back to Vienna. You will be separated from your wife for a very uncertain period, perhaps for long years, perhaps. . . I don't even want to think about it."

"Did your Russian friend inform you that I was *persona non grata* in St. Petersburg?"

"Your question is very logical. The answer is no. You know the political situation. Berlin, Vienna, St. Petersburg are bound tightly together in their defense against the revolutionary atmosphere in Europe. They avoid the slightest disturbances with their allies. They know who your father is. Besides, you haven't done anything wrong or scandalous. . ."

"In that case I can't think of anything to bar my marriage."

"You are utterly mistaken, Count Adalbert. It was friendly talk, and you cannot deny the logic of what he said."

"Who was that Russian?"

Von Nordthal began to rearrange the objects on his desk, though it was perfectly tidy as it was. He pretended he did not hear the question, which he did not wish to answer.

"Was it Prince Igor Effremovich?" Dali asked a moment later.

"No. It's not a diplomatic secret. It was a friendly talk. Colonel Zorkoff. A good friend of mine. A very nice, warm-hearted man. His talk with me was entirely sympathetic. He is concerned about your fate."

Zorkoff's name did not impress Dali, for he knew nothing of the rumors about Dushenka and the czar. He stared at von Nordthal, looking as if he were tempted to ask whether the ambassador was telling the truth. He stood up.

"I thank you very much, Your Excellency. I am sorry that my private affair has robbed you of precious time."

Von Nordthal stood up.

"I'm awfully sorry for you," he said. His voice sounded sincere—almost too sincere, as if he were hiding something. He stared at the floor and for a moment was silent. Then he said: "You have not given me your reaction to what I have told you."

"I will marry her Sunday."

Von Nordthal looked distressed. He put a hand on Dali's shoulder.

"Count Adalbert," he said, "take my advice. Don't go through with the marriage."

"I will marry her on Sunday."

"Is that your last word?"

"Definitely."

Von Nordthal again stared at the floor and remarked, as if to himself: "Let's hope I am wrong."

He offered his hand to Dali, accompanied him to the door, and said: "God help you."

When, after the performance, Dali accompanied Dushenka home that night, he noticed two shadowy figures following them. The secret police? Nothing unusual in that. This was not the first time he had been followed. In fact, every member of the foreign diplomatic corps in St. Petersburg was followed now and then.

Dali and Dushenka had supper in the house, and then Dushenka went to bed. It was shortly after midnight when Dali began to undress. Just as he was pulling off his boots, the doorbell rang. Hearing Nyanya go to the door, Dali asked Dushenka:

"Surely you are not expecting anyone?"

"No!" she said, and climbed out of bed.

The heavy tread of several men sounded on the creaking stairs. The door swung open, and a military police captain entered, followed by two soldiers, pistols in their belts. The

159

captain glanced at a piece of paper in his hand and read in broken German:

"*Sind Sie Graf Dukay?*"

"Ja," Dali answered quickly. Holding a boot in his left hand and half undressed, he cut a weird figure. "*Was wollen Sie von mir?*"

"Get dressed. Put on your boots!" the captain commanded. Dushenka hurried to Dali's side:

"There must be . . . must be some mistake," she said in Russian. "He's my. . . ."

The captain pushed her back with his outstretched left arm—and not gently.

"Get back into bed!" he snapped. He turned to Dali, who stood frozen, a boot still in his right hand.

"Hurry up!"

"*Ich bin von dem Österreichishem . . .*"

"Hurry up!" the captain raised his voice.

Dali was ostentatiously slow, but this was his only resistance. Dushenka again rushed to his side. Her left hand pressed to her throat, the other on Dali's shoulder, she stood over him while he pulled on his boot.

When Dali was dressed he picked up his saber, but the captain relieved him of it. Then one of the soldiers came up to Dali and examined his clothes, every pocket and seam from head to toe. When he found the knife Dali carried in his boot, he stuck it into his own boot.

"Put out your hands!" ordered the captain, and expertly handcuffed Dali's wrists. Then he waved Dali toward the door.

Dali obeyed without looking back at Dushenka. Every man loses his soul when he is unexpectedly handcuffed.

Dushenka, left alone in the room, stood motionless. While the heavy footsteps receded down the steps, she remained frozen in panic, still holding her left hand at her throat and her right in the air, where Dali's shoulder had been. When the door slammed, she screamed:

"Nyanya!"

Nyanya hurried in, deathly pale and wringing her hands.

"Help me dress!" Dushenka commanded, breathing heavily. "Give me my shoes . . ."

"Where are you going?"

"The Glavny Shtub . . . to Prince Igor . . . Get me a carriage . . . a horse . . . Quick!"

"There are none . . . it's one in the morning . . ."

Still in her shirt and with one shoe on, Dushenka limped over to the window, opened it, leaned out and shouted desperately into the silent street:

"Dali! . . . Da-li!!"

The night was dark and still. The Aurora Borealis had folded and put aside its fan of huge silvery feathers.

6

From the direction of Novgorod, the June morning approached St. Petersburg; but the big city was still silent. When the sun rose, shortly after three o'clock, the morning breeze swept immense Petrovski Square clean of little patches of white mist. Zealous sunbeams climbed the equestrian statue of Peter the Great and carefully shined the emperor's huge bronze boots.

Petrovski Square was entirely paved with cat skulls—carefully selected stones from the gravel pits of the Ural's, each with the round shape and the size of the skull of a cat. The stones served as a kind of warning siren for the guards of the Winter Palace. The ironclad wheels of a carriage clattered so loudly over the stones that the sound could be heard a mile away.

At four in the morning, the sentries around the great iron gate of the Palace stopped their sleepy, monotonous pacing and listened. A moment later, a heavy, glided, glassed-in carriage appeared in the deserted square, drawn by three beautiful black horses—a very unusual sight indeed at such an early hour.

The carriage stopped some hundred yards from the gate, and Olga alighted. She showed her papers to an officer of the guards and the entrance gate opened.

Inside the coach, Tonchi silently held Countess Jadi's cold hand, as if he were sitting beside a deathbed. The horrible news about Dali's arrest had reached her at two-thirty in the morning.

Afterward, Dushenka and Nyanya had dressed and run to Tonchi's boarding house. "Let's go to Olga!" Tonchi had proposed. Supporting the two ladies by their arms, he hurried them to Karamsin Street. At the Serebraniy palace, Countess Jadi, Olga and the des Fereyolles came down, half dressed, to the petite salon and there they held a conference. What to do? Who could help? Who?

Olga immediately sent a mounted courier to Prince Igor's headquarters in the Second Cossack Regiment's barracks with a note reading: "Please, come to my place at once!"

The mounted courier came back and reported:

"The military guard was not willing to awaken the commander. Not for a message from anyone. 'Wait until seven in the morning, when his office will be open,' he said."

It was three-thirty in the morning when Tonchi said:

"Colonel Zorkoff would know why Dali was arrested."

"You are right," Olga said while she stood up. "Let's go to the Winter Palace."

And they had gone, leaving Dushenka and Nyanya under the care of Alphie and Rolly.

Now, while she waited for Olga in the coach, Countess Jadi tortured her mind for an explanation of Dali's arrest. She remembered the musicale, when, to the great surprise of everyone the czar had showed up alone, and how he had amused himself for more than half an hour in conversation with Dushenka. But that was weeks ago, and since then the czar had almost disappeared from the picture. Von Nordthal? Alphie had the feeling that the ambassador's friendly advice against Dali's marriage originated in Vienna, but Jadi hardly thought that possible.

"What do you think?" Countess Jadi asked Tonchi after a long silence.

"Nothing. Absolutely nothing," Tonchi said. "The only thing I can think of is that someone sent an anonymous letter to the secret police. You know how, even in Vienna, an anonymous letter to the secret police is enough to warrant an arrest. Spy. Conspirator. Reformer. Liberal. That's enough."

"Do you think Dali is still alive?"

"Oh, please! Please! How can you think of such a thing!" Tonchi said reproachfully. "Dali is a member of the Austrian embassy! He will be freed in a matter of days, maybe even this morning."

But Tonchi was not as sure as he tried to sound. From the

moment he had learned of Dali's arrest, he had been frantically trying to find an explanation. And he had three ideas. First, what he said to Countess Jadi. An anonymous letter. But Tonchi did not really believe that. He was more inclined to his second theory—that the czar was behind it. He had told Dali the day before that he did not like Zorkoff's "friendly" advice. After Olga's party it was obvious that the czar was interested in Dushenka, and wanted her for his mistress, or, more precisely, one of his mistresses. Tonchi could easily imagine how it could have happened. During the routine early morning report, Zorkoff told the czar, among other things, about the Sunday wedding. And the czar, yawning, told Zorkoff: "Stop it." Zorkoff went to von Nordthal. And when the friendly advice did not work, the arrest came. It seemed logical and probable. In that case Dali was not in danger—only his marriage. The arrest? A fabrication. Vienna would intervene, Dali would be freed. But as a *persona non grata,* he would be recalled.

But there was a third possibility, one Tonchi dreaded. The visit to the underground. Dali, like all foreign diplomats, was often followed by the secret police. Did Zorkoff know of the carpenter shop and its secret function? Had he only just found out? Tonchi closed his eyes every time the possibility entered his mind. That possibility sounded more logical than some anonymous letter, even more logical than the czar's desire to stop Dushenka's wedding.

"Here she is!" Countess Jadi whispered. And there was Olga, returning across the Winter Palace's empty yard.

Princess Olga stepped into the carriage. For a long moment she did not speak, but her face revealed a great deal.

"Zorkoff was unusually stiff," she said finally. "He doesn't know anything about the arrest. When I asked him to arrange an urgent audience for me with the czar, he advised me not to press the request. 'I don't want you to be rebuffed,' he said. 'His majesty never interferes in the affairs of the military police.' "

"He was lying," Tonchi remarked in a low tone.

"Of course he was!" Princess Olga agreed. "When I asked him why he had gone to von Nordthal, he said his talk with the ambassador had been absolutely unofficial. 'I spent several pleasant evenings with that charming boy,' he said, 'I liked him very much, I felt it a duty of friendship and comradeship to inform him of a serious obstacle to the marriage he planned.' When I asked him if he could guess the reason for the arrest, he said to me reproachfully, 'How could I? You are the first person who has spoken to me of it!' And then when I asked him to contact the secret police, he shook his head and said: 'You should know that the secret police, according to its strict rules, never gives out any information, not even to his majesty!' "

"Dirty liar!" Tonchi remarked to himself. Countess Jadi had not said a word. Suddenly her shoulders trembled, and with a suppressed scream of agony, she started to sob. Princess Olga embraced her. Tonchi held her cold hands.

"Let's go first to the embassy," Countess Jadi pleaded, when she found her voice.

It was already eight. Tonchi remained in the carriage, while the two ladies ascended the carpeted marble stairs. Von Nordthal left his breakfast and hurried to meet them.

Olga told him briefly what had happened, and asked:

"Do you know of any reason for the arrest?"

"I will go immediately to the foreign minister and demand an explanation," he said.

At seven Dushenka had left for Glavny Shtub, to seek Prince Igor's help. By nine, she had not returned.

Around ten, von Nordthal, coming directly from the foreign office, arrived at the Serebraniy palace. He had received no explanation.

"Is any Russian officer," Countess Jadi asked, as if it were a last resort, "under arrest in Vienna?"

"To reciprocate? No."

"Has our embassy any carrier pigeons to Vienna?"

"Unfortunately, no."

After a few seconds of silence, Rolly asked:

"What about that electric device which was invented in America last year?"

For a moment no one answered Rolly's desperate question. Then Alphie whispered to her: "The Morse machine is not in use yet."

Countess Jadi, her voice betraying her despair, asked von Nordthal:

"What is your advice for me, Baron Heinrich?"

"Neither Your Excellency nor I can do anything here in St. Petersburg. Fortunately, Princess Olga and ... "

A gesture took the place of Prince Igor's name.

". . . our Russian friends will do their best. But we must contact Vienna. I will send a special diplomatic courier to Dali's father right away."

"He is in Berlin. For three weeks. Officially," Countess Jadi said hopelessly.

"Then I would suggest that Your Excellency take the next mailcoach to Vienna. Talk to his serenity, the chancellor, as soon as possible."

"Mother cannot make that long trip alone," Rolly said.

"I am at her excellency's disposal," von Nordthal said. "I will accompany her."

"Why you?" Rolly asked. "Why not Alphie?"

"No, thank you, dear," Countess Jadi said. "Alphie cannot leave you and your child alone. I confess I don't feel strong enough to make the trip alone. May I ask Monsieur la Harpe to accompany me?"

Of course, all the important questions remained unanswered. Would Metternich intervene? Would the czar honor his intervention? It was a bad time, for lately there had been a great deal of tension between Vienna and St. Petersburg. Metternich knew that the czar had his eye on the Bosporus and the Dardanelles, because Russia's fleet was bottled up in the Black Sea, with no access to the Mediterranean. The czar, on the other hand, thought Metternich "too liberal."

Dali's family and their friends discussed these complications. Von Nordthal remarked: "I had the honor recently to deliver a letter from His Serenity, Prince Metternich, to the czar. Politely debating the problem of some unavoidable reforms, our chancellor wrote to His Majesty the czar: 'Sire! Stability is not immobility!' "

"A real Metternich sentence. What was the czar's answer?" Alphie asked.

"Very clever. I should say majestic. No words. Just a golden bust of the late Emperor Francis for the chancellery, reminding Metternich that the reason Francis' reign was so stable was because the emperor had been sitting on the Habsburg throne for nearly half a century absolutely *immobile.*"

"All right, but if we take into consideration . . ." Alphie started a sentence but Olga cut in:

"Gentlemen, this is no time for a long political discussion. The question is: Would Metternich intervene?"

"My humble answer is *yes,*" von Nordthal declared.

Olga stood up and ordered the servants to make preparations for Countess Jadi's long trip.

When they took the mailcoach at noon, Dushenka had still not returned from Prince Igor's office.

"I am afraid he is not in St. Petersburg," Olga said.

Countess Jadi, with Tonchi at her side, was in tears when she bade her daughter and sister farewell.

7

After their departure the afternoon passed without any news. That night in the Lomonosoff Theater, Dimitri Kantemir stepped in front of the curtain and again announced to a full house that because of the slight indisposition of Dushenka Arkadievna Bobak, her role would be played by Katerina Pavlova Ukrin.

While the curtain went up before a disappointed audience, Nyanya returned from the Hotel Doulon, where she had gone to pay Dali's bill. A boy followed her, carrying Dali's two heavy valises.

"Wait in the kitchen," Nyanya told him. "We will need you again."

Dushenka was busy packing. Opened valises lay on the floor, clothes were spread on the chairs. She was struggling with the problem of how to pack her fragile balalaika and the even more fragile Ikon.

The days were so long now that, although it was eight o'clock, the cupola of St. Isaac's church was still bathed in sunshine. The same sunshine caressed the eighteen-foot-thick stone walls of Schlusselburg, Key of the Baltic, a former Swedish fortress on an island in Lake Ladoga, not far from St. Petersburg. The fortress had been turned into a state prison a century before. There was no death penalty in Russia during the reign of Czar Nicholas—only deportation, prison and the stick. At Schlusselburg, political prisoners were in effect buried alive. It was at Schlusselburg that young Ivan VI died in the middle of the eighteenth century. There were no executions at Schlusselburg. But the *palka,* the stick, was regularly used for physical punishment; sometimes a prisoner was sentenced to a hundred strokes, but, out of sheer mercy, the guards applied the fourth or fifth stroke with such force that the prisoners collapsed and died.

Dali was at Schlüsselburg.

When the church bells struck nine, the commander of the prison, followed by the guards, had every cell opened, and he personally supervised the search of the horsehair cover on the wooden bench, the empty drawer of the small table, every corner of the cell, looking for hidden weapons or tools. He mounted a chair and tested every bar of the narrow window near the ceiling to make sure none was loose.

Dali stood by the wall, staring into space as if he were alone. He did not move during the inspection; he did not even glance at the commander. He was no longer a Pálffy Hussar in a bright uniform. He was barefooted, dressed in brown prison garb. The commander, as was his custom, left the cell without a word, without a single glance at the prisoner. The heavy key turned in the lock, the grated door was closed again. The steps of the commander and the guards faded away in the long corridor.

Night fell on Schlüsselburg. Dali lay on his back on the horsehair-covered wooden bench, his hands folded under the nape of his neck, staring into the darkness toward the invisible ceiling.

Why was he here? Why was he arrested? The *B* needle. The *B* needle. Yes, the *B* needle. Was Serge an *agent provocateur?* Was he arrested? And Tonchi? Was he arrested, too? And his mother? And Rolly and Alphie and Olga? If the police caught someone in connection with the *B* needle, his whole family, all his friends would be arrested and exterminated.

He saw no other explanation for his arrest, but the *B* needle. He was not sorry for himself, he was ready to die. He was sorry for his mother, for Dushenka, for Rolly, for Olga, for Alphie.

But if that were so, why wasn't Dushenka arrested and taken

away? Perhaps there had been a house search in Hotel Doulon. But even so, they could not find anything suspicious. He and Tonchi used to burn every letter on any political subject. And he had thrown the tiny wooden tube containing the *B* needles into the Neva. No one knew about the *B* needle but Serge. And Serge did not know either his name or his profession.

Then what was the reason? And who was behind his arrest? Von Nordthal and Zorkoff? With the understanding of his father? A mock arrest? Just to scare him and force him to give up Dushenka?

The invisible ceiling gave no answer to these chaotic questions. Inky clouds were gathering in the summer sky. The air was warm and heavy. There was a faint light at the narrow, grated window, a glimmer of that strange, giant silver fan of the Aurora Borealis. The bells in the tower struck ten.

"No, there is no death penalty in Russia . . ." Dali thought.

The tower struck eleven. No, there is no death penalty in Russia. . . . But a few minutes before midnight, the silence of the prison was broken by a heartrending howl. The *palka!* The stick! The howl came not from a neighboring cell, nor even from down the long corridor. Perhaps it emanated from another floor, but its distance made the howl more mystic, more frightening. When the heinous howl abated, the silence implied the prisoner's death.

Dali's thoughts were febrile, an access of terror.

Another hour passed. When he heard steps in the corridor . . . yes, the steps were approaching . . . he knew that he was going to die.

The steps reached his cell and stopped. A voice whispered: *"Monsieur le Comte!"*

Dali recognized the voice of the commander. He was surprised to hear him speak French, for yesterday morning, when he had been admitted to the prison, the commander had talked to him through an interpreter. Dali went to the door.

"Je suis un ami d'un des votre amis," the commander whispered. "I am a friend of one of your friends. While I inspected your cell tonight, I left a chisel in the drawer of the table. Cut out the grating of the window. You can do it in less than an hour. This is the second floor. We are on an island in Lake La-

doga. There's water below the window. Don't hesitate to jump. A boat awaits you. On the opposite shore you will meet your friends. Good luck, Monsieur!"

His steps faded away in the long, dark corridor.

Dali found the chisel in the drawer. It was a big one, richly greased to lessen the noise. He mounted the table and set to work, slowly but steadily. In what seemed like two hours but was actually hardly more than half an hour . . . the bars came loose.

Resting, as he lowered the chisel, he experienced a strange, sweet feeling, coming through his aching palm, pouring into his body—a feeling he had never known before.

It was *libertas.* . . . *Freiheit.* . . . *Szabadság.* . . . The word freedom had never been more than a theory to him. To be sure, it had always been a theory he held sacred. But now the word had become a greasy chisel, and the muted clinking of metal on stone as the bars came loose in the window.

When the opening was large enough to crawl through, Dali poked his head out, looked around and then climbed out and dragged himself across the twelve-foot-thick wall. He breathed the sweet, heavy air of the June night and listened to the silence. He could hear nothing but the water lapping the shores below him. Clinging to the edge of the wall, he began to lower himself. Suddenly, as he was hanging in the air, a horrid suspicion flashed into his mind. There was no death penalty in Russia, but you could shoot a fleeing prisoner; it was the duty of the guards. Could it be that the commander was an *agent provocateur?*

Or, if the commander really was a friend of friends, who were the friends? Tonchi and someone in the underground? Was the commander of Polish origin? Or had he been bribed by Dali's mother? Or by the Embassy?

Dali looked down. The water seemed more than ten feet below. Was it shallow? Was the bottom rocky?

He plunged. When he surfaced, the desperate strokes of his arms were useless against the strong current, although he was an excellent swimmer. The water was dark; it seemed like the strange darkness of death. He knew he could not stay afloat long. And then he heard the splash of an oar, and two strong arms pulled him up and into a small boat.

The two Russians in the boat did not speak; they were busy with their oars. When they reached the shore, there was a dim bit of early daybreak on the horizon. The first shadow to emerge was Nyanya. Then Dushenka grabbed Dali's arm and whispered:

"Get into the troika. Quick. We have papers to pass the Finnish border. The driver and the horses are from Prince Igor."

Dali turned to say "Thank you" to the two oarsmen and recognized, to his great surprise, Sylvester Bralin, the son of the baker from Novgorod, the young soldier so desperately in love with Dushenka.

When Dushenka had broken the news of her engagement to Sylvic, she had confided to Dali that she feared Sylvie might try to kill him. And well he might have! Now he stood there, smiling, holding the dripping oar straight up as if it were a lance. He seemed happy and grateful that Dushenka had turned to him for help, and he had risked his life fishing Dali out of the water.

He shook a wet hand with Dali, then kissed Dushenka's gloved fingers. Dushenka said to him in a low voice:

"Thank you for everything. *Au revoir,* Sylvie."

Then she turned to Dali:

"Come! We have no time . . . Come on!"

The three fast horses pulling the troika galloped off in the direction of the Finnish border.

The dawn was yet a dark gray, but the lapwing above the marshes was already on the wing, crying sadly.

PRO
PATRIA
ET
LIBERTATE
PART THREE | 1839–1849

CHAPTER SIX

AT EIGHT IN THE EVENING, the mailcoach in which Countess Jadi and Tonchi travelled had only a few miles to go to reach the Finnish border. The other passengers, lulled by the monotonous rhythm of the hooves, were sleeping. But there was no sleep for Countess Jadi and Tonchi.

Countess Jadi, her mind beset by a thousand fears for her son, was in a desperate state. Frequently she would have fainted but for Tonchi, who revived her by holding a small bottle of Eau de Cologne under her nose. Tonchi himself had very little hope. Even if the roads remained dry, the journey to Vienna would take weeks. And even if Metternich should send a courier pigeon to Czar Nicholas, still many things could happen in Schlusselburg Prison within two or three weeks.

The six horses seemed hopelessly slow on the sandy road. The cries of the lapwings above the marshes and the flickering lights of the will-o'-the-wisp turned the landscape, for Countess Jadi and for Tonchi too, into a vivid representation of Russian hell. After sunset they crossed the Finnish border. The two spent an anxious night at an inn. In the morning, Countess Jadi appeared to be at the end of her strength. Her face had a grayish cast, and there were deep purplish rings about her eyes.

They were having their breakfast at the inn when suddenly a pale, unshaven young man appeared, dressed in dirty, wrinkled clothes, accompanied by one old and one young woman. His appearance was ghostly and frightening.

"How do you do folks?" he greeted Countess Jadi and Tonchi. "M . . . My name is . . . " He turned to the young lady: "What's my name, my dear? Oh, yes, David Schillinger . . . show the Monsieur my document, dear . . . I am an itinerant meerschaum merchant from Prague. Let me introduce my wife, Fanny. Say a nice hello, honey."

Then he pointed to Nyanya's toothless grin:

"And that old witch is my lady-companion."

Dali extended his hand to Countess Jadi, who sat speechless, her hand pressed to her throat.

"You look very familiar, Madame. I remember we used to walk together before I was born."

Countess Jadi was too weak to enjoy Dali's whimsical greeting. She broke down and sobbed so hysterically that the mail-coach could not leave for a half hour, to the great consternation of the other passengers.

They slept through most of the day. The other passengers were pressed so close to them in the overcrowded coach that they could not talk much anyway, except of the weather and other neutral topics.

They could talk freely for the first time in the room of the inn where they rested for the night. Countess Jadi and Tonchi wanted to know every detail of Dali's escape.

"Prince Igor," Dushenka whispered, "offered his help under one condition: We must say not a word to anyone, not a single word, even outside Russia. He said he would tell von Nordthal not to report Dali's arrest to Vienna, either officially or privately."

"I won't even tell my husband," Countess Jadi said.

During the evening at the inn, they speculated about the main character in that strange drama. Who was the commandant of the prison, who smuggled the chisel into Dali's cell? What was his background? Why did he act on Prince Igor's request, when it must have been a tremendous risk for him?

"I'm afraid we will never know," Tonchi said at last. "Just as we'll never be certain why you were arrested."

And he told the story of a young British diplomat who one night, five years before, had disappeared from his Moscow hotel. And the Russian foreign office still "has no idea" what happened to him.

"Who were the oarsmen in the boat?" Countess Jadi asked.

"Sylvester Bralin, a friend of mine from Novgorod," Dushenka whispered, though whispering was no longer necessary, "and a friend of his."

Nine days later they arrived in Prague. Countess Jadi changed to the mailcoach for Vienna, and Tonchi accompanied her. She still looked exhausted.

Dali, Dushenka and Nyanya went on toward Buda. But when they reached Possony, near the Austrian border in Hungary, they stopped for a few days rest. After delivering Countess Jadi into the hands of Endre and Flexi in Vienna, Tonchi joined them there. The following day Andris arrived from Zekerd, and after a happy and noisy reunion in the Hotel Griff's lobby, the trio held its first conference in eight months. But the agenda of the conference was hardly more than Dali's and Tonchi's report that their Mission in Russia was a failure.

"For the time being," Tonchi emphasized.

"I think we were mistaken," Dali said, "when we thought that Prince Igor was the man of the future. He is a wonderful man, but he is less interested in liberating serfs than he is in becoming Olga's serf himself."

Two days later they took the steamship *Argot* to Buda-Pesth. Andris was enchanted by Dushenka.

To their horror, when they arrived in Buda-Pesth, Dali and Tonchi discovered that Pesth had disappeared. They were aghast as they looked from the Buda hill to the graveyard that, before the dreadful flood, had been Pesth.

"There . . ." Dali pointed to the Pesth shore and explained to Dushenka, "there stood once the Café Árpád, where I used to play billiards with Andris."

Gesturing grandly toward Pesth, Andris quoted in Latin his favorite French writer, Proudhon:

"*Destruam et edificabo!* I will destroy and rebuild! Catastrophe is the greatest architect. You will see that within a decade the most beautiful *stone* city will stand here, in place of the *clay* city."

"Fortunately," Tonchi remarked, "the Habsburg throne is made of clay, too."

Their conversation, though in French, seemed a new and frightening language for Dushenka and Nyanya. Nyanya had always thought that Habsburg was a city, like St. Petersburg. Dushenka, who had heard the expression "Habsburg Empire" many times, knew that the Habsburg monarch was an individual, like Nicholas or Alexander; but she could not understand what her husband and his friends meant to do about him.

Three days after their arrival in Buda, Count Adalbert Árpád Maurycy Dukay, 24, Roman Catholic, and Dushenka Sonya Arkadievna Bobak, 22, Orthodox, were married in the little St. Priscilla Chapel in Septemvir Utca.

Dali's best man was Andris, and Tonchi gave Dushenka away. There were only three witnesses: Countess Jadi, Nyanya, and a small lady who arrived on horseback at the chapel at the last minute. She was Andris' bride, Irma Alacsy de Alacs. Dushenka, in her bridal veil, looked innocent and very young, Dali and Andris wore their gala hussar uniforms, and Countess Jadi wore violet silk. Nyanya was dressed in the folk costume of the Novgorod district: sulphur-yellow apron, red boots, and blue kerchief binding her gray hair. Tonchi's faded pea-green frock coat, though lace-cuffed for the great occasion, did not add much color to the wedding.

The ceremony was not glamorous or monumental, but everyone was deeply touched. Dali and Dushenka were pale, while Countess Jadi and Nyanya wept quietly.

And the same afternoon, in the same chapel, with the same witnesses, a second wedding took place. The only difference was that the delicate Irma was the bride, and Andris, who had once wrestled a bear, the groom. Tonchi was his best man, and Dali gave Irma away.

Endre and Flexi were not present at Dali's wedding, but they did not mean to snub Dushenka; they just had an invitation to a Schönheim-Altstadt garden party for the same day.

In his congratulatory letter, sent by a special dispatch rider from Vienna, Endre wished great happiness for his son and wrote: "Why don't you move into the left wing of our palace in Buda? There is a great shortage of accommodations since the flood. Your mother is most enthusiastic about your bride. She tells me 'Trishunka' is extremely pretty."

Nothing showed better the distance in Endre's mind between Princess Maria Augusta and the Novgorod girl than his casual misspelling of Dushenka's name. In Flexi's congratulatory letter, her name was spelled almost correctly: "Drushinka."

Dali and Dushenka replied to the letters, but Dali did not accept his father's invitation to the palace in Septemvir Utca, which was too big, too luxurious compared to the little house in Dushenka Ulitza. Instead, the newlyweds moved into a small house in Buda, which belonged to the Gere estate that Dali would one day inherit and was used as an extra guest house for the Septemvir Utca palace. The little house, which dated back to the seventeenth century, was dwarfed in the fashionable neighborhood that had grown up around it; it stood like a poor relation, coldly looked down upon by the mighty palaces and mansions of the Eszterházys, Pálffys, Zichys, and other aristocratic families. In the yard, which commanded a view of the Danube, a stone pavement was framed by flower beds. A sedan chair was kept in the portico, seemingly not in use for many decades, but piously preserved as a reliable witness of the good old days.

Four doors opened from the long corridor: the first to a living room and the adjoining master bedroom, the second to a guest room, the third to the kitchen, and the fourth to the servants quarters. The greater part of the furniture was of the powdered-head-and-pigtail period, with miniature portraits in black oval frames by the dozens; but no man on earth knew any longer who the ladies and gentlemen of the portraits were. In the living room an obsolete harpsichord stood by the wall near a pea-green porcelain oven. The name of the harpsichord's maker was still readable above the keyboard, set in a painted garland of faded flowers.

After inspecting the house and the garden, Nyanya inhaled the heavy fragrance of the flower-beds, looked up at the turtle doves' cage in the portico, and said to Dushenka:

"It reminds me of the Bralin house in Novgorod."

Dushenka explained to Dali that the Bralin house in Novgorod was smaller but had a similar corridor.

One day in July, Endre and Flexi arrived from Vienna. They descended from the height of the Septemvir Utca palace to Dali's small house, and remained there for half an hour. Endre embraced and kissed "Trishunka"; Flexi kissed her fingers. But when Dushenka introduced Nyanya, who wiped her hand on her apron before shaking hands, Endre's face took on the expression of a guest who has been offered a dish he hates, but swallows it out of sheer politeness.

"How do you feel, sir?" Dali asked his father.

"Very well, thank you, my son."

But Dali was surprised to see how much his father's hair had grayed during the nine months since he had seen him, and how much thinner his nose had become. In the first half of the nineteenth century, as in the time of Shakespeare's "Old John of Gaunt, the time-honored Lancaster," a man of fifty was regarded as old. The forty-eight-year-old Endre Dukay had already given Flexi full authorization to sign the vital rental and other contracts for the estate. In the old days, after harvest every year, the twenty odd agents of the Dukay lands and forests would come from their faraway counties and spend three days reading their reports and accounts, lingering for hours over such monotonous items as "two and a half pounds of three-inch nails for the repair of the hog sty in . . . ," . . . "three liters of kerosene for the hair of the house maids, against lice. . . . " The most precise and detailed accounts omitted only those tens of thousands of florins the agents stole yearly from the estate's income.

This was the usual way of managing huge estates, from the Urals to France where the aristocrats had had their lands restored after the French Revolution.

But Flexi's approach was a new one, and rare even for his generation. His friend Solly Rothschild had filled his head with plans to "industrialize" the estate. Endre did not like any reforms, not even in agriculture. But he never objected aloud. Once in a while, when he was in a good mood, he would greet Flexi with a loud "Good morning, Herr Rothschild!" This was his only expression of disapproval. And in truth, he trusted Flexi.

But whenever he thought of Dali, Endre felt a kind of sorrow, anxiety and anger, mixed with sympathy, for his second-born "imperfect" son. His fatherly feeling had built a tragic air around Dali, not only because of his marriage, but in the recollection of his childhood misdeeds, and in the recognition of his restless mind, his "pyromaniac character." "I always felt some dark and fatalistic strain in his nature," he used to say to Jadi and Flexi.

His main concern was Dali's close friendship with Andris. Flexi often had heated arguments with Andris over such questions as conservatism or absolute and hereditary monarchies, but Flexi never spoke of such matters before his father. But Baron Erich Dukay-Hedwitz, Endre's nephew, had also heard Andris' political views, and "felt it his duty" to carry them to Endre.

Flexi's wedding was held in Vienna in the Stefanskirche, which proved to be too small to hold the aristocrats who attended. At their head was Flexi's godfather, Prince Metternich. Among the guests were Alexander, Duke of Teck, and his beautiful duchess, the former Countess Claudia Rhédey, whom Dali had loved so at the age of thirteen. And also among them of course, was Baron Erich Dukay-Hedwitz. Dali and Dushenka had been invited, but they had decided not to attend. Dali did not want to expose Dushenka to the danger of being snubbed by the Schönheim-Altstadts. But Alphie and Rolly did attend. On their way from St. Petersburg to Paris, they spent a week in Vienna. After the wedding party, in the company of a nurse and little Miette (French for bread crumb), their five-month-old daughter, they travelled to Buda and stayed in the Septemvir Utca palace for another week. For Dali and Dushenka they brought back the atmosphere of St. Petersburg.

"How long is your vacation?" Dushenka asked Alphie.

"Very long," said the marquis. "I'm going to Paris to resign my post in St. Petersburg."

2

On the last day of September in 1838, Dali and Dushenka, Andris, and Irma, and Tonchi and Nyanya made an excursion to an ancient inn on top of a hill; it was called The Shepherd's

Pretty Wife. The walk took two hours, but the weather was wonderful and no one minded walking.

Dali and Dushenka, holding hands, headed the procession. Dushenka wore a wreath of orange flowers in her brown, silky hair. As they walked, Dali swung her hand to the rhythm of an old French folksong that Dushenka sang softly: *jusqu'à la fin du monde.*

Some fifteen steps behind them, Andris had engaged Tonchi in a political conversation. Nyanya walked beside Tonchi, while Irma walked at Andris' side.

"The germs of Proudhon's 'I do what I want' doctrine," Tonchi was saying, "may be traced to the forbidden fruit in the Garden of Eden, to the fundamental yearning for happiness in human nature, in every walk of life. This revolution is demonstrated not only in children's misdeeds, but in the vandalism of grownup Sunday tourists."

These last words appeared to be aimed at the fragrant blossoms in Dushenka's hair. The flowers came from Archduke István's royal garden, but not by permission of the archduke. When they had passed the estate, Dali had simply climbed the fence and helped himself to the flowers. Fortunately, no guards had seen him, for they were under orders to give one warning shot and then shoot to kill. Last summer, two students of the deaf and dumb institute had been killed for pilfering one orange.

Jusqu'à la fin du monde. . . . Until the end of the world . . . Dushenka's famous alto sang the refrain of the slightly spicy old song about the most important piece of furniture in human life . . . the bed.

"Did you read that anonymous work *The European Pentarchy?*" Tonchi asked Andris.

"Of course, I did," Andris replied. The work, printed in many Slavic languages and smuggled in hundreds of thousands of copies to the Czechs and Slovaks, called for the union of the five Slavonic races in Europe. This pentarchy was to be, of course, under the "archy" of Russia.

"Well," Tonchi said, "that's the same madness as Fichte's philosophy that all the nations of the world must accept the leadership of the Germans. Look at this beauty!" His mind, accustomed to leaping from one topic to another, now contemplated a captive stag beetle in his palm. "I cannot liberate Poland," he said to the beetle, "but I give you back the sweetness of your freedom."

The beetle opened its shiny chestnut-brown wings, preened its long filmy antennae, and flew from Tonchi's extended palm into the forest.

The sweet scent of the forest was suddenly invaded by the spicy smell of mutton goulash.

The Shepherd's Pretty Wife, a small thatched stone inn, had received its pretty name in the fifteenth century. In those days the valley below the inn, hardly two miles from the royal palace, was a dense wilderness, and a marvellous place for hunting. One day, during a hunt, King Matthias, lost his way and found shelter in a shepherd's small house. The shepherd's wife was pretty and the king was young. The shepherd was not at home. From that day on the king went "hunting" every day. The shepherd was never at home. But the king's many hunting trips aroused suspicion in court circles, and one day, when Matthias entered the house, he was greeted not by the warm kisses of the shepherd's pretty wife, but by a slap across the face so forceful that his majesty lost his balance and fell to the floor. And Queen Beatrice stood over him screaming, "Is *that* what you are hunting for?"

So the legend went.

Patrons of The Shepherd's Pretty Wife were mostly Sunday tourists, lovers, or groups of patriots, who preferred that remote inn to the crowded cafés of Pesth for their dangerous conversations. If the weather was good, the long tables and wooden benches around the small house could accommodate a hundred guests.

"*Delicieux! Delicieux!*" Tonchi whispered to his spoon, enjoying the mutton goulash for which the inn was justly famous.

"The secret of it," Andris explained expertly, "is that a whole sheep goes into the kettle, liver, kidney, heart, lung, udder, head, brains, tongue, teeth, nails, bones, bowels . . . everything, even the wool." Everybody laughed heartily when Tonchi put down his spoon with a glassy look, acting wonderfully as if he believed Andris' recipe.

Spirits were rising rapidly, thanks to the strong greenish-gold wine. Like sea gulls suddenly appearing in the empty sky, gypsy musicians entered the inn's yard. Dali called for the old innkeeper.

"Tell me, Uncle Janos," Dali inquired, "how can you charge only six kreuzers for a double portion of that wonderful goulash, plus three expensive peaches, plus a bottle of excellent wine?"

"Very simple, sir," the old man explained. "I have three sons. One is a guard in the royal orchards, the second is a wine dresser in the Metternich cellar, and the third is a shepherd on the Dukay estate."

"You see," Dali turned to Tonchi reproachfully, "and you were teaching me Adam Smith's economy!"

An hour later, slightly tipsy, he clung to his glass, commanding silence, and stood up for a toast.

"Ladies and gentlemen," he began, in the most solemn tone, "we have arrived at this dinner on the thirtieth of September. Now it's ten minutes after midnight, the first of October. I do not know if Prince Metternich was right when he said that our century was born with the opening of the Congress in Vienna, October first Anno Domini 1814, but I do know that on that same day, twenty-four years ago, twins were born in Vienna, and the second-born received the name of Adalbert Árpád Maurycy. Before you sing a happy birthday to me, let me tell you that I have never been so happy, never in the whole twenty-four years of my life, as I have been since I met and learned to love hopelessly a girl named Dushenka from Novgorod."

A tear ran down Dushenka's cheek as she lifted her glass in response to the ovation that greeted Dali's words.

That morning, October 1, 1838, the rising sun cast an angry eye at the black thatched roof of The Shepherd's Pretty Wife. For beneath the roof, candles were still burning brightly, and six guests, Dali and Dushenka, Andris and Irma, Tonchi and Nyanya, occasionally changing their partners, were still dancing to the music of the gypsy fiddlers.

To have an heir was not so important to Dali as it was to Flexi. Dali's small estate was as nothing compared to the huge Dukay lands Flexi would inherit; and in any case, he was not interested in the inheritance because he did not believe in the future of the feudal system. Moreover, Flexi's bride had become pregnant quite promptly after her wedding. So while Flexi prayed for a son, Dali wanted a daughter.

Early in March of 1839, though Nyanya had told him that the child might come any day, Dali rode one morning to Ararat, where Tonchi was entertaining twenty-year-old Karl Leiningen, a captain in the Leiningen Regiment in Vienna and a cousin of young Queen Victoria. In spite of these "shortcomings" (as Tonchi put it) the tall, extremely handsome German count was an ardent admirer of Kossuth. Tonchi thought it very important to introduce Leiningen to Dali and Andris. The young officer, with only two days leave from his regiment, had just time enough to meet Dali in Ararat.

"I'll be back tomorrow evening," Dali told Dushenka at their farewell embrace.

And the next evening, true to his word, he was back. He delivered his horse to the stable boy, and then hurried to the house. He stopped in the open corridor and listened. Did he hear well? He heard a baby cry.

"*Un garçon!*" Nyanya greeted him joyfully. But when Dali leaned down to kiss Dushenka and shouted jokingly: "Long live my son, the future king of independent Poland and Hungary!" Dushenka remained silent. And when Dali looked at her, he saw tears flowing down her chalk-white cheeks.

"What's the matter? What happened?"

It was Nyanya who answered, half joking, half serious:

"She will never forgive you, Uncle Dali, that you were not here by her side last night! It is her first child. Didn't you know?"

Dali tried to cheer Dushenka, but with little success. But he took the crying baby up in his arms and shouted with fatherly joy:

"Stop that crying, son! No, you aren't the heir of the Dukay estate, but I vow you will be the heir of the much larger estate of Charles Louis Montesquieu, George Washington, Thaddeus Kosciusko, Monsieur Tonchi, Baron Andris Zeker, Karl Leiningen and greatest of all, Count Dali Dukay, *de genere* Ordony, your proud and happy father. Stop that earsplitting noise, will you?"

Nyanya was moved to tears when Dali asked her to be the newborn Dukay's godmother. Andris was his godfather. The baby was named Ádám Andreas Fedor Hyron. Andreas in honor of his godfather, Andris; Fedor, in commemoration of Dushenka's late father; and Hyron, after Tonchi's given Polish name.

When Endre inquired about his grandson's fourth Christian name, Hyron, Countess Jadi told him that Hyron was a thirteenth-century Orthodox Greek saint, which was true.

Two months later, on the second anniversary of his imprisonment, Kossuth was allowed to receive visitors. The trio's names were among the first on the list. When Andris, Dali and Tonchi entered Kossuth's cell, he was not alone. Kossuth's unmarried sister and a young lady none of them knew were already there. The young lady, not so very young and not a striking beauty, was feeding the canaries. Dali immediately guessed—correctly, as he later learned—that it was she who had sent the little prisoners to the great prisoner.

The cell proved too narrow for five visitors. And because more visitors were waiting outside the corridor, the trio's visit was very brief; but the handshakes were long and warm. The trio left the Buda fortress in a depressed mood. Two years in that narrow wet cell had done Kossuth no good. Even the large blue eyes and the strong sonorous voice had become faded.

During the ensuing week, while Dali brooded over Kossuth's condition, a terrible blow struck Dushenka. Nyanya, in her seventy-fifth year, went to sleep one night and never woke up. Dushenka was beside herself with grief. Nyanya had been more to her than mother; she was Dushenka's motherland and her mother tongue. Dushenka had the feeling that with Nyanya's death, the Russian language had become extinct. Dali's Russian was poor and Dushenka's Hungarian imperfect. For the most part, they conversed in French.

Dushenka's new maid, cook, and lady companion was named

Julie. Julie was a remarkable maid. Unlike Nyanya, she could put her hand on earrings, hairpins, gloves, ribbons—anything that Dushenka called for, within a moment, in one or another of the innumerable leather, silver or inlaid jewel boxes which adorned Dushenka's dressing table. But she could not understand the Russian words Dushenka absentmindedly used to her.

A few weeks after Nyanya's death, Dushenka began corresponding with friends in Novgorod.

"I am going to forget my mother tongue," she explained to Dali.

When she informed Sylvester Bralin of Nyanya's death, Sylvie answered in a long letter. "We knew her from our childhood. I can imagine how lonely you are now without her," he wrote. "Is there any chance that one day you will return to Novgorod for a couple of weeks? Only as a visitor?"

Dushenka could go back to Russia any time. But to get out again was another question.

In hopes of cheering Dushenka, Dali suggested that she resume her career. Dushenka hesitated at first. She could not imagine appearing on any stage or in any concert hall as a Countess Dukay. But Dali persuaded her that she should simply use her maiden name. For three months Dushenka took four German lessons every day, and for another four months she practiced the new piano Countess Jadi had given her. She played Mozart, Strauss and Liszt, accompanying herself while she struggled with the unfamiliar German lyrics.

When Dushenka thought herself ready, Dali took her to Vienna for an audition with Herr Robert von Stolzman, manager of the Teater an der Wien. Von Stolzman, a composer himself, was a very dignified man, with the manner of Prince Metternich and the hair-do of Johann Strauss. He was the mighty authority of the musical world in Vienna. During Dushenka's audition, he stared at the floor coldly, his head tilted to one side. A man like Herr von Stolzman had every reason to resent the "great" talents young and rich aristocrats escorted to the try-outs. They were rarely talented, and usually tiresome.

When Dushenka had finished her first aria, Herr von Stolzman addressed his words not to her, but to Dali, as if Dushenka were some supposedly rare object for sale, the authenticity of which he doubted.

"Fräulein Bobak," Herr von Stolzman announced the verdict, "has a lovely alto, but I think it needs at least a year of training and polishing." When they left Herr von Stolzman kissed Dushenka's hand gallantly, but it was obvious that no unknown Russian alto with poor German pronunciation would be welcome at the Teater an der Wien.

Sorrow and idleness are not the best cosmetics. The wonderful indescribable light in Dushenka's face gradually faded away. The eyes had lost their gay twinkle. Her graceful figure began to thicken in response to the rich and heavy Hungarian diet, her little breasts growing large and soft. But Dali did not notice this, and even if he had, would not have cared.

"A penny for your thoughts," Dali said one morning, reaching for her hand.

She shook her head as if she were shaking something out of her hair.

"I don't know why, I've clearly heard the creaking of the stage floor at the Lomonosoff," she said. "One's memories sometimes come back in the funniest forms."

"Are you homesick?"

"Well . . . not particularly."

But she was. She was more and more desperately homesick every day; and it took all of her strength to conceal it, not so much from Dali, as from herself.

Worse, though, than homesickness was another feeling that, try as she might, she could not banish. Dushenka was jealous.

She suspected Dali of having a love affair with a vivacious cousin of Andris' named Eliz Sissanyi. Eliz was one of those rare Hungarian girls who knew the difference between feudalism and rheumatism (as Andris put it). She was exceptionally educated in social science, spoke fluent German and French, and had diligently studied English. "Now that I'm to be a relative of Queen Victoria, I had better learn that damn language fast," she told Dali laughingly. For Eliz was engaged in a flirtation with Karl Leiningen. In Dali's opinion, Eliz was not particularly beautiful, but he enjoyed her sense of humor and admired her patriotism.

Dushenka's jealousy of Eliz was unfounded; but whenever

Dali excused himself to go to Pesth and did not return until late, Dushenka could barely hold back her tears. She knew Eliz attended the Pesth meetings, and she convinced herself that that was why Dali attended them. But Eliz was not Dushenka's only worry. She was jealous of every woman who appeared near Dali, socially or otherwise. She was jealous even of Julie, her maid. If a woman is afflicted with the disease of jealousy, nothing can help her. And Dushenka, born with a constant longing for tenderness, yearning for small expressions of love, found Dali cold.

But of all Dushenka's sorrows, the greatest was her feeling that she had become a burden on Dali's life. However polite and kind Andris and Tonchi were to her, she understood that they thought Dali one of the most important figures in Hungary's near future . . . a man the country needed . . . a young and brilliant man of great moral stature and fine education, with one of the most ancient names in the country. Who would be the leader of the nation, the great reformer, if Kossuth should die in the Buda prison?

In fact, Dali's star was ascending only in Andris' and Tonchi's imaginations. Dali liked to make speeches, but he was far from being an orator. His voice was colorless and sounded rather sad. He never shared Tonchi's belief in his political career.

4

In the spring of 1840, the stillness which had reigned in the monarchy since Kossuth's arrest three years before was suddenly broken by noisy demonstrations against the Habsburg oppression of several Italian provinces. *Morte ai Tedeschi! Evvivan gli Ungaresci!* "Death to the Germans. Long live the Hungarians!" demonstrators shouted.

In order to strengthen the effective forces of the army, Metternich had to summon the Hungarian Diet to vote the conscription of new classes.

"What? Hungarian soldiers against the Italian freedom fighters? Never!" This was the reaction of Hungary. Count Lajos Batthyány joined the opposition in the Diet.

To gain support, Metternich cleverly declared a general amnesty for political prisoners. Most of the freed men left their prison physically and mentally broken. But Kossuth, though he looked sick, was in full possession of his mental and spiritual faculties. What was more, he was tempered, matured, and ready for action. It seemed that his three years in the damp and chilly cell of the Buda fortress were purposeful links in the grandly conceived plan of his life.

Thousands streamed to the Danube bank when he left his prison in the evening. Dali, Andris, Tonchi and his friends had secured 200 torches, and distributed them to the students, who escorted Kossuth to the country hall. Despite his great popularity, he could not get a mandate to the Diet, for he had been released from prison too late.

The Hungarian Diet, the old-fashioned version of a parliament or congress, had more than 600 members. It held its sessions not in Buda-Pesth, but in Pozsony, near the Austrian border, for two reasons: first, to be close to the Austrian troops in case of an urgent dissolution; and second, to be as close to Vienna as possible, because most of the members of the Diet's upper house, the rich pro-Habsburg Hungarian aristocrats like Endre Dukay, lived in Vienna. It did not take these members long to get to the Diet. Those aristocrats who lived in Eastern Hungary generally did not attend, but sent delegates. For long years, as a young lawyer, Kossuth had been such a delegate. But a delegate had no right to make a speech or cast a vote in the Diet.

Coming out of jail after three years, Kossuth had no job and no income, but he refused to accept the more than 10,000 florins his friends had collected for him. Was his refusal merely pride? Or was it political caution? This well-intended charity would tie his hands in his dealings with groups he might one day oppose. His refusal of the money made a profound impression not only on his friends, but on his political foes as well.

But despite his courage, Kossuth was genuinely ill when he emerged from prison. When the first gala celebrations that had greeted his release were over, he accepted an invitation to a resort in the Mátra mountains, not far from Buda, to restore his strength.

The great patriot's release from prison had effectively dampened the fervor with which Tonchi and Andris had begun to speak of Dali's political future, and his subsequent illness had, equally effectively, curtailed the long and frequent political meetings that Dali had been attending. In Ádám's early infancy, though Dali had spoken of his son delightedly, he had paid but little attention to him. But in recent months, with Kossuth out of prison, Dali had spent more and more time with Dushenka and the baby. For the first time since their earliest weeks in Buda, Dushenka felt that she had a husband and Ádám a father.

Now that Dali had discovered his son, Dushenka reasoned, he would never again become so involved in politics as to spend long days—and nights, too—away from home on those boring, dangerous missions. Dushenka could bear anything, loneliness, homesickness and all, so long as Dali was by her side. She would never need to be jealous again, for now, Dali would stay with her, and Ádám, always.

On a very bright and beautiful September morning, while Dali and Dushenka each held one of Ádám's little hands, so that the child formed a link between them, a clatter of hoof beats sounded, rushing up the street to their house, then stopping. A moment later, Andris dashed into the yard, breathless with haste and excitement.

"Great news!" he cried. "Kossuth is back from Mátra! And he's gained 200 pounds."

"What? *Two hundred* pounds?"

"Yes!" Andris said, only now acknowledging Dushenka's presence with an absentminded bow. "He gained thirty-five pounds, and Theresa has about a hundred and sixty-five."

"Who is Theresa?"

"The 'unknown lady' who sent the first gift to his prison, the two canary birds. He married Theresa last Monday."

Dali glanced at Dushenka.

"Well," he said with an ironic little smile, "I always argued with Tonchi that vocation and family life are not incompatible."

And in no time, he was as busy as ever before. During his long and frequent absences, Ádám took to wandering through the house, then out to the stable, then back through the house, his little face puzzled and sad. When he couldn't find his father anywhere, he would finally seek out his mother. Usually, he found her in tears. But he clung to her and followed her wherever she went. His formerly energetic disposition changed, and he became a quiet, passive child.

Dali, caught up in a whirlwind of activity, was too busy to notice such changes. One morning in November, before going off with Andris, he snatched a moment to write in his diary:

"At 3 in the morn. Dushenka gave birth to a seven-and-a-half-pound girl. Dushenka has decided to call her Sonya."

5

Not long after the Congress of Vienna, Metternich had suggested that Emperor Francis declare October 1, the date of the opening of the congress, a national holiday. The emperor had liked the idea, and on October 1 of every year since, a great military parade had taken place on the training field near Vienna. The emperor, the imperial family, the aristocracy, and all the government dignitaries and foreign ambassadors attended, and most of the ladies came on horseback to watch the parade.

A few days before October 1, 1841, Endre asked Dali to ride in the parade as a reserve lieutenant in the Pálffy Hussars. Reluctantly, Dali heeded his mother's and Tonchi's advise not to refuse Endre's request. October 1 was the twins' birthday, and Dali went to Vienna for the annual dinner party in Gisellastrasse.

Dushenka could not help remembering the carefree celebration they had shared on the occasion in the first year of their marriage, Dali's twenty-fourth birthday under the black thatched roof of The Shepherd's Pretty Wife—Tonchi and Nyanya, dancing to the music of the ragged gypsy fiddlers. Folksongs, folksongs, gay and sad old folksongs, the music of which resembled so much old Russian folksongs. Gisellastrasse, the new waltzes played by the elegantly dressed string quartet, and conducted by Johann Strauss himself, was different. Dushenka never attended these festive birthday parties. She was always uneasy in the company of Endre and the Princess Maria Augusta, Flexi's wife, whose exaggerated tenderness seemed to her a reflection on the daughter of a game keeper from Novgorod. And now, Dali would ride in the parade! And among the women he would encounter in Vienna would, of course, be the most beautiful and elegant ladies in the monarchy.

Dali had not noticed the slow erosion of Dushenka's beauty, but she was herself acutely aware of it. And she was convinced, remembering how passionately he had spoken of her grace, her exquisite features, her slender waist, when he had courted her, that these were of paramount importance to him. And so she knew in her heart that he would surely pay court to one of the beauties he would see in Vienna. Dushenka's jealous anxieties were never more misplaced for, as it turned out, the parade on that first of October offered her husband no opportunity for flirtation, but only occasion for grief and remorse.

According to the program, the slow parade of the artillery was to be followed by the goose-stepping Deutschmeister Regiment; then the music of the military bands would precede the climax of the day: the cavalry in gallop. Dali was the only Dukay to ride in the parade. Though Endre, a colonel, and Flexi, a first lieutenant, were cavalry officers in reserve, they participated in the show not in saddles, but in the more comfortable loges, with gilded silk armchairs. Endre was honored to sit in Metternich's loge, and Flexi, with his wife, Princess Maria, occupied a loge next to her Habsburg relatives. Countess Jadi remained in the Gisellastrasse palace. In twenty-five years, she had never attended the grand parade. Each year, she found some reason for staying away, but the real reason for her absence was that she could not celebrate the opening day of the congress that had begun a new tragic era for Poland.

Among the aristocratic ladies who attended on horseback was the exquisite Duchess of Teck, formerly Claudia Rhédey, whom Dali had loved passionately in his youth.

It was eleven o'clock in the morning. The October sky was dressed in clean blue, the sunshine was as yellow as the trunks of the wasps which appeared from the nearby vineyards. The forests of the surrounding Alps wore their colorful autumn costumes for the festive day, contesting with the bright colors of the military uniforms, and the flags and pennants.

"What a glorious day!" Duchess Claudia, in the saddle of her beautiful bay gelding, said to her neighbor, an ill-favored but enormously wealthy baroness. When the baroness offered no reply, Claudia closed her eyes and surrendered her "most beautiful" face to the kisses of the light breeze.

Then the military bands stopped, and so did the talking in the stands. It was time for the cavalry. A trumpet sounded from the west side of the valley, and the first squadron approached like a whirlwind. The Viennese Dragoons were in dark-sea-green uniforms, the silver crests of their shakos, shaped like Roman helmets, glittering in the sun as they flashed into view.

The crowd's breathless silence broke into applause. Some hundred yards behind the dragoons came the Hungarian Hussars. The crowd cheered them ecstatically, and many of the women threw their hats high into the air. Then, one of the ladies' horses became bewildered and reared.

All right . . . all right . . . the lady showed excellent horsemanship as she reined in the dancing horse. Then she petted its neck tenderly, calming the beast. But the nervous animal stood still only for a moment. Then suddenly it bolted into the gap between the dragoons and the hussars and reared again, and . . . oh, Lord . . . Amidst screams from the ladies, awed voices asked: Who was she? Countess Apponyi? No! Princess Auersperg? No! They are both here. . . . Who, then?

When the squadron had passed, the lady lay on the ground . . . a heap of silk, velvet, veil and blood . . . trampled to death by hundreds and hundreds of galloping horses.

She had no face. It was half an hour before anyone could identify the body. It was the Duchess of Teck, born Claudia Rhédey, mother of three, twenty-six years old, and at the peak of her beauty and happiness.

When Dali learned that the victim was Claudia, it so utterly shocked him that he rode back to Buda without even calling on his mother, who always liked to see the twins on their birthday, and recite the traditional family prayer of thanksgiving with them.

Dali was in tears when he told Dushenka what had happened. "I know it was not my fault," he said. "Still, my horse helped kill her." For the first time in many months, he truly yearned for Dushenka's tenderness, for a word of consolation or reassurance from her.

Dushenka did not try to console him. She said nothing. She

was pale, too. She had a cold feeling that it was not the duchess Dali had killed, but herself. Dali had lied to her in St. Petersburg. He lied when he said that she was his first love. And now . . . this horrible accident revealed the truth: his first love—perhaps, no probably—his only love had been the duchess . . . the greatest beauty in the monarchy. It was natural, of course. Perfectly natural. But oh, how he had lied!

A day later Dushenka was horribly ashamed of the rage she had directed at the poor duchess, who had died such a hideous death. Jealousy is a terrible vice, she told herself, if it can reach even to the grave. And she resolved that she would never give way to it again. But at the back of her mind lay the belief that Dali had never truly loved her. It changed her, that belief. She no longer wept when Dali left her alone, and in his presence she seemed more cheerful than she had in months. But inwardly, she was not happier; only changed.

Before Christmas, Dushenka received a large package from Novgorod. The sender was Sylvester's mother. But because Madame Bralin could not write, her letter was written by Sylvester. The Christmas gift was a beautiful balalaika. Dushenka answered the same day:

My dear Aunt Katyushka!
There are many dinner parties in our house given for my husband's political friends. Even if I spoke Hungarian better than I do, I would not understand their conversation. They talk about nothing but politics. Sometimes Dali travels in the country for political meetings, and I am left with my children, Ádám, two and a half years old, and Sonya, thirteen months. Since Nyanya's death there has been no one around me who speaks Russian. But now I am not alone! God bless your wonderful idea, my dear Aunt Katyushka. The balalaika! I am singing again not only to myself, but sometimes to our guests.
Now I will tell you a few sweet stories about my children. Little Ádám asked me yesterday . . .

And there followed a dozen children's stories, the same all over the world. Aunt Katyushka could not read. Therefore the letter was read by Sylvester. That way the correspondence between Novgorod and Buda-Pesth was absolutely innocent.

After Kossuth started his daily paper under the unpretentious title *Pesti Hirlap, Pesth News,* political life in Hungary became very animated. "Hungary's fate is the fate of the Danube Valley, perhaps the fate of Europe," read an article in *Pesti Hirlap,* "for Hungary is the anvil of the two, huge sledge hammers: Fichte's German nationalism from the West, and Russia's imperialism from the East."

The only difference between Vienna's and Buda-Pesth's political thinking was that, as a bulwark against growing Prussian and Russian strength, Metternich wanted the Habsburg monarchy to become the strongest power in Europe, even at the price of the oppression of its subject nations; and Kossuth wanted the same bulwark in the Danube Valley, even at the price of keeping the Habsburg dynasty on the throne. But Kossuth demanded independence and a constitution for Hungary, and reforms. First of all, the liberation of the serfs.

During his three years in prison, Kossuth had read copiously in his cell; he had learned English, and knew all about Great Britain's and the young United States' democracies.

6

In the spring of 1842, Dali spent a whole week in Pozsony, where the Diet was in session. His mission there completed, he arranged to take the boat back to Buda-Pesth. His conscience troubled him, for when he had gone to Pozsony, he had told Dushenka he would return in three days. And now again he had left her alone for a week. Dali found it almost impossible to explain the intricate political situation and the importance of the present issue to the sweet, naïve girl from Novgorod who happened to be his wife.

For the most part the new electric device, the telegram, was used, even by wealthy people, only to announce a birth or a death in the family. The postal clerk in Pozsony looked up at Dali from the brass wheels of his clicking, fantastic instrument in surprise when he read the unusually long message:

"Arrive Monday evening on *Argot* with lots of gifts for you and children. Happy to embrace and kiss you again. Yours as ever Dali."

In the blue twilight the streetlamps were already lighted on the Pesth shore in honor of *Argot*'s arrival. Last time Dali had returned here on the *Argot,* Dushenka had been standing under one of the lamps, waving a large white kerchief. But tonight, she was not there.

"She will come," Dali assured himself. *Argot* had arrived some ten minutes before schedule, because of high water and a steady tailwind. In her days as an actress, Dushenka had learned to be precisely punctual, not only for performances, but for every appointment in her life. She will come, Dali thought.

But at seven, she had not come. The other passengers and the crowd that had greeted them had already dispersed. Dali decided to go home. He gave his heavy valise to a porter, and, crossing the long pontoon bridge, he climbed the Buda hill so fast that the porter could hardly keep up with him.

Dushenka's room was dark and empty.

Holding an oil lamp high in his left hand, Dali entered the bedroom. At first he saw nothing unusual, but then his eye caught the white square of an envelope on the dark bed cover.

"Suicide!" Dali exclaimed, even before he had read the letter. The envelope was open and the address was but: "To Dali."

Dali could hardly recognize Dushenka's handwriting. She had written in Hungarian, which she knew only slightly, and most of the words were misspelled.

"Forgiv me Dali. I am go back to Novgorod. Sylvie you knew the baker's son was here came unexpectedly takes me home. Am sick very homesick. Left Ádám for you took Sonya with I. Forgiv me Dali. Forgiv."

Holding the oil lamp in his left hand and the letter in his right, Dali stood frozen in shock. Then he cried "Julie! Julie!"

When, minutes later, Dushenka's maid entered the room with three-year-old Ádám in her arms, Dali still stood immobile, the lamp in one hand and the letter in the other. At sight of his son, he carefully placed the lamp on the table, pocketed the letter, and asked Julie, so calmly that it seemed as if everything had happened with his knowledge and consent:

"When did they leave? Yesterday?"

"Today. Three this afternoon. With the mailcoach."

Dali nodded and smiled at Ádám, his fingers slowly arranging the little boy's disheveled hair. Then he turned and left the room. Once out of sight, he dashed to the stable, hastily saddled Falcon, and within seconds, he was galloping downhill. "They left at three . . . the mailcoach . . . they are going through Warsaw," he thought. Falcon's flying hooves struck red sparks from the cobblestones in the narrow streets. The blue twilight had turned to dark evening when Dali reached the open highway leading to the north. He whipped Falcon as violently as if he had lost his mind. Was there any hope of catching up with the mailcoach? Was there any hope that the old heavy coach had lost or broken one of its wheels, as it often did? It was not easy for Dushenka . . . her trembling handwriting showed that . . . she was in a dreadful state of mind making her decision. Could she have changed her mind in the mailcoach? Perhaps she was already on her way back in a chartered coach.

The road was empty. Only a thin half moon answered these desperate questions. Dali whipped Falcon more and more violently.

After a half hour, Falcon stumbled, fell and rolled over, throwing Dali far out of the saddle. Bruised but not seriously hurt, Dali got up and turned to Falcon. His expert eyes immediately revealed that the horse's right front leg was broken. He looked around—the road was empty. No trampling of hooves, no rattling of wheels gave the slightest sound. Silence stretched to the faraway horizon.

He knew his duty toward a horse with a broken leg. He pulled out his pistol and shot Falcon through the head. He watched the horse as its delicate legs twitched in an agonized kick. And then, with a loud breath, Falcon expired.

The double-barreled pistol was still smoking in Dali's hand, when he looked around again. He seemed to be asking some question of the still, dark night. There was no answer. The half moon hung, remote and indifferent, in the indifferent sky. Somewhere far distant, a dog barked in the empty world. Dali lifted his pistol with the slow dazed gesture of one who does not know what he is doing, and fired the second bullet into his chest.

Hours later a peasant hay cart came along, drawn by two tired oxen. Three peasants were snoring peacefully in the hay.

The oxen stopped, trembling, before the pool of blood, where Dali lay across Falcon's silky neck.

The peasants took the unconscious Dali in their cart to the nearest hospital in a small town.

Dali's fever was high, but the bullet had just missed the heart.

His condition was serious, but he would live, the doctor reported to Endre.

When Endre received the hospital's report, the family already knew from Julie how Dushenka had disappeared with little Sonya, and how Dali had desperately dashed after her.

Endre's remark was: "I always felt there was some black, fatalistic strain in his nature."

Physically, Dali recovered well. His wound healed quickly, and he was soon out of bed, able to sit in an armchair by the open window. But his mind was near total collapse. What was there left to live for? He had sold his mission in St. Petersburg for love; in Buda, he had sold his love for his mission. The warm sweet jasmine fragrance, floating profusely through the open window, brought back Dushenka's face with a heartbreaking vividness. It had been her favorite perfume.

When Dali left the hospital, he moved to Ararat, and never returned to his Buda house where he had spent four happy years with Dushenka. Weeks later he told Andris and Tonchi that Dushenka's departure had been decided months before, because of her incurable homesickness, and that their separation had been perfectly friendly.

"It wasn't easy either for her or for me," he said. And he added after a moment:

"One never pays back one's life to God in one sum, but in installments."

He paid one of these installments on a May evening, when, strolling in Ararat park with his mother, he suddenly stopped and closed his eyes.

"Don't you feel well?" Countess Jadi asked him anxiously.

"I'm all right," Dali said, and continued their walk.

But he was carrying the pungent scent of a jasmine shrub they had just passed, as a knife in his heart.

It is said that every man lives as long as he wants to live. Dali seemed to have lost his joy of life and the will to live. When he returned to the room in Ararat castle where he had spent his youth, he sent his son Ádám to live with Andris' wife, Irma, who had only a three-year-old daughter.

Except for his early morning ride, now in the saddle of Falcon IV, a two-year-old colt, he buried himself in the castle's library.

At the end of September, he received a letter from Dushenka. It was a letter of warm congratulations for Dali's twenty-eighth birthday. In her poor French, Dushenka explained that the Orthodox Church did not regard a Roman Catholic marriage as valid. She was therefore free without even getting a divorce. And she had married Sylvester Bralin, who had already adopted Sonya.

"Don't be surprised," Dushenka wrote, "if I sign this letter 'Sonya.' It was, you know, Dimitri Kantemir who gave me the name Dushenka. Even in those days at the Lomonosoff, Sylvester always called me by my original Novgorod name: Sonya. Now Dushenka—poor Dushenka—is dead."

Dali answered in a friendly, if less sentimental tone, wishing happiness for her and Sylvester, "who will live in my memory until I die as one of my saviors when I plunged into the water from the Schlüsselburg prison." At the end of the letter he wrote a few sentences about Ádám's health, height and weight, and quoted a few of the boy's *bons mots,* as Dushenka had written about Sonya.

Although Dali tried to hide it even from himself, his mood was one of complete apathy. For months he lost interest in all political meetings and sometimes became aggressive in political discussions.

After the New Year, Countess Jadi brought old Doctor Kunz from Vienna to Ararat to see her ailing son.

"How do you feel, Dali?" the doctor asked him.

"I have a very serious disease, but I have found a much better doctor than you."

"What's your trouble, and who's your doctor?"

"It is a bad case of pig-disease. Fortunately my doctor is the Scottish critic, Thomas Carlyle."

When Countess Jadi left them alone, Dali continued:

"Carlyle says that living only for eating, for digesting, for sleeping, for making love, is a pig philosophy, and this philosophy is found most commonly in rich aristocratic circles."

Old Doctor Kunz put a consoling hand on Dali's shoulder.

"Forget your pig-disease, my boy. You are a young, healthy, highly intelligent pig."

April 12, 1843, the anniversary of the day Dushenka had left him, Dali wrote in his diary:

Tonchi said once that he is a dead man because he was hanged in effigy. It was a joke. But I am in dead earnest when I say that I died after I shot Falcon through the head and wanted to kill myself. Now, after a year, I have been born again as a new man. I made a vow last night, like Buddha or Saint Simon; I will sacrifice my life for a high ideal. Women, family over. I feel it my duty as an aristocrat. I don't want to die a healthy, highly intelligent pig.

Dali read every book of history and philosophy which was not in classic Greek. But he knew Latin, still a living language, even for new jokes. The old saying: *plenus venter non studet libenter* (stuffed stomach does not like work) had recently been extended with *sed vacuus eo minus!* (but an empty one even less). The allusion was to the poor. Despite its humorous side, the saying had already become a battle cry.

In that year 1843, social problems could no longer be solved by psalm singing, or with the circulation of unctious tracts. The *vacuus venter*, the empty stomach, had become a huge, threatening ghost. There were steady hunger catastrophes in Asia—the Chinese, Hindu and the Russian poor sometimes ate the rotten roofs of their thatched houses. And in the seven lean years of a prolonged drought, many people starved to death in Europe, too.

Andris came to see Dali and Tonchi almost every weekend, sometimes in the company of political friends. And he usually found Polish patriots or itinerant German intellectuals in Ararat castle. Since Byron's letters of travels and Goethe's "Journey in Italy," travelling had become virtually compulsory, first of all for writers. As there was a lack of hotels in the country, most of the castle's guest rooms were open for the "immortals." Sometimes for months.

Dali's guests held long symposia at Ararat.

"Subscribe to the *Reinische Zeitung*," suggested Robert Prutz, the playwright from Bonn. "It is a good medicine against blindness!" he added, throwing the small paper on Dali's table. "People in your country don't see what is going on in the new, western generation, first of all in Germany."

Dali leafed through the paper.

There was an article called "Life of Jesus," written by David Frederich Strauss, which stripped the gospels of their sanctity.

"There is nothing new in that article," Dali said. Since the departure of Dushenka, Dali had been in revolt against the Church, even questioning the existence of God. Influenced by the pantheist Spinoza and the positivist Comte, he said to Prutz: "I am afraid that in our day God has been reduced to a universal policeman!"

A second article in the *Reinische Zeitung*, written by George Herweg, demanded higher wages for the iron workers in every country, not only in Germany. A leading article, written by the editor-in-chief, Karl Marx, said:

"Religion is the opium of the people. The people cannot be really happy until it has been deprived of illusionary happiness by the abolition of religion."

"How old is Herr Marx?" Dali inquired, reading the paper.

"Twenty-four, I guess."

"I see . . ." Dali said in the tone of a matured man of twenty-eight.

The literary section published the first act of a play written by Robert Prutz. Now Dali understood why Prutzie, as they called him, always carried the *Reinische Zeitung* in the pocket of his long, shabby coat.

The topic of their symposium was always worthy of serious discussion.

"What is love?" Dali once wondered aloud. "Love is the most selfish of passions. The admiration of our lover is a flattering mirror, in which we happily see evidence of our physical and spiritual perfection. And when our lover leaves us, it is not the lover whom we mourn, but the happy image of ourselves—gone with the broken mirror. Am I right?"

He never mentioned Dushenka's name. But looking at Dali's lonely face, Tonchi changed the subject.

The trio feverishly supported Kossuth's policy, though a Hungarian-Polish personal union was not in Kossuth's program.

"Hungapole," as Dali had once dubbed it, was very rarely mentioned in their talks. Hungapole was dying out, as one of those dinosaurs which lived in the boisterous political dreams of the young century and in the boisterous minds of young men.

Dali resumed his duty as mounted messenger, and now Andris rode at his side more often than he had seven years before, when Kossuth had not yet been arrested and jailed. Spurring their horses from the eastern Carpathians to the sunny hills of the famous Tokaj vineyards, from the Polish frontier in the north down to the southernmost town of Orsova on the Lower Danube shore, they were feverishly organizing Kossuth's followers into clubs and societies under different and innocent-sounding titles, like "Hercules Club for Classic Wrestlers" (meaning the fighters for reforms), "Trainers of Untrained Lipizzaner Horses" (meaning the pro-Habsburg Hungarians), "Botanical Society for the Lovers of Wild Flowers" (meaning the serfs), and so on. Among hundreds of other riders in all of Hungary's sixty-three counties, they posted two confidential agents, trained by Kossuth.

In August, István Varga, one of Kossuth's volunteer secretaries, interviewed a young man who wanted to be a courier. The applicant did not speak Hungarian.

"Because you are a prince," Varga told him in German, "you will receive twice Dali's salary, for he is only a count." Varga, of course, was joking; for Dali received no salary.

"*Danke vielmals, Gnyadigerr Herr!*" said the boy, with a heavy Polish accent.

The new courier was Dali's second cousin, Prince Mycislav Voronieczki. Though only nineteen "Myci" was already an ardent Polish patriot. Myci's hair was carrot-red. An excellent horseman, he was assigned as a liaison between Buda and the Warsaw underground. Myci had not realized that Varga was joking about the salary, and told Dali of the interview, perfectly seriously, adding:

"How much is your salary?"

Weighing the question for a few seconds, Dali said:

"Fifteen florins a month."

"Oh!" Myci exclaimed happily, "then I will receive thirty florins!"

From that day on, Myci received his salary out of Dali's pocket. And the secret police report that went to Vienna read: "Prince Mycislav Voronieczki, a student from the Kracow University, entered into Kossuth's service as a mounted courier. We know that Kossuth is in steady financial troubles, and we do not as yet know the source of the funds used to pay his secretaries and couriers."

While Flexi, in Vienna, planned to double, or even triple the Dukay fortune by building factories and mechanizing the estate, Dali was reading Proudhon's new book, *What Is Property?* He corresponded with some "dangerous" thinkers too, among them Lamartine, the French poet and statesman who had been a liberal royalist, like Dali in his boyish dreams about Hungapole. But Lamartine was becoming more and more democratic in his opinions. The idea of democracy was conquering Western Europe. Even the old Catholic priest-philosopher, Lamnais, dreamed of the advent of a theocratic democracy. Dali's favorite writer was Chateaubriand, already nearing eighty. Dali felt that his own way of thinking resembled Chateaubriand's in its abhorrence of terror and violence.

8

In the summer of 1844, Western papers were in a fever over the brief and unexpected visit of Czar Nicholas to several foreign monarchs. His itinerary included a meeting with the Prussian king, a stop at the Hague, and a meeting in London with Queen Victoria.

"Birds of a feather flock together," Tonchi remarked, reading the papers. "People who live in high towers, don't like earthquakes."

"How do you mean that?" Dali asked.

"Well . . . there are too many reformers in London, like Cobden, and other liberals, to say nothing of Bonn, where Friedrich Johann Spiritza, Karl Marx and David Strauss, to name only a few, are pounding the table and demanding radical reforms."

Rolly and Alphie now lived in London, and Rolly wrote to her mother:

. . . I was among the spectators when the czar came through the entrance of Buckingham Palace. He had aged since I saw him five years ago in St. Petersburg. Bald and bulky. They gave him a review in Hyde Park, and it was really striking when the Duke of Wellington, in the full scarlet uniform of a Russian field marshal, at the head of his regiment, rode past and saluted the queen and the czar. Nicholas rode up to him and shook the old hero of Waterloo by the hand. Nicholas is so tall that Buckingham Palace ordered a specially long bed for him.

"Wonderful hospitality!" Tonchi said scornfully, when he saw Rolly's letter. "England ordered a specially large bed—for Asia!"

In October, Dali went to Vienna for a family dinner to celebrate his and Flexi's thirtieth birthday. Returning to his hermit life in Ararat, he wrote in his diary: "Thirty years! *Trente ans, comme le bon sans-coulottes Jesus Christ!* as Camille Desmoulin said as he stepped up to the platform of the guillotine. His Judas was his schoolmate and best friend: Robespierre. Who will be my Judas? And who will be Tonchi's or Andris' Judas? I don't like Tonchi's plan to visit Warsaw again. After so many years can he still trust all of his old friends in the Polish underground? Times change, people change, time changes people."

But Tonchi was determined to go. Along with his constant remarks about the rising tide of democratic ideals and demands for action in Germany and elsewhere, Tonchi revealed an increasingly strong desire to see Poland, too, producing strong intellectual leaders, who might challenge the power of the foreign overlord; ideas alone would not save Poland, but without ideas, all would be lost. Perhaps the time was not yet quite ripe for open agitation—then, Tonchi would work with the underground. The important thing, he reasoned, was readiness. When the moment came, whether it proved to be a moment for talking or for shooting, Poland should not be found wanting in men and ideas of her own.

Andris shared Dali's misgivings about Tonchi's proposed trip and together they managed to persuade him to wait.

Dali's son, Ádám, still lived in Zekerd, with Andris and Irma. Much as he loved the boy, Dali could not bear to keep him at Ararat, where he would have no one but a servant to act as his mother, and the sight of him would be a constant reminder of Dushenka. The generous fifty silver florins a month Dali paid for Ádám's keep in Zekerd was a great help to Irma, for Andris was, as always, short of money. The first few French words Ádám wrote went to his mother in Novgorod for Christmas.

Dushenka answered Ádám in French:

Your little sister Sonya already speaks fluent Russian, and I am afraid she has forgotten her very few Hungarian words. Tell your father that she is healthy, happy and beautiful, in contrast to old Sonya (me), who is a little unhappy about her weight. I've gained more than twenty pounds since I left Hungary. My husband's bakery is famous for its *piroshki,* a kind of dough stuffed with meat or roasted cabbage. It is delicious but it does not help a lady's figure.

Her weight was a reply to Dali's question as to whether she had seen her old friends at the Lomonosoff, and whether she had any plans to continue her theatrical career.

After New Year's Day, in spite of Dali's warning, Tonchi refused to postpone his trip to Poland any longer and moved his headquarters from Bonn to Warsaw. He was, as he put it, following "the strong undercurrent of the spiritual ocean."

The spring of 1845 was rather uneventful. Kossuth's popularity throughout the country grew steadily, and Dali and Andris were constantly busy in his service. On the first day of May, when they returned from Pesth, after a political meeting, to Ararat, they found young Prince Voronieczki, the liaison between Buda and the Polish underground, at the entrance door, impatiently waiting for their arrival.

"*Er was . . . er was . . .*" he said in his broken German breathlessly, "*er was verhaften!*"

"Who? Who was arrested?"

"The . . . the Monsieur."

"Which . . . who . . . which Monsieur?"

"Monsieur la Harpe."

Pale with emotion, Dali asked:

"Tonchi?"

"Ja."

And Myci told them that when trouble had broken out in Warsaw last week and Tonchi had fled to Lemberg in the Austrian section of Poland, thinking that his papers from the chancellery would protect him there, on the day of his arrival the secret police had picked him up.

Dali and Andris stared at one another in horror. Then Dali exclaimed:

"Let's go to Vienna!"

The next evening they arrived in Vienna on the steamship *Argot*. At Gisellastrasse, they held a secret conference with Countess Jadi. She was deeply shocked by their news. "Poor Tonchi," she said, and she covered her face with both her hands for a long moment. Then she turned to Dali:

"You know that your father would not dare intervene. Why don't you ask Metternich personally? Flexi has been granted an audience next week, to greet his godfather on his seventy-second birthday. Join Flexi! I am sure your father would like to show off his grown-up twins; he can open Metternich's door for you."

"Next week?" Dali said. "I'm afraid it will be too late."

"I am afraid, too," Andris agreed, gazing at the floor.

Countess Jadi stood up.

"Order my coach," she said to Dali. "And wait here. I will speak to Metternich."

She went alone to the chancellery. An hour later she returned, looking dejected.

"Baron Eigler told me that your earliest chance to talk to the chancellor will be at Flexi's audience in the middle of next week. He showed me his serenity's appointment list, and it is already overcrowded."

"Next week . . . next week . . ." Dali shook his head. "Too late."

But there was no other way.

CHAPTER SEVEN

In 1845, METTERNICH, AT seventy-two, was at the peak of his power. Liberal journalists in Paris acknowledged him with such titles as "The Inquisitor of Europe," "The Arch Enemy of Human Rights," "The Hangman of Poland," "The Butcher of Lombardia," to mention only a few.

The golden-white door of the Austrian chancellor's study opened to admit the most important persons in the monarchy and dignitaries from abroad. It also opened, at times, to less-distinguished visitors about whom, for one reason or another, the police felt some concern.

Metternich often used the "system of interviews," even when the report of his secret police labeled a visitor *S.G.* for *sehr gefährlich*—Very dangerous. The erudition of the radical intellectuals he met in these interviews gave him reliable information about what was boiling in Europe, more effectively than the most detailed police reports could have done.

When Metternich decided to grant an audience to the Dukay twins, he did so because he wanted to improve his knowledge of the younger generation.

Flexi appeared for the audience dressed in black coat and English trousers, Dali in hussar uniform. They arrived at the chancellery a few minutes before seven in the morning. Their appointment was set for seven. The vaulted corridors of the chancellery were alive with the buzzing of clerks, couriers, and secretaries carrying big files under their arms, bumping into each other in their haste. At the main door of the corridor, Flexi handed the invitations to an Uhlaner captain in gala uniform, who opened the door before them. The secretary in the anteroom glanced at the two names briefly, and wordlessly opened the golden-white French doors with a humble bow. The ceremony seemed like an unknown rite of some mystic religion.

Beyond the golden-white French doors was yet another door, opened for the twins by yet a third attendant, who announced:

"Their excellencies, the Counts Antal and Adalbert Dukay."

The twins entered—first, the firstborn Flexi, then the lesser Dali. The two visitors stood at the door and bowed deeply to the old chancellor, who was sitting at his Louis Quatorze desk some thirty feet from the door. His serenity was reading a file, and at first did not look up when the visitors entered.

"Father told me," Flexi whispered, "that Uncle Clemi's ears are weakening. Let's make a louder bow," he suggested. Flexi was trying to cheer Dali up, for though he did not know the reason for his brother's tragic expression, he could see that something was wrong. But Dali did not smile. He was scrutinizing Metternich, whom he had never seen before, carefully. He was surprised by the chancellor's youthful appearance. The profuse and carefully arranged locks around his forehead were snow-white, but his face was smooth and fresh. His heavily braided full dress and broad sash, adorned with his most prized decorations, were clearly mirrored in the black marble top of the huge desk, making him a legless, four-armed phantom with two heads, the one above clearly seen, the reflection below only imperfectly visible—exactly as it was with the Habsburg monarchy in these stormy years, Dali thought.

Metternich was reading the secret police files about his visitors.

"Count Antal Dukay, 30. Married Maria Augusta, Duchess of Schönheim-Altstadt. Father of two children. No drinking, no smoking; bets very heavily on horse races, including English Derby, with great luck. Godson of His Serenity the Chancellor. H.C."

The H.C. stood for *hoch* (high) *conservative*.

Metternich looked up, pretending to have just noticed his visitors' presence. He stood and moved around his desk a few steps toward them; his walk was vigorous; his well-formed knees and legs, in their white silk stockings, seeming unchanged from the time of the Congress of Vienna. He offered his hand first to Flexi, then to Dali.

"Sit down, gentlemen."

His voice was clear and, though soft, it carried authority.

Sitting back in the Gobelin armchair, he crossed his legs casually and let his hand dangle over the arm of the chair.

Flexi, as the firstborn and as godson, spoke first:

"We came to express our very best wishes on the occasion of Your Serenity's birthday."

"Thank you very much," said Metternich. Then asked sympathetically: "How is your father?"

Endre was on sick leave for two weeks. While Flexi reported on his father's liver ailment, Metternich glanced into the second report which read:

"Count Adalbert Dukay, twin brother of Antal. Close friend of Baron Andris Zeker, follower of Lajos Kossuth and other subversive persons. Restless, highly nervous. Suspected of epilepsy and pyromania. Had a love affair with Frau Malvin Hugel, wife of a pharmacist in Buda. Last December spent ten days in St. Rokus Hospital with venereal disease. Recently in Frankfurt he drew his sword in a fight with German ultranationalists. G2."

The red G2 meant that politically he was *Gefährlich,* dangerous, but only in the second degree.

Dali would have been greatly surprised by this report if he had read it. He had not spent a single day in St. Rokus Hospital. He had never drawn his sword in any argument; and he had never been in Frankfurt. All fantastic lies. He *had* had an affair with a Frau Hugel, but her name was not Malvin, but Paula. Malvin was her mother-in-law, an old toad.

Metternich finished skimming the report about Dali just as Flexi finished his report on his father's health. His serenity turned to Dali:

"Why don't you like the German nationalist movement, Count Adalbert?" he asked in a benevolent tone.

"I agree with Auguste Comte," Dali replied, "that the growing German nationalism is the new barbarism." Dali knew that Metternich also took a dim view of German ultranationalism, which planned, among other things, to swallow Austria.

Dali's eyes were fixed on the chancellor's face, and however loathesome was the name of Metternich for him, he could not deny that the face revealed a dignity of the soul, a classic harmony of head and heart. "He will give clemency for Tonchi," he thought.

"I don't think," Metternich said, "that barbarism is the right word for nationalism, but I vividly remember that once I wrote Wellington: I long felt that *my* country is Europe."

Bowing as deeply as possible from a sitting position, Dali said:

"I'm glad to hear it, sir. I have always known that Your Serenity has not the slightest touch of race prejudice."

Metternich did not take his blue eyes from Dali's face, but remained silent. There was something about this hussar he did not like. Craggy brow, large brown eyes, finely shaped nose, sensitive lips, his smile set off by an artificial eye-tooth, the face was visibly that of a man susceptible to the most emotional idealism—he looked the very type of the crazy Hungarian whose idol was Kossuth.

Reclining gracefully in his chair, supporting his face with two long fingers, Metternich patiently listened to the second-born Dukay. Along with the nervous aggressiveness in the young man, there was undoubtedly some brilliance; his analysis of changing society, as he traced the development of capitalistic production and the growth of the working class, showed that.

The old chancellor turned toward the flower-covered garden beyond the large window and spoke meditatively, as if he were alone.

"I am a Rhinelander myself. I know what is going on there. My heart bled when I had to sell one of my oldest vineyards to make room for a new metallurgical factory."

"The unavoidable clash between the factory owners and the new working mass," Dali began, but Metternich cut him short.

"Mass!" he exclaimed. "You want to transform the Gospels into speculative truth! Changing *persons* into fragmentary men, into blind, stupid and dangerous masses!"

Hoping to smooth the situation, Flexi interrupted.

"Your Serenity is right," he said flatteringly. "The Hegelian truth is a speculative truth."

"But a new kind of conscience dawns in Western Europe," Dali said, raising his voice, "demanding freedom and independence for all the nations, fundamental rights for all individuals."

"I assume," Metternich interrupted him, "you're a great admirer of Goethe. Well, as I remember, Goethe said, 'Only law can give us happiness.' Law, my friend!" His finger knocked on the black marble top of the desk. "Law!" And when he glanced at the huge renaissance standing clock, it meant that the audience was over.

"I would like to ask a great favor from Your Serenity," Dali said, changing not only the topic, but his tone, too.

"A friend of mine . . . and of my family . . . was arrested in Lemberg. No one knows why."

"What is his name?" Metternich asked in the tone of a man ready to help, and his hand reached for a pencil.

"Antoine Jules la Harpe."

Flexi looked at Dali in surprise. Dali had not told him, or their father, of Tonchi's arrest.

The chancellor's hand stopped in mid-air, then changed its course and fished a file out of his drawer.

"His name was never la Harpe," he said in an icy voice. And lifting the report closer to his narrowed eyes he read: "His real name is Hyron Ty-e-mi-niczky-Yojtkowski. He was hanged twice by the Russians in effigy. You said he was a friend of your family?"

And the chancellor looked at Flexi, who had turned pale at his words.

"He was my brother's tutor," Flexi said. "All of us knew him as a Swiss, very loyal and conservative . . . and . . ."

"And a very dangerous revolutionist!" Metternich said. He turned to Dali, raising his voice: "Have you ever witnessed a revolution? You have not, *mein lieber Freund!*"

In no other language can the phrase, "My dear friend!" be as insulting as in German. The old chancellor's gray face turned red, his faded blue eyes burned with cold fire as he shouted:

"You didn't live in the French Revolution! But I was a student in Strasbourg when parts of butchered bodies were carried through the streets on pikes! And I saw children playing in the gutters—with severed heads! Do you know what a revolution is? The lost illusion of man's dignity. In Paris, after his parents had been guillotined so they would be 'deglorified,' the dauphin, that poor child, was left to squat for months in his own ordure!"

He threw the file back into the drawer, put his fist on his Louis Quinze desk, and said harshly:

"Let me tell you this. I am willing to give clemency to a man who has murdered his father, but never to anyone who wants to murder his fatherland!"

He stood up and, with a brief nod, ended the audience with no handshake.

2

The military prison was located in the left wing of the Lemberg barracks. After the western part of divided Poland, called Galicia, had been given to Austria by the Congress of Vienna, the huge barracks in Lemberg sheltered the Habsburg monarchy's two most reliable infantry regiments, keeping order and peace in that explosive part of Europe. The barracks were named after Archduke Ludwig, one of the crown council's members, who made decisions in the name of the *knödl*-crazy Emperor Ferdinand.

The commandant of the prison, an old Austrian colonel, was having his breakfast at six when his aide-de-camp reported:

"Two couriers from Vienna, with an urgent order from the chancellor."

The old colonel jumped up and with trembling fingers buttoned his collar; he swallowed, grabbed his sword, and hurried to his office.

One of the couriers, a dragoon captain, clicked his heels and reported as he entered:

"My name is Count Otto von Rolsen . . ."

"Your servant," said the old colonel, giving him a friendly hand.

"Herr Oberst," the other courier, an uhlaner lieutenant clicked his heels too, and introduced himself: "My name is Baron Rudolph von Hessenstein, lieutenant of the . . ."

"Your servant," the old colonel interrupted the formality with a friendly handshake. He was neither a count, nor a baron; not even a Von.

Count Rolsen presented him with a large, official envelope of the chancellery, sealed with a violet wax.

"A special, urgent order from His Serenity, Prince Clemens Metternich," he said.

The letter was addressed to the Commandant of the Military Prison, Ludwig Barracks, Lemberg, and—in Metternich's own handwriting—read:

"I have learned that through some mistake Monsieur Antoine Jules la Harpe, alias Herr Hyron Tyeminicki-Vojtkowski was placed under arrest in Lemberg. Give him to my couriers Count von Rolsen and Baron van Hessenstein. I want to talk with him. This is a delicate political matter."

The colonel rang the bell, hastily scribbled the name on a slip of paper and handed it to his aide-de-camp.

"Bring me this prisoner . . ." he said. When the aide-de-camp left, he turned to his visitors:

"He will be here in just a moment."

The herculean dragoon captain, Count Otto von Rolsen, occupying the largest armchair, said:

"We are taking Monsieur la Harpe to Vienna. His serenity wants to apologize to him personally."

"Oh, yes, his serenity is very kind," said the colonel, as he poured cognac for his guests. "In a big machine like ours, mistakes are unavoidable—sometimes even fatal. *Prosit!*"

The chancellery's official stationery had been stolen from Endre Dukay's office, and his letter forged by Dali.

They drank, and "Baron von Hessenstein" asked the colonel:

"How is Monsieur la Harpe?"

"All right, I hope," the colonel said. "I haven't seen him personally . . . we have over 1,500 prisoners. The food is not luxurious but no one starves. And I don't tolerate rough treatment. Any news from Vienna? How is his serenity? I've had the honor to talk with him . . ."

Steps were heard approaching down the corridor, and "Count Rolsen" and "Baron Hessenstein" stood up to greet the prisoner.

The door opened but instead of Tonchi, the aide-de-camp entered with a sergeant-of-the-guards who reported to his commandant:

"Herr Oberst, the prisoner's record showed two previous

Russian convictions. At the request of the Paskievich Barracks in Warsaw, we have handed him over to the Russians."

"When?" cried the colonel.

"Monday last. Major Hahn signed the order."

The colonel waved him away angrily and, turning to his visitors, raised his arms and said:

"I am frightfully sorry. His serenity's letter came too late. Sit, please. I shall write out my report right away."

"No, thank you," said "Count Rolsen," "we will report it to his serenity."

They clicked their heels, gave the military salute, and left.

Dali and Andris were pale as they left the Lemberg barracks.

It was Andris who spoke first:

"If the Russians have him taken over I am very much afraid . . ."

He did not continue.

Dali made no reply.

"Anyhow," Andris said, to ease the tension of their silence, "the colonel is happy. The old idiot will frame Metternich's letter and it will go down in history as a shining proof of the most humane chancellor's delicate treatment of his political prisoners."

To most, it is much less painful to know conclusively that someone is dead than to keep him alive in thought as missing. Was Tonchi still living? There was no death penalty in Russia. Only the *Palkin,* the stick. For Dali it was unbearable to think of Tonchi tied to the whipping post, howling in pain. There was a possibility that he had been deported to Siberia. That was the best he could hope for. Many Siberian exiles survived; they enjoyed the company of other "subversive" intellectuals; and in many cases clemency came unexpectedly soon, sometimes in ten, even five years.

After his unsuccessful venture to Lemberg, Dali wrote to Dushenka. He received her answer within a month:

I went to St. Petersburg and got in touch with all our former friends to learn what happened to Tonchi. Last Christmas, after Prince Igor's marriage to Olga Serebraniy, the two went honeymooning to the Crimea on the Black Sea. It is almost certain that they won't come back. As you must have heard, Princess Olga sold the Serebraniy palace in Karamsin Street, with all its art treasures. But you may not know that Prince Igor likewise disposed of his estate in the Urals. Old Yashvil told me he believes they will live in Switzerland or in the United States. Without their help neither I nor Sylvie could learn anything of T.'s fate.

3

After Tonchi's disappearance, Andris said to Irma one day:

"I am afraid the loss of Dushenka and Tonchi was too much for Dali. One day he is depressed, the next he is too optimistic; his ideas are too brilliant, he is dreamy and confused. He talks constantly of Tonchi, and repeats the words 'Metternich must go! Must!'"

"So what?" Irma asked. "Are you sorry for Metternich?"

"No. I am sorry for Dali. I don't like his look and the way he says 'must.'"

Alone at Ararat, analyzing Tonchi's unknown fate, Dali became convinced that Tonchi had died under the *palkin*. Poor Tonchi was forty-five years old, and in the last months had complained to Doctor Kunz about pain in his left kidney. No, he could have not survived the *palkin*.

In Dali's thoughts it was Metternich who had murdered him. It was Metternich's police who arrested him, and it was Metternich's staff in Lemberg which, out of sheer politeness, had handed him over to Czar Nicholas' torturers.

Whenever Countess Jadi went to the early Mass at Ararat chapel, Dali accompanied her. And when his mother knelt on the stone floor, he knelt behind her. But he did not stare at the pomp of the altar, at the flames of the candles; he did not listen to the hocus-pocus of the *Hoc est corpus;* he stared at the soles of his mother's shoes, as they peeped out from under her long velvet skirt while she was kneeling. And on the empty soles of her shoes, God was written more clearly than in any book. These moments in the chapel crushed all the theories in David Frederich Strauss' Christ-denying "Life of Jesus."

The following year, in May, 1846 the pro-government *Lemberg Nachricht* carried an article praising Count Adalbert

Dukay for his donation of ten thousand silver florins to the SASGL, Society of Advanced Studies of the German Language, at Lemberg University.

Andris knew what was behind the society. It was a cover for a secret "Metternich must go" movement in Poland. Several hundred reliable students and over 1,000 non-student members were drawn from every corner of Poland: tough, veteran Poles who hated Metternich's drastic proposals to Germanize this part of Poland under Austrian occupation.

There were secret meetings at Ararat. The old trio had been replaced by a quartet: Dali, Andris, an army major named Jozsef Nagy-Sándor, and Karl Leiningen. Sometimes Polish patriots participated in these secret meetings, among them the carrot-haired Mycislav Voronieczki, now twenty-one.

"How much is the membership fee in the SASGL?" Karl Leiningen inquired.

"Death on the gallows," Voronieczki answered.

In 1846 Kossuth's star was ascending. His final aim was more than "Metternich must go"; it was the old dream of the nation: "The Habsburgs must go." The Italians in Lombarde-Venetia were no less dissatisfied than the Poles and the Hungarians with the Habsburg rule.

The time had come to act.

In March of 1847, Dali travelled to Poland for a gala performance of the SASGL in Lemberg.

The evening opened with a half-hour lecture by the Austrian Dean of the University, who waved the audience to stand while he thanked God for giving the monarchy the wise and benevolent Emperor Ferdinand and the great chancellor, Prince Clemens Metternich.

The first performer was a student who, in high-pitched tones, recited three long Schiller poems. Then other students, with horrible Polish accents, declaimed poems by Goethe and Johann von Struber (the dean of the university) in German.

Around midnight the final curtain fell. Some twenty students remained, sweeping and cleaning the stage, the hall and the corridors. But when the streets outside were silent and deserted, they went to the basement and locked themselves into one of the deepest cellars, leaving three watchmen, one at the entrance of the building, a second near the basement door, and the third in the narrow cellar corridor leading to the meeting room.

That night Dali participated in their secret meeting. The students asked Dali to obtain an audience for them with the chancellor in Vienna.

"We want to give him a nice, elaborate report about the great achievement of our society," said young Ivor Radowski, a second cousin of Dali's. He stepped closer.

"Do you notice anything suspicious on my coat?"

He was dressed in a richly trimmed black coat, with decorative cords running parallel and horizontally across the chest. But one of the loops was not cloth cord, but black iron, covered with the same stuff; it served as the hilt of a small dagger, only three inches long.

Dali shook his head.

"No, boys, I do not believe in murder," he said.

Passionate voices asked:

"Then how do you propose to stop him? By argument? Poland has been bled to death! We can wait no longer!"

Waving them to silence, Dali said:

"I agree with you that we must stop him. But no murder. Under no circumstances. I have a better idea. How about kidnapping him: Holding him as a hostage?"

The students murmured uncertainly. Several seemed to favor Dali's suggestion, but a few were obviously bent on murder.

"Let's think it over," Dali said. "Tomorrow I will come again with more concrete ideas."

When Dali left the meeting, at one o'clock in the morning, the students remained in the carefully guarded basement to debate their ideas and Dali's. Around two o'clock, three pistol shots rang out—one at the entrance door, one at the basement door, the third in the narrow corridor of the cellar.

Five days later, two lines in the Vienna papers reported the detection of "a childishly planned conspiracy at the Lemberg University against the life of Prince Metternich." The participating students, the story read, were "severely punished."

The newspapers received no more details from the chancellery. But the words in the brief official communique, "severely punished," meant that more than 80 students and some 50 outside members of the SASGL were hanged, and some 200 more were hanged in effigy.

Dali, who had left the cellar before the raid, was not arrested.

In the middle of May, *Die Wienerische Zeitung's* headline read:

"Brichie, the zoo's youngest baby giraffe, ate a lady's hat and died."

On the seventh page along the *Nachrichten* there were two lines: "Count Adalbert Dukay, age 33, committed suicide in the Adler Hotel, Lemberg."

4

Even the most detailed maps of the *Kriegsministerium* in Vienna omitted Heron Island. The only excuse for such an omission was that only a few men knew of the island, which was hardly larger than the ballroom at Schönbrunn.

Heron Island had been named for a heron's nest atop a weeping willow, whose graceful boughs sheltered nearly a third of the tiny island. The island owed its existence to a Mesozoic sea, which had retired from that part of Eastern Europe millions and millions of years before, leaving behind the Danube, Lake Balaton and a few smaller rivers and lakes, as a hastily departing woman might leave her belt, handkerchief, some ribbons or hairpins in the bed or on the floor after a long clandestine night.

Heron Island lay in the middle of one of the ancient marshes, surrounded by a forest of reeds and protected by acres of bottomless mud, capable of swallowing a man on horseback. It took a *pákász*, a marsh dweller, to find the island, for the way was a labyrinth of narrow zig-zagging canals where the translucent water had carved paths through the treacherous mud. The military police, under the command of Major Erich Dukay-Hedwitz, were helpless in that jungle.

Heron Island was ruled by old Imre Kerge, the father of Pista Kerge, who had been killed by Count Leznay. Uncle Imre had a kettle, two knives, two rusty spoons and ten fingers for forks. He used flint and steel, with bits of dry punk, to make his fire. The few florins a year he required to buy tobacco, candles, salt, gunpowder and other supplies came from the sale of aigrette feathers, which ornamented the furred caps of gala uniforms, and of the pear-shaped, freckled, greenish eggs of lapwings, a great delicacy in *Le Tracteur* in Vienna.

It was a clear September morning, in the year 1847.

Old Kerge returned from his dawn fishing excursion in a noiseless boat, bearing a ten-pound pike wriggling on the tip of his harpoon. He started to build a fire, then went to the well for fresh water. The well was the marsh itself; the water in its canals was dirty and yellowish, and had an unpleasant stench. But old Kerge was a *pákász*. He sank a six foot reed into the brackish mud at the bottom of the marsh and sucked up pure, fresh cold water. Then he cleaned the pike, and placed it over the fire. Bodri, his watchdog, followed his every move with her melancholic amber-yellow eyes, her head tilted. For security purposes, she had been trained not to bark.

A daily visitor to the island was Toto, who arrived twice a day, at breakfast and dinner. Toto was always in a hurry, and always disappeared as soon as he had picked up his food. For a long time, Toto seemed the strangest animal in the world: a male otter in the morning and a female in the evening. The mystery was solved when, one day at breakfast, Toto introduced his wife and three children.

When the pike on the spit was thoroughly roasted, old Kerge stepped to the weeping willow, whose golden-green lacy branches, reaching to the ground, formed a leafy tent.

He called out:

"Pálinkás joreggelt!" which meant "Good morning with brandy!"

A moment later a man stepped from the willow tent, carrying on his arm a horsehair cover. The brown locks of his dishevelled hair hung to his shoulder. His thick moustache, shaped like a half-moon, resembled that of a Mongol Khan. His brown beard reached to the middle of his chest. The man yawned, stretched, then rinsed out his mouth and spat water into his palms, rubbing his face, ears and neck. After this morning toilet, he sat on a stone near the fire and had a voluptuous feast on the just roasted fish. Then he lit a big cigar and started to read the

Morning Post. This was strange behavior for a primitive *pákász*, living on an inaccessible island somewhere in Hungary.

The man's appearance was that of a man near fifty: but he was not fifty. According to the wanted list of the military police, he was thirty-three. His name was Adalbert Dukay, five feet eleven, 160 pounds, hanged in effigy last May, dishonorably discharged from the Pálffy Hussars, stripped of his right to his estate and of his title of count.

When this horrible news had reached Vienna, Endre Dukay had collapsed and remained unconscious for hours. No heavier blow could have befallen him.

When the conspiracy against Metternich's life was brought to light, Dali was described as the founder of the SASGL and the source of most of its funds. This description was substantially accurate, and, moreover, it was also common knowledge, not only to the police but to the public.

No one in the Viennese salons had believed the *Wienerische Zeitung's* story of Dali's suicide. This was reported to the paper by Dali's Polish cousin, young Prince Voronieczki, to mislead the police and the public. To Endre Dukay the suicide story was a consolation. When he regained consciousness after learning of Dali's disgrace, he had told Doctor Kunz: "I always felt that there was some dark and fatalistic strain in his nature." And he added: "He was never normal."

Endre's belief in the suicide version was shared by Flexi's wife, Maria Augusta. Flexi himself doubted the story, but he pretended to believe it. Four other versions were told in the salons: Dali had been shot by a Lemberg firing squad; he was locked up in a strait jacket in a mental institution; he had crossed the ocean and established a thriving bordello in Costa Rica, in company with his common-law wife, a Russian prostitute; he was in truth the mysterious Facia Negra, the dreaded bandit in Transylvania, who wore a black silk mask.

Countess Jadi wept—not for Dali, but for young Ivor Radowski, who was shot on the spot when the police discovered the dagger in his coat. Countess Jadi was the only one in the family who knew where Dali was. Through old Kerge, she remained in constant contact with her son.

Shortly before Christmas, when the marsh was frozen solid,

Countess Jadi, using the pretext of a fowl hunt, went secretly to visit Dali. When she saw him, she scarcely recognized him, in his long beard, half-moon moustache, and *pákász* dress. Mother and son spent three hours together.

Christmas was beautiful on Heron Island. The snow was knee-deep and the silence sky-deep above the sea of reed. When twilight fell, old Kerge lighted the candles on the small, decorated Christmas tree that Countess Jadi had brought the week before. The wind was perfectly still. When the flame of one of the little colored candles touched a pine branch, the smell of resin filled the clear, cold air with the warmth of old Christmas evenings. But there was no singing; and no children played around the tree.

Late one morning some six weeks later, when spring had thawed the waters of the canals, Bodri, sleeping near the open fire, jumped to her feet and dashed to the shore, waving her tail excitedly, her amber-yellow eyes gazing northward. Dali expected no one and could see nothing at first. Then a boat appeared, bearing three men.

"The one in the stern is our baron," noted old Kerge, who never needed a telescope.

Yes, as the boat came closer, Dali recognized Andris, then the bearded Colonel Nagy-Sándor and then Myci, Dali's Polish cousin, Prince Mycislav Voronieczki. The three men waved to Dali with wild enthusiasm. Andris shouted a few words, but the wind carried his voice away.

Now the boat was scarcely a hundred yards away. Andris stood up and cupped his big hands around his mouth. With all his strength he shouted:

"Last . . . night . . . the . . . revolution . . . broke . . . out . . . in Paris!"

The day was February 26, 1848.

The three visitors, sitting around the open fire, tried to analyze the situation while they enjoyed a meal of roasted fish, and drank the excellent wine Countess Jadi had sent to Heron Island.

"We saw Kossuth for a few minutes this morning before we came to you," Andris said to Dali.

"He was full of vitality," Myci said, "full of energy and full of plans."

They spoke in German because Myci did not understand Hungarian.

"What was Metternich's reaction?" Dali asked.

"We don't know yet," Andris said. "Most probably the same as during the 1830 Paris revolution. You remember, your father told then that when the first report reached his desk, he sneered: 'The madness of a few!' "

"For Metternich," Dali said, "every revolution is the madness of a few. Only 200 million or so."

"When his serenity is alone in the toilet," Andris added, "he is convinced that he is the majority in Europe."

They laughed while old Kerge opened a new bottle and filled their glasses.

Andris, Nagy-Sándor and Voronieczki left Heron Island when twilight fell. They advised Dali to stay at his hiding place until they knew what the outcome of the Paris revolution in Vienna and Buda-Pesth would be.

CHAPTER EIGHT

ON THAT FEBRUARY DAWN IN Paris, the people chased away Louis Philippe, the last Bourbon king. Prime Minister Guizot was reviewing the alerted national guard when a man grabbed the reins of his horse, and shouted: "Où sont les reformes promisés?" His hand was yellow-brown-black, typical of a tanner. Guizot beat off the dirty hand with his whip, spurred his horse, and rode back to the Tuilleries at full gallop minus his silk top hat.

The crowd pressed on the royal palace. Louis Philippe grabbed his famous green umbrella, and left the palace through a side door, with scarcely any money. The wrath and fury of the mob grew to gigantic proportion. Guizot, "everybody's servant," as he had recently called himself in a speech, fled from Paris dressed as a butler, as "somebody's servant."

In the two weeks after the Paris revolution broke out, the corridors of the chancellery buzzed more feverishly than in the busiest days of the Congress of Vienna. In many rooms, candles burned all night.

The birth of the Second French Republic set the whole world askew, but everyone knew the cause of this revolution. It was not an isolated French uprising. During the last three decades, stimulated by the Industrial Revolution, people everywhere demanded reforms. They wanted to enjoy the marvels of the new technology. They wanted better homes; they wanted to ride the new railways; they even wanted to send telegrams. Poultry farmers wanted to have incubators; everyone wanted something new, useful or even just funny from the Industrial Revolution. At the same time the great success of the young United States' and the South American countries' revolutions for independence and democracy had given not just hope and courage, but real determination to the oppressed nations of Europe. In Venice and in other towns in Northern Italy under Austrian occupation, the streets echoed with the shouts of angry mobs crying "Death to the Germans!" University students formed deputations to the government in Berlin, in Vienna, in Buda-Pesth and even in Warsaw, with demands for reforms. Most magnificent, for the first time in Europe's history, patriots had found a mighty ally in the organized workmen. The active cooperation of the new working class had put the revolutionists into power in Paris. For the first time, a Paris paper used the expression "The glorious new working class." And indeed, it was a new-born class, conceived in the womb of the system of factories and shops.

Growing up, the new working class was taught to walk by Louis Blanc, the socialist leader. In the bloody February revolution, it learned to fight.

In England's House of Commons, Benjamin Disraeli, whose unorthodox speeches were often amusing, said that in France "everything is going downhill at a *railroad pace.*"

"Railroad pace!" the prime minister mused. "Quite a new expression, fitting to the technological era."

Everyone in Europe knew that the Congress Period was giving way to the Period of Revolutions. Everyone knew, except one man, the oracle of Europe: Metternich.

Seeking his infallible opinion of the situation, Lord Ponsonby, the British ambassador in Vienna, was told:

"Don't worry. Nothing will happen. I am receiving information every hour about the Paris situation. The provisional government has opened relief works for the unemployed and the idle who thronged to Paris. They are now digging ditches, and building forts at a uniform wage of two francs a day. The job is useless and the wage is low, but it keeps the discontented busy and prevents any more riots until the conservative classes can regain control."

On March 10, Endre Dukay paid a brief secret visit to the Rennweg villa to see Metternich's third wife, a former Hungarian countess, Melanie Zichy.

"Princess, please don't tell his serenity that I came to see you. I don't like the whispering rumors about the general situation; I would like to suggest to you that you hide all your jewels in a private house, with a reliable friend. The friend should not be an aristocrat. Remember the French revolution."

The following day, Saturday, Andris Zeker arrived in Vienna; and in the afternoon, he witnessed the demonstration of the Polish university students.

The students, led by Dali's cousin Myci, gathered in front of the chancellery. There Myci began an ardent speech against Metternich; from time to time he was interrupted by the steady, rhythmic shouts of his followers: "Met-ter-nich re-sign! Met-ter-nich re-sign!"

The old chancellor's reaction to the demonstration was calm and quick. He gave the order to Baron von Eigler: "Alarm two batallions."

The demonstration was dispersed within an hour. On Sunday morning, Endre Dukay, although he did not feel too well, accompanied Countess Jadi to Mass in Stefanskirche. Both of them stayed on their knees for a long while after Mass. Among the worshipers was Princess Melanie. As Endre had requested, she had kept his visit secret. She had also ignored his advice about hiding her jewels in a private house. "Don't worry, dear," Metternich told her, when she asked him about the situation.

The next day was Monday, March 13. That day, Flexi telegrammed unbelievable news to Rolly and Alphie: "Revolution broken out in Vienna."

At one o'clock in the afternoon, the Austrian government realized the gravity of the revolt. Metternich, at the chancellery, was protected by troops. At two o'clock, all the suburbs were in an uproar. An officer of the "City militia," organized on the spot, brought the emperor the demand of the people for Metternich's dismissal. At that point, Metternich invested Prince Windischgrätz, one of his most determined generals, with extraordinary powers.

Flexi hurried to the chancellery to assist his father in any way he could. Then he ran back to Gisellastrasse to his wife and mother with the latest news. Later, he returned to be with his father. Maria Augusta, with an incessant *"Ach, mein Gott . . . Ach, mein Gott,"* made confused preparations to flee to Linz with their three children—Peter, Ilona and Paul.

At seven in the evening, grenadiers stood posted at the huge wrought-iron baroque marvel of the Burg's main gate. Angry demonstrators pelted them with the foulest abuse, but they stood there, fixed as statues, not moving a muscle. They did not use their rifles.

The Crown Council, called to session only on rare occasions, consisted of Emperor Ferdinand "Der Gütige"; Ferdinand's uncle, the Archduke Johann; and all the cabinet ministers, headed by Metternich.

When "Der Gütige" entered the great council hall, everyone stood. The faces of the archdukes and ministers and generals in the council were pale. Endre Dukay, dressed in a black attila, stood modestly by the wall. He had no seat in the council; he was attending only to demonstrate his unconditional loyalty to his emperor and to Metternich.

There was only one self-assured, smiling, and happy face in the Council, that of his majesty. Emperor Ferdinand V was fifty-five, but his pink face, gleaming with the great wisdom and benevolence of the good-natured idiot, made him appear younger.

Prince Metternich was the first to speak. The seventy-five-year-old chancellor had looked no more than sixty-five two weeks ago, the day before the Paris revolution broke out. Now he looked over eighty. But he was just as eloquent and wordy today as he had been thirty-four years before at Flexi's and Dali's christening.

When Metternich had harrangued the council for an hour and a half without appearing to be near the end of his statement, Archduke Johann pulled out his watch and said:

"Prince! In thirty minutes we must give an answer to the people."

The old chancellor stopped, surprised and angered by the interruption. A cabinet minister who had never liked Metternich broke the silence:

"It has always been his habit never to come to the point."

There was suppressed laughter. And that moment—the moment of that laughter—marked the end of Metternich's power.

"Are you aware, Prince, that the people's first demand is that you resign?" Archduke Johann asked.

Metternich's thin blue lips could still smile, and he calmly replied:

"Highness, when the Emperor Francis lay on his deathbed, I promised him I would never desert his son."

He gracefully bowed to Ferdinand V, who at that moment was trying to catch a fly in mid-air.

Passionate voices filled the council hall:

"You must resign! You are a danger for us all! Resign!"

The old chancellor bowed his snow-white head and said:

"I have ever been the humble servant of the Imperial House. Now, if the imperial family wishes me to resign . . ."

He was sure that Ferdinand would not let him down.

He was mistaken. One of his words boomeranged with a final blow.

"Family? Did you say family?" shouted Ferdinand. "Who is the emperor? I am the emperor! Didn't you know that?"

He beat his chest with both his fists.

"I am the emperor! It's for me to decide! I accept your resignation." And he raged at Metternich as if the chancellor were only Wenzel, his personal valet.

Metternich bowed to the emperor and without another word left the council chamber. He walked to the hall where they were waiting—the representatives of political, religious, and cultural groups of commerce and industry. They came for informa-

225

tion, or they came bearing information; they came for advice, or they came giving advice. In either case, they could not keep away in these fateful hours!

It was after nine. Of the huge retinue Metternich had only lately commanded, only three now stood at his side: his former personal secretary, Baron von Eigler; Endre Dukay; and his godson, Flexi. With immense dignity and calm, the old chancellor announced to the assembled company that he was laying down the office he had held for thirty-five years.

"I have been assured by his highness, Archduke Johann," he said, with a hint of irony in his tone, "that my resignation will be to the advantage of my country. God bless Austria! These gentlemen, will be my last words in this hall: when monarchies vanish, it is because they surrender."

And he left the hall.

Parva domus, magna quies, read the marble tablet above the entrance of Metternich's house on Rennweg. "Small house, great quiet." That night the tablet should have read: *Magna domus, parva quies.* The house was great, but there was little quiet in it. When Metternich returned from the Burg, in the company of Endre Dukay and von Eigler, Melanie looked at him anxiously.

"You must go to bed, Clemi," she said. And indeed, he did look wholly exhausted.

"No, dear. I feel well."

"You must!"

Old Metternich turned to Endre and von Eigler.

"You see. I may have ruled Europe but never Melanie."

He touched Melanie's shoulder with affection. Then, listening to the shouts of the mob in the neighboring streets, he said:

"I don't know what will happen during the next few days in Europe. Thank you, dear."

The "thank you, dear" was for Melanie, who had tied a warm kerchief around his neck.

On his way from the Burg to his house on Rennweg, Metternich had stopped to see a friend, Mr. Wood of the British ambassador's office. There he had secured for himself and Melanie not only passports as an ambassador's butler and cook, but also an English butler's suit. This he now donned, and said with a bitter smile: "I, the faithful servant of the House of Habsburg for a half century, I am now fleeing, like Guizot, as 'somebody's servant.' "

Acting on Endre's instructions, Flexi arrived with ten properly armed Dukay servants. Outside the *parva domus,* although it was raining, Endre and Flexi stood guard. The angry shouts of the mob "Down with Metternich!" shattered the night again and again.

Von Eigler turned to Melanie:

"Princess, you had better go and dress. We cannot stay in this house."

Metternich, standing before a wall mirror, greatly enjoyed his butler dress. He said, rather to himself:

"A suitable costume, after all, for one who has been the faithful servant of the imperial house all his life."

When Melanie appeared, dressed as an ordinary cook, von Eigler pulled out his watch and turned to Metternich.

"We must go, Your Serenity."

Metternich sat down in an armchair.

"I have no money," he said. "I sent a man with a note to Karl. Let's wait until he returns."

A few minutes later the man rushed into the room, hatless and out of breath. Melanie snatched the leather bag from his hand. It contained one thousand golden ducats, sent by Metternich's old friend, Karl Rothschild.

A one-horse, dilapidated cab was waiting before the Metternich house, ready for the great journey ahead.

Melanie tenderly arranged the horsehair cover over the old man's knees, and the cab clattered off into the dark, cold night.

When Countess Jadi informed Andris of Metternich's departure, Andris jumped to his saddle. Reaching Hungary, Andris rode southeast to Heron Island, bearing the great news to Dali.

Metternich left Vienna around a quarter to midnight.

An hour later, in another city another fugitive fled his palace. When the Berlin revolution broke out, Frederick William IV left Berlin in the most fashionable vehicle for fleeing emperors, kings and statesmen—a peasant cart.

The next day, on March 14, at five in the afternoon, revolution broke out in Prague.

The match of Tonchi's dreams had at last been touched to the dry wood, and the fire, flared by the winds of long pent-up frustration, was spreading rapidly—too rapidly to be put out this time.

2

On March 14, at ten, the Café Pilvax in Pesth was overcrowded with politicians, writers, and other intellectuals. Among them was Dali, who, with the help of Andris, had hurriedly shaved off his caveman beard, left Heron Island by boat, and, dressed in a black Magyar dolman, galloped to Buda-Pesth. Andris was with him, as were Colonel Josef Nagy-Sándor and Karl Leiningen.

At a small corner table, in the noisy, crowded café, a young man was writing. He was twenty-five. He wore a thin, dark mustache and a small goatee, and his face had a greenish palor. Sometimes he bit his nails, his dark, burning eyes staring into space as if he were totally alone in the café. He was writing the Hungarian Marseillaise for the revolution, the outbreak of which was being planned around him; it was scheduled for the following morning. "Grab your sword, Hungarian!" was the title of his poem, and the first three lines read:

> Grab your sword, Hungarian!
> Your country calls you!
> Here is the time—now or never!

The sheet of paper was cheap, but his handwriting was beautiful.

"No good, Sándor," Andris Zeker said, standing behind him and looking at the poem.

The poet gave him an angry look.

"Why not?"

"Supposing you are in bed, or just sitting. Before you grab your sword you have to jump to your feet. Am I correct?"

Sándor Petöfi's black eyes looked at the clay inkstand for a second, and he said:

228

"You're right. Exceptionally."

He crossed out the first words and wrote: "Jump to your feet, Hungarian!"

The next day, March 15, 1848, the poet read his poem from the National Museum's ballustrade to a few hundred open hearts and open umbrellas. The rain was cold but the hearts were warm. After Petöfi had read his poem, the black sea of umbrellas went to the state prison to open the jail bulging with political prisoners. With thundering cheers they carried out the inmates on their shoulders. A fragile socialist poet, riding on Dali's and Andris' shoulders, kicked at the air frantically, shouting in fright. He knew nothing of what had happened in the world.

"What are you doing with me? Where are you taking me?"

"We are transferring you, brother, to another jail," Andris said to him. "You have written so many bad poems, you deserve another ten years for them."

"Ach, mein Gott!" Maria Augusta cried, and she wrung her hands when word of the Buda-Pesth revolution reached the Dukay palace in Vienna. Her panic was groundless.

The Hungarian revolution flamed up in a gay, happy mood. It was brief and bloodless.

By the beginning of April there was peace all over Europe. Peace and silence. In Germany, Frederick William IV, who had fled his palace in a peasant cart, returned to it in a royal coach to inaugurate a series of reforms that placated his people.

In Paris, the streets were quiet.

In Vienna, Sunday crowds strolled happily under the bright shining sun. The wurst stands were under siege, old Tyrolians wiped the white foam of beer from their moustaches with their thumbs. The forty-foot merry-go-round in the Prater majestically turned to the melody of a Strauss waltz and the children's cries of glee.

In the new atmosphere, all who had been open or secret foes of the dismissed Metternich, became favorites, notably Prince Felix Schwarzenberg.

These were the first happy weeks of the Period of Continental Revolutions. Not only the people, but the leaders of these revolutions did not care for the *plutôt mourir* idea. Everybody wanted rather to live. In London, political refugees from every corner of Europe printed a proclamation in a dozen languages: *Wszycsy ludzie as bramci!* read the Polish slogan, "Every man is our brother." To Dali, it sounded like Tonchi's shout from his unknown grave.

"Is this an international slogan of the Socialists or French Communists?" Andris asked the omniscient journalists in Café Pilvax. They said that it was not. It was only an outburst of brotherly love in Europe, torn by dissension for so many decades. Old and implacable foes embraced each other, even in governments. Poor Endre Dukay would not have believed his eyes, seeing Prince Eszterházy sitting next to Kossuth in the cabinet.

Paul Eszterházy had contributed several legends to the Eszterházy name. When Miss Pardy, travelling in the monarchy and Turkey in search of data for her new book, had visited the Prince in his Kismarton palace, the gallant Eszterházy had prepared tea for her with his own hands, burning dozens of thousand florin bills under the golden samovar. And once, when a Scottish Duke boastfully told him: "I have 30,000 sheep," Eszterházy had said: "Really? I have 30,000 shepherds." And he told the truth.

This same Prince Eszterházy became secretary of foreign affairs in the new cabinet, headed by Count Lajos Batthyány as prime minister. Kossuth served as secretary of the treasury, and his great political foe, the conservative Széchenyi also accepted a post in the new "revolutionary" cabinet. There was universal friendship, hope and love in Europe. The motto of "Liberty, Equality and Fraternity" had been revived—with, of course, some mild modification here and there. But everyone was urged to forget former quarrels.

After Metternich's departure in the days of the March revolutions, the Vienna court had completely lost its head. Thus it was very easy for Hungary to get every thing that Kossuth had been demanding for years. The Hungarian Diet wrote into law the liberation of the serfs. The general and proportional sharing of taxation was also enforced for the first time in history. Until

1848, a Paul Eszterházy, who owned one-thirteenth of Hungary, or an Endre Dukay, or any other rich aristocrat did not pay any tax. Even a simple nobleman with no title paid no taxes—not even the two *kreuzers* toll for crossing the pontoon bridge between Buda and Pesth. The liberation of the serfs and the general taxation were the "big nails in the Feudal System's coffin" as an editorial put it in the triumphant new press.

With Metternich in exile and the feeble-minded Ferdinand on the throne, and with the Austrian government frightened out of its wits, Hungary easily reclaimed her eastern territory, Transylvania, which in the seventeenth century had become a hereditary Habsburg province. Besides this great territorial restoration, Hungary also received the right of self-determination, with an English-style parliament and government, entirely independent of Austria's. Only the personal union survived. "Der Gütige" remained both emperor of Austria and king of Hungary.

3

When, late in April, Dali secretly appeared in Vienna, Countess Jadi told him:

"We can no longer hide from your father the fact that you are alive. Yesterday I spoke to General Ficquelmont, the new chancellor—an old and dear friend of mine. I confessed to him that you are living. He told me that if you can produce witnesses to swear that your part in the Lemberg conspiracy was motivated solely by patriotism, he will help us to quash the indictment and re-establish your legal rights."

Dali paced the room nervously. So much had happened in these last weeks since he had left Heron Island.

"How is Father?"

Countess Jadi shook her head sadly.

"Doctor Kunz is not at all satisfied. He speaks of biliary ducts . . . catarrhal jaundice . . . I only know that he lives on bismuth and pepsin."

Dali resumed pacing, then stopped again.

"Do you want me to see him?"

With tears in her eyes, Countess Jadi exclaimed:

"Oh, Dali . . . I know it's hard, but we must do it."

Next morning two men presented themselves to see Endre.

"This is my son, Ignatz," old Kunz introduced the young doctor. "Just hatched at Vienna University. They call him Kunzie."

There seemed nothing unusual to Endre in Doctor Kunz's visit. The doctor came to see him every week.

"My son has something interesting to tell Your Excellency. But first, let me ask: "Has anyone ever seen Count Adalbert's grave in Lemberg?"

"Nobody," Endre Dukay replied. "But then, Mozart died over half a century ago, and as you know, no one is sure even to this day in which of the many Viennese cemeteries he lies. Why do you ask?"

"My son has a friend, a young journalist from the *Lemberg Nachricht,* who does not believe the suicide story. Don't get excited, please. Perhaps it's only another of the many rumors we have all heard about Count Adalbert. Take that pill, please."

Young Kunzie had a glass of water ready. Obediently, Endre Dukay took pill and glass. His head trembled and Kunzie politely wiped off the water that had spilled on Endre's coat.

"Now, tell his excellency what your friend told you," Doctor Kunz encouraged his son.

Kunzie was a healthy young man with a round face and a soft, sympathetic voice. The way he held his folded hands on his stomach seemed to indicate that he liked his stomach very much.

"My friend has just come from Lemberg," Kunzie said. "He had heard the rumors that Count Adalbert did not die, and he wanted to investigate; so he went to the Hotel Adler, where, according to the *Wienerische Zeitung,* the suicide occurred a year ago, on April 5, 1847. Am I correct? This man spoke to the manager, the porters, and the maids, and none of them knew anything of the suicide."

Endre Dukay gazed at the floor and said thoughtfully:

"Hotels don't like to talk about suicides or murders within their walls. It is bad for business."

Though he loved Dali and mourned his death, Endre still thought it a lesser evil than the conspiracy to murder Metternich; and the suicide story had the advantage of suggesting that Dali was insane at the time of the conspiracy. Endre clung to it.

"The Adler is a small, shabby hotel," Kunzie continued, "famous for its bedbugs. It hardly seems possible that Count Dali ever occupied a room in that cheap, dirty place."

"My poor son was ever grudging even with the kreuzers," Endre said, a catch in his voice. "I remember once telling him, 'I'm going to buy you a money-throwing machine for aristocrats. So you can live up to the name of Dukay.' " These statements were untrue, but Endre was clutching at straws.

The two Kunzes laughed politely, and young Ignatz continued:

"And another thing, Your Excellency! My friend spoke to several professors at Lemberg University. Now, since Metternich's downfall, they dare speak. They were all deeply convinced that the charge against Count Dali was fabricated. He new *nothing*, absolutely nothing of what was behind the cultural front of that society."

At that last sentence, Endre Dukay's dark face lit up. He jumped to his feet.

"Let's go talk to your friend."

"Sit down!" old Kunz told him. "Her excellency, the Countess is already investigating this story."

"Did you speak with her?"

"Of course, I did. In the early morning."

"And what did she say?"

"She said that in February old Imre Kerge told her that he had seen Dali in a boat, deep in the reeds. Her excellency did not believe it, that's why she did not mention it to you. But last Monday, old Kerge told her he had spoken to Count Adalbert, and that he lives on Heron Island under a false name."

Endre Dukay buried his face in his hands and sobbed.

"Oh, if it would only be true!" he said.

"Won't you take another pill?" Doctor Kunz suggested briskly, and young Kunzie was ready with the glass of water again.

When Countess Jadi arrived an hour later, her husband had recovered from the first shock. The plot worked smoothly.

Countess Jadi had to repeat, over and over again, every word

233

that old Kerge had supposedly told her. On the sofa next to her husband, holding his hand, she finally said:

"Endre, Dali is in Vienna!"

"Did you . . . did you see him?"

Countess Jadi nodded.

"He came to Vienna with his documents to prove his innocence in the Lemberg conspiracy."

Endre Dukay stood up and said:

"Let's go and find him at once. I must see my son."

"Be still, Endre" Countess Jadi said soothingly. "Dali is already on his way here."

The butler served brandy and appetizers. Doctor Kunz looked into his patient's lonely face, and decided that he had had enough preparation. He went to the window and gave a discreet signal.

"What is that noise?" the doctor asked, though there was no noise outside. Someone is coming . . . "

And then the door opened, and there stood Dali! Flexi was by his side. Dali rushed to his father and held him in his arms. The son was pale but his eyes were dry; the father quietly wept.

Countess Jadi and the Kunzes turned away to hide their tears.

During lunch, Doctor Kunz was amazed to see how quickly his patient had recovered. Endre's hands had ceased to tremble, his eyes became brighter, his voice stronger.

Dali had always seen his father as a man given to sudden outbursts of anger, to shouting at his butler, treating his wife alternately with pompous formality and awkward tenderness, and at certain moments, revealing outrageous pride or shameful servility: actually a man capable of very little thoughtfulness and love.

Now he found a father completely changed: a man who spoke calmly and with a sad wisdom, a man deeply loyal to both of his two countries—Hungary and Austria.

"I know," Endre Dukay said to Dali, "that many of your friends, perhaps you, too, have always thought of me as a traitor."

"No! Never, Father!" Dali protested. "A traitor—why?"

"Andris once told me, 'He who has two countries, has none.' He is wrong. Absolutely wrong. For a Hungarian, loyalty to the

Habsburgs is a matter of life or death. Our nation is too small to survive alone. We are neither Germans nor Russians. We are brotherless orphans in Europe—perhaps the Finns are our only cousins."

When he paused the room was silent. Dali had the feeling that Endre spoke to him not merely as his father, but as a man near the grave.

The old man reached for his son's hand. The gesture reminded Countess Jadi of an afternoon in Warsaw, in the Radowski house, in the third week of their acquaintance, when young Endre had reached for her hand, confessed his love and proposed. Now he used almost the same gesture, spoke in almost the same emotional tone. But his words were different now, to his son.

"Promise me, Dali, that you won't ever take up arms against the Habsburgs. Promise me."

Dali remained silent.

"Do you promise?" his father asked again.

"I do," Dali said, hardly audibly.

After a moment Endre spoke up:

"I lived under three Habsburg emperors. Leopold, Francis and now Ferdinand. None of them were angels. We ate at their tables, we danced at their Burg, we went hunting with them, we knew them very well. No, they were not angels. I often said as much to your mother. Do you remember, Jadi?"

Countess Jadi nodded without raising her eyes. She did not remember that Endre had ever criticized the Habsburgs, even once, during the thirty-five years of their marriage.

"There were moments," Endre continued, "when I hated them. For example, when . . ."

He did not finish. He waved his hand and said resignedly:

"It's all the same now."

Flexi placed a consoling hand on his father's shoulder. He knew what the unfinished sentence meant. His father had hated the Habsburgs just last month, when they had humiliated old Metternich and forced him to resign.

Dali could hardly believe what he heard. He had never imagined such words coming from his father. Was this the same man who, eleven years ago, had so triumphantly embraced

Erich, patting his shoulder proudly because Erich had arrested Kossuth?

And as if Endre had read his son's thoughts, he said,

"Thank God, Kossuth's agitation didn't destroy the peace. Now he too realizes that Hungary and Austria must live together in brotherly love. More independence from Vienna? Of course, I would prefer my country totally free of all foreign rulers, but could Hungary survive alone? I think not. And what is our alternative? The Hohenzollerns? The Romanoffs?"

Flexi turned to young Ignatz Kunz:

"Kunzie, you are a young man, tell me frankly how you feel about this important issue. Forget that you are a Jew, forget German anti-Semitism and Russian pogroms. Speak as an educated man, free from prejudice, and tell me, what would you choose: St. Petersburg, Berlin or Vienna?

"Vienna, of course!" Kunzie answered with conviction. And old Kunz nodded approvingly.

Countess Jadi did not show any inclination to take part in the conversation. As always, she simply listened quietly.

"Now, I think," said old Kunz at eight in the evening, "his excellency must retire."

The following morning, Endre Dukay, still attired in the hussar uniform of a reserve colonel, but minus his heavy sabre and supporting himself with a walking stick, appeared in the chancellery with Countess Jadi.

General von Ficquelmont, the new Chancellor, was nearly eighty, but still in good health. When Endre and Jadi arrived, he stood up to greet his old friends, and kissed Countess Jadi's hand. Neither prince nor count, but only a *von* Ficquelmont, the cleanshaven pseudo aristocrat tried to be similar to his great predecessor in everything. He imitated Metternich in his dress, his hair-do, his smile and manner. But he was three inches shorter and some fifty pounds heavier than the "Coachman of Europe," and in the great chancellor's study, he looked like a lovely tame white rabbit in a huge cage, when the lion is absent.

It was in this very same room, at this same desk even, that Endre had spent his lifetime watching Metternich rule the monarchy. Endre glanced at the huge clock at the left and remembered the morning, the first of October in 1814, the busy, terribly busy day of the opening of the Congress of Vienna—when he had been late. Metternich never tolerated a half minute delay on the part of his secretaries, and when Endre had entered the room, clicked his large spurs, and greeted his master with military precision, the chancellor had extended his right arm to point imperiously to the clock. And now after almost thirty-four years, Endre heard his own voice again, breathless with haste and excitement; "Your Serenity, I humbly report that my wife gave birth to a child at seven this morning." Then he did not yet know that Jadi had borne twins.

Endre and Countess Jadi talked quietly with von Ficquelmont about Dali's fate; from time to time during the conversation, Endre covered his eyes and wept. Von Ficquelmont was sympathetic, and they left the chancellery with the best hopes.

It took only five days for a courier from the chancellery to deliver a large sealed letter to "His Excellency Count Adalbert Dukay," inscribed in the most beautiful calligraphy.

". . . and because of the sworn testimony of Baron Andris Zeker

. . . and because of the original text of the letter in which Count Adalbert Dukay *expressis verbis* donated 10,000 florins toward the worthy cause of the advanced study of the German language in Poland . . . and in the possession of clear evidence that he . . . I hearby order . . ."

And Dali was reinstated as legal owner of his Gere estate. His title of count, his rank as reserve captain of the Pálffy Hussars, and his high standing in Vienna society all were restored to him.

4

On the fifth of May, the century-old chestnut trees cast dark-blue shadows across the well kept lawn as the few weekend guests, among them Princess Maria Augusta and her parents, strolled in Ararat park before dinner.

Leaning on his walking stick, Endre walked arm in arm with Countess Jadi. Flexi and Maria Augusta strolled ahead of them, chatting gayly. From time to time, Maria Augusta would throw a pine cone as far as she could and Frou-Frou, her fox terrier puppy would fly after it, sometimes catching it in mid-air, and bring it back to Maria Augusta, hoping she would throw it again.

Endre and Jadi watched their four grandchildren running, laughing, and shouting in the park. Three of them were Flexi's; the fourth was Ádám, Dali's nine-year-old son, who was visiting Flexi's children. That day Dali was not at Ararat. His political work kept him in Buda-Pesth.

As Endre strolled along, his thoughts touched on Flexi's future. Prince Antal? Chancellor of the Habsburg monarchy? Why not?

The purpose of this family gathering was to celebrate the thirtieth anniversary of the Schönheim-Altstadts' marriage. The dinner that night was one of the best ever prepared by the old French chef in the Ararat kitchen. The young, blue-legged partridges were in season, and these were the first item on the menu, served with puree of lentils, tenderly spiced with bay leaves. Then came the wild boar sucklings, boiled in *vin rouge de Bordeaux* and served with roseberry jam and horse radish.

Coffee was served after dinner in the imposing red salon.

While the satiated guests chatted amicably over their coffee, Endre was silent. Then suddenly, the little silver spoon fell from his trembling hand.

"Don't you feel well?" Countess Jadi asked anxiously, peering into his ashen face.

"I apologize." He smiled faintly at Maria Augusta and her parents, as Countess Jadi and Flexi helped him out of the room.

Doctor Kunz was in Vienna. A butler hurried to the village and returned with the barber for a veinesection. Meanwhile, Endre had been put into bed, and Countess Jadi administered leeches to his veins.

Endre took hold of Jadi's hand. He wanted to say something to his wife. His lips moved, but he could not make a sound. Countess Jadi knelt by his bedside, and he put his hand on her head. Then at last, he whispered: "Thank you, dear."

That night, May 5, 1848, Endre Dukay slid gently from a merciful coma into death. At fifty-seven he looked seventy. But he died a happy man. God had given him back his wayward son, Dali. And with his son's innocence proven, the Dukay name was cleared.

5

It was June. Everything was bathed in a golden light throughout Europe. Even for old Metternich better days were in store. Rolly, living in London with her husband, wrote to her mother:

... and I followed Flexi's wish to find out if his godfather would accept any financial support. After their arrival in London last March, they took a modest room in a rather shabby Hanover Square Hotel. When I first went to see them, Melanie made no secret of her worry. Metternich did not receive a single penny from the Austrian government (after thirty-five years of, oh, what service for the monarchy!) Here, in Buckingham Palace, Emperor Ferdinand is fondly called "The Cretin." Melanie told me that the emergency money Rothschild gave them in the last hour, when they were fleeing from Vienna, was running out rapidly. London is rather expensive.

When I heard from Flexi and went to convey his offer of financial support to his old godfather, I found that the Metternichs had already moved into a most charming house on Richmond Green, called the Old Palace. Melanie was beaming with joy. She told me that their financial troubles were over. Czar Nicholas, informed of their situation, sent 100,000 rubles with warm greetings. Melanie said: "We accepted it, of course, only as a loan."

Alphie thought that the rubles were not a generous gesture for Metternich, but the czar's 100,000 *palkas* to the backside of Metternich's longtime rival, Prince Felix Schwarzenberg, author of the slogan "70-million Habsburg empire!"

Rolly's long letter ended, after a few bits of gossip about Queen Victoria, with the optimistic statement that London's diplomatic circles anticipated decades of peace and calm throughout Europe.

But on the very day Rolly's letter arrived at Ararat, Europe's bright sky suddenly darkened.

For the first time, the slogan *"Mort aux Capitalistes!"* appeared, written in flaming red on a wall in Paris, as if traced with a trembling and bleeding forefinger.

And then the great hurricane returned. Only three months before it had seemed that Europe's revolutions were over, the demands of the people satisfied in a half a dozen countries. Now, suddenly, the spirit of revolution rose anew, this time with awesome violence. First it struck in Paris, producing the bloodiest street fighting the city had ever witnessed.

It began when the national assembly took decisive measures and closed the "national workshops," to which multitudes of workers had flocked, pumping the treasury to pay the unemployed for useless labor. "Join the army, or leave the city!" the assembly ordered. The answer was the workers' shout: "Bread or lead!" The government troops gave them lead, and the workers died by hundreds every day on the stone pavements torn up for barricades. The streets were littered with corpses. It was more than a revolution; it was a massacre.

It was the first appearance of socialism on the European stage. At length the well-equipped government troops restored order. Some 4,000 workers were transported to penal colonies without trial. Over thirty newspapers were suppressed, and leading radical writers were imprisoned.

Order was restored, but the horrible "June Days" in Paris left a heritage of implacable hatred between workers and capitalists.

Not only in France. The fire of that hitherto unknown hatred became the first true international phenomenon in those days of blazing nationalism.

Who aspired to sit on the throne of the world? Czar Nicholas? The goateed nephew of Napoleon? The eighteen-year-old Franz Joseph? Vittorio Emmanuele, with his gigantic corkscrew moustache? None ot them. The new Rex Imperator was not a human being; it was a fantastic monster, growing rapidly bigger, with hundreds and thousands of miles of steel tentacles, thrashing wildly in pain while giving birth to a new order—the Machine Age.

The June Days seemed more dangerous for the Habsburg monarchy than the February Paris revolution. The Austrian government realized that it had made a blunder in March, when it gave so much freedom to Hungary. To correct that "blunder," Vienna played a congenial trick against Hungary.

Countess Jadi used the expression "congenial trick" in a letter to Rolly with no explanation. Seven turbulent months had passed since the March revolution before Dali finally found time to explain Vienna's "congenial trick" to the des Fereyolles:

I am pretty sure [Dali wrote them in the middle of October] that Flexi has already informed you from Vienna about what is going on here in the Danube Valley; now it is my turn to give you the view from Buda-Pesth.

Emperor Ferdinand is the target of many jokes, not only in the Pesth cafés, but even among his ministers in Vienna. Baron Pillersdorf, the new prime minister, said in his speech recently: "Our great emperor is our flag!" When he was asked why he called the feebleminded Ferdinand a flag, Pillersdorf said: "Because we are *carrying* him."

Now, the "congenial trick." The camarilla's secret agents encouraged Hungary's minorities to demand independence from the Batthyány government. In the north, the Slovaks; in the east, the Russians and Saxons; in the south, the Serbs and the Croats suddenly became independence-hungry. To give all of them independence would reduce Hungary to a third of her present territory.

On the following pages Dali gave a long account of the rapidly worsening situation. Shooting wars had broken out between the Hungarian troops and the minorities on all frontiers. Vienna's "congenial trick" worked wonderfully. But the Austrian government's support of Hungary's minorities enraged the Austrian people. Reforms for everybody, except *us?* Reforms and independence for the entirely illiterate Slovaks and Rumanians? And no reforms for the highly cultured Austrian people, most loyal to the Habsburgs? The angry question was put in Vienna, in Linz, in Innsbruck, in Graz, in Laibach, throughout the whole of Austria. Reforms for everybody except us?

Meanwhile the attacks of the minorities on all sides truly made the Hungarians "jump to their feet." Hungarian soldiers serving in Austrian regiments deserted the Habsburg flag and joined the *Nemzetörs,* Guards of the Nation, or the *Honvéds,* Defenders of the Fatherland.

Dali's letter reported sad news:

By September the situation had become so terrible that Prime Minister Batthyány called an emergency cabinet meeting. All the members appeared, except Count Széchenyi, who had had a nervous breakdown. The following week two doctors started to take him aboard the steamship *Argot,* to the Dobling mental institute near Vienna. When the ship was around Komarom, Széchenyi suddenly grabbed the rails and plunged into the Danube. He swam ashore, and then started to run . . . into the empty twilight.

You know that in the political battles between Széchenyi and Kossuth I always stood for the "revolutionair" Kossuth, and regarded the "evolutionair" Széchenyi as an old, slow horse with a secret love for the Habsburgs. But now his tragedy threw full light upon his greatness. A man who, seeing the deadly danger of his country, loses his mind is not a madman but the big bleeding heart of a small nation.

The second tragedy—I happened to witness it—occurred on September 28. I had just returned from Vienna. Crossing the pontoon bridge from Pesth to Buda, I saw a great tumult around the open carriage of Count Lamberg. Do you remember him? An old friend of father's, a soft-spoken, polite Austrian who loved the Hungarians. After the Batthyány cabinet resigned, Der Gütige's manifesto dissolved the independent Hungarian parliament, and the crown appointed General Lamberg as Hungary's military dictator. There is no greater blow to patriotism than the violence of patriotism. Angered by the manifesto which knocked down Hungary's independence, a patriotic mob dragged Lamberg out of his coach. When I arrived at the spot to try to calm the rioters, Lamberg lay on the ground. There was a big knife sticking out of his chest, and he was already dead. Seeing the knife stuck in his heart, between his many decorations, I had the horrible feeling that war between Austria and Hungary is inevitable. And I saw myself leading a hussar company attacking the Gisellastrasse, and I saw Flexi leading a dragoon squadron, putting our Buda palace in Septemvir Utca under seige. For the time being I cannot write more.

Dali's premonition about the war was justified. The morning after Lamberg's cruel murder, Count Latour, minister of defense, ordered the five Austrian regiments stationed in Vienna to march into Hungary. But the regiments were immediately attacked and disarmed, with what? With angry shouts, slaps and kicks. Governments always forget that their soldiers are under the command, not only of generals, but also of mothers, wives or girl friends. A mother's shout from a window made a Hansi or Fritzi averse to shooting, despite Prince Windischgrätz's command to shoot. In one suburb, respectable citizens rushed out with crowbars and sledge hammers to dismantle the Tabor Bridge, which was to lead the regiments toward Buda-Pesth.

The old, lame Talleyrand might have stepped out of his grave to exclaim:

"You see? You see again? Remember what I said: 'We must recognize that governments and people are two entirely different things!' "

It seemed that the Austrian people had had enough from the Habsburgs. Observers expected their downfall in a matter of weeks, by the unanimous will of the "loyal" Austrians.

"Too bad," Dali said to Andris, "that poor Tonchi could not witness the collapse of the Habsburgs. No doubt, the Habsburgs are leading the way for the Hohenzollern and Romanoffs into history's sewer."

"And then," Andris replied, "your old dream, Hunpolia, will come true."

Dali did not answer. His feelings were deeply hurt. In Andris' fading memory, the great dream of Hungapole had become Hunpolia.

6

Young Ignatz Kunz, as a medical man, joined the Academic Legion, and reported to Countess Jadi that the Academy for Army Surgeons had a large anatomical display of wax replicas of human organs: brains, hearts, lungs, livers, bowels, and the like. When the students displayed the painted organs on the marble stairs of the Schönbrunn palace, feebleminded Ferdinand was so frightened that he fled the palace in an apple cart, disguised as an Austrian peasant. To reinforce his disguise, he had his cart surrounded by mounted guards and six cannons. The escort seemed so unusual for a peasant that people along the road recognized him immediately. His precautions were unnecessary in any case. The villagers who saw him cheered wildly, crying *"Hoch Der Gütige!"* while his majesty grinned and waved, and shouted in his high-pitched voice, *"Hoch die Revolution! Hoch!"*

By nightfall of the same day, October 6, the rioters had taken over some 60,000 carbines. At three in the afternoon, Countess Jadi, in her room in the Gisellastrasse house, heard shooting from neighboring roofs and windows.

Countess Jadi was pale, almost hysterical. She had spent a sleepless night and here emotions were in chaos; panic, and horror mingled with a hidden hope and joy. Was it possible that this hell would mean a great turn in Poland's fate?

"Oh, Lord! . . . look . . . ," Countess Jadi screamed in horror as she stood looking out her window. "Is that Lati! Yes, it is Lati! . . . Oh, Lord! Flexi! Look!"

Lati was Count Latour, the minister of defense, an old friend of the Dukays. Unfortunately for him, everybody knew that as the head of the secret police, he had been responsible for the arrest, torture, and death of many political prisoners. And it was he who had ordered the five regiments to move into Hungary. The delirious mob recognized him on the street, and before he could reach the safety of the Dukay palace, they snatched him.

Flexi dashed down to the street to Lati's aid. But he was too late. The shouting and howling crowd around him was too large to penetrate. Poor Latour, lifted in the air, was kicking and wriggling as the mob bore him to the *Am Hof*, the "Place of the Court."

Flexi followed, desperately hoping for a chance to intervene. For the first time in his life, Flexi came very near to fainting. As he watched helplessly, a rope was thrown around Latour's neck; the victim screamed like a pig when, held by its ears, it feels the butcher's knife on its throat.

When Flexi returned to Gisellastrasse, he found Dali in his room.

"Don't you feel well?" Dali asked his brother.

For a moment Flexi could not speak. Then he described the scene he had witnessed.

"Horrible," Dali commented.

"Do you remember," Flexi asked him, "Metternich's words during our audience? When he said that as a young student, he had witnessed the bloodthirsty mob in the Strasbourg streets? Now I think it was his memories of the French Revolution that gave him such a tremendous drive against every kind of revolution. Don't you think so?"

"Possibly," Dali answered. "Wounds in body or in mind have a greater influence on our characters than any sermon. But don't forget that Emperor Francis and Czar Nicholas and the Latours and Metternichs made many thousands scream and moan. Don't forget that Tonchi, too, most probably . . ."

"I haven't forgotten," Flexi interrupted. "Still, after what I have seen today at *Am Hof*, I say with Metternich that revolution, blood streaming on the pavements, changes persons into fragmentary men, into blind, stupid, dangerous, bestial masses."

Dali did not answer. He pretended to suppress a yawn, stood up and stretched—the transparent trick of a man who wishes to avoid an argument, fearing his own words.

Many aristocrats thought that Vienna was not safe in those days. Flexi ordered three ox carts from Ararat for the large Ispahan carpets, the two Rubenses and the other paintings, as well as the silver and a few rare pieces of furniture; for he thought the cellars in Septemvir Utca in Buda would be a safer place for these valuables than the Vienna palace.

After Grandpapa Maurycy's death, Jadi had had the life-size portrait of King Bátori brought from the Radowski house in Warsaw to the Gisellastrasse. Now, as the former king of Poland proceeded down the stairs, supported by four delivery men, Flexi turned to his mother.

"It seems a shame to entrust such things to an ox cart," he said.

"Well," Countess Jadi remarked lightly, "that is how all emperors, kings or chancellors flee."

And she tried with a smile to conceal her sorrow at the thought that King Bátori was going to his second grave, however dry might be the cellars in Buda.

The three oxcarts, heavily packed with the valuables, slipped out of Vienna in the last possible hour. Prince Windischgrätz, the toughest of the Austrian generals, gave the order "to choke the revolution in Vienna with a nice necktie." The necktie was his, Prince Auersperg's and Jellachich's troops, closing in and tightly encircling Vienna.

When Kossuth and his generals learned of Windischgrätz's plan, they dispatched all available Hungarian troops to Vienna to help the revolution. But the Austrian forces held the advantage. On October 30, a few miles from Vienna, at the village of Schwechat, the liberating Hungarian troops were defeated.

Next day Vienna's revolutionaries surrendered.

The curtain fell on Act I of the Hungarian War for Liberty.

CHAPTER NINE

IN THE FIRST DAYS OF NOVEMBER, Vienna was as calm, its mood as *gemütlich,* as in the happiest days during the reign of Emperor Francis. The waiters in the Papagei and other cafés served as politely and bowed as deeply as if they had not been revolutionary sharpshooters only a week before.

This greatly encouraged the court clique, led by Archduchess Sophie, "the only male member of the Habsburg family," mother of young Franz Josef. At the end of November, Prince Felix Schwarzenberg became the new prime minister. As a young diplomat, Schwarzenberg had been sent home from London in disgrace because of his scandalous adultery. And a few years before the war, Metternich had fired him from the diplomatic corps when Schwarzenberg, as an Austrian envoy in Naples, had had to flee from several outraged Italian husbands.

Schwarzenberg, as the head of the Austrian government, decided that the "congenial trick" to incite the minorities against the new government in Buda-Pesth had not worked well enough. The time had come, he thought, to mobilize the whole Austrian army and start an all out war against Hungary, whose freshly acquired independence, after three centuries of Habsburg rule, was becoming more and more dangerous to the dynasty.

The previous April, when the Habsburg court was in a panic after the March revolution, Emperor Ferdinand had made a solemn oath that he would never revoke the independence he had granted to Hungary. In a deeply devoted Catholic Austria, the emperor could not break his oath. The only solution was to force the emperor to resign. But Der Gütige liked being emperor. He was so fond of the ceremonies attached to his rank that, when he was asked on his fiftieth birthday what kind of national gift he would like to receive, he answered with a shy grin: "Crown me every Sunday."

Still there was a simple way to get rid of the benign idiot, Ferdinand. He signed every paper his ministers put on his desk. He liked his signature so much that sometimes he signed the same document twice or even three times. But he never bothered to ask what the documents were about. A story told in Vienna held that one of his lackeys had a document signed by Der Gütige appointing Felix Schwarzenberg as prime minister, and an hour later Schwarzenberg had another paper signed by the emperor which appointed the lackey foreign minister. The story was not too far from the truth.

On December 2, Ferdinand unknowingly signed his resignation. Archduchess Sophie's dream came true. Her eighteen-year-old son, Franz Josef, stepped to the throne.

On December 7, after hearing a fiery speech by Kossuth, the Hungarian parliament rejected Franz Josef as Hungary's Apostolic king, and declared his occupancy of the throne unconstitutional.

Three days later, Franz Joseph appointed Prince Alfred Windischgrätz commander-in-chief of the Austrian Army, and ordered him to march against Hungary.

One morning, in his Olmütz exile, Der Gütige took his personal valet aside and whispered:

"Could you tell me, Wenzel, who is the emperor of Austria?"

"Franz Josef."

"Since when?"

"Since two weeks."

"And who am I?"

"Your Majesty is the emperor-in-chief."

"Then why do you want to leave without permission from me?"

"Your Majesty is in reserve, like myself. I was called to the colors."

"Is there a war?"

"Yes, Sire. A regular war."

"Against Russia?"

"No, Sire. Against Hungary."

"Who is the commander-in-chief?"

"Prince Windischgrätz."

"Win-disch-grätz? Good Lord! He's a cretin."

Der Gütige was wrong. Windischgrätz was not only the best of the Austrian generals, but, however tough as far as discipline was concerned, he was also a gentleman, and very benevolent as well in his dealings with a defeated enemy.

When Windischgrätz moved against Hungary, Flexi faced a terrible dilemma as to which side he should take. Unlike his godfather and his late father, Flexi did not see in Kossuth the irresponsible demon behind a hopeless war. He did not hate Kossuth. But as a man of reason, he was very much afraid that this war, however justified, would drag Hungary to her doom. He knew from his friend, Solly Rothschild, that the financial and economic structure of the Kossuth army was too shaky to sustain a war for many months.

On the other side, Dali and Andris were not alone in maintaining absolute faith in final victory. Not only the serfs, the peasants, the workers, the middle class and the intelligentsia, but many aristocrats stood behind Kossuth; and they, too, ready to die for freedom and independence, joined the *Honvéd* tricolors. They brought their servants, horses, and carts with them, all badly needed for the war. Now it seemed that the whole nation had indeed jumped to its feet, with the exception of a few in Vienna, who remained loyal to the Habsburgs.

Flexi suffered such torment in trying to make his decision that Countess Jadi began to fear for his mind.

In Ararat, the family, along with many of their friends, held a conference, Flexi was under heavy pressure from Dali's sanguine, pro-Kossuth friends: Karl Leiningen, the cousin of Queen Victoria; József Nagy-Sándor, the luxuriantly-bearded general; Count Andrássy, a young hussar officer who was a close friend of Andris.

Dali and Andris said nothing while Flexi was under siege. Dali had anxieties of his own, as terrible as Flexi's were to him. He had given his word to his father that he would never take up arms against the Habsburgs. What could he do? If he had to remain idle while others fought, he thought he would commit suicide, or go mad.

Flexi paced the room restlessly. However Vienna-educated, however, "castrated of his Magyar feeling," he could not forget that he was *de genere* Ordony. Nor could he help but remember that his mother was a Pole.

Countess Jadi's pale, green eyes, now paler than ever, followed Flexi's slow steps.

"Without material support from the Dukay estate," said the bearded Nagy-Sándor, "the second cavalry brigade for our national army cannot survive."

Flexi stood before the baroque clay stove, his arms crossed behind his back. His voice was solemn.

"Let's remember the disciples who said: 'He followeth not with us' and Christ rebuked them: 'Forbid him not, for he who is not against us is for us.' " At this, Andris spoke for the first time.

"Flexi," he said, "we have to be in camp before nightfall. We have no time for sermons. What is your decision?"

"I wish to remain neutral," Flexi said, and looking at Dali, he added; "I think my brother will be neutral also."

Everyone looked at Dali, except Countess Jadi and Andris. But Dali remained silent. He did not even move.

After a few seconds, Flexi said to him:

"You promised your father . . ."

There was more sadness than reproach in his unfinished sentence; but the word "promise" brought Dali to life.

"I did *not* break my promise," he said, "I did not and I am not about to take up arms against the Habsburgs. Nor are any of us! Our revolution in March was bloodless, and it ended with a sincere understanding with Emperor Ferdinand."

Then his voice became bitter:

"It was the Habsburgs who took up arms against us!"

Like a shadow, Countess Jadi slipped behind him. As he raised his voice, she placed a calming hand on his shoulder.

"Do we have no right to defend our fatherland?" Dali demanded.

At that everyone jumped up, and everyone began to talk at once:

"That brat! That young Franz Josef! And Sophie, his mother! Who broke Ferdinand's solemn oath? Who gave the order to start a regular war against us?"

Flexi remained calm, almost smiling. Countess Jadi pleaded: *"Bitte, bitte, meine Herren . . ."*

Andris' voice boomed above the clamour:

"Felix Schwarzenberg!"

Bitter accusations sounded against Prince Felix Schwarzenberg, Austria's new prime minister, who had ordered the war.

General Nagy-Sándor turned to Flexi:

"Count Antal, you should have seen the mobilization! Poor peasants came with only their horses. And you should have seen . . ."

"The only thing I can promise," Flexi cut in, "is that the Dukay estate won't give a single horse or cart, or any provisions to the Austrians."

He rang the bell and said to the servant who responded:

"My coach! I have to go to Vienna right away. And tell Mr. Pogány I want to talk to him."

The servant bowed and left.

So cold and firm were Flexi's words that to continue the argument seemed for his friends not only senseless but humiliating. Everyone stood silent, looking any place except at Flexi.

Dali looked at his mother. Still in mourning for her husband, Countess Jadi wore a black robe that made her hair look very grey. But she was still slender and beautiful as she stood immobile, with quiet dignity. There was a look of sorrow about her, a silent reproach against the whole world. It was impossible for anyone in the room to look at her without thinking of Poland.

Papa Pogány, one of the Dukay estate's bailiffs, was seventy, a man with paprika-red cheeks and snow-white hair. He seldom wore anything but tobacco-brown trousers and a braid-trimmed Magyar dolman. Old Pogány could remember Flexi as a baby, had even spanked him several times. Now he stood at attention before his master and addressed him as "Your Excellency."

"Uncle Pali," Flexi told him in a firm voice, "I appoint you as my deputy and charge you with all the affairs of the entail during my absence. In this unfortunate war between Austria and Hungary, I have declared myself absolutely neutral. Therefore I strictly forbid you to give any provisions to either the Windischgrätz or the Kossuth army. Do you understand my order?"

"Yes, Your Excellency!"

In the tense silence Flexi's look was fixed on old Pogány's eyes as if he longed to say something more—and different. And, as though Papa Pogány understood that silent look, the old man repeated in a lower tone:

"Yes, Your Excellency."

Flexi waved his hand to his guests and quickly left the room.

After a few seconds of deep silence, Countess Jadi spoke.

"Let's go to the dining room. Time for you gentlemen to have a bite."

Only Papa Pogány did not move. The invitation was not meant for him. Countess Jadi remained by the door, and when General Nagy-Sándor started through it, she touched his arm, stopping him; then she stepped out herself, closing the door behind her.

Left alone with the general, Papa Pogány said to him:

"How many horses do you need, General?"

He flashed out his shabby note-book and, with a pencil hardly longer than his thumb-nail, wrote down the number of dry beans, peas, lentils, horses, oxen, cows, sacks of wheat, rye and oats, bales of hay, kegs of beer and cases of wine, boxes of candles, and carts that General Nagy-Sándor requested. At one item Papa Pogány's pencil stopped:

"Five hundred sheep? Let's make it two thousand, General. We have so many sheep we could block up the Danube with them. No, sir, I am not generous. War is war. It could happen that Windischgrätz would take Ararat. I'm afraid he wouldn't ask my permission for the provisions."

After he pocketed his notebook, he said:

"May I ask you, General, a great favor? When, tomorrow, your men come for the delivery, I will protest and shout. Would you be so kind as to have me tied to a tree?"

"With great pleasure, *Tekimtetes uram*," said the good-humored general, using the title of middle-class people. It meant "Your Dignity."

Then Nagy-Sándor joined the other guests in the dining room. While the general had been talking with old Pogány, a new guest had arrived, dressed as lieutenant of the Honvéds. He had not attended the discussion of the afternoon because he did not speak a word of Hungarian. He was Myci, the carrot-haired young Prince Mycislav Voronieczki, who had come from Poland with old General Josef Bem to join the Kossuth army.

The black-sealed bottles of old wines restored the good mood of the company.

An hour later the group of six, General Nagy-Sándor, Karl Leiningen, Gyula Andrássy, Dali, Andris and Myci, rode out of the park in the darkening twilight.

Alone, Countess Jadi stood by the window and watched them go. The silence that fell when the sound of the hoofbeats receded seemed to ask: Where will their ride end? How many will ever return?

2

December of 1848 was extremely cold. The Danube was frozen "down to the bottom" as the saying went. Patrols found no enemies in that world "turned into glass," but sometimes they found partridges frozen to solid ice. Dali, riding with Andris along the Danube shore carried a frozen red deer in his saddle. The north wind shot millions of tiny needles into the two men's faces. The wide collars of the long, gray military coats were pulled up to their ears.

In front of Dali and Andris rode two officers. The bright green feathers on their shakos told the world that they were generals. The taller one wore long, white whiskers, the shorter a white straggling beard. They looked seventy.

"I'm afraid," Andris remarked, "that these two kids will catch cold."

The shorter general was Arthur Görgei, commander-in-chief of the Upper-Danubian wing of the new Honvéd army; his taller comparison was Karl Leiningen. The thirty-eight-year-old Andris called them "kids" with justice. Görgei's beard and

Leiningen's whiskers were white not with age, but with snow. Görgei was thirty, Leiningen only twenty-nine. The two were regarded as the most talented generals of the War for Liberty.

Petöfi, "the poet of Liberty," was only twenty-five. The volunteer drummers were young boys—one of them only fourteen. His name was Imre Kerge, and he was a nephew of the late Pista Kerge.

The whole of the Kossuth army was very youthful and, generally, untrained. Windischgrätz's troops were old veterans, with less willingness to die, perhaps, but with far more training. Austria's generals were old—Windischgrätz himself was over sixty—but they did not quarrel with each other. Contrastingly, the young Hungarian generals quarrelled constantly.

Andris was an aide-de-camp to Görgei, Dali to Leiningen. The four officers were riding to inspect their troops, a force of 30,000 men armed with nearly a hundred cannons. Imposing numbers when one recalls that Kossuth had created that army out of the thin air in less than two months. The trouble was that the Honvéds' line along the Austrian-Hungarian border as thin, and the clothes of Görgei's men were also thin—too thin for the cruel cold. Their food rations were small, as were their twelve-pound cannons, compared to the Austrians fine provisions and giant twenty-eight-pound guns. Windischgrätz had over 100,000 troops, and all were well clothed.

On the cold morning of December 18 Görgei's troops received a hot shower. At the small town at Mosony a torrential downpour from Windischgrätz's 300 cannons hit the Honvéds.

Leaning on the neck of his horse, Andris galloped along the line of infantry to deliver Görgei's command for immediate retreat.

The thin line of the snowed-in "Defenders of the Fatherland" broke like a white clothesline as the hussar squadrons, galloping wildly, fled the attacker. The trumpets blew the signal of the retreat: ta-taaaa . . . ta-taaaa. . . . The sound mixed a panicky scream with a heart rending sob of farewell. Farewell to the hope of victory, farewell to the dead and wounded, men and horses alike, whom they had to leave behind. More than a quarter of their small twelve-pound cannons were also lost.

Next day a heavy snowfall slowed the advance of the Austrian troops. Without stopping to rest, even on Christmas eve, Görgei lead his defeated army to the east, to the defense of Buda. He hoped to meet the south wing of the Honvéd army, which was on its way north.

Papa Pogány's generosity to the Kossuth army proved to be a providential. On December 20 the advancing Austrian troops took Ararat, but found no provisions. With them came Baron Erich Dukay-Hedwitz, now a dragoon colonel. Erich immediately took over the entail's management. When he arrived at Ararat castle, Countess Jadi and old Pogány were already on their way to Buda.

Windischgrätz advanced slowly and cautiously, at a rate of some ten miles a day, through the deep snow. On December 27, he put up his headquarters in the village of Bicske, scarcely twenty miles from Buda-Pesth, and began preparations to besiege the city.

The next day, a deputation headed by Count Lajos Batthyány, who had been the first prime minister in the short-lived independent Hungarian government, arrived at Bicske to open negotiations with Windischgrätz for an armistice.

It was only eleven years since that horrible January night in 1838, when the great flood had swept away Pesth's clay houses. During those eleven years, the back-breaking work of thousands of masons, carpenters, locksmiths, glaziers, upholsterers, and every kind of laborer had built a new Pesth. A new bridge across the Danube, a marvel of stone and steel, was just about to be opened for public use. To let Buda-Pesth perish, to expose its women and children to the fiery tempest of Austrian cannon, would be the most cruel stupidity.

Batthyány regarded the possibility of an armistice very hopefully. He had often met Windischgrätz in the Viennese salons; and he was the best mediator for another reason, too. He had been the first prime minister of independent Hungary after the March revolution, and in September he had resigned that post because he did not agree with Kossuth's no-compromise policy.

But the Austrian general's aide-de-camp informed the Hungarian delegation that the commander-in-chief would grant them an audience under one condition: Batthyány must leave the headquarters immediately.

It was a severe blow to Batthyány.

"Your Excellency," the aide-de-camp said to him, "was one of the promoters of the March revolution in Buda-Pesth."

"Of the *bloodless* March revolution," Batthyány pointed out. "And I was appointed prime minister by the emperor."

"Well," said the aide-de-camp, scratching his ear; the gesture conveyed his opinion of the feebleminded Ferdinand. "Besides any political resentment, there is a deep human wound in his serenity's heart," he continued. "During that same week in March, when the Czech revolution broke out, his serenity's wife was cruelly killed in a Prague street."

"Yes, I know. I was shocked when I heard it," Batthyány said. "But I don't see the connection between Prague and my . . ."

The aide-de-camp raised his hand, politely but firmly indicating that he was not in a position to discuss the matter.

Batthyány returned to Buda-Pesth. The other members of the delegation remained at the Austrian general's headquarters for several days as Windischgrätz's guests.

The people of Buda-Pesth were not informed about the result of the negotiations, but they were not at all alarmed. Most of the officers of the army enjoyed a few days leave. On New Year's morning, gypsy musicians went from house to house, playing old folksongs or the latest Vienna waltzes, and collected some silver coins just as they did in the happy years of peace. In quiet Buda, the air of the old Russwurm pastry shop was filled with its usual warm fragrance of vanilla, of freshly roasted coffee, or puffy, glistening sweet breads. The small, vaulted shop was filled with the same people as ten years before, when the Russwurm had been a favorite meeting place of such celebrities as Franz Liszt, with his bright green gloves and black mane.

In Pesth, in the National Theater, the blond and pretty Fräulein Helen Hoch had no idea whether she was an Austrian or a Hungarian. She had been born in Vienna, of an Austrian father and a Hungarian mother, and had grown up completely bilingual, an immeasurable advantage for a young actress. She was a feted member of both Austria's *Wiener Teater* and Hungary's National Theater in Buda-Pesth.

One January night, Dali and his mother attended the theater, along with Andris and Irma and General Leiningen and his wife Eliz. They had come to the theater to see the famous Helen in the leading role of a patriotic play in which she sang the new soldier song, "Lajos Kossuth sent a message. . . ." Every night, thunderous applause and a standing ovation greeted the song.

As Helen reached the middle of the famous song, a man dashed into the theatre and shouted at the top of his voice:

"The Austrian troops have entered Buda-Pesth!"

The three officers, Andris, Leiningen and Dali, dashed out, mounted their horses, and galloped away to investigate the news.

When they met a small rear-guard of their own troops outside the city, they found that the awful story was true. Their army, which was supposed to defend Buda if the friendly negotiations for an armistice failed, was in retreat to the north. The south wing, the Honvéd's third army corps, advancing toward Buda with 12,000 troops, had encountered the Austrians and been so badly beaten that it could not unite with Görgei's army. The young general, a man of sudden decision, gave up his plan to defend Buda and withdrew his army. And, during the first act of the patriotic play, Windischgrätz's army had noiselessly entered the snowed-in-city without firing a single shot.

The ladies left behind in the Dukay box understood the situation when the bilingual Helen dropped the Hungarian Kossuth song in the middle and swung into Hadyn's *Gott erhälte*, the emperor hymn. Was she a traitor? She was not. She was only a half-Austrian and half-Hungarian, loyal to both lands or either, depending upon the demands of the changing situation.

During intermission, the Austrians took as war prisoners all those in the audience who were wearing the uniform of the Honvéd army and all civilians who sported the Kossuth beard. When the curtain fell, Austrian officers, already intermingled with the audience, applauded enthusiastically.

Baron Erich came with the advancing Austrian troops to Buda-Pesth. During intermission, he appeared in the Dukay box to greet the ladies, and stayed to chat with them amicably.

The next morning, when Erich informed Countess Jadi that the Septemvir Utca palace would be used for Windischgrätz's headquarters, Jadi did not resist. The commander-in-chief, an old friend, graciously left a suite of rooms at Countess Jadi's disposal.

The fall of Buda-Pesth made headlines in the European press. The Pope, the king of Bavaria, and the king of Hanover, to say nothing of young Franz Josef, sent Windischgrätz the highest decorations. An old comrade, the Duke of Wellington, wrote him: "Since Napoleon, no maneuver had been planned and carried out more successfully than yours."

On January 8, an Austrian officer appeared at the home of Lajos Batthyány, saluted politely and said: "On the command of His Serenity Prince Windischgrätz, I take Your Excellency into custody."

And before the surprised Batthyány could say anything, the patrol, with fixed bayonets, surrounded him, and he was led away.

3

There was peace in Buda-Pesth, but Dali and Andris, at the rear of the Görgei army as it retreated slowly to the northeast, were in steady engagement with the pursuing Austrian troops.

Finally, on January 31, Görgei stopped at the famous vineyards on the Tokaj hills and, like a cornered beast, fought back; the fighting was ferocious. The remaining seventy-eight small cannons thundered, the rifles in the frozen hands of the untrained infantry cracked constantly, and the heavy swords of the hussars flashed in the cold, bright air.

The Hungarians' faith in their ultimate victory was unquenchable. And for the first time since Windischgrätz had crossed the Hungarian border in December, the Austrian troops were beaten—and badly beaten. The first victory! Everybody was drunk with excitement—and with the world-famous Tokaj wine, offered to the victorious Honvéds by the ecstatic population.

"Historians will never find out," Countess Jadi wrote to the des Fereyolles in London, "whether the change in Windischgrätz's treatment of the jailed Batthyány was due to my steady pleading with him or to the Tokaj victory. I think it was the latter. Anyhow, he has given Antonia and little Emma permission to see Lajos every day. The pontoon bridge has already been removed, as it is every December, and the new Chain Bridge is not yet open to the public. So every day Antonia and Emma cross the Danube twice in a small boat, struggling among the ice-floes, from Pesth to Buda and back."

Young Emperor Franz Josef was critically wounded—not physically on the battlefield, but mentally by a crazy scheme of Prime Minister Felix Schwarzenberg's. The headlines of the Vienna papers spoke of: "The 70-million Habsburg Empire!" And the rest of Europe thundered and sneered. Louis Napoleon, president of the French Republic, was furious. "Small and rocky Austria has hardly 5 million inhabitants," he stated. English papers called Franz Josef "the arrogant Habsburg brat." In Berlin, Frederick William IV and a young Prussian giant, thirty-three-year-old Count Otto von Bismarck, pounded the table in their rage. "Does Franzie include the whole of Germany in the 70-million Habsburg empire?"

Metternich, in his exile in Leipzig, told his friends: "Maniac rule. It worries me to see the dynasty's future in his hands."

Flexi held the same opinion of Schwarzenberg as his old godfather. He kept his promise of neutrality. When, in January, he was called to the colors as a dragoon lieutenant in reserve, he asked old Doctor Kunz for a medical certificate stating that he had a sick heart. It was true, if not physically, at least metaphorically. With his wife and three children, he retreated from Vienna to his father-in-law's remote castle in Bavaria.

When, in February, Dali was slightly wounded on the left thigh by a shrapnel splinter, Andris' wife Irma appeared in Bavaria with Dali's ten-year-old son, Ádám, and a letter from Dali.

"If I happen to die on the battlefield," Dali wrote to Flexi, "please, take care of my only son. Ádám stutters slightly but our army doctor, young Kunzie, tells me that he will lose this defect of speech when he reaches sexual maturity.

"Educate him in the spirit of the Blind Boar."

In Ararat castle there was a life-size portrait of their great-grandfather, Ferenc Dukay. The old warrior had lost his left eye in Rákóczi's war for liberty against the Habsburgs. In their childhood Dali and Flexi had called the old, morose man

"Blind Boar," because even his ears and forehead seemed to be hairy on the sooty oil painting.

The spring of 1849 was filled with historical events. The greatest was the resurrection of the Honvéd army, which emerged like the phoenix from its own ashes, bagging one victory after another. *Apó,* Hungarian for "Little Daddy," was the pet name given the fragile old Polish general, Josef Bem, who had fought in every Polish revolt during his lifetime. He had been wounded nine times in his life, and always led his boys into the wildest fire himself.

In forest-clad Transylvania, the eastern part of Hungary, Apo Bem silenced the Rumanian and Saxon minorities who, with the help of the Austrian troops, were harassing the Hungarians.

"The secret of Little Daddy's victories," Andris explained, "Is that before every battle he makes a stirring speech to his troops. Since he speaks no Hungarian and they understand no Polish, Apó speaks in broken French and they don't understand that, either."

"Little Daddy is a wise man," Dali said. "He knows that the more unintelligible the speech, the more enthusiastic the audience."

They laughed. Everyone now laughed at witty remarks and pointless stories at which they would not even have smiled in the days of the retreats. The mood was high in every Honvéd camp.

When rumors said that Franz Josef would go to St. Petersburg to ask Czar Nick the Stick for help, the camp theater ridiculed the meeting in a brief, dramatic sketch.

In the playlet, a trumpet signal served instead of an opening curtain. Then, young Franz Josef, weeping and wringing his hands, dashed to the stage, which was marked "Winter Palace," bewailing the Honvéds' victories and the names of Görgei, Leiningen, Nagy-Sándor, and even Andris Zeker. Franzie held both hands at the seat of his brand new emperor's trousers, indicating that something dreadful had happened. He was accompanied by his tutor, the Black Prince of the Mountains. Schwarzenberg's role was played by a gypsy corporal whose pockmarked face was smeared with oily soot from the cannons' barrel to make it as black as possible. Archduchess Sophie stood behind her son, carrying a large night pot in case of another emergency. The "only male member of the Habsburg family" was dressed as a woman and sported a strong black mustache. Her role was played by a hussar sergeant.

At Franzie's shout "Help! Help!" a nearly seven-foot-tall private appeared on the stage in the part of Czar Nick the Stick. Franzie fell on his knees before the great czar, still covering up his seat.

"Help please, Uncle Niki!"

Taking in the situation with the trousers and pinching his nose, the czar asked, with a strong Russian accent:

"Vot is yer trouble, zonny?"

It was the black-faced gypsy (Schwarzenberg) who answered:

"That lousy Kossuth is coming to take Vienna. Help us crush his army with your big stick!"

"Oh, I will faint," cried the mustached Archduchess Sophie, "if I do not sit down!"

And she sat down on the nightpot.

Since the time of Pericles, when in the golden days of Athens the open-air Dionysus Theater had accommodated over 20,000 people, no larger audience had ever attended any theatrical performance than the audience that watched the "Meeting in St. Petersburg." More than 10,000 ragged Honvéds, shivering in the cold March wind, rolled with laughter when her imperial highness, Archduchess Sophie sat down on the nightpot. From the back rows, hussars watched the performance on horseback; and when the horse whinnied, it seemed that they, too, were screaming with laughter.

"Help you? Fer how much?" asked Nick the Stick.

Again, Prince Schwarzenberg answered for Franzie, who was weeping.

"We'll sell you, Sire," Schwarzenberg bowed deeply, "the pride of our monarchy and the future of the whole western world. Very cheap, Sire."

"Shame on yourself, you loafer!" cried a voice from the audience.

"Who was that?" asked Schwarzenberg angrily.

"I am Prince Metternich. I am talking from my London exile!" replied the same voice.

"Death to the Romanoffs!" another strong voice cried.

"Who was that?" bawled the czar, waving his big stick.

"I am Prince Czartoryski. I am talking from my Paris exile. I am waiting for the happy day when, like your father Paul, you will be bludgeoned to death by your own people, and your corpse cut into small pieces, will be thrown into the Don, the Volga, the Lena and all over the Russian steppes."

The czar collapsed, and while a drummer beat the mournful signal of an execution, the characters disappeared from the stage on all fours. It was the end of the play.

"Confess," Andris said to Dali, "that you are the anonymous author of the masterpiece."

"No, I am not," Dali protested.

As if in answer to the play, the first Russian troops broke into southeastern Hungary through the Carpathians. But Apó Bem threw them back into Bukovina.

In the hectic days that followed, Dali scribbled only a few words in his diary.

March 27

Letter from Mother. The Diet in Vienna released Sch'berg's crazy plan in connection with "The 70-million Habs. emp." with the abolition of all frontiers. Headline in Vienna papers: "Hungary ceased to exist!" Ha-ha!

April 6. Camp Isaszeg

Victory over Jellachich!

April 10

Jamj's audicious attack crushed a whole Austrian corps.

W-grätz's troops are in retreat on every front. Good-bye, Freddy.

April 21

General Guyon lead us against the ancient fortresses of Komarom. We liberated that large city on the Danube shore some fifty mis from B-Pesth. With very little fighting.

Ararat, April 23

Last night Erich fled from the castle and joined the retreating Aust. troops. It was a strange feeling riding alone in the alley, then into the park, to "liberate" the deserted castle. I entered my former room alone. Within a half hour the park came alive—five people, then twenty, then more. They were deserters—former servants whom Erich called to the Austrian colors.

261

Next day, chasing the retreating Austrian troops, Leiningen's and Nagy-Sándor's hussars defeated the third squadron of the Viennese Dragoons. The village of Zekerd was only three miles from the battlefield, and Andris invited his comrades to his own home for dinner.

Spring had conquered the fields and gardens. Young flowers curtsied in the stiff breeze, old trees, fanning themselves with their leafy branches, looked like old ladies with ostrich fans. Across the river, which curved around the shoulder of small park where the lemon-yellow *colza* bloomed, the fields showed bright patches of red and blue—the uniforms of dead hussars and dragoons, in clouds of flies.

Around noon, the officers of the brigade sat talking in the living room of the Zeker castle. The only lady in that martial group, Baroness Adrienne Zeker, was sitting on the lap of one of the officers.

"Adrienne!" her mother shouted for the third time, from the kitchen. The weevilly lentils were still unselected, the quail and partridge were unplucked, the nuts unpounded in the wooden mortar.

"Adrienne!" Irma called. But whenever her father was at home, Adrienne had eyes and ears for no one but him. So she ignored her mother's call, and clung to her father's thick neck.

Adrienne was now nine-and-a-half. Irma held that a woman needs dignity in her name, and refused to tolerate silly pet-names. But alas, Adrienne's dignity suffered greatly from the two missing front teeth in her steady grin. Her pigtailed hair was brown and, despite the originally neat braiding, dishevelled.

While his brother officers discussed the Austrian retreat, Dali watched the little girl clinging to her father's neck, her lithe body nestling against his red hussar uniform. The scene brought a gleam of tears to Dali's eyes. He thought of his lost little Sonya. She had been not much more than a year old when Dushenka took her to Novgorod. Soon she would be nine; perhaps she too wore pigtails, and was missing a front tooth or two. But her tender arms twined not around Dali's neck, but around the neck of Sylvester Bralin.

"Do you want to marry me?" Dali asked Adrienne.

She hid her grin with a pigtail, then shook her head.

"Why not?"

Adrienne studied Dali's large silver spurs, his wide saber, his waxed moustache.

"You are too old for me," she lisped.

The guests laughed at this, but Andris told Adrienne seriously:

"You don't know, my dear, that your pedigree entitles you to marry into the highest ranks of Hungary's nobility. You may be poor, but your family is as distinguished as Uncle Dali's."

Andris would not have been a true Hungarian had he not taken every opportunity to boast of the ancient origin of both the Zekers and the Alacsys.

"I'm afraid," said Dali, "that compared to Karl, we are all waiters from the Papagei."

They laughed.

"Did you ever dance with Victoria?" Brigadier Nagy-Sándor asked Karl Leiningen.

"Never," said Karl. "When she ascended England's throne twelve years ago, I was eighteen, a cadet. Mother asked me . . . Asked! . . . Commanded me to write her a letter of congratulation, and address her as 'Dear Viki!' "

"What was the answer?" Andris asked.

"Well, it wasn't addressed 'Dear Karl'. It was only a printed card, 'Her Royal Majesty . . . graciously asked me to thank you . . .' signed by the stereotyped seal of a secretary," Karl said, and they laughed.

Brigadier Nagy-Sándor smoothed his big brown beard thoughtfully and asked Leiningen:

"What is your feeling Karl? Supposing we win the war . . . ?"

"Sup-pos-ing?" Andris cut in reproachfully, but Nagy-Sándor ignored him, continuing to Leiningen:

". . . and we become independent, what will the Western powers' attitude be toward our republic?"

"I don't think," said Leiningen, "that dynasties like the word 'republic.' A small Hungarian republic would be left alone . . . a toad in the eyes of the highest thrones of Europe."

"So you think," said Brigadier Nagy-Sándor, "that we would be in a better position as a kingdom?"

"Oh, definitely," Andris interrupted again, looking at Dali.

"Gentlemen," said Brigadier Nagy-Sándor with a smile, "before we elect a king, let us win our war."

A deep silence followed his words.

The ringing of a brass mortar broke into the silence.

"I'm getting hungry," said Andris, in the tone of a host, and he went out to the kitchen; his voice and Irma's reached the ears of his guests indistinctly.

Two of the officers invited to dinner at the Zekers had not appeared. One had been killed in the morning battle, the other now lay in the village school that had been converted to a field hospital, where young Ignatz Kunz, as a surgeon of the brigade, was hard at work.

While Andris was with Irma in the Zeker kitchen a boy dashed in and cried:

"The doctor needs a big sharp knife."

"What for?" Irma asked.

"To amputate a hussar's leg."

"Bring it back, sonny," Irma called out, as the boy snatched the knife and ran off. Then she turned to Andris.

"Go tell your guests that dinner will be served in ten minutes," she said.

People are adaptable. They can grow accustomed to any situation, however dreadful, when they are given no choice.

Irma's dinner was never served.

Trumpets sounded an alarm. Within seconds, the hussars were in their saddles. Commands filled the air like pistol shots, while a hussar scout, sword drawn, reported to Brigadier Nagy-Sándor the perilous situation at hand.

At the last moment, Dali lifted Adrienne's light body in the air, kissed her forehead, and whispered:

"Goodby, Adrienne."

The Brigade disappeared in a dust cloud, moving toward a small forest where the enemy, separated in small groups, readied itself to launch a sneak attack.

The official history of the Hungarian War for Liberty of 1848-49 occupies many volumes. Reliable sources are filled with contradictory data, turning heroes into scoundrels, scoundrels into heroes, martyrs to traitors, generals to fools, defeats to victories, enslavement to liberation . . . in a word, it is history. To read the official war documents of the *Staats Archivi* in Vienna, or in Buda-Pesth, would take years, and leave one with an incurable headache: Better to rely on the diaries of what witnesses there were, and hold no illusions concerning their accuracy.

Dali continued scribbling some notes in the small black journal he carried in his saddlebag.

In Camp
Apr. 25, 1849

Since we left Zekerd, I have not seen a chair, a table or a bed. In the left pocket of my dolman I found three walnuts, a piece of dry bread and a baby mouse. Andris solved the mystery for me. Adrienne! As a childish prank, she used to smuggle provisions into her father's pockets. Good to know somebody on this earth loves me.

Andris brought three cats in a cage. He says if you let a cat look once at a mirror and see himself, he will return to that spot even from thousands of miles away. In this way, he uses cats as carrier pigeons. Yesterday he wrote at length to his wife, Irma, and to Adrienne, and placed the letters in one of the cats' collars, which are hollow hoses.

Apr. 26

Headquarters in a farmhouse. Rain. Stinks like wet dogs or swine. Much talk.

"What would you answer, Karl," I asked Leiningen, "if at the Last Judgment you should be asked why you joined Kossuth's army?"

Karl, eating his third soft-boiled goose egg—his favorite breakfast dish—said calmly:

"For three reasons. First, I met a Hungarian girl. Second, I fell madly in love with her. Third, I married her. Please pass the salt."

He did not mention his strongest reason . . . the lines of Petöfi which he carried always in his wallet.

For Love I sacrifice my life.
For Liberty, my Love.

"What would you do," I asked, "if, in the middle of a cavalry attack, you should suddenly find yourself up against your brother Rudolph?"

"We would behave like gentlemen," he answered earnestly. "My brother would kill me or I would kill him."

Apr. 27

After the battle of Vac sitting in a ditch enjoying the sun of the first warm day, I dozed and dreamed my head was carried off by a large cannon ball. I felt myself leaving this life. Oh, what a wonderful feeling!

Every day I come to hate more the three words: heroism, patriotism and goulash.

Day after day the provisions grow worse. More horses and men are lost. War is not what I expected. At night, large dinner parties and long speeches, gypsy music, singing, dancing, card playing. The next morning, shots. Fun and horror. Horror and fun. Last Wednesday Brgdr. Nagy-S. won a small battle at Vác and lost a large stake at the poker table the very same evening.

Passing a potato field at full gallop, saw yesterday a yellow mare standing in a pool of blood. Bringing urgent dispatch could not stop to relieve the beast. This morning I passed the field again. To my horror the mare was still there, the pool three times as large. No human being can suffer with the dignity of a horse in pain. Rewarding the mare for her bravery I drew my pistol and shot her through the head. Andris told me Major F. did the same thing with a screaming hussar who had lost both of his legs, because the army surgeon was performing his duties in another area. Act of mercy.

Apr. 28

Slight fever. My armpits are swollen from a dose of kerosene Kunzie prescribed as a preventative against lice.

At three o'clock this afternoon, heard artillery fire in the northwest. Kossuth had already arrived in a light hunting coach in the company of General G. He has aged much in these five months.

General G. led the way to the top of the hill. With his walking stick he pointed south, then north and west, explaining the difficulty at the start, and the sudden victorious outcome of the first battles.

May 3

Victory at the village of K.

Our strategy worked wonderfully. Long, thin line of infantry attacked with loud hurrays, sounding trumpets and beating drums. Then, as the enemy came forward, our cavalry drew in and overrode their troops like a herd of boars trampling corn.

After morning Mass, relaxed over cards. Austrians in full retreat, along the front. Instead of chasing them, Görgei decided to move toward Buda.

May 9

The siege of Buda is in full swing. We bombarded the city from the Svab Mountain, two miles off. It is not a good feeling when you are compelled to bombard your own house. (Mother may still be in Septemvir Utca.) Some of our cannon balls weighed twenty pounds. But I was hit by a 200-pound Catholic priest. He was climbing a ladder against the fortress and I after him. He carried a sword in his right hand which is not a help when climbing. He slipped and fell from the top of the ladder; his sword missed my neck, put a deep gash in my shoulder.

May 20

I am still in the Rokus Hospital. Mother was with me for several hours. I had not seen her since January. She was in good health, although she had lost two molar teeth and a few small jewels. Her teeth were extracted by an old barber in Buda, her jewels by a light-fingered Deutsch-meister sergeant who lived in the palace, one of W-gratz's staff. Batthyány already is in an Austrian jail (Laibach?)

May 31

First day out of hospital. Dined with Helen (Hoch) in Blue Bottle Inn. Food horrible, drink mediocre, Helen excellent. She is singing again in the theatre, of course, in Hungarian. With the Honvéd tricolor in her hand, she was a smash hit with the song: "Lajos Kossuth sent a message. . . ." Now the whole world knows what the message was. Long live the victory of world democracy!

June 3

Last week young Franz Joseph and his mother Sophie fled to Olmütz from Vienna. Question of days that we will capture Vienna. (Let's hope without bombarding the city.)

June 5

Gorgeous sunny morning. June! At 10 P.M. Kossuth entered liberated Buda-Pesth in an open coach, drawn by six white horses. His wife rode at his side. A company of hussars followed the coach, covered with flowers the cheering crowd threw at them. Hussars' swords drawn, their horses dancing. Overwhelming ovation as they rode by.

All drunk with victory.

In the drama of the Hungarian War for Liberty, Act two ended with Kossuth's star at its zenith. Act three began with its slow eclipse, when the huge, ghostly shadow of Russia appeared above the Eastern Carpathians and, for the first time in history, Russian troops moved onto Hungarian soil. It was June, 1849.

Dali's diary gives but a vague account of the great drama:

Camp T. June 7, 1849

Bad news. Vienna papers write: Franz Josef, accompanied by Prime Minister Prince Felix Schwarzenberg, met Czar Nicholas I, accompanied by Marshal Prince Pashkevich, last week in Warsaw.

On May 21, 22, 23 the emperor of Austria and the Czar of All the Russias agreed on terms for the Russian army's intervention into Hungary's "riot." As commander-in-chief, Pashkevich will act independently from any Austrian generals, but provisions will be paid for by Vienna. To crush the natural fortresses of Hungary, the hard nutshell of the Carpathians, with a huge pincer, Pashkevich will come through the northern, Luders through the southern passes.

I have a bad feeling that our laugh last March in the camp theater may have been too early. But the general mood is not panicky. In the camp I hear the names of Lamartin and Cobden, and other great names of the Western World, who have sincerely said "my heart goes with the Hungarian people." I do not believe the czar will interfere. And if he does, the whole Western World will declare war against Russia and Austria. They cannot let Hungary perish between the Habsburg and Romanoff despots.

June 9

The German papers say that huge Russian armies are moving toward the northern and southern Carpathians. At the same time there isn't any news in any foreign papers about any move from the Western World.

Are we to be left alone again, as in the past centuries in our wars for liberty?

Last night I went with Andris to the National Club to learn Kossuth's opinion of the Russian move and the reaction—or lack of reaction—of the Western diplomats. We could not get into the club. Thousands besieged the entrance. Everybody wanted to talk with Kossuth.

June 17

The days are long. Midsummer nights. Short nights. Sleepless nights.

June 20

Found Mother kneeling, so deep in her prayers that she did not hear when I entered.

Reorganized Austrian Army, led by Baron Haynau, moving now toward Buda-Pesth.

July 2

Hot days. Only the news makes us shiver. Görgei failed to break through Haynau's line advancing from the west. He was wounded in battle. Buda is in danger. Mother moved to Ararat.

July 3

Erich recaptured Ararat. Haynau ordered an investigation against Flexi (needless to say on Erich's suggestion), claiming Flexi had sabotaged the Austrian army's demands for provisions.

July 10

Yesterday Kossuth and his government fled from Buda-Pesth.

July 12

Andris and I both now assigned to Leiningen's Third Army. Together with the Seventh, Görgei led us toward Vác, only twenty miles north of Pesth on the Danube's elbow. Görgei's head still bandaged from recent wound. Lieutenant D., the painter, made a picture of him: riding a black stallion in the golden rye field, red trousers, snow-white head (the bandage), bright-green ostrich feather on his general's hat, blue sky in the background. I do not like it. Too beautiful.

July 13

Pashkevich's army is marching towards Vác from northeast.

July 14

2 P.M. Rumors, rumors that Haynau's troops entered Buda. Cossacks approaching from northeast.

6 P.M. Rumors proved true.

West and East! Germans and Russians! No escape either for Hungary or Poland.

Sleepless night.

July 15

Russians captured Vác. Görgei ordered us (Leiningen's corps) and the First Corps (Nagy-S.) to recapture the town. Heavy fighting for six hours. Many casualties on both sides.

At eight in the evening we chased the last Russian out of Vac. Exhausted by the fighting and the scorching heat, we fell asleep in the grass. Night was dark. At ten an alarm. Pashkevich's counter attack failed to recapture Vac. This is the third night we have slept less than two hours.

July 16

Gen. Richard Guyon commander of the Southern Army (Fourth

Corps). Congratulations. He is the finest Hungarian type—of French origin.

July 17

Another 170 Poles joined our brigade; they will be led by Myci (Lieutenant Prince Mycislav Voronieczki).

Bem Apó greeted his compatriots with a speech: "My dear sons! As a Pole I am proud of you. Now, I hope you will not try to outdo your brave Hungarian comrades in the realm of steady, heroic quarreling with each other. I want you to know, there *is* an enemy too."

This innuendo referred to the steady quarrel between Kossuth and General Görgei.

July 18

Further news from Buda-Pesth. Several Cossack officers appeared in the streets. They are museum-crazy. Prof. K. director of the Natural Museum reported: "Sixteen Russians came. Didn't pay the 5 Krz. entrance fee. Didn't take anything away. They were only interested in the bottles in which we kept frogs, lizards, snakes, human embryos in spirits. They drank the spirits but did not touch the frogs or embryos. Damage negligible."

July 19

After the battle near the S. river, we dined with four Russian officers. They examined our horses, checking teeth, knees, hoofs, everything. Major Count Vladimir Dorosheff from the Third Cossack Regiment, offered 300 rubles for Andris' black gelding. Andris said a flat "no!"

During dinner the bargaining went on, as well as the vodka. At 600 rubles Andris reached out his big hand to the Russian: "That's a deal." Major Dorosheff paid out the rubles in six golden hundred-ruble coins, which I remember well from my days in St. Petersburg.

This friendly exchange, the dinner and horse sale, occurred while we were war *prisoners!* Yes, war prisoners. In the early morning battle, our company at left was cut off from the brigade and we found ourselves among the Cossacks, thicker than fiddlers in hell. Thus the Russian dinner.

After dinner, around midnight, our Brigade broke through the Russian line. Alarms, trumpets, commands. Tables and chairs overturned . . . Andris and I jumped into our saddles and galloped through the broken Russian line to our headquarters.

Later Andris said: "I feel like a horse thief. No time to repay Dorosheff those 600 rubles. And he was a nice fellow too!"

Mother has forwarded a letter from Dushenka and a few lines from Sonya, too! The letters were dated May 19, when they first learned of the Russian mobilization against Hungary. "We have tears in our eyes" Dushenka wrote, "whenever we spell out the word Hungary, and even when we only think of your country." Mother has closed the Septemvir Utca palace and moved to Vienna, where our Gisellastrasse palace is deserted too.

July 26

Hot day. Our batallion, under Andris' command, ordered to defend Verestorony Pass in the southern Carpathians, where Russians pour into Hungary. My confiscated Gere estate is not far from Verestorony; but I have no time to visit my estate agent.

Verestorony, July 27

The fight has been on since daybreak. No trenches in the rocky ground. Cossacks do what we do: jump saddle, horses lie down, use mounts as cover—oh, God of Horses, forgive our horrible sins!— rifles across the horses flanks.

Cossacks are too many.

6 P.M. Big loss. We have to retreat.

Andris takes a severely wounded young drummer into his saddle.

Order to join Gen. Bem. He was beaten by southern Russian army. Little Daddy's primitive but very busy cannon factory, melting bells and casting gun barrels, has been destroyed by the Russians.

Stifling heat. Bad food. Spent the night in the house of a genuine Calvinist minister. He and his family: simplicity and dignity.

July 28

Gen. Bem's headqu. near Segesvár. Old man at 63. Can't ride. Wounded again. Lame, right hand in sling, sees troops in coach. His adj. Petöfi. Soldiers call the poet "fellow with big pen." But he has only small pencil, sheets of paper, open neck, white collar, no hat, no discipline. At inn asked him for newspaper when finished. He threw it on the floor and snarled: "You can pick it up . . . that's where I found it." Could not call him to order because he (26) prom. to Major and I (34) still Captain. Don't like him since his poem, "Let's hang all the kings!" *Why all?*

July 29

Sleepless nights for us all. Report 16,000 Cossacks and twenty-four cannons on the surrounding hills. We are only 3,700 scattered in small villages and cornfields. Provisions poor. Not even goulash! Population Saxon, pro-Habsburg. Fear the wells poisoned. Very hot day. I don't know the degree. There will not be peace, because we count in Celsius (1-100°), the Russians in Réaumur (1-80°) and the English in Fahrenheit, which is Sanscrit to me.

July 31

Forest. Don't know where. Don't know how remained alive yesterday. Chaos in the valley, chaos in every mind. Hardly remember what happened.

Began after lunch. Talk of excellent Russian gen. staff with many *German* generals. At 2 through field glasses spotted Gens. Skaryatyn and Ohrendorff in the hills studying valley, deciding where to launch attack. We had only a few small cannon. Gen. Bem handled them himself. Salvo.

Skaryatyn fell. We guessed the worst. The revenge of his soldiers would be dreadful because he was very popular.

3:15. As if the sides of the hills had slid down with uprooted forests of *pikas*. Cossacks attacked from all directions. The ring closed. Took no war prisoners. Killed everyone they could catch. Outside ring, our troops ran every which way. Lasted maybe two hours, maybe less, I don't know. Gen. Bem fainted. Andris ran with him in his arms.

No more horses. All shot or wounded or taken. I hope my Falcon galloped back to Ararat. Sunset. Hiding in bushes on hill.

Kunzie pointed down valley. Man was running up the road, open shirt, hatless, Cossacks coming on at a gallop, overtaking him. Petőfi.

When they were almost upon him, the poet stopped, turned and flung open his arms . . . a brotherly embrace or a plea for mercy? A *pika* went through his heart and he fell under the horses' racing hooves in a cloud of dust.

Aug. 2

Forest clearing. Do not know name of village down in the valley. Of thirty-nine here, seven were wounded. Told to go south to Arad, a larger town of 15,000 or so, for regrouping of our Army.

Aug. 11

Kossuth and five members of the gov. arrived last night. He is in terrible shape. Pale, unshaven. Running fever. Took water in trembling hand. Then called a cabinet meeting. Leiningen, Andris and I were invited as observers.

The meeting explored every possibility of saving the desperate situation. To continue the fight is hopeless. Someone suggested offering the Hungarian crown to Czarevich Alexander. Unanimous protest. To whom, then? The Sultan and the King of Sardinia sympathize with us, but militarily they are too weak to help.

Everyone looked at Karl Leiningen. Great Britain!

Kossuth suggested a Coburg prince, one of the prince consort's relatives. He said:

"The British, Cobden and others, have already demonstrated their sympathy. They are fully aware that either pan-Germanism or pan-Slavism, either a 'Habsburg empire of 70 million' or '100 million Russians' sooner or later would make Great Britain 'Small Britain.' "

"I also feel," Karl said, "that Buckingham Palace would welcome a Coburg on the Hungarian throne. Albert is a Saxe-Coburg-Gotha. What about Albert himself? He is young, ambitious. He would be the strongest tie to Great Britain."

"Albert is a German nationalist," someone remarked.

"Then perhaps Adelaide Louisa," Karl suggested. "The oldest daughter of Victoria. She is nine. A young queen always brings peace and luck to her country."

"What about the Chinese Queen Mother?" Andris asked with bitter irony.

I did not say a word, but I strongly felt during this debate that the Hungarian throne is being exhibited like a ragged armchair in an antique shop. And there is no buyer. The price is too high. Perhaps a new war.

Anyway they asked Karl Leiningen to write to his cousin, Queen Victoria. He was instructed to emphasize that Hungary had ever been a *kingdom*. Neither Buckingham Palace nor the British people like the word "republic." Hungary wishes to continue her peaceful existence as a kingdom, with a constitution modeled after Britain's.

Aug. 13

The candles were burning the whole night in the tanner's house where we live. Around a large table we were writing letters. Karl (Leiningen) to Queen Victoria, Major Marky, although he is no cousin to Louis Napoleon, to the French President. Marky has a different view of Buckingham Palace. He is a republican; also, his French is excellent. Andris was writing to his wife and little Adrienne. I, to my mother.

No one talked. Only the spluttering of the quills broke the silence as we wrote. And Karl whispered once, to ask me: "How do you write Great Britain? With one "t" or two?"

It was five A.M. when Andris placed our two letters in the "mailbox," along with the six golden hundred-ruble coins he received from Major Dorosheff for his horse. The mailbox, of course, is Frenchie's collar, a hollow tube around her neck. Frenchie is the last of the "courier cats."

"She will find her way back to Zekerd," Andris said, "and Irma will forward your letter to your mother."

Andris held the cat in his big hands, looked into Frenchie's yellow eyes, smoothed her shiny fur, then kissed her head. . . . He placed her tenderly on the ground and said:

"Goodbye, Frenchie. You know the way to Zekerd, don't you? You know Mama Irma and little Adrienne."

There were tears in Andris' eyes. Frenchie did not move. Since she had left Zekerd four months before she had been kept in a cage. Her sudden freedom seemed to confuse her. She looked suspiciously around the yard, measuring the height of the wooden fence. Then she jumped and disappeared.

Világos, Aug. 14

At four General Görgei summoned all the officers. Told us the situation hopeless. From the west, Haynau's troops; from the east, the Russians. The ring closed. Only two choices. Surrender or die.

"I don't feel," he said, "I have the right to sacrifice the lives of more than 30,000 comrades without asking your advice. I am for surrender. Our last remaining weapon is to *humiliate* the Habsburgs. Therefore, we should surrender not to Haynau, but to Rudiger, the Russian general. Now, gentlemen, talk this over among yourselves and let me know your decision within an hour."

Gen. G's headquarters were situated on the top of a hill, in the small house of a wine presser. The fateful conference was held in the yard.

Gen. G returned to the house and we went down to an orchard on the hillside to vote on the question: "surrender or die." We were over a hundred, including the general staff.

The first speaker was Andris:

"Comrades!" he shouted. "I am not willing either to surrender or to die. There is a *third* solution. The sultan will welcome us. We can reach the Danube in two days. To the south, the ring is not closed yet."

"Hopeless!" Bgdr. Nagy-Sándor shouted. "The ring could be closed in an hour. Our chief is right. I vote for surrender."

A heated argument began. Karl [Leiningen] spoke:

"Comrades! I too vote for surrender. But not, of course, to the Austrians. If we surrender to the Russians, we will be treated as war prisoners. General Rudiger is a gentleman."

"But of German origin!" shouted someone. "He will hand us over to Haynau!"

Others said that Haynau's army was closing the ring from the South and that it was too late to fly. "Capture by Haynau means instant death on the gallows. Already we have been declared criminals in Vienna."

A few—I won't mention names—wept. And there were three who looked up, not to the Heavens, but to the trees, to see if there were any plums or pears left on the branches. Men are different. Two ate, one pocketed the fruit, not listening to the debate. They behaved like calm children among the shouting grownups. Perhaps they had lost their reason.

The voting, of course, was not on "surrender or die," but on surrender or flight to Turkey.

The window of General G's room was open, and one could see him pacing the room. Around five a trumpet signaled that the hour was over. Those who voted for surrender to the Russians, the majority, went back to General G, led by Brgdr. Nagy-Sándor and Karl.

Andris grabbed my arm:

"Let's go!" he said. And we went down the hill with those who had voted for the flight.

After a hundred steps or so, a pistol shot was heard from the orchard. Then another. We stopped and listened. General G appeared in the window as other shots rang out . . . two, three . . . then a volley.

This was the answer of those who did not wish either to surrender or to flee. They shot themselves through the head.

I could not move. I was all but petrified. I had a strong desire to die, too.

Andris pushed me:

"Let's go!"

And we ran downhill with the others.

5

Two miles beyond Orsova, the mighty Danube, now 4,000 feet wide, opened her arms to embrace the island of Adah Kaleh. The fleeing veterans of Kossuth's defeated army prayed to reach the picturesque little island, with its golden orchards and white minarets, which was the northernmost outpost of the Ottoman Empire; for the island offered safety from Franz Josef's and Czar Nicholas' ravaging armies.

The Kossuth-*hunds,* a term coined by Prince Schwarzenberg, traveled by night, to avoid both Haynau's military police and the Saxon pro-Habsburg citizens. Haughty and stupid Hungarian officials had always treated Hungary's minorities as inferior races. The proud Saxons in Transylvania so hated the Hungarians that, after the battle of Segesvár, when the Russians ordered them to inter the dead on the battlefield, the Saxons, to simplify matters, interred the still screaming wounded, too. A mass grave received all the corpses—among them "the man with the big pen," whose body was never found.

The fleeing veterans moved in small groups. Three of these nocturnal "hounds" were Dali, Andris and young Kunzie. The three men had neither swords nor pistols, only saddlebags, which they carried on straps hanging from their shoulders. Dali and Andris wore their ragged hussar uniforms. Fortunately, Kunzie had left his blue surgeon's uniform in Arad and had donned civilian clothes. Moreover, he had false documents too, which enabled him to enter the Saxon villages to obtain food and drink.

At daybreak these three found themselves in a forest of beech. As Kunzie prepared to visit the nearest village for provisions, Andris said:

"We will wait here. Make a sketch of the terrain, so you can find us."

"I'll return by noon," Kunzie said, "and I'll try to bring you back something to wear."

When Kunzie had gone, Dali sat on a fallen tree trunk. Andris, searching his bag for the remains of yesterday's food, said:

"I wonder if Frenchie has arrived by now. Cats are most intelligent creatures. I have known them to hitch hike in carts and coaches, and even trains."

When Dali offered no comment, Andris spoke again, this time in his most casual tone.

"Let's make an agreement, Dali. If I die first, you take care of Irma and Adrienne. If you die, I will care for your son, Ádám."

Dali nodded but did not speak. Andris yawned. The mighty yawn transformed his stern, tired face.

In his bag Andris had found bread and some crusty sheepsmilk cheese. Dali spat out the lukewarm water from his canteen. It was stale.

"Hand me your canteen, I'll go fetch some water from a spring."

"All right," said Andris, "but don't go too far." He brushed the crumbs from his trousers into one hand.

"I'm going to bed," he said with another yawn. "Bed" was the wonderfully soft couch of fallen leaves. But before he lay down, he scattered the crumbs about eight feet away.

"Otherwise the ants will eat me up," he explained his strategy. "You don't know about survival in the fields and forests. You have no idea how to entice the enemy from . . ."

"From" was the beginning of a snore. Exhausted, he fell sound asleep. But in a few seconds he jumped up, slapping his bull neck, shouting obscene hussar curses. His neck and face were covered with big ants. Dali laughed quietly.

"Here, use kerosene," he said handing Andris a small bottle. When Andris, duly smeared with kerosene, was asleep again Dali covered him with fern and burdock, not to protect him from the ants, but to conceal his red hussar trousers, not exactly the ideal costume for Kossuth-*hunds* in hiding. The look on Dali's face and his gentleness as he covered his sleepy comrade expressed more clearly than any spoken word his friendship and love for Andris, who seemed to him now more like his own brother than Flexi ever had.

Then Dali waded upstream, at times waist deep in lacy fern. The gurgling of the brook under the ferns sounded like the cool, rhythmical breathing of the sleeping forest. It was a wonderful feeling for him to be alone now, between the high columns of the beech trees and beneath their lofty branches. He walked noiselessly, so as not to disturb the cathedral-like quiet. Following the brook, Dali emerged at length in a clearing by the shore of a spring-fed lake.

The sun came up, but disappeared, as a lady would disappear behind a Japanese screen when she rose, to make her toilette. The forest was sunk in gloom. After a while, she reappeared, more radiant than before, and examined every line of her face in the small silver mirror of the lake.

Dali wondered when he had seen this clearing and this lake before. It looked familiar. He sat on a rock and enjoyed the beauty of the morning. Golden shafts of light filtered through the old trees. The cool air carried the scent of mushrooms, and of fallen leaves. In the silence, a thrush called.

Dali felt tired, but not sleepy. As he sat on the rock, tiny fragments of memory swarmed over him like ants—mostly memories of sounds and smells; the crack of gunfire on the Segesvár battlefield; the smell of a little cheese shop near the Lomonosoff Theater in St. Petersburg; the sound of Dushenka's voice, as they had sat by the clay stove in her little house, eleven years ago: Dushenka's sweet musical voice.

The spring gurgled sleepily: *Nessun maggior dolore, che ricorde* . . . "There is no greater sorrow than to recall, in misery, the time when we were happy." As a boy Dali had studied Italian under Tonchi's direction. The line from Dante's *Inferno,* saddened him, as he tried in vain to remember the last words.

Shaking off his reverie, he filled the canteens with the ice-cold, silver water of the spring, and started back to Andris. He had not gone far when he caught sight of the fleshy young horse mushrooms peeping out at him from the dark ferns. He was hungry. When he returned to Andris, his cap was filled with the white "caps of the forest dwarfs."

Andris awoke, wiped his mouth with the back of his hand and threw off his cover of ferns. Stretching, he gave a great yawn, looked around, and asked:

"Kunzie?"

"He has not come back from the village," Dali answered and proudly began handing Andris mushrooms, one by one. Roasted mushrooms would have been a treat, but they could not risk a fire. At night the light would have given them away, while by day the smoke would be visible for miles. But in the saddlebags they carried salt.

"There's nothing more delicious than fresh, raw mushrooms with a little salt," declared Andris, wiping his mustache right and left, and popping the mushrooms into his mouth. Then he laughed quietly to himself.

"What are you laughing at?" Dali asked.

"A story Kunzie told me the other day. About the rabbi and the horse." He laughed so heartily tears came to his eyes while he told the story:

"One morning the rabbi . . . his wife . . . wait a minute, not his wife."

Andris could never remember a story, but he always told them anyway.

They went on devouring the mushrooms with great gusto.

"My little Adrienne . . ." Andris said, after a long silence, but he did not finish. His thoughts were far away.

Then Dali spoke:

"Mother once told me a story about you. A good one. You were three or four years old when we newborn twins were shown to you. Do you remember what you said?"

"No. I don't."

"You pulled at your mother's skirt and asked: 'Which one are they going to keep?' "

Andris laughed heartily.

"Now," Dali added a moment later, "I can tell you. I have the feeling 'they' will keep Flexi!"

Andris made no reply to this prophecy. He could think of none. Again, the two were silent for a time. Then Andris said suddenly:

"Dali! I have made up my mind. I return to Zekerd."

Dali's jaw dropped.

"What?" he exclaimed.

"I can't go on with you. I must go home. I can't leave Irma and Adrienne alone. No servants. Not a horse or a cow. They will starve."

"Are you crazy? You will be caught, and you know what . . ."

"Yes, I know, but don't worry about me. You had Heron Island; I have Druga."

"Druga?"

"Don't you remember Druga? Years ago I told you that I had discovered a cave, some 200 yards deep, hardly a mile from the house. Cool in summer, warm in winter. The mouth is only large enough for one man. Before the revolution I collected and hid five rifles and a lot of ammunition there. I could defend myself against a whole Haynau regiment. And no one would find me. No one except Irma and Adrienne."

Dali did not speak. He was tired and homesick too.

"You know how things are," Andris continued. "Whatever the terror, there will be days, perhaps weeks when I can come out and work in the fields. Even in daylight sometimes."

"But Zekerd is some 300 miles off," Dali remarked. "A long and dangerous journey to make."

"Leave it to me."

Dali smeared his face, neck and hands with kerosene against the ants, before he went to "bed."

"Take my sofa," Andris offered laughingly, pointing to the fallen leaves which bore the outline of his body.

"Another thing!" he said, when Dali was lying down. "If I go home . . ." He did not finish. Dali was asleep.

The sun stood high. Andris pulled off his shirt to take an "air" bath. His barrel chest was as hairy as that of a bear.

Suddenly he whirled. Was someone coming?

"Kunzie," he thought.

It was not Kunzie. A man with a rifle stepped out of the bushes, and Andris had no time to hide.

A gamekeeper, thank God. The sweat-soaked-ribbon of his hat was decorated with trophies: stag's eyetooth, lynx's ear, bear tusk. He seemed more frightened than Andris.

"Agyonisten," Andris greeted him in Hungarian, in a calm, friendly tone.

The man was so astonished by this unexpected meeting with a "bear" that he could not speak.

"What's the time?" Andris asked.

The gamekeeper, his eyes on Andris's red trousers, did not answer. Obviously he did not understand Hungarian.

"Sprechen Sie Deutsch?" Andris asked.

"Natürlich" the man said proudly, as if there were no other language in the world. Then he asked in a less friendly tone:

"What are you doing here?"

"We are hunting for whales!" Andris said, laughing. Then he said seriously:

"The war is over, my friend. We are trying to get home, and live in peace with our families. Have you children, brother?"

"Yes, I have, but . . ." The keeper heard a noise at his back and swung around.

It was Dali, half awake, who had risen and was staring at the visitor with a sleepy stupid expression.

"Have you a *map* of this forest?" Andris asked. The game-keeper's pale blue eyes narrowed suspiciously, but when he saw that these two were unarmed, he reached into his bag and pulled out a ragged map. Andris took it.

"Now, let's see." He studied it. Then he made a sound which was half a grunt and half a laugh. He beckoned to Dali and pointed to the upper left corner. *"Jadi Forest,"* it read. "1765 acres. Mostly beech. 146-XM. Dukay Estate III."

Now Dali knew why the clearing and the lake were so familiar. When he was ten his father had brought him here on a hunting party. This forest belonged to his own Gere estate.

Was the gamekeeper still his employee, in the rapidly spinning roulette wheel of war? Only two months before, in June, when Kossuth entered Buda-Pesth in an open coach drawn by six white horses, that gamekeeper was certainly his employee. But many things had happened since last June. Who was the owner of the Gere estate now? Who was the owner of Hungary? One thing was sure: it did not seem advisable to tell the Saxon gamekeeper who Dali was.

"Thank you," Andris returned the map and Dali said with an ironic smile:

"I hope you don't mind if we walk through that forest. Do you smoke?"

He offered the gamekeeper one of his last cigars.

"No, I don't smoke," the man said, "and you had better not either."

"Of course, not," Andris agreed. "A forest fire in August is no joke."

The man left without another word, but sent back over his shoulder a last frightened, hostile look.

"What a world!" Andris grumbled as he leaned against the mossy tree. Then he began a political monologue.

"Minorities! The plague of mankind! Minorities in every country, all over the world. Like a knifeblade in the flesh. No way out for the minorities, they are poisoning your blood. . . ."

"And we are poisoning their lives with our stupid nationalism," Dali remarked. "I cannot blame that gamekeeper if he does not like our red hussar trousers."

Kunzie returned with a dozen eggs and bread, but with no clothing. Perhaps in the next village. When he heard of the meeting with the Saxon gamekeeper, he asked uneasily:

"Do you think he will report us?"

"To whom?" said Andris. "There's no Austrian garrison around here. Nor are there Russians."

"You are mistaken about that," Kunzie said. "I saw a Russian patrol in the village."

"Garrison or patrol, Austrian or Russian," Dali said, "let's go. I don't feel safe in *my* forest." And he laughed.

They set off again, 100 steps apart, far enough to help the fugitives to resist the temptation to talk. They made contact with whistles, imitating the thrushes: "Come-on-out!"

It was twilight when they came out of the forest. Kunzie, leading the way, lay down in the grass and cautiously looked around a yellow stubble field. There was no sign of human life on the horizon. He whistled a "Come-on-out." To his right Dali stepped out of the woods, but remained behind a tree. They were waiting for Andris, who walked on the left.

Andris was less cautious. He stepped out, seemingly lost in thought. He looked around for his friends, standing erect, his red trousers plainly visible in the yellow stubble field.

A volley rang out from the bushes nearby. Behind the tree, Dali dropped to the ground for shelter; Kunzie still lying in the grass, pressed his cheek to the soil.

For perhaps an hour, until darkness fell on the yellow field under a half-moon the three remained motionless on the ground. Then Kunzie timidly whistled to Dali and Dali answered him: "Come-on-out."

They heard no whistle from Andris. Kunzie, on all fours, cautiously made his way to Dali; then together they crept a hundred yards to the left.

Andris was lying face up, his eyes open.

"Are you hurt, Andris?" Dali asked, but he knew the answer. Not only were Andris' trousers red, so was his shirt—red with blood. While Kunzie bent over his heart, Dali had the feeling that his own heart had stopped beating.

"He's dead," Kunzie whispered.

Dali remained motionless. Kunzie pulled the signet ring from Andris' finger, then went through his pockets. But they contained nothing of value—no wallet, coins, papers—only a few mushrooms, a half-eaten apple, and a broken pocket knife. Kunzie closed Andris' eyes with a professional gesture. Still, his manner was tender, as if he were noiselessly closing the door of a room in which someone dear had fallen asleep. He handed the signet ring to Dali.

"Let's see what's in his saddlebag," Dali whispered.

There was neither testament nor letter to his wife or daughter. The bag bulged with miscellaneous items Andris had collected during their flight. He had picked up anything at all that he had thought might prove useful in the uncertain future. Among the treasures the worn saddlebag produced were a small empty bottle, short pieces of rusty wire, a rag that had once been a shirt, a crooked spoon, a length of horsehair which Andris had used for nooses to snare birds, a fishing line with hooks, a pack of worn cards to kill time, an assortment of stones for ammunition. Andris was a master at stone throwing; last week he had killed a pheasant.

Dali put every item back into the pigskin bag, which carried the same coat of arms as the signet ring, with a seven pointed crown—only seven because he was only a baron.

"Was he the last Zeker?" Kunzie asked.

Dali, his eyes on Andris' quiet face, seemed not to hear the question. A few moments later he asked:

"What did you say?"

"Was he the last of the family?"

"No. He has one child, a young girl."

"The Zekers were a very ancient family, weren't they?" Kunzie said. "Once when I asked him who his ancestors were, he told me that his grandfather on his mother's side was a famous gypsy bandleader, and his father's father was the wise rabbi in Lemberg. He never gave me a straight answer."

"Well, he told the truth," Dali said, "when during an argument he said to me: 'You shut up. In the thirteenth century the Dukays were serfs and swineherds on the estate of the Zeker barons.' "

Now as Andris lay on the ground at their feet, the male line of the Zeker family, after seven centuries, was extinct.

They had no spade to bury him. Tomorrow would be hot again. And the heat would bring ants and green flies, clouds of them. And vultures, circling high, then closer and closer to earth.

"We must cremate him," Dali suggested.

They set to work. There was a haystack nearby.

"It will make a big flame. We must run after we light the stack," Kunzie remarked.

Just as he had that morning, Dali covered Andris with fresh fern and fragrant burdock. The hay was dry but its scent filled the air. When Andris' body was entirely covered, they added dry branches to the hay. They then lit the stack and ran away like pyromanic children.

The half moon had disappeared in the dark clouds. After some 200 steps, Dali stopped and looked back.

It was an awesome sight. Against the black wall of the forest, the huge orange and scarlet flames blazed high in the air over the pyre.

"A funeral for a king," Dali said. They watched until the flames died. Then Dali spoke again:

"That is the way I would like to leave this world."

"Let's go," said Kunzie, "we must reach Orsova before dawn."

Dali raised his arm in a salute to the embers and ashes.

Then they headed south.

Bluish light struck the distant mountains like the edge of a hatchet, trying to split the darkness.

Soon, the warm summer rain caught them.

PART FOUR | IN
EXILE
1849–1856

CHAPTER TEN

THE NIGHT OF AUGUST 18, 1849
was starless. Near Orsova, the southernmost town of Hungary,
several hundred Hungarian officers waited on the shore of the
Cserna, a river that flows into the Danube. The group was silent
as the night itself. Occasionally the river's surface was broken
by a carp or whitefish throwing itself out of the water to escape
from a pike or jacksalmon and falling back with a splash. Then
the dark, warm summer silence would close over the sound.

The group of the fleeing Kossuth-*hunds* were silent, but if
turbulent human thoughts could be heard, thunder would have
filled the night, the hills would have rolled as in a dreadful
earthquake.

Fear and hope mingled in the exhausted souls of Kossuth's
followers. Painful memories crowded the men's minds: memories of the beating hooves of the attacking 16,000 Cossack
horses, pouring down in shiny brown-black torrents from all
sides of the Segesvár hills; memories of the gruelling imbroglio
the week before in the Carpathians, when General Count Vec-
sey gave orders to push all the Hungarian cannon into a deep
gorge before his 8,000 men surrendered to the Russians, and the
seventy-seven cannons—all of them cast of melted bells from
small village churches, the enchanted bells of peaceful noons

and sweet Christmas evenings—thundered down the rocks breaking wheels and barrels into pieces, ricocheting off the chasm's walls with unearthly sounds, sounds never to be forgotten.

And other memories brought deeper pain: memories of wives and children, of parents and neighbors, friends and pet dogs and cats, the sweet smell of fresh milk oozing from the cows' udders as they returned from the pastures in the golden dust cloud of the sunset—memories, memories, unbearable pains of nostalgia in that dark night. They could not see each other's faces in the darkness, so many wept silently, their tears flowing down their mustaches and into their matted beards. Some, lightly wounded, wore bandages: on their foreheads, on their hands; on a bootless foot.

Dali and Kunzie sat on the river's bank, exhausted by their four days' walk since Világos the past Tuesday.

The night was dark and silent. In Dali's mind the volley which, the night before, had killed Andris, sounded again and again, mixed with the shotlike sounds of dry wood snapping in the big fire that had been Andris' funeral pyre.

The awesome conflagration that had burned Andris to ashes became in Dali's imagination, the cremation of a whole nation.

To Kunzie, sitting next to Dali in the darkness, the future was far less grim. He was ten years younger than Dali, only twenty-five. And though he spoke a faultless Hungarian and had spent many happy days in Buda-Pesth, he had been born and educated in Vienna. He did not share Dali's vision of the "cremation of a whole nation," and even if he had, he would not have suffered over the idea the way Dali did. This is not to say that Kunzie had joined the Kossuth flag in a frivolous or insincere spirit. But Kunzie was not a Hungarian, he was a Jew. And like the other non-Hungarians of German, Polish, French or Serbian origin, like generals Leiningen, Bem, Guyon or Damjanich and so many others, Kunzie joined Kossuth's war for what it represented: the cause of democracy throughout the world.

The silence of the night was finally shattered when someone cried:

"He is coming!" The others listened, then caught the rhythmic sounds of trotting hooves. A signal torch was lit and waved. Now the creaking wheels could be heard.

The peasant cart came up to the waiting group and stopped. Lajos Kossuth alighted. His cart was followed by thirty other carts, bringing the fleeing state officials and the representatives of the defunct Hungarian Parliament.

In the dancing light of the torch, Kossuth seemed a ghost of history as he lifted his round, ostrich-feathered hat, to the cheering group. He was forty-seven years old, but looked sixty. On his bearded face and in the large blue eyes was written the evidence of sleepless nights.

A Turkish colonel, dressed in a blue, French-style uniform, and wearing a red fez, stepped up to Hungary's regent, saluted him, and said in heavily accented French:

"Donnez-moi votre sabre, s'il vous plaît."

While Kossuth took off his sword, the Turk said apologetically:

"Seulement une formalité, Votre Sérénité."

The Turkish Colonel came from Adah Kaleh, the small island opposite Orsova in the middle of the Danube, the northernmost outpost of the Ottoman Empire.

Kossuth handed over his curved sword of honor in its red velvet scabbard, and then turned to the man standing next to him.

"A glass of water, please," he said.

No, he was not going to make a speech. He was just suffering from thirst, having travelled since early morning under the blazing August sun.

Kossuth was led to a tent to rest, and after some refreshment, he was to take a boat, with three of his ministers, to the island of Adah Kaleh where, on Turkish soil, they were safe from Haynau's troops. Abdul-Mejid, the young sultan, had already offered political asylum to every politician or soldier fleeing from Austria, Germany or Russia. The Ottoman Empire was engaged in a cold war with the great European powers over control of the Bosporus and the Dardanelles.

Bego Mustafa, the Turkish oarsman waiting on shore, had no idea who Kossuth and his friends were, and he did not care. He cared only about getting his fee, 25 kreuzers for each passenger.

289

Dozens of other boats were already on their way to pick up the thousands of Hungarian soldiers, but the stream was very strong, and rowing up from Adah Kaleh, some four miles away, took more than four hours of back-breaking effort.

As the three ministers climbed aboard Bego Mustafa's boat, Kossuth remained ashore. Twilight deepened. He was only a shadow of himself now. Then he raised his hand as if to command silence before speaking. There was no need to command it. The men gathered at the riverbank awaited his speech with baited breath. When he spoke, his strong voice broken, he said only three words:

"Forgive me, Hungary."

"Forgive me," he repeated, and half-suppressed sobs sounded in the shadows around him.

That was all. There was no time for a speech—an Austrian or a Russian battalion could have been on the march to Orsova to overtake them.

Kossuth leaned down, picked up a pinch of earth, and put it into his purse. An ancient habit of emigrants who leave their country forever. Then the regent of Hungary joined the others in the small boat. The oarsman helped him aboard, and the boat pulled out into the broad river.

Two days later, after nightfall, Dali had to take part in a funeral.

Three shadows walked in the procession. Bertalan Szemere, who had followed Batthyány as free Hungary's prime minister, István Varga, Kossuth's private secretary; and Dali. Varga and Dali had been selected for this secret task for two reasons. First, both were more than ten years younger than Kossuth and Szemere, and both were capable of handling the shovels in the stony ground; and second, they were regarded as the most reliable men to keep a secret, whatever the torture, in the event of capture.

During the procession, the haze-faced Bertalan Szemere carried the coffin of a small child.

"Let me help you with it," Dali suggested politely. Szemere did not answer, but shook his head. Outside the town, they passed a small cemetery.

"How far must we go?" Varga asked, sounding tired. Again, Szemere just shook his head. For weeks he had sometimes behaved as if he were losing his senses. But after thirty more steps, he pressed the heel of his right boot into the soft earth and said:

"One thousand! I am counting the steps from the milestone in front of the steam mill. We must know exactly where we bury it."

The wooden box contained no body. In it was the 849-year-old Saint Crown, symbol of the nation's supreme constitutional power, given to the saint, King István, sovereign of the nomad Magyars, who had forced his pagan people to take up Christianity.

The heavy crown was a gift from Pope Sylvester and Dukas, the Byzantine emperor, on the occasion of István's coronation in the year 1000 A.D. It was ornamented with seventeen sapphires, twenty-three rubies, nine large topazes, and hundreds of pearls. It was valued, as Szemere put it, at 849 golden years of Apostolic Kingdom in Hungary's history. It was an 8½-pound, dome-shaped masterpiece of Byzantine goldsmithing, with a cross on top. This great national treasure had been in flight many times over the centuries, from invading enemies, from quarrelling pretenders to the throne, even from the throne's financial troubles. In the fifteenth century, it had been smuggled in a velvet cushion to Vienna and pawned to Emperor Frederick. In the sixteenth century, it had been captured by Sultan Soleyman. In the long years of the Turkish occupation, during its many flights from camp to camp, the crown's cross had become bent. Superstitious people took this as a bad omen for Hungary's future. During the Seven Years War in the seventeenth century, hidden in a pigsty in the village near Ararat, the crown miraculously survived a great fire. At the end of the eighteenth century, when Emperor Leopold promised Hungary a constitution, the crown returned to Buda in a triumphal procession, to the thunder of cannons, the blaring of military bands, and the tears of cheering crowds. In 1805, in the bottom of a peasant cart, the crown fled from Napoleon to the church of an eastern town. And in January of 1849, when Windischgrätz occupied Buda-Pesth, an old woman pushing a handcart had carried off the Saint's Crown, concealed under smelly, half rotten potatoes. This time the crown was fleeing from young Franz Josef.

The small group, led by Szemere, walked on the riverbank in

solemn silence. Only a few stars trembled on the river's smooth surface.

"One of you, boys, certainly will survive me," Szemere told Varga and Dali, "and you can tell the coming generation where we buried the crown. They will badly need it for a *real* Magyar king."

"Despite his victory in battle," Dali said, "Franz Josef cannot be the legal king of Hungary if the Saint's Crown does not touch his brow during the coronation."

Bertalan Szemere pressed his heel again into the sand, and announced solemnly:

"One thousand-eight-hundred and forty-nine steps! We will never forget the number of this year!"

Then he turned to Dali and Varga, who carried shovels on their shoulders.

"Dig the grave under that old willow."

"Don't say grave," Varga said to him. "There's no use in such pessimism."

The shovels worked almost noiselessly for a half hour. Then, without any ceremony, they lowered the box into the hole. Dali and Varga carefully leveled the ground, concealing the freshly turned earth with gravel and fallen leaves.

Commanding the small Orsova garrison was an Austrian major, who remained in his house pretending not to see a single one of the 4,000 Hungarian soldiers who, on the night of August 17, outnumbered the whole population of the town. Hour by hour, the Kossuth-*hunds* continued to arrive in small or larger groups. The artillerymen had no guns, but most of the hussars and infantrymen were armed, they were desperate. "Leave them," thought the major, "to Field Marshal Haynau." Haynau's well-equipped battalions, he knew, were on forced march to Orsova, prepared to lock Hungary's last gate to freedom. The major had six children. And those six sleeping children "defended" the remains of Kossuth's army on those nights.

Next Sunday afternoon, the fishmarket was deserted. But the timetable of the huge sturgeons who travelled upstream from the Black Sea to spawn, ignored holy days, and thus it happened last night that churning the dark water they found themselves, eleven of them, in the *varsa,* the eons-old V-shaped labyrinth of a long wooden fence in the middle of the river, strong enough to resist the mighty tail and conical snout of the "viza," that giant of the sturgeon family, that swimming factory of the pea-sized, world-famous Romanoff caviar. The viza reaches a record length of eighteen feet, weighing nearly a ton. The eleven caught last night were mere six footers. Laid on the sandy shore, they looked like victims of a careless boating party.

Dali, Varga and other shadowy figures of the refugees were watching the lucky fishermen, when a courier arrived with word of Haynau's rapidly advancing troops. He was Countess Jadi's most reliable servant. He came from Vienna, and brought a letter for Dali. It was dated August 12, 1849.

When I learned [Countess Jadi wrote] that the only way was Orsova, I had to write, hoping my letter would find you. I plead with you, Dali, come home. Enclosed are papers that will enable you to reach Heron Island, the only safe place for you at this time. And *not far from me!* Come home, Dali! I am horribly lonely. I know, much better than you, what the danger is. Still I say, Heron Island is a better place for you than Turkey or any faraway country where my helping hand cannot reach you.

I just came from Vienna where I led a delegation of the wives of the generals who were captured. Eliz Leiningen was to be the speaker, but poor Eliz fainted in the anteroom as we awaited the audience. So it was I who spoke to Schwarzenberg. I spoke briefly, and, I think, to the point, because the wives of the generals were sobbing loudly. When I pronounced the word clemency, Prince Schwarzenberg interrupted me briskly. Oh, Dali, it was horrible! A devilish grin appeared on his handsome face. I always thought he was the most handsome and charming man in Vienna. Now he said to us, rubbing his hands joyfully:

"Clemency? Of course, clemency. There will be a lot of clemency. But first, we will make a little hanging."

The sobbing behind my back immediately stopped. We left the room in deadly silence. It was an ice-cold silence in which, I think, all of us preserved our pride and dignity.

I went to the Burg and requested an urgent audience with the young emperor. My audience was denied. Then I asked for an audience with his mother, Archduchess Sophie. Denied, too!

The end of the letter repeated "Come home, Dali! Don't go to Turkey! I want to see you every week on Heron Island!"

While others boarded the now-arriving Turkish boats, Dali lit a candle and read his mother's letter again, sitting on a bench. Kunzie stepped up to him.

"Come, your boat is ready."

Dali scribbled a few lines to his mother.

Recvd lettr. last minute. Cannot return. To reach Heron Island even in civ. clothes and false dcmts seems impossible. Old Kerge served in my co. Can't find him fear he was killed at Segesv. Kunzie (young Dr. Kunz) is with me but Andris no longer. Poor Andris died during our flight. He was killed by Russian patrol night before last. I made a vow . . . Poland too . . . you will underst. . . . *plutôt mourir*. Pray for the downfall of the czar.

"Try to help Andris' family. I promised. His little daughter Adrienne was his last thought, and his wife Irma. Will write from Turkey through French diplomats. Good to think that . . .

Impatient shouts came from the shore:

"Come on! Come on! . . . Where is Captain Dukay?"

. . . my son, Ádám is with Flexi in Bavaria. Tell Flexi I am proud of him. I hear he refused a post at Haynau's side. God Bless you, Mother.

He folded the letter and gave it to the courier.

Kunzie stopped before they took the boat.

"Let's not forget . . ." he said, leaning down to pick up a pinch of earth as Kossuth had done.

"No, I won't do that," Dali said. "I'm sure I'll come back."

The two climbed aboard the small boat.

There were six other officers in their boat. Many little yellow lights were pitching on the water, the lamps of other boats coming from Adah Kaleh to pick up other comrades.

"To leave the country," Dali remarked, "is much easier than to come back."

"Why?" asked a voice near at hand.

"Because we are going downstream."

When the eastern part of the sky began to brighten, the white minarets of Adah Kaleh appeared, the symbol of the Ottoman Empire.

294

Two days later, when Haynau's troops reached Orsova, the town seemed empty. They did not find a single Kossuth-*hund*. Only the numberless corn cobs, littered under the bushes and on the shores of the Danube and the Cserna, revealed that the remains of the fleeing Kossuth army had passed that way, surviving by eating up the cornfields around Orsova.

2

Adah Kaleh was packed with the refugees. Snow-white minarets, golden orchards, veiled Mohammedan women and red-fezzed Turks decorated the small, green island. The islanders greeted the Hungarian soldiers with wide grins under their black fork mustaches, and offered them fruits, halvah, honey cake and finely cut tobacco. Their harems' grilled windows were high up under the roofs, to make climbing up and peering in impossible for such godless Christian males as Captain Isten Balogh.

Army humor had dubbed Captain István Balogh "Isten" Balogh. *Isten* is God in Hungarian. One third of Balogh's six-foot stature was covered with a huge, gray beard: he looked like Zeus. Though well over forty, Isten Balogh was still strongly attracted to the opposite sex, and he was a champion drinker. The previous February, during the battle at Kapolna, he had been badly trampled by fleeing horses. While he lay unconscious, Kunzie had treated his black and blue thighs by applying cold compresses of industrial alcohol. Left alone, Isten Balogh had recovered consciousness and grabbed the washbasin at his bedside, drinking all of the industrial alcohol it contained. He later declared it delicious.

The morning after the Kossuth-*hunds* had arrived at Adah Kaleh, in the garden of the Aziz minaret, Isten Balogh stood on a stone sarcophagus and lectured to a large audience. He had been a college teacher in civilain life; old habits die hard. Though his lecture offered little information about Turkey, everybody liked his strong baritone voice and his way of talking.

"Mohammedenism is the official religion in Turkey, but don't worry comrades, the Turks are not bigoted; there are Catholic and Protestant churches, and synagogues too, in this great country. In my opinion Mohammed was the greatest prophet because he ruled that every man has a right to a number of wives and provided the easiest rules imaginable for divorcing one or another—or all at once, if one wishes to start fresh."

"Long live Mohammed!" shouted the audience.

"The Turkish ladies," Isten Balogh continued, "are veiled, because they are so beautiful that if they went about unveiled they would not be safe for a moment."

"How do you know that, Captain?" Dali asked, and the audience laughed.

It was the first good laugh since Vilagos.

The essence of Isten Balogh's lecture was a brief summary of Turkish history. For many centuries early in the history of the western world, the Turks were mighty nomads on the steppes of northern Asia, at the foot of the Altai Mountains. As they grew in numbers and power, they became land hungry, and waged frequent wars, first in Asia, later in Europe and Africa as well. At the end of the thirteenth century, their young leader, the brave Othman, whose name means "bone breaker," proclaimed himself Sultan; and beginning at that time, the well-organized, wonderfully trained and paid Turkish army started to break the bones of Europe. Since then, in honor of Othman, they had called their quickly growing territory the Ottoman Empire. In the middle of the fifteenth century Mohammed II occupied Constantinople and renamed it *Eis-ten-puli* ("Into the city!"), honoring the battle-cry of the brave Turkish troops who had successfully beseiged the city. The new name soon softened to Istanbul. At that time, Turkey was the greatest political and military power of the world. In the eighteenth century, the then Sultan Mustapha became alarmed at the growing strength of Russia, and from then on Turkey and Russia, if not always at war, were never quite at peace. So it was that the remains of Kossuth's army, who had fought against the Russians, were warmly welcomed by the Turks.

Dali resumed his diary.

Adah Kaleh, August 21
It is our third day, breathing the air of freedom here. Kossuth and his entourage took a passenger steamboat yesterday, but no one

knows where to. Lacking maps of the lower Danube, we even don't know the names of the Bulgarian towns on the shores.

Widdin, September 5

Large town of 25,000 on the Danube's left shore. Arrived last evening on a Turkish passenger boat. Widdin is in Rumania, one of Turkey's Danubian principalities.

Hundreds and hundreds of tents along the Danube shore for our camp, 3-4 officers, 8-10 soldiers for one tent. Bread, meat, firewood available in open canteens. Wine and brandy too.

We are four in our tent: Captain B., Kunzie, Cornet Z. and myself. Our Generals live in Widdin in a rented villa.

September 12

I was told that only General Bem knows the secret of the whereabouts of Kossuth. Yesterday I went to Bem and asked him.

He paced for a time, then stopped and turned to me:

"Can you keep a secret?"

"Of course, General!"

"Well, I can too," he said, and walked out of the room.

Funny old man. But I realize that it was the only answer he could give me. Widdin is swarming with Austrian and Russian spies, disguised as consulate employees or journalists, commercial travelers and pretty commercial "ladies." Prime Minister Lord Palmerston's order to the English fleet to enter the Dardanelles is regarded in the world press as a success for Kossuth. The Burg and the Winter Palace want to grab Kossuth at any price.

September 20

Late evening rumors that Ambassador Prince Radziwill, the pro-Habsburg Pole, appeared in Istanbul to renew Austrian demands for the extradition of all of us. Sultan Ab-dulMedjid [writing his name in Turkish way—*dul* is the same as the French *de* or the German *von*] a young and brave man, refused the demand, though Vienna has Russia's backing. The more public opinion in France and England sympathizes with Kossuth and the rest of us, the more firmly Vienna and St. Petersburg strive for Kossuth's and our destruction.

Kunzie is 100 per cent sure that the sultan will not hand us over to Haynau's gallows. Isten Balogh and others are not so sure. Neither am I. The Turks have suffered many defeats by the Russians in the past decades. Though Turkey still exercises suzerainty over the Danubian principalities, Rumania, Bulgaria and Serbia, and also over Albania and Montenegro in Eastern Europe, she would suffer a deadly blow if Russia, and Austria declared war. Even to think of it is a nightmare. Sometimes I feel that Andris was right when he changed his mind and, instead of Turkey, wanted to go back to his family and hide in the Druga cave. His death, in the fraction of a second by an unexpected volley, was a blessing compared to Haynau's gallows, which await us if the sultan should be compelled to extradite us.

September 30

The French consul in Widdin told me yesterday that, after three-days trial, those Generals who decided to surrender last August, (among them Nagy-Sándor and Karl Leiningen) were condemned to death; but he added that under the pressure of the Western powers, first of all France and England, Emperor Franz Josef is ready to grant clemency.

When I brought the news to our tent camp, my comrades again split into two groups: the optimists and the pessimists. Among the optimists, the younger officers went so far as to talk about leaving Widdin and walking through Rumania to Hungary to surrender. They say even as much as five years in the Olmütz fortress is better than our uncertain future in Turkey. The pessimists (Captain Isten Balogh among them) argued that the nineteen-year-old emperor will not have the last word on clemency; and that the Black Prince (Felix Schwarzenberg) and Franz Josef's mother, that blood-thirsty vamp, Archduchess Sophie, will decide—and decide against clemency. I am optimistic about clemency. French diplomatic news always proved reliable in St. Petersburg.

But the possibility of our extradition (and Haynau's gallows) still hangs over our heads like the sword of Damocles.

October 14

Great day of fateful decisions! This is what happened.

In the early morning a large steamship arrived at Widdin from Vienna, bringing a small force under the command of the Austrian General, von Hausleben. He immediately sent to our camp emmissaries who spoke Hungarian. When we grouped around them, they told us that full amnesty is waiting for us at home. Money and land for the poor to start a new life.

"Comrades!" one of them, a handsome lieutenant, shouted, "I am your brother, I am Hungarian on both my father's and my mother's side. I serve in the Austrian army, because I know, just as many sober Hungarians know, that our small nation cannot survive without Austria. Come home comrades. What fate awaits you here? Look at these graves!"

He pointed to the cemetery not far from our camp. During the two months we have been here, over 300 comrades have died of typhoid fever. There are no wells near our camp. The "golden-brown" Danube is our drinking water.

"Come home, comrades! Your parents, your wives, your children are waiting for you!" shouted the lieutenant, and many of his listeners sobbed. He had a strong, warm voice. He was not a professional orator, but his words sounded so sincere that they touched my heart. I thought of Mother's "come home" letter, that I received in Orsova. I thought of the promise I gave my dying father.

I left the group, almost in fear that I would break down. I walked to another group where a colonel of the Viennese Uhlans, a short man, stood on a chair, speaking in a fairly good Hungarian:

"Comrades! My name is Count Rudolf Leiningen. I am an Austrian officer of German origin. Still, I am a great admirer of your heroic fight. But now it is over. I am authorized by General Hausleben and our prime minister, Prince Schwarzenberg, and Field Marshal Baron Haynau to tell you that full amnesty is waiting for you . . ."

I elbowed closer to the colonel. He said he was Count Rudolf Leiningen, and Karl's twin brother was an Uhlaner. But I have met Rudi, a six-footer, several times in Vienna. It is possible for a young man to grow taller in a few years, but no tall man becomes shorter by a foot after he reaches thirty. And I remember that last summer Karl told us that his brother Rudolf did not speak a word of Hungarian; for that matter, Karl did not speak it well. This uhlaner was not Rudolf Leiningen.

I saw through the trick. Everybody in our camp knows that Karl Leiningen is under a death sentence, together with the other generals, and has been since last September. Hausleben wanted to show us that the condemned's twin brother expects clemency, and thus strengthen our belief in the amnesty.

"I must warn you, comrades," shouted the fake Rudolf Leiningen, "the future awaiting you in Turkey is very black. The dignity of the Austrian and Russian monarchies cannot allow, cannot tolerate, even at the price of a new war, the defiance of the Sultan."

"Colonel!" I interrupted him, shouting as loud as I could, so every one in the group should hear. "Will you be kind enough to tell us who you are? I happen to know Count Rudolf Leiningen personally."

The colonel pretended not to hear my words. But when he finished his speech, he stepped down from the chair rather quickly I thought, and went directly back to the boat. Angry shouts and whistles followed him.

But the real storm of whistles broke out when our men noticed General Hausleben returning from the town, in the company of the Austrian consul.

Hausleben got back to the steamboat safely, but not before the consul ran to the Turkish barracks for help, fearing that our soldiers would attack the steamboat in their fury. A Turkish major appeared with a company, but he showed no willingness to intervene. He said to the consul, as solemnly as if he were quoting the Koran: "Every man on earth has the right to whistle."

The situation was more tragic for us than for Hausleben. The camp is now split between the great YES and NO: between the hysteria of homesickness and the *plutôt mourir*. The latter shouted they would rather die. They do not believe in the full amnesty and other promises. "Beware, brothers, beware that dirty trap!" shouted Isten Balogh, standing on a bench. He quoted Kossuth's message of last Sunday. Kossuth is still obsessed with the idea of a European war against Russia; naval action by England and France in the Black Sea would be very effective, with the coordinated help on land of Poland, Hungary and Turkey. "Don't lose hope, comrades!" Isten said. "The day is near when we will pay the czar for Segesvár!"

But many voices cried: "Let's go home! Let's go home!"

At three in the afternoon two other steamboats arrived.

Around five, those who had decided to go home boarded the boats. They made three full boatloads, while angry whistles, obscene curses and farewell shouts were heard from the shore: "Tell my mother . . . !" "Tell Erzsi . . . !" . . . tearful messages to parents, wives, children . . . Everyone made so much noise that dark clouds of cormorants and wild ducks rose on distant shores in panic.

Those who could not decide, stood wordless, watching the feverishly fueled boats. And there were men on the boat's decks, standing wordless and dead pale too, fixing their eyes on their comrades left on the shore.

When the steam whistles screamed and the big paddle wheels started to churn the water, something heartrending happened.

Five of those on the shore dived into the water and frantically swam toward the boats, and at the same time three men on the boats plunged into the Danube and swam for shore. Then the hellish noise stopped and only commands were heard, while rescue ropes flew from the decks and from the shore as well. The three from the boats were pulled to the shore, but only four from the shore reached the boats. One man, Corporal Benke from my squadron, was drowned.

More than 2,000 men went with Hausleben's boats.

October 15

This morning the empty tents in the camp look somehow like a cemetery. I had a nasty surprise when I learned that Istvan Varga, who helped dig the grave for the Saint's Crown last August, went home with Hausleben's boat. He has a wife and three children in Hungary. He is a very honest man. But Schwarzenberg knows that he was Kossuth's most reliable secretary, and will guess that he knows where Kossuth hid the Saint Crown. Will he be tortured?

3

On October 16, before the soldiers at the Widdin tent camp had recovered from the shock of losing so many comrades on the previous day, they received another terrible blow.

A French courier brought the latest mail to Dali, and to many of the other Kossuth-*hunds,* and the letters bore horrible news. In summary, this is what they said:

Together with the thirteen generals, Marshal Pashkevich had delivered to Franz Josef a message from the Czar: "I leave the fate of the prisoners in Your Majesty's hands, but I find extending clemency desirable." The message did not originate with Czar Nicholas, nor with Pashkevich. It was suggested by the Russian General Rüdiger, to whom the Kossuth army had surrendered at Világos. Good soldier that Rüdiger was, he suggested clemency in recognition of the heroic gallantry of the thirteen captured generals. Rüdiger had been so favorably impressed that, after the surrender, he gave a dinner party to the generals, after which Leiningen wrote to his wife: "My dearest Lizzie—the Russians treat us wonderfully. It is a question of weeks, perhaps days, until you, my sweet Lizzie, and our three children will be in my arms." Karl Leiningen was the youngest of the generals, only thirty; but Gorgey had expressed the view that, in case of his own death, Leiningen should be his successor as a commander-in-chief.

When the nineteen-year-old Franz Josef read the czar's note suggesting clemency, he said briefly, "No clemency."

Why was that angel-faced, blond, blue-eyed, devoutly Catholic emperor so unshakeable? He was angry and humiliated that the Hungarian generals had laid down their weapons, not at the feet of his own Baron Haynau, but before a *Russian* general, stealing the glory of victory from the Imperial Austrian Army.

And thus the fate of the thirteen was sealed.

They came from different races. Eight of them were Hungarian, three German, one Polish and one Serbian. They came from different classes of society, from the middle class, from the peasantry, from the aristocracy.

They were more than Hungarians. They were more than Europeans. They were the noblest, most romantic product of the noble, romantic century.

Countess Eliz Leiningen had asked Buckingham Palace to intervene on behalf of her husband. The palace had declined. The British ambassador in Vienna, a close friend of Flexi's, showed her the official response from Buckingham Palace.

"Count Karl Leiningen," the letter read, "is not a cousin of Her Majesty. One of his distant uncles, Prince Ernst Charles Leiningen was the first husband of Queen Victoria's mother. Her Majesty, whose father was her mother's second husband, Edward, Duke of Kent, has no Leiningen blood in her veins."

The trial of the generals began September 21 and ended four days later, with death sentences decreed for all thirteen.

The day of the execution was October 6.

On October 5, thirteen Hungarian ladies, led by Countess Jadi, were granted a special audience by Baron Haynau, head of the military court. Among the ladies were Irma, Andris' widow, some middle-class women, and two peasant girls, all dressed in deep mourning veils, representing the nation.

The audience lasted hardly a minute. When all the ladies lined up before Haynau, Countess Jadi spoke.

"We thirteen women are willing to marry the thirteen men condemned to death."

The others repeated her words in the rhythm of a Catholic Mass: ". . . marry the thirteen men condemned to death. Amen."

Baron Haynau was not surprised. He nodded and said, in a soft polite tone:

"*Ich danke vielmals.* . . . thank you for coming."

The thirteen ladies left the room without a word.

The visit was a kind of ancient rite still practiced in the

Orient, a last, and hopeless, effort to save the lives of men already standing beneath the gallows.

As it happened, by special clemency of Franz Josef, four of the doomed were not hanged. They enjoyed, instead, the dispensation of *Pulver und Blei:* powder and lead. Less humiliating than hanging. In the early morning they died before a firing squad.

The gallows awaited the remaining nine. Count Karl Leiningen was the fifth. The ninth and last was "Old Beard," General Josef Nagy-Sándor.

The place of execution was opened to the public at three in the afternoon. There were not many spectators, mostly youngsters. Those who witnessed the execution gave descriptions of the fantastically brave behavior of the condemned; the descriptions were somewhat exaggerated. Some of the condemned gave heart-rending patriotic shouts as the ropes tightened. Others behaved as human beings. Leiningen, as he walked to the gallows, wept. Old Damjanich's knees had not strength enough for that last walk, so he was politely supported.

The hangings were over by six o'clock. It was already twilight. A breeze dishevelled the hair and beards of the hanged men. The area was deserted.

Countess Jadi's letter was dated October 10th, 1849, in Vienna, where she was staying with Countess Eliz, widow of Karl Leiningen. She wrote:

I had to break the terrible news to Eliz. Even at the last moment, she still hoped. Besides Karl's belongings—his signet ring, silver watch, notebook, purse (with 39 kreuzers)—his jailers turned over five letters Karl had written to Eliz. A sixth was addressed to his brother-in-law, Leopold Rohonczy. I copied it for you . . . [Countess Jadi finished her letter with the following words:] I must be very apologetic for my last letter, in which I pleaded with you to come home. But no one, no one even in the most pro-Habsburg circles in Vienna, could have imagined the horrors Schw. and Haynau have instigated. There are rumors that the terror is raging in Buda-Pesth too. Names are circulating by the dozens. I am very anxious for your cousin, young Voronieczki, who, since September, has been awaiting his fate in the Neugebaude prison. Two weeks ago I met Tony [Antonia Zichy, Batthyány's wife] in Vienna, and she told me that Haynau had not allowed her to see her husband in Olmütz, but Lajos is already on his way to Pressburg, and he will be acquitted. In spite of this only good news, I must tell you my feeling: Do *not* come home, however bad your situation is in Turkey. Let's wait until the tempest of revenge is over.

Karl Leiningen's last letter, written to his brother-in-law in the condemned cell on October 6, 1849, at 6:15 A.M., read:

My dear, good Poldi!
My presentiments after the death sentence did not deceive me. My situation is grave, horribly grave. Before the day is out I shall have ceased to live. Well, goodby my dear old friend. I pray to God to give me strength in my last hour. Please, convey my regards, and my farewell to all my good old friends. Oh, God! Watch over my poor wife. The four condemned to the firing squad have just gone to death—the volleys still echo in my heart.
Next, it is our turn—once more farewell till we meet in a better world. God bless you all, my gallant comrades—goodby—goodby.

Your Karl.

When Kunzi entered the tent, he found Dali lying face up, the letters still in his hand, his eyes full of tears.

Two days later, a letter from Flexi brought more bad news. Twenty-five-year-old Prince Mycislav Voronieczki, Dali's cousin, who had been captured in August in the battle of Temesvár, was hanged in Pesth, together with old Baron Perényi and many other patriots. Carrot-haired Myci was the last male descendant of the ancient Voronieczki family.

But most heartrending was the fate of Count Lajos Batthyány, first prime minister of the short-lived Kossuth government.

As Flexi related the story, Field Marshal Windischgrätz had written a letter to his brother-in-law, Prime Minister Prince Flexi Schwarzenberg, suggesting clemency for Batthyány. The result was a letter to Haynau, signed by young Emperor Franz Josef, but written, of course, by Schwarzenberg: *Es ist mein Wille dass die Todesstraffe. . .* "It is my will to carry out all the death sentences with no delay."

On October 5, Batthyány was brought from Olmütz to Buda-Pesth for trial. The military judges, lined up on each side of the great hall where the trial was held, formed a "street," at the end of which stood the chairman colonel with the prosecutor major. Batthyány, heavily chained, was led to the open end of the "street." The chairman handed a black-sealed envelope to the prosecutor, who opened it and read the sentence. High treason. Death.

Batthyány paled and stepped back. He had been sure of acquittal. The chairman broke the small, symbolic white stick; a drum beat loudly, and Batthyány was led to the condemned cell on the second floor. The execution was scheduled for seven o'clock the next morning, October 6, the same day the "thirteen martyrs" were executed at Arad. October 6 was the first anniversary of Count Latour's murder during the Vienna revolution. Baron Haynau and Prince Schwarzenberg insisted upon October 6 for the mass executions—revenge for Latour's death!

When twilight fell, a Svabian peasant woman appeared in the corridor of Batthyány's prison cell, stating she had permission to sell bread, fruits, and fresh water to the prisoners. She knocked on Batthyány's cell door.

Next morning at five, when the goaler went in to awaken Batthyány, he found him lying on the floor in a pool of blood. The peasant woman had been his sister-in-law, Carolina Zichy, and she had smuggled a knife to him. During the night he had cut his throat and his neck on both sides. It was the only way he had to escape the humiliation of hanging; but he had not died. The prison doctor asked that the execution be postponed. Even the hangman was unwilling to hang a man with such dreadful open wounds on his neck. Now everyone, even the jailers, hoped that the death sentence would be remitted. But the only "clemency" granted permitted *Pulver und Blei* instead of hanging.

At six in the afternoon, dressed in black with a light-blue silk cap on his bald head, deathly pale from the loss of blood, Batthyány was led down to the prison yard. He leaned heavily on the arm of the Hungarian Catholic priest, for he was not strong enough to stand alone. A drum beat continuously while the sentence was read again. Then as the last part of the ceremony, the chairman shouted three times: "Clemency for the condemned! Clemency for the condemned! Clemency for the condemned!" But of course no one answered. The priest blind-folded Batthyány's eyes with a white kerchief and Batthyány knelt. When the officer drew his sword, and shouted the command to fire, Batthyány shouted too, but in French: *'Allez Chasseurs! Allez!* Come on Hunters! Come on!'

Six riflemen stepped forward and fired. Two bullets went into his chest, two into his stomach, one into his heart, and the sixth into his forehead, blowing out his brain through the back of his skull.

Prince Windischgrätz and Baron Haynau were both very angry after the execution—Windischgrätz because he had wanted clemency for Batthyány, Haynau because Batthyány was *only* shot and not hanged.

Every decent Austrian regarded Schwarzenberg and Haynau as sadists, and those aristocrats who were loyal to the Habsburgs were very much afraid Franz Josef would soon regret that he had surrendered to their influence.

The whole West was nauseated when news of the executions reached Paris and London. The pressure on Buckingham Palace, which had refused to try to save Karl Leiningen, was so great that Queen Victoria was compelled to order a one-day official mourning in the palace for Count Charles Leiningen-Westburg.

An unfortunate Austrian judge-advocate went to trial himself, because he had absentmindedly left on his desk a "play of pencil" he constructed during the trial of the thirteen generals from the letters of their names: Leiningen, Nagy-Sándor, Damjanich . . . and the "onomasticon" read *"Pannonia! Vergiss Deine Toden Nicht, Als Kläger Leben Sie!"* "Pannonia! Never Forget Your Dead! They Are Alive As Accusers!" Pannonia was the name of the one-time Roman colony, now the territory of Hungary.

One afternoon, in the first days of November, when a heavy fog lifted from the Widdin shore, the crows and the gulls, drifting in the high, strong wind, were surprised to see that the large camp of tents had disappeared.

Turkish boats had carried its occupants down the Lower Danube, deeper into Turkish territory.

The ultimate destination of the exiles was Istanbul, but they journeyed there in slow stages, with long sojourns in towns along the way.

That first such stop was in Shumla, a big town on the right shore of the Danube. Shumla was in Bulgaria, over which country the Turks still exercised suzerainty. Although the Bulgarian language is Slavic, the people were more closely related to the sultan's subjects than to the czar's.

The Bulgarians are Slavs and yet not Slavs; before they settled down between the Danube and Istanbul, they were an ancient Turkish race of nomad horsemen around the Volga. When they came into conflict with the stronger southern Slavs, they were oppressed—so much so that, early in their history, they lost their native tongue.

The first feeling the veterans noticed about Shumla was the abundance of wonderful vegetables around and inside the town. Their rich, steadily irrigated soil made the Bulgarians the best vegetable gardeners in Europe. The second thing they noticed was the abundance of mendicant Moslem friars called dervishes. Many of the dervishes had been rich men, but had resigned their fortunes and abandoned striving for pleasure and luxury, except the greatest luxury: absolute freedom. The dervishes thought themselves entirely independent of any discipline other than their own. They had three orders: the Howling Dervishes, the Twisting and Dancing Dervishes, and the Itinerant Dervishes. Their *sheykh,* a tall, slender, white-bearded man with a rope around his camelhair robe, a handsome figure with blazing black eyes, told Dali: "Perhaps to your Western eyes our way of life seems strange, but following the first command of our Koran, we are happy to be as humble and obedient as a corpse in the hands of a corpse washer."

At the end of November Madame Kossuth and her three children arrived at Shumla. But still no one had seen Kossuth since Orsova. A company of Turkish Infantry escorted Madame Kossuth and the three children to Kossuth's Shumla headquarters. The great patriot had to be strongly guarded against Russian and Austrian would-be kidnappers.

During their long weeks in Shumla, the veterans of Kossuth's army, nearly 2,000 in number, were scattered in the neighboring villages, billeting with friendly or not so friendly Bulgarian peasants in small mud-houses. Most of the hussars, former heroes on the battlefields, became champions in stealing the *kokashi*, the cocks from the poultry yards. And the pretty Bulgarian women were in danger, too. The officers lived in shabby barracks in Shumla. They were told that there were bigger and better barracks being readied for them in Istanbul. For political and security reasons, Kossuth and his closest advisers were not going to Istanbul.

On their first Christmas in exile, the veterans provided their barracks with small trees and tried to observe their old traditional celebrations. But every one was melancholy.

Everyone mourned the lost past, the mothers, brothers, wives, children they had left behind. And everyone worried about the future. Dali was not the only one in the group who had slept very little since they left Orsova. Isten Balogh used to ask them every morning: "Well, boys, how did your rhinos behave?" They gave the name rhinos to their tortured thoughts: black rhinos thrusting huge tusks into their hearts and brains through the long sleepless nights. Their worst anxiety was still the prospect of being turned over to Baron Haynau. How long, they wondered, could the sultan dare to grant them sanctuary?

The week after Christmas Dali received a letter from his mother. She wrote that the Gisellastrasse palace in Vienna was called the "House of Widows" because Antonia Zichy, widow of Lajos Batthyány, and the other widows of the martyrs were her guests there. Countess Jadi had gone to Zekerd herself to break the horrible news of Andris' death to Irma. She acknowledged Dali's obligation, and promised to support Andris' family "until you are able to," she wrote.

Countess Jadi enclosed a letter from Irma: "Frenchie, the courier cat," Irma wrote, "arrived safely with Andris' letter and the rubles. When the cat arrived (Aug. 19) Andris was already dead, but I did not know it then."

A few words were added below Irma's signature: "God bless you, Uncle Dali! Adrienne."

Andris' only child would be ten now, Dali thought. Her writing was shy; some of the small letters resembled tiny violets, the o-s and a-s, little bedbugs.

Andris' handwriting had always looked as if the letters were written with a hussar sabre. What had he said in his last letter to his wife and little daughter? Probably that he would see them soon, Dali thought.

On January 2, 1850 Dali wrote in his diary:

Good news!
We are saved. At least for the time being.
I led a delegation to Kossuth, wishing him a happy—a happier— New Year, and he informed us that Pasha Heyreddin, brother-in-law of the sultan had just come to tell him the sultan's answer to the renewed Austrian and Russian demands for our extradition. Said the sultan: "The remains of the Hungarian army are the guests of the Ottoman Empire, and our historical traditions honor first of all the guest's right."
"Long live the sultan!" we shouted three times.
Kossuth told us that he is learning Turkish. "We don't know what is in the future, we don't know for how many years Turkey will be our second fatherland," he said, and added with a smile: "After all, we do have a lot of Turkish blood in our veins."
During our conversation, Kossuth said a few encouraging words about the future, and spoke about his mission: to keep reminding the conscience of the world of the bestial cruelties practiced by Franz Josef after he had crushed the Hungarian war for liberty. Kossuth was neither sad nor joyful. He is the rare type who can lose everything but still maintain his dignity.

In the first week of February Kossuth and his retinue left Shumla for Kiutahia, capitol of the Sandshak, a Turkish district. A villa in a residential street awaited Kossuth, and there he was "interned" with his family for the "short time until the Habsburg and Romanoff dynasties will fall down," as Kiutahia's Turkish commander told him.

Kossuth explained his decision to stay in Kiutahia by saying that he did not want to abuse the sultan's hospitality by causing more difficulty for the Turkish government than was absolutely necessary.

"For political reasons, I shall remain here in this remote town," Kossuth said. "In Istanbul, with its many foreigners, I would be a much bigger red flag to the bulls of the Habsburg stable."

On the evening of March 10, Dali and others of Kossuth's officers bade him farewell. Next morning they were to leave Kiutahia for Istanbul.

On their last evening with the great man, Kossuth told his followers that he was considering leaving his Turkish sanctuary, if only temporarily, to present his case to the people of those Western countries that had been most sympathetic to his war for liberty.

"Has Your Excellency decided where to go?" asked Isten Balogh.

"Oh, yes," said Kossuth. And his large dark-blue eyes brightened. "First of all England. According to letters I have received from London, not only such liberal British friends as Mr. Cobden and others, but even her majesty's foreign minister, Lord Palmerston, are very sympathetic to the cause I represent. Is there anybody among you who speaks good English?"

Dali was the only one who raised his hand.

"If and when I make this journey, Count Dukay," Kossuth said, "I hope you will accompany me to England."

"It will be a great honor for me, Sir," Dali answered.

Later he told Kossuth that his sister, wife of the French diplomat, the Marquis des Fereyolles, lived in London's Mayfair. Her husband was assigned to the British embassy.

CHAPTER ELEVEN

ON THE SECOND ANNIVERSARY OF the bloodless Hungarian revolution, March 15, 1850, the Hungarian veterans entered Istanbul. The next morning Dali and a group of his comrades went sightseeing. Several French tourists joined their group, and, out of sheer politeness, Captain

Isten Balogh lectured in his heavily accented French rather than Hungarian. He knew everything (from a German guide book) of Istanbul's history, and its monumental buildings.

The comrades were always short of cash money, and Isten's lecture was so well received that he decided to work as a tourist guide. Within two weeks, he had provided himself with an arm-band reading "GUIDE, Speaks French, German, Hungarian, Rumanian, Latin, Classic Greek."

Soon afterward, he told Dali of a fat lady client who had approached him at the main entrance of Haga Sophia and said to him in Rumanian: "Will you guide me to Haga Sophia?" Isten Balogh led the lady through narrow streets for an unnecessary half hour, lecturing her on Emperor Justinian, Empress Irene, and the Isaurian dynasty. After their circuitous walk, they again arrived at Haga Sophia, and he said: *Voila, Madame!*

The lady was so enchanted that instead of the one franc fee he asked, she gave him a louis d'or.

By the end of April Dali's diary contained the following advice on Turkish etiquette:

Do not touch your cap with two fingers when greeting a Turk. In Turkey this means: "I would be awfully glad to prick out your eyes with these two fingers."

Pull off your boots before you enter the house or tent of a Turk. You will find your host sitting in Turkish fashion in the middle of a beautiful rug. He will greet you by touching his forehead to the ground.

Turks introduced *kaveh,* which is *café* or coffee, to the world. You will get *kaveh,* (with no sugar) and *tshibouk,* the Turkish pipe with long handle, sometimes over six feet long. Turks are the most hospitable people. But don't make too much noise sipping your coffee, and don't puff too big rings from the *tshibouk,* or the pasha's eunuch will kick you out.

Don't put the empty *findzsa* (cup) on the rug. Hold it in an elegant way, however numb your hand. Be polite to the servants. If a eunuch brings you a glass of lukewarm and rather dirty water, thank him in the following way: touch your chest with your palm, then your mouth with your forefinger, then your forehead with your palm. After you have drunk the water, every one will shout three times *Affietler olsum!* (To your health) and you will shout: *Evalla!* (Thank you!)

While conversing, try to smile all the time. You are completely free to say anything. You needn't fear that the pasha will be insulted, because the interpreter will translate only pleasant things; otherwise *he* would be beheaded.

Until their arrival in Istanbul, the refugees wore their ragged Honved uniforms. Now, the hospitable sultan provided them with new Turkish military costumes: a red fez with a hanging black tassel and a light-blue jacket and trousers, tailored after the style of the French army.

The first time the veterans wore their new Turkish uniforms, Dali met Isten Balogh in the street. He said to him, fixing his eyes on his fez:

"Excuse me, sir, you look very familiar to me. You are a dry-fruit peddler from Buda-Pesth, aren't you?"

"Yes, sir," Isten Balogh answered. "And I recognize you, too. But where in the hell did you leave all the rugs? *You* are an itinerant Egyptian rug merchant, aren't you?"

The refugees enjoyed not only their new Turkish uniforms, but their salary too. For officers 300 piasters a month, when a pound of beef cost a half piaster, and as Isten Balogh put it, "a 150 pound girl for a night ten piasters, not even one kreuzer."

One night they went to the *Blue Camel Cabaret*. The star was a fat, black Armenian Venus, dressed only in a necklace, red sandals and hat-sized black pubic hair. In her navel was a small silver whistle which she blew by pulling in and out her big navel muscles. Then she smoked a tiny pipe by the same ingenious agency. "It's a dirty trick," Dali said and left the show in disgust. But Isten Balogh and Major Marky enjoyed it very much, suffocating from laughter.

In order to avoid extradition, the refugees had to disappear. But how? Where? Very simple, said the young sultan Abdul Mejid, with real Oriental wisdom. Their names in the Turkish army rosters were changed to Ali, Mohmed, Ozman, Suleyman . . . and so on.

"Baron Haynau could find them now," said Pasha Heydrin, "more easily in the Silver Desert of the Half Moon than in our Istanbul barracks."

Dali changed his name to Ussein Zounguli.

On an August sunset a young girl came to the well on Ibrahim Square. She filled her jug, unveiled her face and smiled at Dali. Her left breast was uncovered, a snow-white masterpiece. Dali could not help dashing toward her, but she disappeared as quickly as a gazelle. Her Mussulman father appeared from the thin air and offered his young daughter to Dali as a wife for five hundred piaster. Dali agreed to pay two hundred, half of it in advance.

"Wait here at the well. She'll be back in five minutes," said the father, and disappeared.

So, too, did Dali's piasters. The girl never came back.

A few days later, Isten Balogh told Dali:

"If you happen to see a pretty girl at the well on Ibrahim Square, and her Mussulman father wants to sell her to you as a wife, don't give him a red piaster in advance."

"No, I won't," Dali said. "What do you think I am, an idiot?"

One day, on Damascus Place they saw a well-dressed, convicted man receive 50 "sticks." To the quick rhythm of drums two women administered the punishment. The victim walked off, limping. He was convicted of homosexuality.

"A rich Syrian lady's dress," Dali wrote in his diary, "is a narrow kaftan, bright blue silk trousers, golden moccasins. Pea-sized diamonds and rubies glued with resin to her face. Fingernails canary-yellow. Her most charming idea of beautification: miniature male sex organs tattooed on her lovely chin."

On September 30 the *Journal de Constantinople* revealed that the Rothschild firm had given a 220-million ruble loan to the Russian government. Upon reading the story, Kunzie quoted the following poem:

> Money is money, my little sonny,
> And a rich man's joke is always funny.

Kunzie, as a Jew, did not like the idea of Rothschild's money going to Nick the Stick because the czar was a self confessed anti-Semite, and described the Jews as the most dangerous race, after the Poles and Finns, within the borders of his empire. Kunzie feared that Nicholas would use Rothschild's loan to finance new pogroms.

Letters from home brought further depressing news. When Dali was a child, their servants in Vienna, in Buda and in Ararat castle had specialized as lackeys, butlers, valets, hunters, chefs, cooks, kuktas, cupbearers, scullions, pages and so on. Now, Countess Jadi wrote, in the large palace in Vienna she had only an old and deaf butler and one young housemaid. Irma, Jadi reported, had no help of any kind.

His mother's letter informed Dali that the Ararat estate, managed by Erich, was in very bad shape. Erich was now convinced that he would be the legal heir in a short time; but he was very busy, as commandant of the military police in Hungary, chasing the "Kossuth-*hunds*" all over the country. His men stabbed every haystack with their long bayonets, and searched every cave with torches. In Transylvania, when the first policeman entered a cave through a narrow opening, a volley rang out from inside the cave, and the opening was blocked by the dead policeman. Erich ordered many kegs of gunpowder and had the cave blown up. Among the ruins, the police found the corpses of seventeen Kossuth veterans. When Dali read this story, he thought of Andris. When Andris said he had plenty ammunition in the Druga cave, he had forgotten the possibility of being blown up.

Countess Jadi had visited Flexi's family in Bavaria. Together with Flexi's eldest son, Peter, Dali's son, Ádám, had received his first riding pony. "Last Sunday," she wrote, "Ádám fell out of the saddle, his right foot caught in the stirrup. The same thing happened to you when you were a child, and Falcon galloped away dragging your head along the ground. Do you remember? But this time Flexi caught the pony after a few steps, and Ádám, though head down, was not hurt. No other news in the family."

Spring lengthened into summer, summer into fall. The time passed uneventfully for the exiles.

One day in October, Dali wrote in his diary:

Last night again endless talk. "Exiles," said Isten Balogh, "don't experience the tragic storms which stir the soul of greatness. Neither in politics nor in literature. I am horrified by our confused political talks and quarrel." And Kunzie said, using medical words: "Exile is a sickbed, a hemophilia of memories, often accompanied by pernicious anemia of morals." At these words, he looked at Cornet Zih, who still has not paid back a friendly loan, in spite of his "word of cornet honor."

And two days later, Dali wrote:

Sleepless night. Rememb. Dushenka with my two favorite lines from Shakespeare's Tempest:

> Sir, she is mortal,
> But by immortal Providence, she's mine!

Alas, I had to correct the Bard:

> But by immortal Providence, she *was* mine!

In November Kossuth wrote them from Kiutahia that he had received a letter from New York, from Colonel László Ujházy, which he forwarded to General Guyon. Ujházy urged Kossuth to visit the United States. He found the sympathy of the American people fantastic.

Dali knew Colonel Ujházy very well. He was a brave hussar on the battlefield and highly imaginative, but unfortunately he couldn't write correctly even in Hungarian.

Ujházy's long letter read:

I was greatly encouraged by Senator Oates, who wants to introduce a bill requiring that every Hungarian freedom fighter receive a few hundred acres to start a farm. The United States Government owns millions of acres west of the Missouri, stretching bigger than the whole of Hungary, where herds of bisons graze. I spoke with an American government official, very high up, and told him that our forefathers had made a fatal mistake, when coming from Asia almost a millennium ago: they settled in that part of the Danube Valley which was to become the bloodiest battleground between East and West.

The official listened to me eagerly when I presented him with my vast plan! To bring over 5 million Hungarians doomed to death by German and Russian imperialism. Patterned after New England, we can establish New Hungary in the American West. I told him that it is in the best interest of the United States to spread civilization to the Missouri grasslands and sow the land with 5 million tough Magyars who have proven themselves, again and again, ready to die for freedom and democracy.

"A wonderful idea!" said the official. Then he took out a pencil and paper and began jotting down calculations. "The only trouble is," he said, "that our biggest steamship the *Franklin,* can carry only 300 passengers. For 5 million Magyars we would need some 20,000 ships. And we don't have them."

Tomorrow I will go to the Ocean Steamship Company, which recently added the *Washington* and *Herman* to their fleet. They are building bigger and bigger ships all the time; in ten or twenty years, we could bring our people to the great Missouri Valley.

Ujházy said at the end of his letter: *Ubi bene, ibi patria*—our country is wherever we are well off.

In the middle of December word came from Aleppo that General Bem was dead. Mussulmen came to his bier, touched the coffin, then kissed their fingers. They regarded him as a saint.

There is nothing more democratic than a Turkish funeral. Be he a pasha or a beggar, passersby in the street carry the coffin for a few steps, one group after another.

In Istanbul many comrades wept when Isten Balogh read the report of "Little Daddy's" death. Dali was even more saddened than the others. For him, General Josef Bem was the incarnation of Poland's tragedy, who, in his old age, came to fight for Hungary's freedom.

On Christmas Eve a new game made its appearance—Little Baccarat. One by one each player would grab a handful of lentils from a pot in the middle of the table and count it, under the watchful eyes of the other players; if he got 379 he had a *schlager*, a hit. If he got 281, he could grab a second "card." If the two grabs came to over 410, he had lost. Very exciting. Cheating was impossible. Counting took time, but to the Istanbul exiles, time was cheap.

2

In the early months of 1851, conversation among the refugees revolved exclusively around Ujházy's Missouri Valley scheme. Many had come to view the Missouri Valley as a Garden of Eden. Others said that Ujházy was not only a dreamer but an idiot. Dali did not participate in the argument. It saddened him that such a remote scheme should generate such violent heat among his comrades.

In the first week of January, the pressure from Vienna and St. Petersburg became so strong that the sultan was finally compelled to "expel" Kossuth from Turkey. The deadline for his departure was September 15. Pasha Heyreddin, who went to Kiutahia personally to inform Kossuth of the sultan's decision, apologetically explained that the last Austrian-Russian demand contained polite but definite threats of war if the sultan did not yield. The Austrian ambassador had represented to the sultan that Kossuth's asylum in Turkey not only injured the pride of the two victorious powers, but was also regarded as a hostile act because the "criminal" (Kossuth) was organizing a campaign against Austria and Russia in the world press from his headquarters in Asia Minor.

On February 8 good news came from Kiutahia. Kossuth's friends in England were arranging a lecture tour for Kossuth there and most probably also in the United States. The "Great Journey" to America, as Kossuth called it, depended on the American government. Kossuth was working on the list of his followers—about twenty—who would accompany him to England. Dali's name was seventh on the list.

One day in March Dali and a few comrades went to see the famous Howling Dervishes, who stood in a semicircle in the Mosque, their faces pointed fixedly at the *imarat,* which indicated the direction of Mecca. There were strong, handsome youths and white-turbaned old men among them. They began their rhythmic singing in a low tone, bowing alternately to right and left; they kept it up for hours, the singing becoming gradually louder, until at length sweat glistened on their foreheads and their mouths foamed as they howled: *La ilaha ill'llah!* Then exhausted, they collapsed.

"Some even die," their Turkish guide told them.

"They made a very deep impression on me," Dali wrote to the des Fereyolles, describing the scene. "Whoever is God, He is in the very depth of the Howling Dervishes. I understand they smoke opium, which produces pleasant sensations and hallucinations. The dervishes we saw in Bulgaria belonged to the Dancing and Twisting Order. This was the first time I ever saw the Howling Order. It was fantastic, and heartrending.

"One day I will enter that order. I have much more reason for howling than these poor devils."

On June 8, Kossuth wrote to Istanbul with great news. Senator Foote of the State of Mississippi had moved in the Senate that the Government offer Kossuth asylum in the United States and send a warship to Kiutahia in Asia Minor to fetch him and his entourage. Dali ordered a black Hungarian *attila* for the "Great Journey." He felt sorry for Kunzie, who was not on the passenger list. Kunzie still dreamed of going to his relative in Philadelphia, who could surely help him to become a successful doctor in the United States.

The American frigate *Mississippi* arrived on August 20 and circled the shores of Asia Minor, waiting for the sultan's consent to fetch Kossuth and his comrades. Two days later Sultan-Abdul Medjid gave his consent.

The French consul told Dali that news of the *Mississippi*'s arrival had been acclaimed with delight in France, in England, in America and all over the free world, and had provoked horrified amazement in Vienna and St. Petersburg. The French consul thought that Russia and Austria might sever diplomatic relations not only with Turkey but with the United States as well.

On August 23, leaving behind him his name as Captain Zoungouli, Dali took the boat for Kiutahia. In his passport he was again Captain Count Adalbert Dukay; now he had a new title as well: "Hungarian Freedom Fighter."

Kossuth's headquarters in Kiutahia was teeming with foreign correspondents. He was now the focus of the world press. An American newspaper, *The Sun*, compared him to Lafayette, and reported elaborate preparations for Kossuth's reception in New York.

On the morning of August 24, two years after Kossuth and thirty-five other rebels, including Dali, were hanged in effigy, the frigate *Mississippi* arrived at Kiutahia and hoisted the Hungarian tricolor in Kossuth's honor.

After lunch Dali went to the harbor to have a look at the *Mississippi*. She was the mightiest warship in the world—a sidewheeler carrying powerful twenty-four-pound guns whose fire was capable of piercing two inches of iron.

The *Mississippi* was scheduled to sail on September 1, 1851.

Dali arrived at the harbor at nine. There was a crowd for the farewell, including a Turkish company in gala uniform. Pasha Hayreddin, brother-in-law of the sultan, ceremonially returned to Kossuth the sword of honor which had been taken from him before he stepped on Turkish soil at Ada Kaleh two years before. The pasha spoke no foreign language, but at the end of his brief Turkish farewell speech he proudly shouted a few Hungarian words which he had painstakingly learned for the occasion: *Isten veled barátom!*—Good-bye, my friend! Alas, the pasha's Magyar pronounciation was so poor that it sounded like: *Este feled garatom!* which meant "Around evening my throat!" But there were tears in the pasha's big, black eyes when he embraced Kossuth.

Kossuth answered in fluent Turkish. He had learned the language during the two years of his exile. He thanked the sultan and the Turkish people for the hospitality and friendship he and his comrades had enjoyed in the great Ottoman Empire.

Representing the United States, the American consul gave Kossuth $2,000 in an envelope for small expenses during the long journey. Deeply moved, Kossuth thanked him but did not accept it, saying that he had been able, in the past two years, to save almost all the high salary he had received from the Turkish government.

Then, they walked up the gangway to the Free World. On board the *Mississippi*, the captain greeted Kossuth with a brief speech, addressing him as President of Hungary. Kossuth replied in fluent but rather flowery English.

After the reception, Kossuth explained to his new American friends that he had learned his English during his three years in the Buda prison by reading Shakespeare and the King James version of the Bible.

Then, at a signal, the *Mississippi*'s whole body trembled, the huge paddlewheels started to churn the dark water into white foam, and, to Dali's inexpressible joy, they were en route.

The brief story of the Great Journey was written in Dali's diary.

Marseilles, September 16

No roses without thorns.
Huge crowd waited for Kossuth at the Marseilles harbor, but he was not allowed to leave the ship. Why? We do not know. Strong

police cordons barred the way of the enthusiastic French who wanted to come aboard and shake hands with Kossuth. Thousands wanted to hear Kossuth and shouted: *"Vive Kossuth! Vive Kossuth!"*

He had to make a speech. He spoke in excellent French.

After his speech and the great ovation that followed, the crowd threw flowers at him which, alas, fell into the water. But several ladies' hats and even three women's shoes landed on the upper deck.

September 18, Gibraltar

Kossuth was advised to accept the invitation to England before going to New York. We will go to England aboard the Spanish *Madrid* instead of the *Mississippi,* will postpone our trip to America for two weeks.

September 23

Arrived in Southampton. Despite the size of the crowd, I managed to spot Alphie and Rolly and their daughter, Louise, born in St. Petersburg thirteen years ago. I wouldn't have recognized Louise. Little Jules, 3, was standing on Alphie's shoulder to see better. This is the first time I have seen him. After the gala reception and festivities in Kossuth's honor we went to Brompton Road behind Hyde Park to the des Fereyolles' apartment.

September 28

Alphie told me that when Queen Victoria was informed about the "republican" Kossuth's "too warm reception" in Southampton by the British liberals, Cobden and others, she wrote a letter to Prime Minister Lord John Russell telling him to prevent Lord Palmerston, secretary of state, from receiving Kossuth, who was on his way to London. According to Sir Charles Greville, Palmerston answered the prime minister's letter: "There are limits to all things, I do not choose to be dictated to as to whom I may or may not receive in my own house."

Prime Minister Lord Russell summoned the cabinet immediately. Twelve of the members sided with him, one with Palmerston. Overwhelmed, Palmerston agreed not to receive Kossuth.

October 25, 1851

It is scarcely believable what Kossuth can do with an audience. Even the conservative papers (who have no liking for him) speak of him as a man of indomitable courage and eloquence.

October 28, Picadilly

This morning I saw Queen Victoria and the prince consort riding in an open coach. Victoria's pink parasol seemed to symbolize the pink sky of the future. The crowd cheered the young royal couple. Karl Leiningen once told me that Prince Albert's pet name in Paris was "the Prince from the Box." The French pronunciation of *"le Prince qu'on sort de la boite"* is exactly the same as that of Prince *Consort (qu'on sorte)*—chosen. Victoria chose him from a pool of extremely handsome German princes, perfectly trained for European thrones—tall, blond, blue-eyed, honest and elegant. He is a Saxe-Coburg, not only German but pan-German. Grenville told Alphie that when the news that the czar's Cossacks had crushed the Kossuth army reached Buckingham Palace two years ago, Albert gleefully drank a toast to Nick the Stick.

October 30

Richard Cobden writes in *The Times* of Kossuth: "He is most certainly a phenomenon. Not only is he the leading orator of this age, but he combines the rare attributes of a first-rate administrator: high moral qualities and unswerving courage. This is more than can be said of Demosthenes and Cicero."

November 3

Wonderful news in the *Morning Post*. Baron Haynau, whom the press of the free world called "The Hyena of Brescia," arrived in London last week for a rest after the ordeal of signing so many death sentences in Buda-Pesth. His long, hanging, screw-shaped moustache became very well known through caricatures.

"Last Monday," writes the *Morning Post,* "he was dining with a girl in a fashionable Soho restaurant. A few sturdy Britons, delivering beer kegs to the restaurant, recognized him.

" 'You are Baron Haynau?' one of the delivery men asked politely.

" 'Yes, what do you want?' Haynau asked.

" 'You are the "Hyena of Brescia," are you not, sir?'

"Háynáu sprang to his feet.

" 'What an impertinent . . . !' "

He did not finish. He was interrupted by a mighty slap. Women screamed, chairs flew through the air, tables turned over. The kegboys beat Haynau and threw him out into the street.

God bless the English kegboys.

November 20
Southampton

277' long, 45' in the beam, 24' in depth. Motor power a pair of side-level engines. *Humboldt* is the largest, most beautiful American steamship. The day after tomorrow we will bid farewell to England.

Ninth day on the ocean. And we have another long week on the gray waves. No appetite, though the *Humboldt*'s kitchen is fine. All seasick. The waiters are black, dressed in white; the maids are white, dressed in black.

4.

December 5
Staten Island

It was a very great moment when the gigantic brown mass, the hills of a large island, emerged from the evening mist. America! We will arrive in a few hours. I asked the captain the origin of the name Staten Island, and he said: "When Henry Hudson arrived here, one of his Dutch officers, seeing land, asked: 'S'tat en island?' Hudson said yes and the island was christened."

"The old man is pulling everybody's leg," one of the officers told me later. "Originally the island's name was Staaten Eyland in honor of the States General of the Netherlands."

It was already dark night when, after sixteen days on the gray and stormy ocean, we arrived at Staten Island harbor. Music, torches, a large cheering crowd. Reporters and many Yankees, climbing up the rope ladders. Reception in the ship's salon. Reception a little bit too warm. A tipsy Yankee slapped Madame Kossuth's backside with a jovial "Hi, Hunkie!"

December 6

Clear winter day. The chairman of the city council and other high officials arrived at Staten Island harbor from New York; after several speeches we were told: Hurry up, thousands are waiting in New York.

We boarded the *Vanderbilt* at 10 A.M. sailed through the dense forest of flags, masts, sails, cheers and hurrahs, military bands and roars of cannon from every direction. Arrived at the Battery at noon. The cheering went on. People went mad while we were led through Castle Garden.

The crowd broke through the police line, the mob was uncontrolled and so excited that we lost Madame Kossuth. (Later we found her in a nearby millinery shop buying a half-dozen new hats.) Mayor Kingsland greeted Kossuth. The speeches were lost in the shouts, but the "Great Exile's" tragic and majestic figure, in black-velvet *attila,* round hat with an ostrich feather, silver belt, and sword of honor, made a tremendous impression—not only on the ladies. After the speeches, Kossuth mounted a beautiful black stallion and, accompanied by General Sanford, inspected the troops of New York. The soldiers greeted him wildly, twirling their caps on their muskets. Then the procession started up Broadway, Kossuth in an open coach drawn by six white horses. The street was decorated with American, Hungarian and Turkish flags. All windows were thrown open—one building had eight floors! flowers and cheers from above—all the church bells ringing. Never have I seen so many people—several hundred thousand, at least—as we rode up Broadway to City Hall, where a gala tent awaited the hero of the day. After the parade, Kossuth fled City Hall through a side door. The crowds, so eager to express admiration, endangered his life.

Small dinner in Irving House. No more speeches. Mayor Kingsland said he would urge formal recognition of Hungary's independence, and General Sanford added that he would organize committees in every regiment to support the Hungarian cause. General S. knew, and faultlessly pronounced, the names of all the 13 generals. He said that he had received the list from the late President Zachary Taylor, a great soldier himself, at the time of the hangings.

December 11

Municipal dinner. Kossuth spoke: "Is there anybody in your great country who can show me a single word in George Washington's writing which speaks of non-interference or indifference? George Washington offered *neutrality* whenever two or more countries are fighting. But he never said that the United States should remain indifferent when a foreign despot interferes in the affairs of a sovereign nation. In this case, the very basis of human rights was attacked—the base on which the greatness of the United States rests." And Kossuth quoted Washington's letter to Lafayette: "If only we might enjoy twenty years of peace, our country will be able to stand up against any despotic power in the world."

Standing ovation.

Mr. Simeon Draper made the last speech.

"I believe," he said, "that my speech will be a great success for I have to announce that a gentleman who prefers to remain anonymous has just offered one thousand dollars to help build up the new Kossuth army."

A roar of applause greeted him.

December 12 to 20

Every day one or two delegations, Columbia University, schools, charity organizations, etc., and speeches, speeches, speeches. After the delirious welcome in New York we look forward to our Washington trip.

A distinguished Quaker lady, Lucrecia Mott, approached Kossuth, asked him why he does not raise his strong voice against slavery in the South.

The same afternoon, Kossuth was visited by a Blackfoot Sioux Indian chief, who said that all Hungarians were *mekams,* bosom friends of the American Indian. As a token of his abiding friendship for Kossuth, the chief offered him a feather costume, said to be 300 years old. His wife looked older than the costume.

Christmas 1851

Catholic priests (first of all the Jesuits) make violent attacks on Kossuth in their sermons: "The dangerous Hungarian adventurer." The echo of Vienna? Or is it just because Kossuth is Protestant?

December 27, Washington

I just learned that the name of the Congressman who, two years ago, raised his voice for our cause and was subsequently attacked by an anti-Semitic paper in Vienna, is not Linkohn but Lincoln, and the horse-trader Jacob in Hungary was never his father.

I have received the full text of his resolution. It reads:

"Resolved, that in this present glorious struggle for liberty, the Hungarians command our highest admiration and have our warmest sympathy.

"Resolved, that they have our most ardent prayers for their speedy triumph and final success.

"Resolved, that the government of the United States should acknowledge the independence of Hungary as a nation of free men at the very earliest moment consistent with our amicable relations with the government against which they are contending.

"Resolved, that in the opinion of this meeting, the immediate acknowledgment of the independence of Hungary by our government is due from American free men to their struggling brethen, to the general cause of republican liberty, and not violative of the just rights of any nation or people."

Alone in my room I read this resolution over again and again, and I am not ashamed to admit that I wept. The resolution was presented to a mass meeting on September 12, 1849. On that same day Karl Leiningen, Nagy-Sándor, all the 13 generals were condemned to death.

December 28

Cold day and cold reception in the White House. The late president Zachary Taylor, who died suddenly the summer before last, was a great soldier and a great admirer of our War for Liberty. Mr. Fillmore, who is now president, showed complete ignorance of Hungary during the brief audience. He uttered no word of official recognition of the justice of Hungary's cause, nor did he hold out any hope that the United States would support Hungary in its fight against despotism. The audience was a disastrous anticlimax to the fervent welcome of the American people.

After the audience, Kossuth said: "Men, you forget the most powerful word in mankind's fate. *Protocol!* We cannot blame Fillmore. Austria is one of the major powers of Europe. President Fillmore could not do more for us without creating a serious diplomatic incident."

It was true. In fact, the Austrian envoy did protest when Daniel Webster said: "We shall rejoice to see our American model upon the Lower Danube and on the mountains of Hungary."

One hope remains: the Senate has invited Kossuth to address it.

January 1, 1852

A series of articles describes Kossuth: "Five feet eight inches, slender, not too strong. Face long, forehead broad but not high, dense locks falling over it. Hair and beard dark brown. Moustache medium, mouth small and narrow, eyes, light blue—" "I have never seen such eyes"—writes Henry du Puy, "they are extremely far apart, giving his face a peculiar, I should say superhuman expression. He wears a tobacco-brown long jacket, tight-fitting black breeches and comfortable wrinkled boots. He speaks as if unprepared, slowly, but with vigor, in a wonderful, powerful voice. An extraordinary soul radiates when he speaks. His wide blue eyes are very intent and spiritually warm."

January 5

We all firmly believed that Kossuth's speech in the Senate would perform miracles. He was warmly received; the Senators one by one shook his hand and asked him questions. What was his Governor's salary, what kind of pomade did he use on his hair and beard, was his curved sword a real weapon or just an ornament? And so forth. They chatted with him amiably on various topics for more than an hour, but he was not given the rostrum to make his speech.

January 7.

My letter to the editor of *The Sun:*
Dear Sir!

Forgive me my hair-splitting. The word Hungarian does not derive from the word *Hun* but from *on-ogur,* an ancient tribe in Asia. The name lives in the German *ungarn* or in the Italian *ungherese,* as clear proof that we Hungarians have nothing to do with the Huns, meaning barbarian hordes of many races.

Sincerely yours,

Adalbert Dukay,
(no relative of Attila, Ghengis Khan or Prince Pashkevich.)

From January 10 to April

Triumphal tour to Annapolis, Harrisburg, Pittsburgh. Kossuth plans to buy 40,000 muskets at $2 apiece. Then he went to Cleveland, Columbus, Dayton. In New Orleans there was no greeting, no delegation. We smelled "fight" at the mass meeting, but Kossuth's eloquence proved to be irresistable, his inexplicable magnetism did the trick. The crowd became most friendly in the end. Then Cincinnati, Madison, Indianapolis, Louisville. Hundreds of pamphlets, thousands of editorials about Kossuth—streets, squares, cities and countries were named after him. Kossuth hats and Kossuth beards became the fashion. Children were named after him. Then to St. Louis, sailing down the Ohio River. Alas, the name of the steamer was *Emperor*. In Concord, we again met a hostile crowd, but we formed a protective wall around Kossuth. After Albany, Buffalo and Syracuse we returned to Washington. His popularity reached its peak during the triumphal tour through New England. Then it began to drop.

Disillusionment followed disillusionment. Madame Kossuth tried to surpass Empress Eugenie and Queen Victoria in dignity, which did not work well in Cleveland. In Pittsburgh she had a heated argument in a millinery shop where she insisted on half-price purchases as the "great Kossuth's" wife. By the end of April the stature of some persons in Kossuth's entourage had shrunk to the size of General Tom Thumb in Mr. Barnum's Museum of Curios.

The Kossuth "show" also found a dangerous competitor in the enchanting Miss Jenny Lind, possessor of the "most beautiful voice and prettiest legs of the nineteenth century." Her concerts, a succession of triumphs, were a bigger drawing card than the appearances of Kossuth. In Providence, Rhode Island, *one* ticket for her performance brought $650, while the gross receipts at the Kossuth mass meeting the next day amounted to less than $400.

The glory of the Hungarian War for Liberty faded. Members of the committee were quarreling, backbiting. And a sinister question arose: How much was embezzled from the collection for a new Kossuth army? And who were the embezzlers, who deprived Kossuth of the 40,000 muskets he intended to buy? Kossuth sailed for London under the alias of Mr. Smith. He left New York a fugitive; in his entourage were the gentlemen responsible for the scandal concerning the collection.

326

This past March the des Fereyolles moved from London to Paris. Tomorrow I will sail for France.

I read last December that the number of Hungarian immigrants to the U.S. between the end of the eighteenth century and autumn of 1851 was 158. Now, this number will be increased by those in our party who have decided to remain, among them one of Kossuth's sisters, who married a Pole named Zulawski. Thus *Hungapole* has been realized, in miniature, on their farm in New Jersey's Orange County. The small farm was presented to them by an admirer of Kossuth.

Something else will remain, too, of our great dreams. At a crossroad in the Missouri Valley, a signpost reads NEW BUDA. Ujházy's flaming imagination lured more than seventy veterans from a hopeless exile in Turkey. New Buda grew in imaginations into a city of golden palaces. But when they arrived, they found only a few empty log cabins. Pioneer life proved too hard for Madame Ujházy; she died. Now László Ujházy has wandered to Mexico, seeking fabulous but imaginary gold mines.

The New Buda signpost in the Missouri wilderness stands like a cross at the grave of Utopia.

No nation can be reborn in the womb of another nation, whatever is the richness and vastness of the new country.

CHAPTER TWELVE

IT WAS APRIL, 1853.

Dali was dining in Montmartre at "Le Rat Mort" with Rolly and Alphie and enjoying a *haricot de mouton, parfait noisette* and the intellectual sweetness of Paris.

"Istanbul," he said, "is the mystical city of heaven; New York the 'federation of matter, industry lording over art,' and Paris is the only true city on earth—in love, cuisine, politics, in every way and walk of life."

"That's the truth," Alphie responded.

"Dali, it's so good to hear you say something cheerful for a change," Rolly said. "But why do you look so glum, if you're happy here?"

"I've just heard the most depressing news from London. I knew, of course, that Kossuth had taken work to support his family, but today, for the first time, I learned what kind of work."

"What is it?" Rolly asked.

Dali did not answer immediately. Then he said:

"He goes about from door to door, hat in hand, selling fire insurance policies. Oh, please, don't misunderstand me! He has to have an income. Whatever he is selling, he will not sell his dignity. Honest work makes a great man greater."

There were tears in Rolly's eyes. And in the silence Alphie remarked:

"History is the greatest inventor of irony. He who years ago set fire to a nation is now selling fire insurance policies."

Dali had received Dushenka's last letter more than two years before, in June of 1851 in Istanbul. In the fall of 1853, through Alphie's diplomatic channels, he heard from her again. This was her sixth letter since she had left Dali. She had borne Sylvester Bralin a fourth child. Their first was Olga, the second and third two boys, and now again a daughter. Together with Dali's daughter, Sonya, there were now five children in the baker's house in Novgorod. Sonya was thirteen now. She was five-three, weighed 114 pounds, and was very beautiful, Dushenka reported, "except for her big nose, which she inherited from you." Dushenka sent a watercolor portrait of Sonya, painted by Sylvie, whose hobbies were playing chess and painting portraits.

Dushenka's letter ended sadly. "Oh, Dali," she wrote, "I cannot tell you my sleepless nights for my first child. Ádám was not yet three when I left him in Buda. Since then, his birthday has been just like his funeral for me every year. I have no hope that I will ever see him, or you, again in this terrible world. There is no photographer here in Novgorod, but I think that in Vienna, though it is awfully expensive, your mother or brother could have a photograph of Ádám made. Send me one, please, or if you cannot do that, maybe your people have a painter friend in Vienna who could make a drawing of my lost son."

Dali placed his lost daughter's portrait on his desk. The water color, though executed lovingly, was far from a masterpiece. Sonya's eyes were too blue, her cheeks too pink, her mouth too tiny and her nose too big.

Dali's heart contracted as he looked at the portrait. This Novgorod baker's painting, this was all that remained to him of his only daughter. And he asked the same question Dushenka had asked about Ádám: "Will I see her again in this terrible world?" And Ádám—what did he learn of Ádám? The boy was already fifteen, and was being brought up with Flexi's four children. Dali had not set eyes on him in four years.

Dali was still brooding when, at five o'clock he arrived at the des Fereyolles' apartment. Rolly was entertaining the usual company, for the most part Alphie's diplomatic colleagues, aristrocrats, scientists, writers, composers. Among them were a few new faces.

Rolly came up to Dali with an elderly man. "This man *insists* he was present at your christening."

"I attended that party myself," said Dali, with a mock serious expression, "but I do not remember you, sir."

They both laughed.

"I know," the old man said. "Your twin, Antal, behaved wonderfully—he slept through Metternich's speech. But you were screaming like hell! My name is Chambonnas."

Dali clutched his hand.

"Chambonnas! I was twelve when my tutor gave me your wonderful memoirs. You are the only man to set my name on the pages of history."

The talk of the group turned to literature. Names of young writers were mentioned. Dali had never heard of them before. When someone mentioned the Goncourt brothers, Rolly remarked: "I cannot imagine how they can ever write an article together." Chambonnas replied: *"Très simple, Madame.* Edmond writes the vowels and Jules the consonants."

Chambonnas exhibited a vast knowledge of French history. Moreover, he drew on his own life at the courts for intimate reminiscences to embelish his stories. He was a typical salon chatterer, and regaled his audience with gossip—such as the time Louis XVI, a few months before his execution, made little pellets out of the dirt between his toes and sent them in small envelopes to his favorites, just for fun. Then the conversation turned to the recent technological inventions, the horseshoe-making machine . . . friction matches . . . the ice-making machine . . . then the magazine gun . . .

"And artificial limbs!" a voice put in, ironically stressing the connection between the two inventions.

"I was seven," Chambonnas said, "When my father first took me to the Champs de Mars. I remember it was June. Before a large crowd, the huge Montgolfier Balloon, inflated with hot air from a fire fed with chopped straw, rose in the air . . . yes, yes, it rose, rose . . . and almost disappeared."

A tall scientist remarked: "Those peasants who destroyed the balloon that landed in their field were right. A balloon moves with the wind. To control its movement is impossible. And propelling machinery would be too heavy."

He was one of the designers of the first iron-clad war vessel in history, *La Gloire*.

During his stay in Paris, Dali had learned to enjoy these gatherings at Rolly's house. They kept his mind off the failure of Kossuth's revolution, and his hundreds of comrades still languishing in Istanbul. But today, he could not enter into the spirit of the party. Thoughts of his lost children haunted him. And Andris' daughter, what of her?

While the other guests conversed around him, Dali felt alone, and sad. At last he excused himself and left the party early. He wanted time to think.

The next evening he went to the rue Capucine, and told Rolly and Alphie:

"I have come to a decision."

"Good," said Alphie. "That's always a fine feeling. What was the question, and what did you decide?"

"I have decided to go home."

"Home? Where do you mean?"

"Austria. Willensdorf. I want to see Âdám. I want to see my mother and Flexi. I will have to obtain a false passport."

Rolly and Alphie looked at him as if they thought they had not heard well. Then Alphie said, with true patriotism:

"Gibbon wrote that if he were only independent, he would always live in Paris. And I could quote Hume or Walpole . . . or

330

Thomas Jefferson, Franklin, Fulton and other great men. If Paris is good enough for Prince Czartoryski, why do you want to leave?"

"Where will you hide in Austria?" Rolly asked anxiously. "Have you forgotten there is a large price on your head?"

"No, I have not forgotten that. But I promised Andris I would look after his wife and little daughter. Mother and Ádám, perhaps, could come here, but Irma and Adrienne couldn't get passports. But I can see them in Vienna, I think. In any case . . . "

Rolly interrupted him:

"Nothing is further from my wish than to doubt the loyalty of your friends, but don't forget, please, that they are sick. Terribly sick."

"What do you mean by that?"

Rolly looked at her husband, then turned her face away. Alphie carried on her thought:

"The temptation, *mon cher* Dali!" the marquis exclaimed. "Friends in despair are friends no longer. How much is the price on your head?"

"Twenty-thousand florins," Dali said modestly.

Rolly turned to Dali again:

"You survived prison in St. Petersburg. Then Heron Island, then the battlefields. Then almost two years in Turkey. Were they not enough for you? At your age you need and deserve a decent, comfortable life. Here, with us . . . "

"Yes, I know," Dali said, "but I gave my word to Andris. I want to be a gentleman."

"Hopeless," Alphie remarked. "May I ask you *who* is a gentleman, in your esteemed opinion?"

"Please! We are talking about a very serious question," Rolly called Alphie to order, in a tearful tone.

But Dali was ready with his answer.

"A gentleman," he said, "is a man who is always fair, but his fairness is never planned."

"Mon Dieu!" the little Marquis exclaimed. "You want to be a gentleman in a world where all of us are meticulous scoundrels, with the greatest concern for fairness!"

"He has another motive," Alphie said pensively, when he was left alone with Rolly.

"Yes, I know. Homesickness."

"More than that. Last week I told him a story I heard from the Italian ambassador: that our emperor is considering a meeting with old Czartoryski and Kossuth. In case of a war, we will badly need the revival of wars for liberty in Poland and Hungary."

On the first of October, in the close circle of the des Fereyolles family, Dali celebrated his thirty-ninth birthday.

The following day, October 2, 1853, he boarded the Paris-Strassbourg-Vienna train.

2

At a suburban station before Vienna, Dali was the only passenger to leave the train. The journey from Paris took three and a half days. Alphie had furnished him with a French passport under a false name, but still, Willensdorf was a much safer place for a reunion than the Dukay palace in Vienna where Countess Jadi was now living. Most probably, the palace was under surveillance—perhaps from behind an innocent-looking window-curtain of a neighbor in the pay of the Austrian police. Eliz and Antonia were steady guests in the palace, sometimes for months at a time. Eliz was the widow of Karl Leiningen, and Antonia was the widow of Lajos Batthyány. And Myci's mother, Princess Laya Voronieczki, an impoverished widow, was "employed" in the Gisellastrasse palace as Countess Jadi's lady companion. Although they were not disturbed, one could suppose that the police kept an eye on the "House of Widows."

Confidential couriers with letters or with messages from Hungary, from Poland, from Turkey or France, met Flexi's or Countess Jadi's reliable butlers or friends in Willensdorf, where the Dukay hunting lodge had neither tenants nor neighbors.

After a three hour walk, Dali reached the village at twilight. When he cautiously rang the bell of the hunting lodge, it was Flexi who opened the door. He had brought Dali's son, Ádám, from Bavaria.

The brothers embraced in silence. Then Flexi, seeming

deeply moved, led Dali through the vaulted corridor whose walls were covered with ibex antlers. He opened a door without a word, admitted Dali, and then withdrew, closing the door behind him.

In the center of the room stood Countess Jadi, holding the hand of fifteen-year-old Ádám. Dali set down his valise by the door, walked up to his mother, and kissed her thin, white hand; then he took Ádám's pale face between both his hands, looked deeply into the boy's dark eyes, and kissed his forehead. Turning again to his mother, he asked:

"How are you, mother?"

"Thank you, Dali, I am well," Countess Jadi answered, with a faint flash of a smile. Her lightly powdered hair was attractively gathered up in a red net; she stood erect, her chin high. She looked much older than her fifty-seven years.

Dali's "How are you, mother?" and her cool answer did not betray a want of emotion. Their brief speeches clearly revealed that their hearts were in their throats.

Dali's eyes returned to Ádám. The boy, with his big, soft hands and feet, had the shape of a human male who is neither child nor man, whose voice was too thick for his thin neck.

The boy turned away, blushing. His father's eyes seemed to him to register every unsightly blemish on his face and forehead, tortured to blue-red between two thumb-nails in a desperate beautifying effort before a mirror. But Dali's eyes did not see the pimples; he was trying to imagine that youthful face in four years, in ten years, with a mustache, and framed in a silky brown Kossuth beard. He saw that face under a top hat, then under a hussar shako. Then he asked his son some questions about his reading, his studies, whether he had a dog: questions with no bones, no flesh, serving the same purpose as the idotic questions an artist asks of his model, making the boy's face relax while he answered.

What would be the fate of his only son? Would he live as dangerously as his father? Purpose is the only value, the only flame, the only beauty in a man's life, Dali thought. Purpose and danger go together—

The door opened again and Flexi walked in, seeming the

very answer to Dali's thoughts—a live, well-dressed, antithesis: "In time of danger, move as little as you can."

"Go now to your room," Flexi told Ádám, in a fatherly tone. Reluctantly, the boy left the room, looking back at his father from the doorway.

"Let's go to the dining room," said Countess Jadi.

The table was set for Dali only. While Dali sat down to eat, Flexi asked him:

"Did you read in the papers of the great sensation? The Saint Crown has been brought to Vienna."

"What!" Dali and Countess Jadi asked, with the same bitter surprise.

"Yes," Flexi said, "the crown has just been discovered at Orsova, after four years of desperate searching by the Austrian police and hundreds of soldiers."

"Oh Lord," Countess Jadi whispered, "then Franz Josef can have himself crowned legal king of Hungary."

Dali, remembering his misgivings in Widdin when he had learned that István Varga had gone home with Hausleben's boat, asked Flexi:

"Did someone betray the crown's secret hiding place?"

"It was not in the papers," Flexi said, "but I met Erich yesterday in Vienna and he told me 'confidentially' that a 'great Hungarian patriot,' a certain István Varga, told the police that he and some others walked 1,849 steps from the milestone in front of the Orsova steam mill to the Cserna river's shore to bury the crown. The number of the steps was a reminder of the tragic year of 1849," Varga said.

"Was he tortured?" Dali asked.

"Erich would not say. I only know that he was arrested, and interrogated, and now he has a good job with the police."

"He has four children," Dali said, as a last and hopeless effort to find some excuse for Varga. "Why was he arrested? What made the police think he knew where the crown was?"

"He was drinking in a Pesth inn and boasted to his close and 'reliable' friends," Flexi said. "And so he was brought to Vienna."

After a long silence, Dali asked:

"Any news from Andris' wife, Irma?"

334

"Not for more than a year," Countess Jadi said. "Last Christmas I sent her some money and invited her and her daughter to Gisellastrasse for as long as they wished to stay, but, of course, they could not get passports."

"I must get in touch with Irma somehow," Dali said.

"What is your plan?" Flexi asked him. "We have a suggestion for you. The false passport Alphie gave you is not too good in Austria, you know. But it is perfect in Bavaria. We can put you in the house of our forest engineer. You would be close to Âdám, and you could see Mother whenever she visits us."

"I accept," Dali said.

Countess Jadi laid her hand over Dali's in a gesture of thanks.

"Your confiscated Gere estate," Flexi said, "is now a state property, managed by my former estate agent, old Paul Pogány, who does his best to see that you will get something from the income as in the past. Erich, custodian of my entail, too, is not too good at mathematics. You won't be left without some income."

The conversation became more general.

"In America," Dali said, "I saw that a mighty, young and vast country could be built up on a revolutionary, democratic theory. You know what Jefferson said?"

"What did he say?" Flexi asked.

" 'The tree of liberty,' " Dali said, " 'must be refreshed from time to time with the blood of patriots and tyrants.' That is what Jefferson said."

"If liberty is a tree," Flexi said, "it has not grown too high, however generously refreshed by all the revolutions and bloodshed in Europe. Remember the French Revolution—*all* the French revolutions. Or in our own lifetime, Warsaw . . . then the October revolution in Vienna . . . you witnessed both of . . ."

"I am speaking of revolution, not merely bloodshed," Dali said. "Our March revolution was bloodless, yet its harvest was very rich. It was the sin of the Habsburgs . . ."

"Let's leave that topic, Dali," Countess Jadi said, fearing that the talk would end in hot argument between her sons.

"We are not arguing, we are only philosophizing," Flexi said. "Dali agrees with me that in a revolution, such horrors as, for example, hanging Latour in the street, destroy more liberties than they produce."

Dali nodded and said:

"But you have to concede that the revolutionary flame burns for the right reasons: more bread, more freedom, more human rights," Dali stressed.

"Yes!" Flexi agreed. "The trouble is that poverty, general poverty cannot be eliminated on either a lampost or a guillotine. In the past, whenever the traditional authority, however imperfect has broken down, the poor have been left in the darkness of their misfortunes, at the bare rocky bottom of the economy."

"The American revolutions were not revolutions in the sense you are talking of—in the European sense. They were free of the mass furor, because they were not motivated by hunger. No fearful spectacle of human misery, no haunting veil of mass poverty hung over them. They were highly successful because they were able to concentrate on political freedom."

"Well, as far as I know," Flexi said, "at the time of the American Revolution the population was 4 million and the electorate a mere 6 per cent."

"Try that roasted duck," Countess Jadi offered the dish to Dali, who ate hardly anything during this conversation.

"Even your favorite philosopher, Hegel, said that violent revolutions are an inevitable part of the historical process," Dali remarked.

"Who told you that Hegel was my favorite philosopher?"

"He was the father of the divine state, wasn't he?"

Flexi laughed.

"You know who is my favorite philosopher? Solly. Solly Rothschild. Last month visiting us in Bavaria, he advised me to start a porcelain factory on my wife's small estate, where they have just discovered an excellent white clay."

It was already midnight. Before retiring, they agreed that the next day Countess Jadi would go back to Vienna, and Flexi, Dali and Ádám would go to Bavaria.

Dali could not sleep. He heard the shy ring of the bell at the entrance door. It wasn't a visitor . . . only the extra edition of a

Vienna paper placed under the door. The huge headline read: "Turkey Declares War Against Russia."

The day was October 5, 1853.

Next morning the steaming breakfast in the dining room waited for Dali in vain.

When Flexi knocked on his door, there was no answer. His room was empty. On the table, a hastily scribbled note read:

"A trunk with my clothes will arrive from Paris in a few days. Please, send it after me, together with my hussar uniform and the black Hungarian *attila* to Irma's address in Zekerd. God bless all of you."

3

Two days later, Dali crossed the narrow Lajta River, the Austrian-Hungarian border. He had crossed it many times in his life. First, as a baby in his mother's arms; next, sitting on the coachman's seat when he was three; then, driving the famous Dukay's four-in-hand when he was ten. He had always crossed it by the stone bridge at Bruck, almost every week going from Vienna to Pesth, or to Ararat and back, by coach or on horseback. Each time the police on duty had saluted him in military style, for they knew whose son he was.

This time, on the night of October 8, 1853, he did not use the bridge. The police stationed there would salute him with handcuffs if they saw him. A circular in German, Hungarian, Slovak, Serb and Rumanian, signed by Baron Erich Dukay-Hedwitz, brigadier general, offered 20,000 florins for him, dead or alive.

Dali crossed the Lajta a mile south of the bridge. He did not have to swim, for the river was not more than twenty feet across and barely up to his knees. He waded through the water, as noiselessly and expertly as a deer. The October night was dark and windy.

It was a strange feeling to be again in Hungary after more than four years, a strange feeling and, despite the danger, a wonderful one. But he did not kneel, he did not kiss the soil. He was worried because the stony bottom of the Lajta had caught the heel of his left foot and wrenched it off. He was a man who had kept his pride in the face of many hard circumstances, but still, a missing heel does not enhance the dignity of a man's walk. As Decartes theorized, physical discomfort, however insignificant, never gave comfort to man, however great his soul.

Dali headed east toward Zekerd. Slowly he made his way through the deserted autumn fields, avoiding the villages where barking dogs might give him away. He slept in forests, and his shabby fur coat proved to be a blessing.

On the third night, he passed the village of Doborjan, Franz Liszt's birthplace. In a couple of hours, he approached Andris' house in the neighboring Zekerd. In the starlight, it was easy to recognize the long lane of poplars leading to the small park.

It was nearly midnight. In the village, the little houses were sleeping under their blackened thatched roofs. Only the village carpenter was awake, his saw droning a monotonous lullaby for the sleeping village.

With a stick in hand, Dali was ready to defend himself if the dogs would attack him. He remembered Andris' *komondors,* the two big, vicious cattle dogs.

But no dogs barked in the silent night. What happened to Irma?

The Zeker house had altogether six windows facing the park.

Dali wondered which window was Irma's bedroom. He remembered that the first room on the right of the entrance hall was the sitting room, occasionally converted to a guest room.

The house seemed deserted. Irma and her daughter might live with relatives now. Or perhaps Irma had been jailed; her tongue always was a danger. Or perhaps she was dead.

If she is living, Dali thought, she will be the same Irma. She will do nothing to harm me. Or . . . is she a new Irma, the one Alphie pictured . . . 20,000 florins is a great sum.

There were many possibilities lurking behind the castle windows. But now there was no retreat.

Dali went up to the window he considered most likely and rapped gently at the wooden shade.

"Taa-taa . . . ta-ta-ta-. . ."

Once, twice, and once again, louder each time. But there was no answer. No candle was lit. Dali wondered if the place might be deserted after all. No dogs barked, no sound came from within. Dali tried once more. Then the window was raised a little and the shutters pushed open. Irma spoke, in a trembling voice:

"*Wer ist da?*"

The question, in German, showed that her first thought was the Austrian Military Police.

"Dali," he whispered, "Are the police within?"

No reply.

"Don't you recognize my voice?"

"Yes, I do," Irma whispered, "but I cannot admit you. Go away, please! Only last week two families were taken because they sheltered former Kossuth officers for a single night, after they had broken out of jail. Please go, I implore you!"

"I understand you," Dali said as he left the window. For the first time, he realized that he was more likely to harm this defenseless lady than to help her. He had anticipated every possibility except this one.

He left the window, trying to walk without limping, as if the missing heel on his left boot were the only loss he had suffered.

Then he heard what he thought was the window again, and Irma called:

"Dali! Quickly, the kitchen door. I will open it. I must talk to you."

"Give me your hand," said Irma. "I don't want to light a candle." She led Dali through the kitchen, heavy with the odor of smoke and cooking grease, then through the glassed-in corridor to the parlor, faintly lit by the light under the picture of the Virgin. The dim light revealed a second figure, standing ghostlike in the doorway, wearing a long white gown. Obviously, the girl looking at him had jumped from bed terrified at the sound of the knocking.

"We have a visitor, Adrienne," said Irma. "Go to my bed for the night, and I shall give him yours." The ghost disappeared as she was bidden, on noiseless bare feet.

"Now tell me all you can about Andris' last days and hours," Irma said.

For half an hour Dali told the story of their flight in the woods. He repeated the last exchange between them and described their last moments together. And then Andris' death. And the pyre—the huge magnificent pyre.

"Jadi wrote me you were in America and Paris. Why did you return to this land of sorrow and danger? For homesickness?"

"Don't you know that Turkey has declared war on Russia?"

"Oh! Is it true?"

"It is. Great things could happen very soon."

"You think a new war for liberty?"

"That is why I returned. To be here at the right moment. But now tell me what happened to you afterward?" Dali asked Irma.

"Oh, my good God!" She said in a petulent voice. "I cannot tell you everything now. God has punished us all."

Rapidly, Irma gave an account of the miserable time they had had. Then she placed an earthenware plate before Dali.

"Help yourself . . . just hard boiled eggs. You must be terribly hungry. Tomorrow I will prepare . . ."

"Do the police often raid?" Dali asked.

"No. But when they come, it's horrible. House search, everything. I will tell you tomorrow. Come now, I will take you to Adrienne's room where you will sleep. You must be dead tired. There are no police in the village now, so don't worry, they won't come this night. I will wake you for breakfast and then I will tell you something very important. Good night and good rest."

Left alone, Dali spent no time wondering what the "something" was. He was already half asleep from fatigue.

4

The next morning, Irma brought Dali's breakfast to him on a tray. Dali was already up, looking out the window.

Now as they greeted each other in the sharp morning light, they covertly examined one another's faces. After four years Irma had changed. Only her waist remained supple and young. She was not yet forty, but her rough hands and broken fingernails spoke not only of hard household tasks but of spades and sickles as well. Her steady little smile, whenever she was listening ". . . that smile, you know, she holds it like a violet in the

340

left corner of her mouth," as Andris had put it, that smile had entirely disappeared, along with the light in her chestnut colored eyes. She had become an old woman with a closed, bitter face. On her neck, once too proud, a red scar betrayed a recent operation.

"After you are finished we will go to the front room. As I told you there is something you can help me with."

"First of all—take me as a paying guest. There is my purse on the table. Take from it as much as you need for the household," Dali said, while he enjoyed his breakfast.

After these past exhausting days the goat's milk in the clay jar and the baked and quartered pumpkin, steaming in a basket, brought back memories. It tasted much better than any meal in those expensive restaurants in Vienna, Paris, London or New York—places where no one honored the pumpkin, the *manna* of the poor.

"I will be back soon," Irma said, brushing his shoulder as she left the room.

Her voice concealed something, and it seemed to Dali that her "violet smile," however faint, had flashed momentarily.

What does she plan to say? What is it she wants? What does this lonely, widowed Irma need from a Kossuth-*hund,* who may bring danger to her house?

She is healthy and very probably sex starved. And she lives alone with her daughter, with no servants. She needs a man who can handle a horse and help out in the fields. She wants . . . and quite naturally . . . to be a wife again.

These were his reflections as he gulped down his breakfast and gazed out the window. Anticipating what she might have in mind to ask him Dali searched for a way to refuse the suggestion without hurting her feeling or her pride. She was, quite definitely, not the woman for him, sexually or as an ideal. He liked her as he always had, as the wife of Andris, and he would do anything for her except to marry her. Physically she was too small for his taste and as a character too huge, too overwhelming, with her steady high-pitched voice.

When Irma reappeared and led him to the living room, a surprise awaited him:

"Reverend Hapek," Irma introduced the village priest.

Reverend Hapek was a man of medium size, about Dali's age. His face and its expression revealed nothing either good or bad, about his personality. His Slovak nose was short and his round face was the color of dough. In addition Hapek's face was covered with tiny, black pimples, like poppy seeds on the dough. In build he was muscular but not fat. He had rough short nails, apparently bitten down during his meditations on good and evil. In a word, the reverend was a man of the Scriptures: "Blessed are the poor in spirit." This was the impression he made on Dali.

When Irma began to speak, her voice sounded sad and tired, "I have told the reverend everything that has happened to us."

Reverend Hapek sat with his hands folded across his stomach in an attitude of heavenly calm. As he looked towards the window his modesty was attractive. It seemed to say: "I am present at this intimate meeting as God's humble servant, for the purpose of helping, but only if the problem bogs down in the morasses of human life." His demeanor was in itself a sermon.

"A horrible blow has fallen upon us, Dali. God forgive me, but it is better that Andris is dead than alive to know of this."

She wiped away her tears, and said:

"You remember Bundi and Rába, our two big watchdogs. They shot them."

Dali bent toward her, "What is it?" he asked, with great concern.

"Oh, it's horrible, horrible," Irma cried. "The Austrian police! God punish them! And God will punish them."

Dali glanced at the reverend who sat nodding toward the window.

"I will keep no secrets from you, Dali," Irma went on. "I will tell you everything. Last July, early one evening Austrian mounted police came here. Two broke into the house while a third remained outside, watering the horses, I thought. I was in the kitchen, doing the dishes. I bolted the kitchen door and hid there; they were very drunk. Thank God, Adrienne was out of the house. Thank God, I thought. I thought so until last week. Last week only did I learn. May God punish them! May God punish him, that third one, who was watering the horses! While the other two were searching the house, that third one, God

342

punish him, found Adrienne in the stable where she had hidden herself in the hay. My poor child! Not quite fifteen then. She did not know what had happened to her. She did not tell me a word, poor shy, frightened, innocent girl. We bathe in the kitchen every Saturday night and last week in the wooden tub I noticed. Oh, Dali, you will understand why I said it is better that Andris is dead. Adrienne is pregnant. In her third month." Irma paused, then dropped her hands, as she had dropped her voice. "And then Adrienne told me about that night."

Reverend Hapek's face was still turned toward the window, his eyes taking in the pale October morning and the park. Irma turned to him with a tortured look.

"Please tell him. You can say it better than I. Please tell him what I want. I have no more strength . . ."

The reverend spoke to the floor, raising his eyes only once. He spoke in a steady, almost cold voice.

"Four years ago, a few days after the battle, an old peasant came to my rectory and reported what was rather usual, that he had found the corpse of an Austrian in his field. I went out and prayed while he dug the grave. I opened the soldier's purse and gave his two florins and a few kreuzers to the peasant for digging the grave and making a wooden cross. The soldier's birth certificate and other papers I took home with me."

While he spoke Irma had covered her face, sobbing quietly.

"Heinrich Stenkl was his name. Born in Linz in 1812. In civilian life a piano tuner, now with the rank of *Stabsfeldwebel*. Officially this man is listed as missing, not dead, in the *Kriegsministerium*. Her excellency's idea is that we should ask Herr Heinrich Stenkl to marry Adrienne."

Now Dali understood what his part was to be in this strange drama. Reverend Hapek continued:

"Her excellency, the Baroness, is looking for a man, a friend, who would be willing to take the part of the dead Heinrich Stenkl before the altar. I am willing to perform the ceremony. And I am willing to write out a certificate stating that the marriage took place in our church, not tomorrow or next week, but last June. Adrienne's child will be born after the proper interval of the marriage as the legal child of Herr Heinrich Stenkl. I am willing to make that forgery. God will forgive me.

God, yes . . . the cardinal, no. But who will know? Besides the four of us—the baroness, Adrienne, you and I—no one but God."

Again he turned toward the window as if saying: "It's entirely up to you what you will do. I will say nothing to influence you."

"Do it, Dali," Irma cried. "I have no one who would do it for us, no one but you."

"This is what is in my mind," said Reverend Hapek, before Dali could answer. "Stenkl is dead. After the wedding he will return to his grave. Heart attack. Adrienne will become a widow. I will write out the death certificate and you may carry it in your pocket to prove you are free. Free in any legal or other respect."

During this scene, Dali did not make a move. He looked down at the Turkish rug, thinking.

When the priest had finished, Dali stood up. Panic flashed in Irma's eyes. She feared he might simply walk out of the room without a word.

Dali's face revealed nothing as he went to the window and stood with his back to them. His posture natural, he sought solitude for his thoughts. He gazed into the park. The emptiness of the sky was broken by a flock of crows, flying above the trees against a strong headwind.

Dali's meditation took hardly more than five seconds. He turned to Irma and said, "Call in Adrienne."

Irma jumped and flew to the door.

"Adrienne!" she called into the corridor.

Dali turned as the girl entered. Yes, she was different from the little girl with pigtails and a missing front tooth, the little girl with thin arms twined around her father's neck so passionately only a few years ago, the little girl Dali remembered. Now she was a grown young woman. Taller than her mother, with long neck and broad shoulders inherited from her strong father, leggy and slender, she had a splendid stature. She did not look like the unfortunate child, shy and humiliated, that her mother's hysterical lamentations had led Dali to expect. There was a dignity about her. She seemed fully aware of her situation, but her integrity was not compromised. Her silky chestnut hair was bound tightly in a simple blue kerchief, her straight, finely chiseled nose turned up slightly. She was not a striking beauty, but she was beautiful. Her youth, her simplicity, her sad pride, perhaps her fate beautified her.

Dali went to Adrienne, and took both her hands.

"Do you know who I am, Adrienne?"

"Yes, I do. Mother told me."

Dali nodded. "I don't blame you if you don't recognize me. I was the best, I think the very best friend of your father. Perhaps you remember when I saw you last in this very room. You had two ugly pigtails and one of your front teeth was missing. Let me see your teeth now."

Adriene smiled with tears in her eyes. The tears came only because Dali had mentioned her father. Her smile showed the pearly teeth of a healthy young girl.

"It looks all right now," said Dali with mock seriousness, and he continued, still holding her hands.

"You were sitting in your father's lap, when I asked: 'Adrienne, do you want to marry me?' You said a big NO. And when I asked you why not, you lisped: 'Because you are too old.' Do you remember?"

Adrienne did not answer. She bowed her head and looked at the floor. She knew of course why she had been called into the room.

"I am sorry, my dear," said Dali, "that I cannot remove the quarter of a century of difference in our ages, but take me now, as an old man, as a sort of father, when I ask you again . . ."

He paused for a moment and forced a smile when he asked:

"Do you want to marry me, Adrienne?"

Adrienne did not answer. She bowed her head still further, leaving beautiful lines running from under the kerchief down the nape of her neck to her shapely shoulder. She did not want to show her tears. She said a hardly audible "Thank you" and walked out of the room, her head lowered; they could hear the sharp clapp-clapp down the stone floor of the corridor, the clapp-clapp of her scuffs as she walked back to the kitchen.

Dali returned to the window and watched a peacock as it flew at the time-blackened fence, carrying the heavy burden of the useless pomp of its tail.

The priest and Irma did not look at each other. Reverend Hapek resumed staring out the window, and Irma quietly sobbed.

5

The night of November 3 was dark and silent; by ten o'clock, there was only one light lit in the village of Zekerd. It was a single candle, burning on the altar of the small Catholic church. The wedding ceremony was as simple and brief as it could be. Reverend Hapek had told Dali beforehand, with his customary morbid humor:

"There will be no music, for two reasons. The rust has eaten the organ pipes and the ants and ravens have devoured the hands of our organist, who was killed, God knows on which battlefield."

Still there was music of a sort. The panes of the two windows in the church had been broken, and the November wind made a mouth organ of them, with the poplars in the churchyard serving as flutes and violins.

Adrienne wore no bridal veil, simply a Sunday dress. Dali was dressed in a plain black suit. In a pew Irma knelt and prayed.

Father Hapek gabbled only the most necessary Latin. After the ceremony he donned his golden white pall and quickly put on his heavy *bunda*, the sheepskin coat of the shepherds, the smell of which, when wet, was said to be strong enough to kill a wolf.

A peasant cart waited outside. Hitched between the shafts was Falcon, Dali's horse. Reverend Hapek had sent a reliable peasant to Dali's Gere estate with a message from Dali to claim this latest Falcon. Now the Reverend himself took the reins in hand. Irma and Adrienne sat in the rear, and Dali arranged a rug over their knees.

"Take care of our house," Irma said gently.

"I will." No more words. Dali waved as the cartwheels started to creak and the carriage took off through the mud. It would be dawn before Adrienne Stenkl, her mother and the priest arrived in the village of Reske, some twenty miles away, where Irma's aunt lived. Earlier Irma had sent a long letter to Aunt Fanissa,

346

tardily informing her of Adrienne's marriage. "You know our situation, dear," she wrote. "In June when the happy event took place I had no servant to send with a letter to you. Heinrich comes from a noble Austrian family, and now, I am sure you will be very glad to hear the happy news that Adrienne is expecting a baby in April. I thought we might now accept your kind invitation to visit you for a few months in your lovely house and to ease your loneliness. There is no midwife in Zekerd, as you know, and it would be a great help to us . . ."

Aunt Fanissa's answer was, of course, an enchanted, "Come!"

Dali remained in the dark before the church while the tiny yellow star of the cart lamp disappeared at the far off bend at the end of the village. Then he went back to the Zeker house. In his room he lit a candle and put an envelope on the table. In the envelope was his "fee" for the part he had played in the wedding, the oddest fee ever paid for such a performance. It was the death certificate from the Zekerd rectory register which stated that he, Heinrich Stenkl, had this morning died of a heart attack.

The dough-faced village priest, so Dali thought, had a mind worthy of a great Viennese lawyer. The death certificate was assurance to both Adrienne and himself. To Adrienne it meant she would return to the house as a widow with her legal child. Some day she would remarry. And Dali, however he might feel about it, would have no claims on his fifteen-year old wife in a conjugal bed. Nor would he have any obligation toward the child. He was free, now, as he had been the night he arrived in the village, and yet he had been able to fulfill his promise to Andris' to look after his wife and daughter. The name of the young Baroness Adrienne Zeker de Zekerd was now as clear as crystal glass.

It had been decided that Dali would not leave the house, at least not the park, until Irma and Adrienne returned. If village children climbed the high stone fence, he would hide in the house. In that small village, where everyone knew everyone else, any stranger would be noticed at once, and word of his presence might reach the ears of the Austrian military police.

Every morning Dali chopped wood for a couple of hours. The winter was hard and the lovely porcelain ovens ate up a lot of wood. Once a week Reverend Hapek came to the house for a game of chess. There was something about the priest which Dali distinctly did not like, something other than his habit of chewing his nails and something other than the poppyseed pimples on his face. Dali could not tell what it was. During their game of chess both of them occasionally concealed a yawn. Neither was a very good player. It was all simply a cure for the painful boredom they both suffered. After the game they would try to converse for a while, and then the priest would go home.

Only once did it happen that they left the chessboard untouched and instead talked until midnight. The topic was Turkey's war against Russia. Public opinion in Europe was not taking it very seriously, Hapek reported. Turkey alone? Just a beagle barking at the huge Russian bear. While France, Austria and Great Britain remained neutral, one could not really call it a war. A battle had not yet been fought on any frontier.

Dali's view of the situation was quite different. France's *Gloire* the world's first iron-clad war vessel, 583 feet long and with a weight of 26,000 tons, trained her big guns on the Winter Palace from the Neva—or at least she did in the imagination of her designer.

In Italy, the bold sailor, warrior and revolutionist, Giuseppe Garibaldi ordered new red shirts for his followers in the mountains and determined to make the king of Naples form an alliance with the king of Sardinia, to prepare the way for a union with southern Italy. Napoleon III had promised that the *Gloire* would free northern Italy from Austria.

The walrus-headed Otto von Bismarck dedicated the whole of his genius to the one supreme task of putting the Prussian stamp on all of Germany, including great parts of the Austrian Empire. These were the days when he wrote in his diary: "The great questions of our time are decided not by speeches and votes of majorities but by blood and iron." These words did not sound like "Happy birthday to you, Franz Josef." Austria was like a bone stuck in Prussia's throat.

Dali thought the new situation worth considerable discussion, not only with Father Hapek, but with Tonchi and Andris. Pacing his lonely room in the deserted house Dali sometimes turned to an empty chair and shouted at an imagined Tonchi:

"No, no . . . You are too optimistic, Great Britain would never declare war against Russia."

But as Christmas approached, it was Andris who, more and more, occupied Dali's thoughts: brave, bold, laughing, powerful, gentle Andris. In the empty house that had been Andris' castle, everything Dali looked at seemed a reminder of his dead friend. He thought of Andris celebrating Christmas here with Irma, and with Adrienne, when she had been a baby, and pictured the little family, united in love and purpose, jovial and warm together. And now Andris was dead, his ashes long since scattered through the air of the Jadi forest, absorbed into leaf and mold, mingling with the dust and the dampness of the forest's ferny floor. And now here was Dali, married to Andris' little girl, to give a name to Andris' grandchild. That was how Dali thought of the infant: not as the bastard of an Austrian soldier.

A few days before Christmas, a man stood before the gate of the Zeker house.

"I am a friend of Baroness Irma. My name is Josef Buza."

Dali led the visitor into the house. Joe Buza placed a small basket on the table.

"You're Herr Stenkl, aren't you?"

"Yes, sir," Dali answered modestly.

"This basket is for you. Christmas pastries from your wife, Adrienne."

Joe Buza, about thirty-five, was a big, angular fellow with no trace of the gentleman about him except for an oversized signet ring with his family crest. Surveying "Herr Stenkl" from head to toe, his glance seemed to say: "You don't deserve a baroness." Then he stomped through the rooms of the house, as if Irma had asked him to look around and to make sure her furniture and carpets were still intact. Before he left he offered his hand to Dali without looking at him and said: *Au revoir,* which was meant to give Herr Stenkl the impression he also spoke French. Which he did not.

One morning, a few days after Christmas, the gate bell rang again.

"I am a locksmith," said the visitor. "Last summer I left a big new file in the kitchen."

The man was about thirty and had an open, friendly face. One of his legs was a wooden peg ending in a rusty iron ring. He was a war veteran.

"Sit down and rest," Dali said to him in the kitchen, after he had found his file. Dali provided a jug of wine, bread and some hardboiled eggs. For two months now, with the exception of Father Hapek and Joe Buza, Dali had not had a chance to exchange words with anybody.

As soon as they started to shell the eggs, the young Zeker dog appeared from nowhere, putting his soft paw on the visitor's knee and looking at him with pleading eyes. The locksmith scratched the dog's ear with great affection.

"That was a nasty job I had to do," he said, "when the Baroness asked me to shoot those two giant watchdogs last summer."

Dali's hand with a glass remained in mid-air.

"Was it you who shot the dogs?"

"Yes, unfortunately. It happened that Bundie, the male became mad, and bit the bitch. There was no other way. The baroness gave me a big, double-barreled pistol . . . it belonged to the late baron, you know. I shot them both."

Dali had a sudden horrified feeling the locksmith was telling the truth.

"I was told," he said evenly, "that the dogs were shot by the Austrian police during a raid."

The man chewed, swallowed and said calmly:

"I don't know, and I won't ask you who the dirty liar was who said so. Austrian police! There have been no Austrian police around here for over two years!"

After the locksmith left the house, Dali paced his room furiously. He realized that he had been trapped and that Adrienne had not been raped at all. He became so enraged that he rushed out, hatless and coatless, to grab that dough-faced priest by the throat and to shake the answer to it all from him.

But before reaching the gate, he stopped, realizing that he was helpless in Irma's hand. With a prize of 20,000 florins on his head, he could hardly afford to cause that kind of trouble. He returned to his room and cooly resolved not to mention the locksmith's visit. With Heinrich Stenkl's death certificate in his pocket, he was almost out of it. In a few weeks he would leave the house and Zekerd forever.

Dali remembered when Irma had said, shedding grateful tears, that it was Reverend Hapek who had taught Adrienne to read and write. What other lesson had he also taught her? Dali thought. In this remote village, this crypt of boredom . . . every afternoon a young girl goes to the parish house where the lonely priest . . . Oh, yes, the story reveals itself. Adrienne had confessed to her mother that she was pregnant. And then Irma roared to Hapek: "You cannot marry my daughter . . . but if you don't find a way out for us I will go to the cardinal!"

The Austrian police, the raid, the rape . . . indeed it had been Irma and Hapek who raped the truth.

6

On the last day of February in the new year of 1854, Dali stood in the living room of the Zeker house and watched through the window how the snow fell in big flakes like pinwheels. The sight transported him in his mind to another snowy night, sixteen years ago, to the Winter Palace reception, and to his first meeting with Dushenka in Bolshoy Park, on the skating rink. Then he was rudely jolted from his reverie by the harsh ring of the bell.

At the gate stood a man from Reske with a letter for Dali, addressed to "Herr Heinrich von Stenkl." Irma's letter was brief. "Last night your wife gave birth to a six and a half pound boy. Both Adrienne and your son are in excellent health."

With another letter, the messenger went to the parish house to Reverend Hapek.

Dali had seen nothing of Hapek since the locksmith's visit. He was a veritable prisoner in the Zeker house.

Then on a cold February day, Falcon raced into the park, drawing the sleigh, driven by Father Hapek.

Irma's and Adrienne's faces were glowing from the wind and cold. Dali helped the ladies out of their "footmuffs," then searching through the robes and furs, he asked: "Where is the baby?"

After a moment Irma said, quietly: "He died two days ago of colitis. We buried him last night."

She collected their belongings in silence, then she continued:

"Well . . . it is over now. Poor child. He was christened Rudolf. It was God who took him. And it is the best solution for us all."

Her words sounded so sincere that Dali realized with a sudden pang of conscience that the conspiracy to saddle him with the child had existed only in his imagination.

There were other surprises waiting.

"Dali," Irma said, when they were alone in the living room, "God bless you for what you have done for my unfortunate daughter."

There were tears in her eyes.

"As far as I am concerned," Irma continued, "spring is coming, the fields will need ploughing, and I have no servants, no oxen, no money . . . I cannot live without a man. I am only thirty-seven, and I think I am not ugly, am I?"

She raised her eyes to Dali, who felt that he was being caught again.

Then the whole picture suddenly changed.

"I am going to marry Joe Buza," Irma declared. "He is a heavy drinker, sometimes he gets rough, but he has six good oxen, three horses, two hundred acres next to my small estate. And a watermill on the Ipoly, too."

Relaxing, Dali said:

"You are a clever and strong woman, Irma. God will help you."

"Now, about you, Dali. If there is a man in the world whom you can trust it is old Pogány, the bailiff of the Gere estate. I wrote him from Reske. He's waiting for you."

Hapek came in from the stable and went to the fire where he stood, rubbing his hands.

"Father Hapek agrees with me that you can trust old Pogány. I will give you back Falcon, and you can travel by horseback."

When Irma went out to the kitchen, Dali looked at the priest and thought: That is the man who fathered Adrienne's child.

"A man was here recently," Dali said casually, "and he told me there was no raid on this house, and no Austrian police were around here last June either."

He fixed his eyes on the priest's dough-face, waiting for his guilty reaction.

"Of course, not," Hapek replied. "The baroness invented the

story. Quite naïvely too. Adrienne is a devout Catholic. She had confessed the truth to me. I said to her: 'Adrienne, go tell your mother!' She did not go. She did not tell. Hysterical scenes, even beatings, followed. You know the baroness. But Adrienne did not tell her mother who had fathered the child. So the baroness made up the story. She is a mother. She wanted to lessen the shame."

Dali studied Hapek. A different man stood before him. His calm tone, his steady eyes, his every word bespoke the truth.

"Why didn't you tell Irma the truth, then, if Adrienne would not?" Dali asked.

"I couldn't. I am a priest. Two years ago, my dear brother, Paul, a prelate in Buda, was found in his bedroom, murdered and robbed. A week later a man came to my church and confessed the crime. I could do nothing but tell him to go to the police as the only way in which he could ease his conscience. He is still at large."

Dali walked to the window and looked out at the park. It was natural that Adrienne would not tell her mother who had fathered her child. Doubtless she loved him and was afraid that Irma would be furious enough to kill him. Yes, Irma could be capable of doing such a thing.

That night, as Dali was collecting his few belongings and packing his saddlebag for the long journey, he was happy to be leaving his "prison." Life in the Zeker house would change too. His bedroom would go back to Adrienne, and the silent house would be filled with Joe Buza as if he were not one but at least a dozen persons.

It was almost midnight when there came a soft knock on Dali's door.

Wearing a black robe, her hair bound with a black kerchief, Adrienne entered the room like a shadow. The mourning costume emphasized the whiteness of her skin. She held her hand to her heart as if afraid to lose it. Her outspread fingers resembled a white star.

"I have come to say goodby," she whispered. But it was obvious she had not come only to say goodby.

"I want to thank you, Uncle Dali, and to ask you a great . . . a very great favor."

"I will do anything I can for the daughter of Andris Zeker."

Adrienne bowed her head. The line of her neck suggested sorrow.

"What is your trouble, Adrienne?"

"Take me with you to Gere."

Her shoulders shook and she burst into tears.

"I can't stay here! I can't live here under the same roof as . . ."

She could not continue. Dali took her hand.

"What happened to you?"

Trembling, Adrienne burst out:

"Last June! My mother's birthday! The day of my death!"

She paused, then went on.

"We had dinner guests, mostly men. The table was set outside under the big oak. We had no servants and I had been helping since dawn preparing it all . . . I served the dinner . . . I ran to the cellar to replenish the wine. We had many overnight guests . . . I was to sleep on the kitchen floor that night on a mat. I was so tired I could hardly throw off my shoes or undress, and I fell asleep. Around midnight."

She broke off and looked up at Dali in the candle light.

"Go on," Dali said.

"I was awakened when something heavy covered me," said Adrienne. "I tried to push it away, half asleep. Something tickled my face . . . a mustache . . . and I smelled wine and tobacco and a bad tooth, and there was hot breath on my face. He covered my mouth when I tried to scream. I struggled to rise but he held me down. When it was over he grabbed me by the hair and lifted me up and shook me. 'If you tell your mother, or anyone, I'll kill you! Do you understand?!' Then he threw me back and hurried out, bumping into the cupboard on the way. The kitchen was dark."

"So you don't know who the man was?" Dali asked.

"Of course I know. I recognized his voice."

She went on in a cold voice. "It was Uncle Joe."

"Buza? Josef Buza?"

Adrienne nodded, her eyes fixed on the floor. Then she said:

"If I stay in this house, he will try it again."

She fell on her knees and cried:

"Please . . . please, Uncle Dali, take me with you."

Dali helped her up, but had no ready answer. Adrienne, thinking his silence meant refusal, offered what she must have thought was her greatest asset.

"I can play the piano," she said with twisting lips, and without waiting for a reply she continued: "If I stay here, he will try it again, and I will take father's hunting knife and kill him, and then mother would kill me because she . . . she loves Uncle Joe desperately."

Again she fell to her knees:

"Take me, please . . . take me with you to Gere!"

7

In the middle of the nineteenth century it was not an unusual sight on the roads to see a man on horseback with a lady in his lap. It was not even uncomfortable, especially for such excellent riders as Dali and Adrienne.

When Irma went to wake Dali at five in the morning, the agreed departure time, she found the room empty. Supposing Adrienne already to be in the kitchen preparing coffee she went there but found it dark. She lit a candle and saw the note left on the table:

"We have gone to Gere. I will write you from there. Love. Adrienne."

"Good Lord!" Irma exclaimed joyfully. "It looks like a honeymoon.

Early March is a very dead season for peasants, farmers and hunters as well. Since they left Zekerd before sunrise, they met only one peasant cart drawn by a cow.

At eight o'clock "Herr and Frau Stenkl" arrived in Komárom and took the steamship to Buda-Pesth. Falcon found a comfortable companion, a bay gelding, tied to the kitchen wall on the lower deck. Adrienne was so exhausted she could hardly eat her dinner, and immediately fell asleep in the cabin.

Dali could not sleep. A heartrending hour awaited him. The steamship was scheduled to arrive in Buda-Pesth at midnight. Dali stood on the upper deck when the ship sided to the station raft on the Pesth shore, and the passengers left the ship. Only a few remained to continue their trip further down the Danube.

After the passengers disappeared, Dali had the feeling that this one hour's pause at the station while the ship took on coal, water, oil and food—was like spending an hour in his own grave. Everything was so strange. The lonely lamp. Its poor light on the forsaken shore was the same as twelve years ago, when arriving from Vienna, he did not find Dushenka waiting for him as she usually did. That night she was on her way already back to Russia—and Sylvester Bralin—with little Sonya.

Further up on the shore stood the Café Árpád, rebuilt after the flood. It was still open and the click of the billiard balls resounded whenever the door opened. Most probably, Dali thought, the table and the balls were the same as when he had played with Andris.

Across the Danube among the contours of the starlit roofs of the small renaissance palaces, stood the gothic tower of the Matthias Church, like a shepherd guarding his petrified flock. To the left of the tower the steep roof is the cardinal's . . . no, that is the Eszterházy palace . . . and to the right of the tower . . . one . . . two . . . three . . . the fourth is the roof of the Dukay palace in Septemvir Utca.

Dali's eyes returned from the Buda hill to the Pesth side, where further on appeared the huge, black square of the Neugebäude, the New Building where Mycie Voronieczki, old Baron Perényi and so many others were hanged . . . and not far from the entrance to the Neugebäude, his eyes bound and kneeling before the firing squad, Batthyány's last shout in the silent night—Allez chasseurs!—resounded in Dali's mind.

But everything was so unreal in the starlight, and so far from his present life as Herr Stenkl.

Next morning one half of the 300-mile trip was over. They changed the steamship for Falcon's saddle. After two days of an uneventful ride, the blue airy shape of the Carpathians appeared invitingly on the horizon.

Dali's confiscated Gere estate in southeastern Hungary, was rich in deer, boars and brown bears but poor in harvesting land. Fortunately, Baron Erich Dukay-Hedwitz, as curator and bailiff-in-chief of all the Dukay estates, was not a hunter. He was never in Gere and there was no danger that one day he would knock on Papa Pogány's door unexpectedly.

The only danger in Gere was Mama Pogány, a sweet old lady with a chignon no bigger than an onion. Taut as a cymbal string, her thinning gray hair revealed an ivory scalp under the blue net. The danger for Dali lay in Mama Emma's warm heart. She had an overhelming desire to share everything with her friends, with her guests, with the poor villagers, even with strangers. Flour, lard, sugar, dried fruits, kerosene, purgatives, linens, everything, and first and foremost any and all secrets told under oath. In such a village as Gere, where nothing upsets the monotony of life, a secret is like a jewel. And a jewel is no jewel if it cannot be worn, displayed and admired.

Papa Pogány did not share Herr Stenkl's secret with Mama.

During their first dinner, Mama Emma feigned concentration on the service, but cast occasional glances at the new "forest engineer" and his pretty young wife.

After dinner she led the Stenkls to the four-room cottage set aside as their headquarters.

Adrienne had no idea for how long Dali planned to honeymoon at Gere, nor his intentions toward her for the future. She was disillusioned that, the night after her confession in Zekerd, Uncle Dali slept on the sofa without touching her, except a fatherly kiss on her hair.

One day a letter arrived from Irma addressed to Herr Stenkl. Joe Buza had disappeared from her life. Not voluntarily. Only three days before the marriage, in a suburban inn in Buda-Pesth, Joe was stabbed to death in a drunken brawl.

Usually, news from outside was slow to reach Gere. But on the night of March 31, 1854, Dali's presence there brought the remote little village unexpectedly close to the world. Late at night, a mounted messenger galloped through its quiet, dark streets up to the Pogány house and, hastily demounting, pounded on the door.

He bore a telegram from the nearest post office. It was addressed to Herr Heinrich Stenkl, and came from Paris. Dali's hand trembled when he read: "On 28 March Great Britain declared war on Russia. Rolly."

Within seconds the house was awake. Dali and old Pogány fell on each other's necks and wept. No greater event could have happened. France and Turkey and a vacillating Austria were nothing against the czar. But now the mightiest power in the world had declared war on Russia.

Shivering in the candle light as the ovens slowly warmed the cold room, Dali dressed hastily. No doubt, the New Order was at hand, the reconstruction of Europe.

"There are three possibilities," Dali explained to Pogány, while he bolted down the hot midnight supper Adrienne had prepared for him. "First, if Austria does not join the Western allies against Russia, the Habsburgs will go down with the Romanoffs. Second: if Austria—perhaps on the advice of old Metternich—sides with France and Great Britain, Franz Josef must change his policy. He must give Poland and Hungary their independence—or else."

"What's the third possibility?" Adrienne asked, when Dali did not continue his theory.

"The third possibility is," said Dali slowly, "that Austria and Russia would fight together again. I believe that, too, would mean the fall of both powers."

Meanwhile, the excited messenger, apprised of the contents of the telegram, dashed through the village and knocked on the windows: "Great Britain declared war on Russia!"

Peasants threw on their clothes, jumped into saddles, and spread the news from village to village. Annunciation Day had fallen only a week before, on March 25. Now, the news was like another salutation of the Angel. Great Britain had declared war on Russia!

When Dali finished his midnight supper, Adrienne threw some of his things together, and then went out to saddle Falcon for him. She knew that Dali was leaving the house before sunrise. She wondered if he would ever return. She heard the messenger's shouts in the dark night: "Great Britain declared war on Russia!" It sounded like the wrath of heaven in that sad and poor village—the wrath of heaven for what Czar Nicholas had done against Hungary five year ago at Segesvár . . . the wrath of heaven for the death of my father, thought Adrienne . . . and the wrath of heaven for what Franz Josef had done with the Thirteen Generals and so many martyrs.

Next morning, Adrienne's husband died with a single motion of Dali's hand when he reached into his pocket, drew out Herr Stenkl's death certificate, and handed it to Adrienne.

"My dear child, I'm afraid your widowhood begins as of this moment," Dali told her laughingly. "When next we meet, I fervently hope, Hungary will be free. And you—you will be really married then."

Adrienne accepted the death certificate in silence, her eyes on Dali's face.

Mama Emma was not present at Herr Stenkl's early departure. After violent embraces with Papa Pogány, and two warm kisses on Adrienne's forehead, who flung her arms around Dali's neck and kissed him, Dali mounted Falcon, and waved the final farewell. Then he disappeared at the turn of the valley on his way to Istanbul.

PART FIVE | THE
CENTURY
DIES ON
HORSEBACK
1857–1914

CHAPTER THIRTEEN

Riding on the deserted, meandering roads high upon the southern Carpathians, Dali's mind was full of memories. He remembered a day in 1849, when he had ridden alongside Andris in the retreat; they were to regroup their forces and . . . to meet their fate six days later at Segesvár. There was a young boy in Andris' saddle, one of the volunteer drummers, his left leg badly wounded by Russian shrapnel. Andris was taking him to the next hospital. After nearly five years, not only the boy's dead pale face, but his arms too, almost in a childish way clinging around Andris' bull-neck, came back to Dali vividly. Had the boy survived his horrible wound? Dali did not know. To join the army, a boy had to be eighteen. But this boy had been only sixteen. Such a lad would write the number 18 on a piece of paper, put it in the sole of his boot, and truthfully say to the recruiting officer: "I am *over* eighteen." And a gypsy boy who did not want to go to the battlefield, would hide the same piece of paper in his bushy hair and swear: "I am *under* eighteen."

These memories were mingled with others in Dali's mind. He lived over again some hearty laughs with Tonchi and Andris. The duel, the pistol loaded with feathers. Then on the small stage of his memory, fragments of landscapes appeared: an old stone bridge in Vienna; the skeleton of a poplar tree, killed by lightning in Ararat park, standing as black as death among the raving green, orange and purple riches of life; the letters *Anno 1563* carved on the flat stone above the door of Dushenka's house in St. Petersburg; the square in Warsaw, suddenly lit by the flash of gunfire, and the frightening statue of a rearing horse jumping out of the darkness for a split second; the cracking mazurka of the brass band on the skating rink in St. Petersburg . . . there she flew away in the mist . . . Dushenka. Hundreds and hundreds of little fragments of his life invaded his mind. He felt his mother's sad and tender hand touching his cheek farewell; he smelled the strong fragrance of the jasmine bushes in the hospital's garden when his mind was near total collapse after Dushenka had disappeared, and felt her silky hair and naked body in bed. So much was lost, forever lost to him, he thought. What was it worth to live?

The deserted road offered no answer to his turbulent thoughts.

Around noon, the pass leading into Turkish territory was only five miles away when Dali suddenly stopped Falcon. To his left the chasm ran boldly down to a depth of a thousand feet. The air was crystal clear, and at the bottom Dali could see the toy cannons. Yes, at this distance they seemed only tiny toys. Broken wheels and broken gunbarrels spread over the slopes all the way to the bottom. Dali looked down the chasm for several minutes. Toys, toys, toys! Every Hungarian weapon, every bayonet hammered out of straightened scythes, every cannon cast from the only bell of a small village church, every regiment of Kosciusko, Czartoryski or Kossuth, seemed a tiny toy compared to the size and number of giant Russia's weapons and armies. But now, at last, the czar faced the whole Western World.

When Kossuth had left Hungary at Orsova in 1849, he had leaned down and picked up a pinch of dust. Dali had not followed his example. He had been sure he would come back—if for nothing else, to fulfill the promise he had given Andris to take care of his family. Now Adrienne was nearly grown. Would he ever return to Hungary? This time he did not know. As he neared the pass, he dismounted and, bending swiftly, almost furtively, snatched up a pinch of dust. Then he mounted Falcon again, and galloped on.

The Verestorony pass was guarded only by a wooden sentry box and three Austrian soldiers. The *Feldwebel*, whose rank was equivalent to a sergeant, carefully examined Dali's papers, which were Herr Stenkl's, minus the death certificate he had given Adrienne.

"*Wohin gehen Sie, Herr Stenkl?*" asked the Feldwebel.

"I am going to Varna. If you have a wealthy, bachelor uncle from whom you hope to inherit a fortune, however far he lives, you have to visit him often, don't you?"

The Feldwebel and the two corporals laughed heartily. They were from Vienna and, noticing Dali's Viennese accent, they became friendly. Dali spent a good half hour with them, sharing their lunch, the *profunt*, the hardtack that was the worst military bread of the world, and some *konzerva*, boiled meat.

"Are you going, brothers, to join the Turks and the Western powers in the war against Russia?" Dali asked.

"The hell with the Turks *and* the Russians," the Feldwebel said. "We would like to join our wives and children at home. Was it not enough for us to fight, and now to guard and chase the poor Hungarians? For five years now!"

Leaving the border line, Dali shouted back from the saddle:

"People and government are two entirely different things!"

"They *are!*" the three Austrians shouted back, laughing but emphatic, knowing not that it was Talleyrand's famous sentence during the Congress of Vienna.

Dali crossed the Danube by the evening raft and stopped for the night in the brick house of a Turk on the opposite shore. During his two years in Turkish exile, from August 1849 to September 1851, he had learned to speak Turkish fluently. At this point Herr Stenkl became, once again, Captain Zoungouli. Next morning his host would not accept a single piaster for the generous dinner, with wine and brandy, and the lavish breakfast he had given Dali. Even in the smallest villages, everyone already knew that Great Britain had made common cause with Turkey against the czar. Now there would be some fighting, at last. Everyone was very busy sharpening the curved Turkish swords. Knowing that "Captain Zoungouli" was going to

Istanbul to join the Sultan's army, Dali's host regarded him as more than an ordinary guest. Bidding farewell to a *friend,* the host accompanied Dali on horseback for the traditional one mile distance from the village. After the final good wishes and handshakes, the host did not return home immediately. Man and horse remained immobile, like an equestrian statue, the host fixing his eyes on the departing friend until the friend had disappeared on the horizon.

It was twilight when, some days later, Dali arrived in Istanbul. As he tied Falcon to a tree in the muddy street before his old barracks, he saw, to his great surprise, a new marble tablet set in the wall. The glittering gilded letters read: *Independent Hungarian Government.*

This impressive tablet had appeared on the shabby wall during the previous week, when all Istanbul had heard that Great Britain had declared war on Russia. One of the two modest barrack rooms had become the office of the Independent Hungarian Government. Dali found his old comrades in the middle of a conference. When he walked in, he was greeted with embraces and animated shouts: "Long live Dali Dukay!"

Dali was surprised by this warm reception, and he was deeply touched. He looked around at the faces of his friends. Two and a half years had deepened wrinkles under eyes and across foreheads.

"You look wonderful," Kunzie said, and patted Dali's shoulder, but Dali knew that these two and a half years had left traces on his face, too.

"Where is Szemere?" Dali asked.

The name of the last prime minister of independent Hungary hung in the air for a few embarrassed moments. Dali was sure that, behind the new marble tablet outside on the wall, he would find Szemere as the head of the revived Kossuth cabinet.

"Didn't you see him in Paris?" Isten Balogh asked. "He is sick." And he added after a moment: "Depression."

"More than that," Kunzie announced, with the authority of a man of medicine.

Former Prime Minister Szemere was on the way to losing his mind. His country's tragedy had been too much for him.

More comrades appeared at the club when they learned of Dali's arrival.

"Who is the new prime minister?" asked Dali.

"We were waiting for you," said Isten Balogh, and again there were lively exclamations: "Long live Count Adalbert Dukay!"

The exclamations brought back the same mixed pride and fright he had felt when, before their mission in Russia, in the heyday of the trio's secret conferences, Andris had turned to him and said: "You are a Hungarian *de genere* Ordony. Your mother has Polish royal blood in her veins—have you ever thought of . . . ?" He had silenced Andris with a gesture, but the unspoken end of the sentence was clear for Tonchi too: ". . . of accepting the crown of the united Hungarian-Polish kingdom?" Now the leadership was offered to him again, in a more modest but not less dreamy form.

"I am greatly honored by the trust you put in my very limited abilities, but too much optimism is always dangerous," Dali said. "May I suggest that the tablet read, 'Independent Hungarian Government *in Exile!*' We are not yet in Buda-Pesth."

The motion was accepted unanimously by the "Parliament in Exile."

"Who are the cabinet ministers?" Dali asked.

After an embarrassed moment of silence, Isten Balogh said:

"We have not yet been able to agree on the candidates."

The tone of his voice revealed that there had been many loud arguments, perhaps even fistfights, about these delicate questions.

"For the most important post of foreign minister," Isten Balogh suggested, "taking into account his exceptionally wide knowledge of foreign languages and great experience in world politics, to say nothing of his high education and unquestionable integrity, I have a candidate, and I am sure our parliament will vote for him unanimously."

"Who's that?" Dali asked.

Isten Balogh, smoothing his big white beard, answered seriously:

"My well-known modesty forbids me to mention his name, sir."

He drew a great laugh, and the tense atmosphere changed into the exultant mood which had prevailed since last week, when Great Britain had declared war on Russia. Salvation seemed even more real now than it had during Kossuth's triumphal tour of England and the United States.

Dali, in hiding at Zekerd as Herr Stenkl, had had no access to newspapers. He knew little of the background of Great Britain's declaration. Now, the comrades told him of the events that had prompted Britain to exchange her long-standing passivity in the face of Russia's menacing power for active war. After the New Year of 1854, Prince Gorchakoff's Cossacks had invaded the Danubian principalities under Turkish suzerainty and Admiral Nahimoff had destroyed the small Turkish fleet in the Bosporus: thus had Turkey's solitary act of defiance brought swift Russian vengeance.

All this was of no moment to Britain until Admiral Nahimoff's fleet, drunk with the victory in the Bosporus, sailed into the Black Sea, violating its neutrality. Great Britain protested with an ultimatum. Czar Nicholas did not even answer it. Did he know that Nahimoff's warships, in windstill, could move only by oars, while the British fleet was already equipped with screw propellers? So was the fleet of France, which declared war on Russia a week after the British declaration.

The candles burned until the small hours, bottles were emptied, but the reunited comrades talked on. The details of the triumph and failure of the "great journey" to America, Dali's sojourn in Paris, then hopes and predictions for the near future in the new situation of world politics, were still being discussed at four in the morning.

2

The story of the Istanbul exile, as the comrades told it to Dali, was very depressing. Soon after Kossuth's departure, the days of warm friendship with the Turkish government were over. The exiles had become a burden, not only financially but politically too, to the sultan's army. They lived in extreme poverty. To get a job was not easy. Cornet Zih was lucky to be one of the sultan's coachmen; but the young sultan was a passionate driver, and whenever he drove the fast grays the coachman had to run after the coach.

A group of officers started a farm they called Little Missouri Valley; it failed, because these officers were lawyers, government clerks or schoolteachers in civilian life, and knew nothing whatever about farming. Others opened small restaurants and cafés, but none of these ventures survived the first year. A sergeant opened a barber shop, which flourished because the sergeant not only gave beard trims and haircuts but furnished call girls for the foreign diplomats, too. One lieutenant was successful in the metal arts and sold home-made Byzantine medals to the tourists—as genuine antiques. The comrades donned the Turkish uniform only on the first day of every month to pick up their salaries; then they went back to their civilian occupations, or to the opium peddlers.

Kunzie had hung up his doctor's shingle, but he made only a meager living because the Turks would not visit a foreign doctor. His patients were mostly fellow exiles, who had no money.

When the news reached Istanbul of Kossuth's fantastic reception in 1851 and his successful tour of the Western World, the general opinion of the exiles was that Hungary and Poland would regain their independence within a year. The failure of the Kossuth mission was not without consequences for them. Two lost their reason, and several others became the victims of opium.

Then, when the news reached Istanbul that Great Britain had declared war on Russia, the exiles suicidal mood swung to wild optimism. Salvation seemed closer and more real than ever.

Yet despite their excitement at knowing that Turkey, Britain and France were at war with Russia, there seemed little for the exiles to do. Czar Nicholas had selected Turkey's Danubian principalities as the scene of the war, and the Turkish and French armies had been dispatched to Varna, in Bulgaria. But once there, the troops remained inactive. The war seemed at a standstill.

In Istanbul, the exiles lived in a fever of anticipation, yet with little real activity. One day, one of their members, a Major Marky, who had served with Karl Leiningen as an engineer, took Dali aside and confided: "I have invented a new, fantastic weapon. The 'locolry.' "

"What is that?" Dali asked.

"I need your word of honor, Dali, that you won't tell it to anybody," he said. "No—I'm not afraid that someone will steal the idea. I am afraid of ridicule.

"But every great, revolutionary idea was greeted with ridicule. The steam engine, the match, gunpowder—everything. I'll tell about the locolry only to you. You're an imaginative man."

He looked around and whispered, his eyes burning:

"I made the word locolry out of locomotive and cavalry. Imagine a huge locomotive filled with riflemen. A horse carries but one soldier, the horse's body is soft and vulnerable, it is an easy target. I have a new idea, especially against the Russians. Imagine a hundred Orthodox churches on the battlefield with onion-shaped, bright-colored cupolas that swiftly move on wide wheels. Their bells are ringing, and at the same time a dozen cannons fire from every cupola. Imagine the Russian soldiers! They are superstitious. Their churches! Their churches are attacking them, their churches are shooting at them. A dozen, even a single locolry will make them run—no, they won't run, they will fall on their knees, and they will follow our heavenly —do you get the idea?—our *heavenly* command to fight on our side against the czar. Now listen."

He took out of his pocket the locolry's secret blueprint and started to explain its construction, using technical words which Dali did not understand. His hand trembled, his eyes rolled wildly.

"I am telling you, Dali, with a dozen locolry we could destroy the whole Russian army. Look at it . . . "

Major Marky, Dali learned, had been consuming a great deal of opium.

In June Dali received a letter from his mother. "I am glad to learn from Irma's letter," she wrote, "that her daughter Adrienne, who, as you probably know, last year married a certain Herr Stungel or Stenkl, has become a widow and now is

370

engaged to young Kalman Kende, from a nice and rather wealthy family."

Countess Jadi then went on to tell Dali the latest news about Ádám, whose health and behavior were both fine, and concluded her letter: "Flexi is very optimistic about the future."

Flexi's own letter, which also reached Dali in June, reflected this optimism. "You remember," Flexi wrote, "I mentioned to you in Willensdorf that Solly Rothschild had advised me to start a porcelain factory. Now I am thinking of going into this industry, because the geologist has indicated that the clay on my wife's estate, though hardly more than two thousand meager acres, is very rich in a rare mineral element, which has no value except that it is excellent for glass and china painting. In honor of the newly discovered planet Uranus, it is called uranium."

The fever of the war left the Austrian government cold. They were preparing another small Congress in Vienna, and hoped that Austria would successfully play the great role of the Angel of Peace at the conference table. Austria was exhausted, her treasury empty. Threatened by the northern Italians under Habsburg rule and by Prussia's growing power, Austria could not decide which side to take in the present conflict, and furthermore, had no desire to go to war again.

At the same time, Czar Nicholas had wearied of the shadow war near Varna, and had decided on a new locale for his confrontation with the West: Crimea.

The Crimean peninsula, washed on the west and south by the Black Sea and on the east by the Sea of Azoff, formed the most southerly portion of the Russian Empire.

With its length of 200 miles, and a breadth of 130 miles, with its healthy climate, hard winters and dry summers, with its rich grasslands, its mountains and its beautiful scenery, Crimea was a true Garden of Eden.

News came constantly to Istanbul. Once the stage was set, the director of the new world drama, Prince Menshikoff, commander of the Russian troops, was ready for action.

One morning in August, shortly before sunrise, Dali set out with his group for Crimea, by way of Varna and the Black Sea. He and his comrades were dressed in their French-style Turkish uniforms, and their saddles, like those of all the officers in the Sultan's army, were sky blue.

After the past three turbulent but idle years, it was a great feeling for the group to be riding forth to fight again.

3

The curtain rose on the great drama on September 4, 1854, when the combined fleets of Great Britain and France, forming the mightiest armament ever conveyed by sea, appeared off the coast of the Crimean Peninsula. The disembarkation had been completed within two weeks.

There was no entry in Dali's diary about the siege of Sevastopol that followed. Day after day great detonations thundered, and the whole peninsula trembled as in an earthquake when the Russians, loading hundreds of tons of gunpowder aboard the largest ships of their fleet, sank them in the mouth of the harbor in order to erect a wall under the shallow water against the fleet of the allies. An army of reinforcements under Menshikoff's command more than once tried to break the allied lines which already ringed the city. Both sides showed enormous courage.

"Humor and immortal heroism are first cousins," said a French captain to Dali, who was jealous of the miraculous charge of an English Light Brigade at Balaklava, when 700 British cavalrymen repulsed the attack of Menshikoff's many thousand Russians on the English base.

"No English general could have given the command for such an insane charge—700 against some 70,000," said the captain. "The Light Brigade simply misunderstood the command, and to everyone's surprise, the result was a miracle, a complete victory over the Russians."

Ten days after Balaklava in the "Soldier's Battle" at Inkerman, on November 5, 1854, the allied troops won another victory when, during the dark of night, they drove off a Russian surprise attack. Dali had not participated in either action. Restlessly, anxiously, he awaited a real opportunity to fight. None seemed to appear.

For long weeks nothing happened. Early dawns above the

Sevastopol hills blew cold air from the bay. There was no snow yet, but sharp morning frost crunched under the soldiers' boots. Occasionally the bark of a cannon sounded against the distant murmur of the sea. Soldiers with clanking muskets passed to relieve the night guard in the hussar camp on the slope of the Malakoff mountain. Every morning Kunzie hurried to the nearby camp hospital, where he worked as a surgeon. Dali watched a Turkish soldier creep out of his dugout, wash his weather-beaten face with icy water, and then turn to the violet horizon to say his morning prayers: *La Il-la . . . allah . . . illa . . . haaa-laa . . .*

After the New Year, Dali wrote to Isten Balogh in Istanbul:

There is nothing more terrible than idleness. For nearly six months nothing has happened to us. We came here to fight against the czar and we are fighting only on the chessboards. I am sick of boredom. Italy joined us in the war a week ago, but so far we have not seen a single Italian soldier. No activity, no news, nothing.

A few weeks later there was important news. On March 3, 1855, an official French dispatch said:

Nicholas Pavlovich Romanoff, Czar of all the Russias, his territory invaded by English, French, Turkish, and Italian troops and a group of Hungarian Hussars, took the disaster as a personal humiliation and affront and was stricken with a severe chill. Yesterday, at the age of 58, he gave his soul to the Creator. He will be succeeded on the throne by his son, Alexander II."

Dali vividly remembered the young crown prince; tall, rather handsome, with German features and princely German manners. In 1838, Alexander, as crown prince, had been only nineteen, though he had looked twenty-five. Dali remembered his remark about Dushenka after the first night of *Cupid and Psyche* in the Lomonosoff Theatre: "Mademoiselle Bobak does not need to sing. She herself is a song." Reading the obituary of the czar, Dali felt all his memories of St. Petersburg come back with painful vividness. The great reception in the Winter Palace, his secret talk with Prince Igor, his great "mission" in Russia, his first meeting with Dushenka. All these fateful days and hours seemed now to be frozen in the depth of the past seventeen years like the millennia-old mammoth corpses deep in the eternal Siberian ice.

"What would have happened," Dali wondered, "had I killed Czar Nicholas seventeen years ago in St. Petersburg?" Crown Prince Alexander was only thirty in 1849. As the new czar, would he have followed his despotic father's policy of pouring the sea of the Cossack regiments into Hungary, crushing the war for liberty? Would there now be a Crimean war? Could the death of a single monarch change the course of history? No, it could not. Yes, it could. A single century, carrying the life of the whole of mankind, is like the life of a single man, affected by the slightest coincidence. "Supposing," Dali thought, "I had been looking in another direction when Dushenka fell on her knees at the skating rink. I would never have met her, my whole life would have turned into another . . . " There was no end to his chaotic thoughts during his sleepless night in his camp tent.

The death of Czar Nicholas did not mean the end of the Crimean war. Unnecessary and stupendous losses were suffered on both sides. The inefficiency and corruption of the Russian officials made the supply and provisions of the fighting troops miserable; and the connection between military centers in Russia and the peninsula, since there were no railways, was very slow.

In these months of 1855 there were only fragmentary notes in Dali's diary, most of them without date or location.

Did not see Kunzie for ten days . . . English 56,000 shrunk to 17,000 because of some mysterious gall-bladder disease . . . Salvos of Russian battleships, when they learned that French General Mayran had been killed, successfully repulsed an allied attack . . . Daily 120,000 shrapnel from 8,000 cannon . . . a wonderful feeling to be again on Russian soil, and without a permit from the czar . . . 3 rockets signal general attack 48 battalions at 2 P.M. Boats stand sideways for firing all cannons then turn other side, fire again while loading empty cannons. Damaged boats left to sink, crews swim ashore . . . Gorchakoff has 2,200 cannon on boats . . . Most of Sevastopol population gone . . . Rumors that in the Caucasus the brave Tsherkes and Turkman tribes are ready to revolt against Czar Alexander II . . . Last night I dreamt that with the victorious allied troops I would appear in Novgorod . . . Dushenka and my daughter Sonya greeted Lord Raglan with flowers in the name of the liberated Russian people . . . I am afraid Sonya does not speak a word of Hungarian . . . The Russians have built three-fold dams around Sevastopol for their infantry and artillery . . . 23,000 French, 25,000 English troops have arrived as reinforcements from Varna . . . Letter from Mother brought by a small French steamer . . . long optimistic speech by Lord Raglan . . . Another 8,000 Turkish troops have arrived . . . Their religion teaches them that a Mussulman soldier killed on the battlefield goes immediately to Heaven."

In June, after the fruitless February and April assault, there was a third attack against Malakoff, the Round Tower. Though it presented a lofty and distinctive target to the allied artillery, the assault was fruitless again. Malakoff was a sort of earthen citadel armed with nearly a hundred guns of different caliber. It stood hardly a mile from the south harbor and threatened the allies' anchorage.

One morning in July, a Russian officer, well mounted and attended by three Cossacks, was seen coolly riding along a cliff, noting in his memorandum-book the number and disposition of the allied fleet in the southern harbor.

The Russian officer and the three Cossacks rode along the cliff within rifle range, unmolested. Dali volunteered to capture them. With five hussars, he went after the Russians, but narrowly escaped capture himself when the fleeing Cossacks lured him too deep into the peninsula toward a small wood where some fifty Cossacks were hiding. When the Cossacks emerged from behind the bushes and galloped toward Dali and his hussars, the British vessels Sampson, Fury, and Vesuvius and three French steamers opened fire. Their shelling was so accurate that the Cossacks returned to their hidden camp in the small wood.

"Anybody wounded?" Dali asked his five hussars.

"Nobody!" came the answer.

"You're utterly mistaken, boys," Dali said. "*I* am wounded."

He had a bullet in his right thigh, but he rode back to headquarters without falling from his saddle.

"There is a French steamer to Istanbul tomorrow morning," said General Guyon when Dali reported to him. "You will return to Istanbul."

"Why, sir?"

"You are limping, Captain."

"So what?" Dali asked. "We came here to fight and not to run!"

General Guyon laughed, and ordered Dali to the camp hospital, where Kunzie took care of his wound.

Three weeks later Dali was still limping, but he was out of the hospital in time to witness the capture of Malakoff, which virtually terminated the siege of Sevastopol. The Russians, aware that further defense of the city was impossible, withdrew to the northern side of the harbor, blowing up all Sevastopol's defenses as they went.

With the fall of Crimea's capital Russia was beaten.

In the following week, in the company of Kunzie, and, of course, Falcon, Dali took the small French steamer to Istanbul.

He wanted to be back with his comrades for the first of October, to celebrate his forty-first birthday, and to celebrate the victory.

"The Heaven has opened in thirteen directions," he quoted the oriental saying; he foresaw a brilliant future as a result of Russia's defeat.

4

On his return to Istanbul, Dali gave up plans for a celebration. He was shocked to learn that Cornet Zih, only twenty-seven, who had never lost his sense of humor even in the most terrible times, had died a dreadful death.

"One day he was arrested in a bazaar," Isten Balogh recalled the tragedy. "He had smeared glue outside the bowl of his long-handled meershaum pipe before he entered the bazaar. While the merchant turned for the desired merchandise, Cornet Zih's pipe touched the merchant's supply of piasters, kept on a wooden plate. His trick worked well in the first two shops. In the third he was caught. We took up a collection and paid the merchants, but the next day he disappeared. In the last days he had no shirt under his ragged jacket, and he was barefooted. He kept a live mouse in his pocket and before he bought opium he gave a small dose of it to the mouse, to be sure the drug was genuine. If the mouse did not suffer convulsions, he would fly into a rage, and beat the peddler who had sold him the opium.

376

Once he told us all, very soberly, that Buddha, Christ, Mohamet, and all the great inventors, Lavoisier, Stefenson, Volta, all of them saw *Nur*, the Arab Light, because they were all hashish-eaters. He said that the Jews were extremely clever because Moses in the desert fed their forefathers for forty days with hashish."

"How did he die?" Dali asked.

"Someone saw him dashing into the desert in a spell of exaltation. When he didn't come back, we organized a search party. We thought he must have lost his way. A week later we found him dead, starved to skin and bones, his body burned by the blazing July sun."

"Where is he buried?"

"In the Magyar cemetery."

After a silence, they talked about the bright future. The discussion went on every night. Dali belonged to the group of absolute optimism. But when, in November, the Russians were still fighting and Austria had still not joined the allies in the war, the optimists started losing ground.

At Christmas Dali received a letter from Countess Jadi.

After relating all the family news, she wrote:

"The bell on old Metternich's door is ringing daily. His former foes are seeking his advice, and so is young Franz Josef."

The last sentence in the letter read:

"I feel more strongly than ever that our dreams will soon come true. You know what I mean."

The same evening Major Marky appeared in Dali's room.

"I think that Andris' funeral on the pyre, as you described it to me, has something to do with the fact that Hungary is now on her way to resurrection," Marky said.

"How do you mean?"

"The greatest teaching in Islam," Marky said, "dates back to Amed Rufai in the fourteenth century. It says that after the death of a nation, the resurrection comes through a great fire. If someone is willing to die on a pyre for the sake of his compatriots, the nation will be resurrected. Ancient Hungarians used to burn a white stallion on a pyre—just to keep away the national death."

Dali did not reply.

377

"The siege has ended. Russia is defeated," Marky went on. "Now the allies will march north from the Crimea. Their next stop is Moscow."

"I'm afraid you're too optimistic," Dali said.

"Optimistic? Too optimistic? Why."

Dali did not answer. Marky's voice was too passionate.

In February, when the French, German and even the English papers wrote that the peace negotiations most probably would end in a compromise treaty, there were shouts, desk-poundings and bitter laughs and nervous sobs among the exiles. On March 15, the seventh anniversary of the "bloodless and glorious" Hungarian revolution, Dali made a speech to his comrades. He said: "I believe in God. I believe in His justice. I strongly believe that our God did not allow the blood of the Thirteen Generals, the blood of Count Batthyány and Prince Voronieczki, the blood of Baron Andris Zeker and of so many comrades, to be shed in vain. In a few weeks at the Paris conference table, the victorious Great Britain, France, Turkey and Italy will dictate the terms of the peace treaty. In a few weeks mankind's greatest . . . "

There was no exalted ovation when Dali finished his speech. Major Marky was the only one who jumped to his feet and applauded.

After that dinner party of March 15, Dali was in a very depressed mood himself. And as he later said to Kunzie:

"I was silly enough to swallow a hashish candy that Marky gave me."

The hashish made Dali so limp that his comrades had to put him to bed. Kunzie tried to mesmerize him, drawing his fingers, with the lightest possible touch, from Dali's forehead to his toes.

As Dali later told Kunzie, he didn't know if he was awake or asleep. He walked in the *Jennah*, the Turkish "Garden of Lust," which was located in the Missouri Valley. He entered the garden through a huge golden gate which led to Hungapole. At the left, across the Missouri River, the Chain Bridge was a perfect copy of the new *Lánchid* in Buda-Pesth. He walked through Buda, and in Septemvir Utca his mother waved her kerchief from the balcony of the Dukay palace. Then he arrived in Ararat park where large herds of bison were grazing. Farther along, the sand on the banks of the Missouri River was pure silver, the gravel emerald and ruby, its fragrance that of his two favorite perfumes: lily-of-the-valley and violet. The water was cold and sweet, its foam shone like the stars. Then he met the ladies of the *Hu-ral-oyen*, but he did not know what *Hu-ral-oyen* was. Their voices sounded beautiful, their snow-white breasts were uncovered, and their eyes were blacker than any he had ever seen.

Yet it was not a dream. He heard their voices as surely as he felt their hot skins when he made love to them.

Now Dali knew why poor Cornet Zih, Major Marky and so many others had become the victims of the hashish candy and the opium pipe.

But the end of his utmost happiness was horrible. As the sun moved to the middle of the sky he began to melt. He melted away under the blazing sun. Nothing, nothing, not a single drop remained of him. He had to make a desperate effort to be born again. But only after long and painful hours of darkness did he struggle out of a womb which was rather a cave than human.

"When I was 'born' I started to cry," he said to Kunzie. "I was cold, I was hungry. The light hurt my eyes. When you brought me a portion of ham I started to vomit because the ham was hairy and when I touched it, it started to mew. I fell back on the pillow in such sadness as I had never experienced in my life before. I sobbed incessantly."

The next morning, after forty hours of heaven and hell, Dali was still dizzy. When his friends tried to help him out of bed, he warned them that his left leg was made of glass and that it would break.

When, finally, he was back to normal, he gave Kunzie his word of honor that he would never again swallow a hashish candy.

On March 20, 1856, the peace treaty was signed by Great Britain, France, Turkey, Italy and Russia. But the "deadly blow" Dali and the optimists had awaited fell, not on the despots, but on democracy in Europe.

Russia emerged from the lost Crimean War more powerful

than she had ever been before. Major Marky sobbed hysterically in the club. Dali put a hand on his shoulder and said:

"Don't cry, Major. The sceptre of the Russian Empire is decorated with the stolen Orloff diamond, once the eye of the main Idol in the Temple of Serigham in India. Don't cry, comrade. The blinded idol will soon take a terrible revenge upon the Romanoffs."

But Dali himself felt the terms of the Paris treaty as a deadly blow.

5

"There is no reason to doubt that, in another campaign, the Russians might have been driven entirely out of the Crimea, and the Romanoffs out of the Winter Palace forever," said eighty-six-year old Prince Adam Czartoryski to Alphonse des Fereyolles when Alphie visited the great Polish exile in Paris.

The treaty guaranteed the neutrality of the Black Sea.

"For how long?" asked Czartoryski. "Is the Black Sea in the back yard of Buckingham Palace, or deep in Russia?"

Later he said:

"Russia was beaten by the allies, but she lost nothing. Nothing! Even Sevastopol was given back to her! The Romanoffs and Habsburgs remain firmly on their thrones. I'm very much afraid that the fate of Poland and Hungary has been sealed forever."

In his letter, Alphie told Dali of his talk with Czartoryski. And he added bitterly: "Great, great, great result! The treaty said that the Christians in the Ottoman Empire remain under the protection of the sultan. Now we Western diplomats congratulate each other warmly, pretending we believe this religious problem was the cause of the bloody Crimean War. Where is the limit of the Western World's stupidity?"

"France and England," Kossuth wrote to General Guyon from his Italian exile, "could have secured Europe forever from the ambition of Russia, but in their councils there prevailed the absurd prejudice that for this war the help of despotic Austria was indispensable. They left Hungary and Poland to perish, and the Western mountain gave birth to a miserable little mouse on the table where the Treaty of Paris was signed."

The letter went from hand to hand among the exiles. In the following weeks the consumption of opium increased greatly.

There was bad news in the papers. Now the new czar, Alexander II, was able to concentrate on Russia's dangerous internal affairs. The extermination of the rebellious Tsherkes, Turkmen and other brave Caucasian tribes began the very day after the treaty was signed.

The terror in Russia, and even more in Poland, increased.

In the following days Dali's depression so worsened that Kunzie felt it his duty to tell Countess Jadi, who was staying in Bavaria with Flexi and his family. Countess Jadi wanted to set out for Istanbul immediately, but it was not so easy as her motherly heart imagined. To get a visa to Paris for her meant months and months of waiting, and repeated applications, and the answer to most of the applications was a single word: Denied.

"Buy me a forged visa," Countess Jadi pleaded with Flexi. In those days it was the only way, even in high society, for an emergency trip. But Flexi refused. He was not worried about an arrest, but he was worried about his mother's health. Countess Jadi had celebrated her sixtieth birthday in February, and though she was not sick, she was not so strong as she had been as a younger woman. Flexi believed that the long and complicated journey to Istanbul, first by coach from the Schönheim-Altstadt castle to Munich, then by train to Marseilles via Paris, then by boat to Istanbul through the Mediterranean would be too much for her. She was convinced that she ought to go, but at length had to surrender to the decision of the family conference.

"Let us ask Alphie to visit Dali," Flexi's wife, Marie Augusta suggested. "He, as a diplomat, could travel more easily than any of us."

And so it happened that one April morning in 1856, Alphonse des Fereyolles arrived in Istanbul.

He went directly to the exiles' quarters and introduced himself to Doctor Kunz. They knew one another's names very well, but they had never met before.

"How is Dali?" Alphie asked when they were seated.

"He is sick," Kunzie said. "He is sick like all of us. Disenchanted, disappointed, despairing."

Alphonse des Fereyolles nodded.

"The compromise treaty in Paris was a terrible blow for us." Kunzie went on. "Three of our comrades committed suicide. Three out of eighty-seven officers. Many of our people have become opium addicts."

"Dali too?"

"No. He tried it once, but he had a dreadful hangover and he gave me his word of honor he would never try it again."

"To quit smoking, gambling, drugs . . . or a certain woman . . . word of honor . . ."

"No, Dali does not take drugs. I'm positive."

"Does he drink?"

"No. Occasionally a few glasses of wine, but he has never been a heavy drinker."

"Is there any woman now in his life?"

"None. Women are cheap in Turkey. Sometimes he has casual affairs with ladies from the diplomatic corps, but he does not have a mistress."

"In your opinion, in his present state of mind, does Dali have any inclination toward suicide?"

"Absolutely none. Last May there was a lot of talk about suicide," Kunzie said. "Dali's contribution was: 'To die for the future is a virtue. To die for the past is cowardliness.' No, Dali has no thoughts of suicide."

"His health?"

"He has no organic disease. I found his heart and lungs in good condition when I examined him last week. He was complaining of extreme lassitude and some kind of occasional brain fog. Well, it's not a disease. It is a mood. All of us here are suffering from that Istanbul disease, as we call it."

Dali entered the room. Alphie jumped to his feet. Dali hurried to him, and the two embraced.

Kunzie strolled casually out of the room, leaving them alone.

"I am on an official trip," Alphie said diplomatically. He did not mention Kunzie's alarming letter. Dali's appearance was an encouraging surprise. The last time he had seen Dali, three years ago in Paris, he had been twenty pounds heavier, and his face had an unwholesome pallor. Now he looked lean and fit, and his face was as tanned as that of an active cavalry officer should be. The Turkish uniform gave him an exotic and elegant air. His voice was softer, his look warmer than in Paris. He seemed touched by the message Alphie brought from Rolly asking him to live with them in Paris, but he said: "I want to stay with my comrades."

The fragile little marquis, with his characteristic French vitality and intelligence, sought to dissuade Dali.

"*Ecoutez,* Dali! If you are lost in the Sahara with a comrade who needs your help for the last few miles, you have to stay with him and help him, even if you risk your own life. That's solidarity. But if you are lost in the desert of the world with millions of fellow prisoners and you refuse your chance to escape, that's *not* solidarity, *mon cher ami.* It's stupidity."

Dali did not answer. His brother-in-law tried another argument.

"I saw Czartoryski recently," he said. "You know he now lives in Paris. The old exile . . . he is nearing ninety . . . told me that the only thing which keeps him alive and in good health is his hope for a liberated Poland. In Europe, you would be near the great leaders of your people, you could share their thoughts and hopes."

Dali did not answer.

A few days later the marquis left Istanbul, promising Dali that at Christmas he would be back with Rolly, and probably with Countess Jadi and Ádám, too.

6

One morning Dali, Kunzie and Isten Balogh were surprised to see Major Marky in a new outfit. He was talking on a street corner with a group of the Howling Dervishes, and he wore a rough, long shirt with no collar, red-striped camel-wool trousers, and a black, yellow, and blue hat. It was the costume of the Dancing and Howling Dervishes.

"I am afraid," Isten Balogh said, "he has changed not only his dress but his God, too."

"His Istanbul disease is getting worse and worse day by day," Kunzie remarked.

Dali did not say a word. He watched the inventor of the "locolry." Major Marky was on the brink of losing his mind.

After the long dawn of the Age of Technology in the seventeenth and eighteenth centuries, mankind was feverishly occupied in exploiting all possible applications of the new marvels. The greatest efforts, of course, were concentrated on the greatest of human problems: how to kill. Among the weapons was a miniature silver pistol with compressed air, for use against fleas. And there was a huge cannon, ordered by Catherine the Great, so big that a tall Russian soldier could walk through its barrel. Many of these new ideas never reached the factories. They were too fantastic; their inventors suffered from excessively lively imaginations.

This was the case with Major Marky and his wonder-weapon, the locolry, now already hopelessly buried in its first, sketchy blueprint. But Marky's imagination was burning and churning with greater and greater heat, under the influence of his greater and greater consumption of hashish candy.

One hot July evening, more than a hundred dervishes, who had come to see in the tall, skinny, foreigner a superior man with the hypnotic power of leadership, obeyed his command and followed him to the gate of the Magyar cemetery. When he raised his right hand, the procession came to an abrupt stop. A three-minute silent meditation followed while the dervishes stood immobile, like dark statues against the setting sun. Major Marky's eyes, wide open, stared to the empty horizon of the Black Sea. He had taken an unusually large dose of hashish. Flies were crawling over his face, but he did not move. When the flies crawled into his eyes and walked over his eyeballs, he did not even blink.

At the end of the meditation, Marky ordered the dervishes to make a pyre. The dervishes broke the stakes of the cemetery's rotting fence, and had a big pyre ready within minutes. When it was lit, the howling sect of the Great Exaltation started their delirious dance, circling the pyre and howling louder and louder: *"La illah! . . . Al-lah . . . illa . . . ha-laa!"* Then, Major Marky climbed onto the pyre, his face gleaming with a strange and ecstatic happiness, as if he had already arrived at the gate of *Jennah*.

But the spiraling tower of the pyre's black smoke had alarmed Istanbul's firemen, and a blue and red fire engine, drawn by wildly galloping horses, pulled up within moments. The firemen broke through the whirling chain of the dervishes and dragged Major Marky down from the pyre before the flames had touched him. He was unconscious, but he had no burns.

When Dali, Kunzie, Isten Balogh and other exiles arrived at the scene, the growing darkness made the pyre, its huge flames fed by the easterly wind from the sea, an appalling sight. The pumps of the old fire engine were too weak for the roaring flames.

Marky was carried to the Turkish military hospital.

Around ten, the last flames of the pyre died, and the black, velvety July night closed in over the city.

Kunzie remained at Marky's bedside in the hospital, while Dali sat on a wooden bench in the hospital's corridor.

Shortly after midnight, Kunzie appeared in the corridor and said to Dali: "He just died."

Dali stood up and nodded. He said nothing.

A few days later a rumor went through Turkey that seven Magyar hussars had burned on a pyre in Istanbul. Seven is a cabalistic number in the Orient. When the rumor reached Thracia and the Kurd districts, and later in Persia, the seven men were not Hungarian hussars but Tserkeses and Turkomans whose rebellious race the new czar, Alexander II, had decided to exterminate. The numbers were now spoken of as seven times seven, and the pyre death had now occured not in Istanbul, but on the peak of the highest mountain in the Caucasus. The farther the legend spread, the larger grew the number of martyrs and the size of the pyre. In Bokhara and among the Uzbeks, it was said that the pyre was built of ancient forests on the top of the Himalayas, and it was so huge that it lit the furthest corners of Asia and of the Far East, where the oppressed and unfortunate roamed.

7

At the end of Sptember, Dali received a letter from Flexi, who wrote:

I strongly believe in a general amnesty in the near future. I thought of you, Dali, in relation to my planned glass and porcelain factory. I would be glad to see you as the general manager of that factory, which may grow to be the biggest in Europe. This position would mean for you, financially, more income than you can hope for from your Gere estate. You are still young, Dali. We will be forty-two on October 1. Don't forget that our Dukay grandfather was fifty-seven when he remarried. I hope you have not given up the thought of a second marriage. Maria Augusta has two very fine ladies in mind for you. . . ."

Dali answered the letter the same day:

Although we are twins, only you will be forty-two next week. Age does not depend on the number of years one has lived, but on what one has lived through. In that respect, I hope you don't mind if I boast that I am eighty-four.

Thank you, Flexi for your kind thought for my future in your factory, but I don't feel qualified for that high position. And please convey my most grateful thanks to Maria Augusta for thinking of me. Alas, I really feel too old for a second marriage. I am too old and—I'm telling it only to you—I think I am sick. Something is wrong with my famous health, but don't alarm Mother, our poor, sweet Mother. Doctor Kunz says that I have no organic disease. But sometimes my whirling thoughts give me strange headaches—strange because they do not resemble any ordinary headaches. It seems to me that this is the sign or symptom of my extreme tiredness.

Last Monday, during my solitary stroll along the Golden Horn Bay, suddenly I felt such a weakness that I had to sit down on a boulder, and although a dead and rotting dog lay only a few feet from me on the ground, giving off a suffocating stench, I couldn't move for a long time. Later, resuming my slow walk in the twilight, I had the strange feeling that the whole world, the whole of mankind is nothing but a huge, dead, rotting animal. No, I am not having a nervous breakdown. But since the shameful Treaty of Paris, even Alphie's letter says that in the glorious and victorious France there has been much gloomy talk.

Here there are many dire warnings that the Western World is hurtling toward disaster on its worst wave of impotence and stupidity. I know that it is an insult to the greater and more civilized part of the world to exaggerate by such prophecies of doom, but you cannot imagine the emotional intensity of that small human community in which I live. Rolly's last letter reproached me for not accepting her invitation to live with them in Paris. I lived there for almost two years when I returned from America, and I don't mean it now as a sermon when I say that 'Man lives not by bread alone.'

You certainly will understand that my mind could not escape (either in a fine Paris restaurant or in the luxury of a Bavarian castle) the thought of how Cornet Zih, Major Marky and many other comrades have died here, in a morbid exaltation of patriotic desperation. I am not hoping for such a solution for myself. But I cannot help thinking that these men are the victims not only of hashish, but of the historical reality of our century. I cannot help but remember the fates of such noble figures as Lord Castlereagh, Count Széchenyi, and now, as the rumor says, Bertalan Szemere, the last prime minister of the Kossuth cabinet.

If I have any disease, I don't say that it is the disease of our century. But I think I'm close to the truth when I say that my disease is caused by the realization that my whole life has been a terrible failure. I was not good as a hero. When I was sixteen, my 'participation' in the Warsaw revolution was but a childish adventure. I was not a hero, either, in our War for Liberty, or in the Crimean War. I don't want to say that I am all guilty because I didn't die on the battlefields with a bullet in my stomach. Still, I have the feeling that everyone is guilty who survived that cataclysm or remained sane.

But don't take my letter as a farewell. After my strange dizziness last Monday, Kunzie ordered a large glass of hot, red wine (three times a day) with plenty of honey and black pepper, and now I feel fine again.

Do you remember Olga's story of what happened when we were born? Olga asked the midwife, Frau Oberfelderkämpfer, Which is the firstborn? And when she answered, Olga thought she was not sure. In the general excitement of delivering twin boys instead of a girl, she had forgotten to notice which was the firstborn.

Therefore you and I have never known if you were me or I were you. Remember what Mother once said to us in Septemvir Utca, when we were ten years old. With tears in her eyes, she drew us both to her and said: 'I have never thought that I had twin sons. You are two in reality, but one in heart, one in soul—you are my *only* son!' and she embraced us both laughingly. Do you remember?

Don't forget that embrace, Flexi. That *only* son of hers will survive us. If I am to die first, I will live in you.

But for the time being both of us will celebrate our forty-second birthday tomorrow. Don't forget to tell my son, Ádám that . . ."

Dali did not finish the sentence because Kunzie entered his room.

"How do you feel, Your Excellency?" Kunzi asked his routine question, jokingly giving Dali his title.

"Thank you, Mr. Doctor-in-Chief," Dali said, "I feel fine."

Kunzie informed Dali that the comrades had arranged a festive dinner party to celebrate his birthday, and "to torture you with endless speeches." Then he added:

"Fortunately, Isten Balogh wrote a poem to toast you. He read it to me. The poem is long and rich in selected obscenities, to keep the party in high feather."

The next day, October 1, 1856, at five in the evening, some sixty comrades appeared for the party. The tables had been set in the yard because the only room available proved to be too small even for six guests. The guests brought along with them their knives, forks, spoons, glasses and plates; but the food, drink, and tobacco was provided by The Bank of Exile (meaning Dali's pocket) as it had been on the occasions of other such gatherings.

By half past five, the comrades were drinking and singing old folksongs. But Dali had not arrived. Kunzie and Isten Balogh went over to the next street, where Dali lived in a thatched house he rented from an old Turk. The door was open but Dali's room was empty. So was the yard, and so was the small stable, except for Falcon, who was neighing loudly.

Kunzie and Isten Balogh went back to Dali's room to investigate. There they found Dali's unfinished letter to Flexi, and while Kunzie held it in his hand, Isten Balogh read it over Kunzie's shoulder.

"It doesn't sound like a suicide letter," Kunzie said. Putting the letter down, Kunzie went to the kitchen, followed by Isten Balogh, who did not exclude the possibility of suicide. They climbed to the attic, then down to the cellar. Isten Balogh was preparing his nerves to find Dali hanged or lying in a pool of blood. But Dali was nowhere about.

Seeing the old Turk returning home, Kunzie shouted at him across the large yard:

"Did you see the captain leave?"

"I saw him in the morning," the old man shouted back, "when he returned from his ride."

"Did he say anything to you?"

"Nothing. He only said before I left that there was not enough hay."

Falcon's neighing was heard again from the stable. Now he was clearly complaining that he had not got any hay today.

The old Turk went toward the small haystack in the corner of the yard. Then he shouted in a frightened voice:

"Here he is!"

Kunzie and Isten Balogh dashed to the haystack.

Dali lay on the ground, face up, the pitchfork fallen out of his hand.

His eyes were open, staring, but sightless.

Kunzie bent down gently and closed Dali's eyes, in the same expert manner he had employed when he had rendered the same service to Andris Zeker seven years before, and with the same solemn tenderness.

Standing over Dali's body, Isten Balogh took off his red Turkish fez.

8

When the exiles, still awaiting Dali's appearance at their celebration, learned that he would never come for dinner again, the gay singing broke off. In deep silence, they gazed at one another, each keeping his own thoughts to himself, many with tears in their eyes.

Kunzie and the old Turk laid Dali on a large table, which served as a temporary bier in the center of the yard. For a pillow, the old Turk put Falcon's bag of oats under Dali's head. Then he extended the right arm of the body, as if Dali wanted to offer his friends his open hand for a last handshake. It was an ancient oriental tradition, to allow the dead this last mute farewell.

The comrades filled the yard. Slowly they passed the simple bier, each stopping for a moment to touch Dali's extended cold hand. Then they walked away.

After the last comrade had passed, the old Turk folded back the extended arm, before death should make it stony.

The festive birthday party that night became a funeral feast. There were no speeches, no singing, no loud talk, no laughter.

Isten Balogh's obscene poem remained in his pocket unread, and Captain Vay did not open the shabby case of his violin, which he always brought to such gatherings. The night was quiet except for the usual Istanbul sounds. Two dogs barked at each other across a great distance, as if they were quarreling from two distant stars in the cloudless sky. From a house across the street, the carpenter's saw and hammer were heard. Kunzie, who organized the funeral, decided on an oak coffin.

The next day they buried Dali in the Magyar cemetery where Cornet Zih, Major Marky and so many others of the remnants of the Kossuth army were buried. The ceremony was performed by an old Armenian Catholic priest. Then the comrades sang the Latin psalm: *Nos habemus unum amicum bonum* . . .

Besides the nearly seventy comrades, there were women in the mourning crowd, the wives who followed their husbands into exile in the fall of 1849. The sole representative of the Istanbul diplomatic corps was the French clerk who had handled Dali's letters through the French embassy.

And there were two ladies, standing by the grave as far from one another as they could: a beautiful Tsherkes girl from one of the bazaars which sold rugs, ancient copper, silver wares and love; and a tall lady, seemingly from the exclusive Pera district, with an aristocratic profile, elegantly dressed and looking as if she felt herself the only mourner in the whole cemetery. No one knew them. Dali carried their secrets to the grave.

After the psalm singing, Isten Balogh laid a wreath of red roses on the grave. On its ribbon, black letters read: "To our beloved Prime Minister in Exile."

Everybody had come to the funeral with a few flowers. Now they placed them on the grave, and left the cemetery in silence.

On the unpainted wooden cross was written:

Count Adalbert Árpád Maurycy Dukay
1814-1856

When the telegram reached Vienna, the family decided not to tell Countess Jadi that Dali had died. She was over sixty, and losing her strength so rapidly that the doctor had ordered her to remain in bed.

A few days after Dali's funeral in Istanbul, his belongings

were sent to the des Fereyolles in Paris. There were two large canvas bags. They contained the tattered hussar uniform he had worn in the War for Liberty; the black attila, almost new, which he had ordered for the "great journey" with Kossuth in England and America; the bright-blue French-style Turkish uniform; a shabby civilian suit which he had worn in Zekerd while he was Herr Heinrich Stenkl; a box of letters from his family and friends, and another box of letters from unknown ladies; an egg-sized ivory miniature of his mother painted in Warsaw when she was young; and the water color of his daughter, Sonya, done by her step-father, Sylvester Bralin. Among the small items were his golden pocket watch, his silver pocket knife, scissors for pedicuring, a deck of French cards for solitaire, a large notebook, and some forty Hungarian, German, French and English books.

His horse, Falcon, was sent back to Paris together with the two canvas bags.

On a shiny April morning in 1857, some six months after Dali's death, Countess Jadi called for Dali's son, Ádám, who at eighteen was a perfect image of his father at that age. As she did every week, Countess Jadi started to dictate a letter in answer to a recent letter from Dali which, though it was dated in Istanbul, had been forged by Flexi.

"I feel so much better now," Countess Jadi dictated to Ádám, "that I strongly hope to see you very soon, perhaps in June, either in Paris or in Istanbul. Last week, Flexi visited his godfather—he was eighty-four in March—and Metternich told him that great things are to come, and . . ."

In the middle of the sentence she slowly closed her eyes, and never opened them again.

CHAPTER FOURTEEN

THE SECOND HALF OF THE century, known as the "Victorian Peace Period" to the world (the "Franz Josef Era" in the Danube Valley, and the "Count Flexi Epoch" in the four Dukay domains), was almost uneventful in terms of revolutions and romantic wars for liberty in Europe.

The voice of the century's early decades had been the voice of Petöfi, who had sung:

> I wish to die on the battlefield
> Among those who are dying for you:
> Freedom of the World!

Heaven had granted his wish. Soon after he wrote these lines, he was killed at Segesvár by Russian Cossacks at the age of twenty-six.

The voice of the century's second half was that of Tennyson, who consecrated his genius to the noble service of humanity and, ennobled by the Queen, died at the age of eighty-three as Lord Tennyson. He had a lovely vista of the future when he sang about the approaching and much happier twentieth century:

> . . . when the war-drums throbb'd no longer,
> And the battle-flags were furled
> In the Parliament of Man:
> The Federation of the World!

A few months after Dali's unromantic death in Istanbul, Tennyson's optimism seemed justified to many sober minds. Here and there a few promising rays penetrated Europe's darkness. The terror in Hungary lessened. It raged only in the barbershops. If the Austrian *Polizei* caught a Magyar in the streets with a Kossuth beard, he was escorted to the nearest barbershop, from which the hairy patriot emerged with a cleanshaven loyal Austrian face.

These were the days of passive resistance in Hungary. In a most loyal small town, the "Butchershop of Archduke Albrecht" depicted the head of a boghorn ox on its large signboard, the ox's face, with its bulging eyes, curiously resembling that of His Imperial and Royal Highness, Archduke Albrecht, Viceroy of Hungary.

In Buda the window of the "Grocery of the Two-Legged Black Dog," displayed a large gold-framed picture of young Emperor Franz Josef, wreathed with garlic. Underneath the picture, where the icon night light should have stood, was a small green bottle of rat-poison.

But the most effective weapon was the misprint. Thanks to its patriotic printers, the mourning nation often found something to laugh at in the papers. The single omission of the second acute accent in Franz Josef's title, *Ausztria császára*, meaning Emperor of Austria, changed the emperor's title to "Excrement of Austria." Fortunately for the printers, these misprints escaped the eyes of the Austrian censors, whose Hungarian was poor.

In 1858 Franz Josef's young and beautiful Empress, Elisabeth, who was known to be deeply sympathetic with the Hungarian tragedy, produced her first child, a blue-eyed boy. Ecstatic commentators predicted a long and happy reign for the newborn crown prince Rudolf.

In 1859, in a secret agreement with Victor Emmanuel, Napoleon III promised to help Northern Italy throw off the yoke of the Habsburgs. Franz Josef's hesitant, two-faced policy toward the West and Russia had alienated him not only from Great Britain and Prussia, but from Czar Alexander II as well. Misprints in the Hungarian papers multiplied rapidly.

Lajos Kossuth, who had once sold fire insurance policies in London, now lived in Italy and was selling the fire of liberty. A secret meeting with Napoleon III produced a plan to revive the Hungarian War for Liberty; it was to be a knife thrust in Franz Josef's back while French troops were pouring into Northern Italy.

"The emperor was so enthusiastic about the idea that he lit

393

his tobacco (neatly curled in thin paper and called a *cigarette*), one after another by the lamp chimney while we talked," wrote Kossuth to one of his friends.

In June, 1859, Napoleon and Victor Emmanuel entered and liberated Milan; but the revived Hungarian War for Liberty remained only a dream.

"Poor Dali," Flexi remarked, "would have died a second death learning that news."

Old Metternich responded to this dreadful blow to the Habsburg monarchy's prestige in his own grandiose style: the Italian and French troops entered Milan on June 8, and three days later, on June 11, 1859, Metternich died in his Rennweg palace. Now real *magna quies* fell upon the *parva domus*. Just a few months before his death, Metternich had cheated Czar Alexander I, Talleyrand, Lord Castlereagh and other greats of the Congress of Vienna for the last time. They had left to posterity only flattering oil portraits. At 86, Metternich surrendered himself to a photographer's desk-size outfit, equipped with recently developed light-sensitive collodion and glass plates. The result was one of the most beautiful photographs of the day. It told the truth about him. The perfect likeness of the old chancellor revealed the dignity of the eighteenth century. But Metternich wore the latest fashion of the nineteenth century, striped trousers and English cutaway, with elegance, and betrayed not a sign of weakness or old age. With its high brow, its forceful and aristocratic nose, the face was that of a great actor—an actor who as a youth had played Romeo, in manhood Richard III on the stage of world politics.

Two years later, at the ripe age of ninety-one Prince Adam Czartoryski died too, in exile in Paris. His dreams of Poland's liberation were not realized, but by then Hungary's future seemed hopeful. In 1866, an editorial in a Buda-Pesth paper said: "While the Industrial Revolution sank the first cable deep in the Atlantic Ocean, in the ocean of Hungarian tears the first blueprint of our country's new constitution was laid in Vienna."

The "no mercy!" Franz Josef had become conciliatory, because Austria badly needed the Hungarian hussars.

In these years Thomas Carlyle worked feverishly on his volume about Frederick the Great, as if he knew in advance that the coming decades would bring glory to the Prussian sword. Bismarck wanted Austria, so influential in German affairs in the "Metternich decades," pushed out of German territories. At the Prussian Diet he announced his purpose with brutal frankness: ". . . not by speeches and votes of majority, but by blood and iron!"

In June, 1866, Prussia declared war on Austria, and in the decisive battle of Königgratz Austria was miserably defeated.

Soon after suffering this defeat, Franz Josef agreed to rule two separate and independent states: the Austrian Empire and the Kingdom of Hungary, each having its own constitution and its own Parliament, one in Vienna, the other in Buda-Pesth. The "Reconciliation" in 1867 became the miraculous rebirth of Hungary.

The same year, Claudia Rhédey's son Francis, Duke of Teck, married Adelaide, the niece of Queen Victoria. Flexi and his wife were invited to the royal wedding in London. Although Francis was not *ebenbürtig* (of equal birth), Queen Victoria gave her permission for the marriage. Chatting kindly with the new relatives, she told Maria Augusta, glancing at the tall and elegant Francis, who had inherited Claudia's raven-black hair:

"I am glad to have this young man in our family. Our unrelieved fair hair and blue eyes make our blood lymphatic, don't you think so?"

After the Reconciliation, Franz Josef and Queen Elisabeth were legally crowned with the Saint Crown. The solemn pageant at the coronation in Buda-Pesth marked a unique moment in history, a moment when both a sovereign and a nation enjoyed the sweetness of genuine forgiveness.

On the day of the coronation clemency was extended to all the Kossuth-*hunds,* with the exception of the *hund*-in-chief. Lajos Kossuth was not permitted to return from his Italian exile. The decision—as Western liberal papers stated—unquestionably reflected the fact that Kossuth was too great for Franz Josef. The last remnants of the Kossuth army, among them Dali's former friends, Doctor Ignatz Kunz (Kunzie) and Isten Balogh, returned to Hungary after eighteen years in exile.

One September morning three months after the coronation,

when the trees in Ararat park had donned their most colorful vestments, Baron Erich Dukay-Hedwitz, the custodian of the estate, asked old Pogány, who, after Dali's death, had returned to Ararat:

"What is that?" His silver-handled crop pointed to a heap of large pigskin valises.

"His excellency Count Antal and his family will arrive from Bavaria to take possession of the castle and the entail," reported old Pogány, as if Flexi's return were the most natural thing in the world.

That morning Erich did not go for his usual ride in Ararat park. Turning back to the stairs with slow steps, so that he should not, even to himself, seem to be fleeing, he returned to his suite. There he feverishly packed his belongings. He left the castle within an hour. He was a gentleman. He did not take any treasure from the castle with him except the prettiest maid, who had been his mistress in recent years.

In October, 1867, a great double wedding took place in Ararat castle. Flexi's eldest son, Peter, married a Baroness Zoskay; and Ádám, Dali's son, married a commoner, Klara Marky, daughter of the late Major Marky.

Placing a resplendent seal on the Reconciliation, the royal couple visited the castles of Magyar aristocrats. In 1868, at eleven on a bright spring day, a trumpet sounded from the tower of Ararat, signaling that the royal coach had entered the park. Fifty-four-year-old Count Flexi, dressed in a gala Hungarian uniform with a cherry-red velvet *dolmány,* an egret feather on his zibeline cap, hurried from the door to the gilded coach, drawn by six horses, and took the arm of the slender Empress Elisabeth. The thirty-eight-year-old Franz Josef stepped nimbly from the coach. A third passenger, a colonel, then darted out, pulled at the skirt of the empress and whispered something to her. The colonel was nine-year-old Crown Prince Rudolf. Franz Josef wore a mourning band on the sleeve of his marshal's uniform in memory of his younger brother, Maximilian, who had died the year before in Mexico, the only Habsburg emperor to fall before a firing squad.

During lunch, although Gustave Flaubert called the trend of this decade "steammania," and the first wagons-lit had already created an international sensation, the conversation between hostess Maria Augusta and Empress Elisabeth, also a great equestrienne, was only of horses.

After lunch, the royal family was led to the marble stables where, following tradition, black coffee and cognac were served. Carpets and armchairs had been set up in the carefully cleaned stable. The stable master reported all the data on the horses, races, ages, parents, and grandparents. When the Empress admired a beautiful gelding and asked if it was for sale, Count Flexi pleaded with her majesty to be gracious enough to accept the horse as a gift.

When the royal entrourage was leaving the marble stables, one of the horses lashed out with its heels. Fortunately its hoof only brushed Franz Josef's coat. Maria Augusta, as a polite hostess, wanted to have the horse shot instantly, but the empress pleaded for its life. The stable boys, telling the story later, said that the frisky bay mare was Falcon V, the daughter of Dali's one-time battlehorse, but this was thought to be a legend rather than a fact.

On April 7, 1869, Edmond and Jules, the Goncourt brothers, wrote in their diary in Paris:

They say that Bertholet, our great physicist, predicts that in 1969, a hundred years from now, thanks to discoveries in physical and chemical science, men will have learned what constitutes the atom, and will be able at will to extinguish and light up the sun as if it were a gas lamp. And the great chemist, Claude Bernard has declared that man will be so completely the master of organic life as to compete with God. He will create life. To all this we raise no objection. But we have the feeling that, when this time comes, God, with his white beard, will come to earth swinging a bunch of keys, and say, the way they do at five o'clock in the saloon, "Closing time, gentlemen!"

After long years of unbelievable effort, Europe and the Far East were brought nearer together by the opening of the Suez Canal in November, 1869. In December, Dr. Ignatz Kunz was baptized, and magyarized his name to Imre Kun. "Kun" meant an ancient Turkish tribe. Kunzie wrote it proudly, in remembrance of his years in Istanbul.

The brightness of the great peace period in 1870 was marred

by a war between France and Prussia, but it lasted only six weeks. The great battle of Sedan actually ended the war with the capture of Napoleon III. The war parties in France and Prussia, who were looking for a pretext for conflict, found the "bloody sword" under the vacant Spanish throne. Prussia wanted a Hohenzollern king, but France did not like the idea of having a Prussian prince on the Spanish throne. After Paris surrendered in 1871, France was declared a republic for the third time; and in the former palace of the French king at Versailles, Prussia's King William was proclaimed emperor of the newborn German Empire.

Two years later mankind's fundamental problem emerged in Francis Galton's theory: eugenics. The problem was not only quantity, as Malthus had thought a half century before, but quality. There are, Galton said, too many hereditary diseases, too many sick people, physically and mentally.

In the first part of the century, newspapers were too costly to spread news effectively among the masses. *The Times* of London had then cost eighteen cents a copy—the price of a good dinner in those good old days. In the latter half of the century, low priced dailies were available in every village throughout Europe. The press, publishing every sort of useful information, was a blessing to millions. A Buda-Pesth illustrated magazine published sensational pictures of two hitherto unknown creatures: one the recently discovered wild man in Africa, scientifically called gorilla-gorilla; the other Masayoshi Matsukata, a statesman from the mystic Empire of the Rising Sun. The accompanying article stated that after six months in captivity, the gorilla had learned fluent English, and the Japanese statesmen was so intelligent he could write with his left foot. There was no limit to the "true" stories of the new world press.

Mankind no longer had any great problems. In India the huge population crevasse created by the latest famine, in which one fourth of the people of the Crissa district perished, was rapidly filled by the amazingly high birth rate. In the British Polo Club in Delhi, the only topic discussed was whether there should be a change in the rule limiting the height of the ponies to fourteen hands.

The Dowager-Empress of China, with the infant Emperor

Kuang-Su in her lap, threw her most beautiful smiles to the Western ambassadors. To Europe's ruling class, Hindu *parishas* and Chinese coolies were only "unskilled laborers" with no human souls. Africa? Good for a few safaris for elephant and lion hunters. Trouble in Kenya? The British Foreign Office sent a single clerk; and he challenged the witch doctor who had incited the native rioters.

"Let's see," the Briton said to the witch doctor, "which one of us can work the greatest miracle?"

When the witch doctor agreed to the contest, the Briton opened his mouth wide, and with one grab, and without any howl of pain, he pulled out all of his 32 teeth. Placing his denture on the table, he said to the witch doctor: "Try the same!"

The natives ran the witch doctor off and bowed before the British clerk.

The young United States of America had a different way of showing its growing power. At the Centennial Exposition in 1876 in Philadelphia, a new miraculous electric device was exhibited. Its name, derived from two Greek words, was *telephone*.

On January 1, of the next year, 1877, Queen Victoria was proclaimed Empress of India, with all the pomp and magnificence of ancient Moguls. But the brilliance of the great peace period was again marred by war. When Russia decided to undertake the defense of the Balkan Slavs, the sultan was beaten by Czar Alexander II so badly that Turkish rule in Europe seemed to come to an end.

The outcome of the Russian-Turkish war in 1877-78 did not disturb Flexi's business ventures. The Trieste-Istanbul Steamship Company, the San Francisco Chemical Corporation and the Melbourne-Sidney Railway—were shrewdly guided by his old friends in the London Rothschild House. The Dukay estate, at the height of its economic achievements, was ready for a great task; to serve as model for the estates of progressive aristocrats throughout Europe.

The embodiment of the conservative aristocrats' "pig philosophy" was a great pig (as caricatured in a Brussels comic paper), the corpulent, bearded Albert Edward, Prince of

Wales, "that rascal of a turf-winding, boozing, rowdy . . . " as an Australian paper called him. The article did not diminish the prince's popularity, but such freedom of the press made Great Britain greater.

Mankind was happy, except for some terrifying moments.

. . . and it was a terrifying moment [Flexi wrote his wife from London]. Hungary was leading an inch or two when Lord Haddington's Fever II jumped on him, and Tom, my jockey was dragged off the saddle and tumbled to the ground. Hungary ran away and fell head over heels, two legs broken. You can imagine my feelings. I am not superstitious, but now I am sorry that I called the colt Hungary. But I was a hundred per cent sure, you and our stablemaster, too, that this grandson of Falcon VI would win the Derby and bring Hungary fame and glory.

Dr. Imre Kun (Kunzie) in 1878 wrote a paper titled "The Duct System of the Gall Bladder and Liver," which earned him a professorship at the Pazmany University in Buda-Pesth, and the same fall, when called to the bedside of the Empress Elisabeth for a consultation, he received a praedicatum to his name; thereafter he was Professor Imre Kun de Kunfalva.

Patriotic Hungarian university students, at the suggestion of Professor Kun de Kunfalva, erected a marble tombstone in Kerepesi cemetery for Prince Mycislav Voronieczki; for by now, nearly three decades after his martyrdom, the small wooden cross on his unkept grave had fallen down. Mycie's tombstone preserved the memory of the extinct Polish family.

In the following three years the list of dead became richer.

In 1879 Baron Erich Dukay-Hedwitz, retired colonel of the dragoons, was one of 132 victims of a railway catastrophe between Vienna and Innsbruck. He was seventy-one, a bachelor.

In 1880, Sonya Bralin, the former Dushenka Arkadievna Bobak, whose marriage to Dali had been annulled in 1842 by the Orthodox Church, died in Novgorod at sixty-three. She had been suffering from heart disease. The flag on the Lomonosoff Theater flew at half mast the day the onetime star of *Cupid and Psyche* died.

Two years later in 1882, Czar Alexander II, who after the first night of *Cupid and Psyche,* had said: "Mademoiselle Bobak does not have to sing—she is herself a song," after twenty-six years on the Russian throne, died a most horrible death. The son of Nick the Stick, believing himself a liberal, travelled unguarded. The streets were never closed when he left the Winter Palace. One March day, near the Ekaterinski Canal, an elderly, shabbily dressed pedestrian hurled a bomb before the open royal carriage. When the czar, uninjured, left the carriage to inspect the wounded horses, an eighteen-year-old girl flung a second bomb at the czar's boots, from a distance of five steps. Although both the czar's legs were blown off, it took him hours to die. His one-time mistress, Princess Yaravskaya, cut her famous very long blond hair that Alexander had so loved and placed it in the czar's coffin with the simple note: "From your Katya."

In the following year of 1883, Karl Marx died at sixty-five, in London, alienated from all his friends. European papers called communism an extinct practice of primitive society, antedating the early Cretans; and later a pious but unsuccessful experiment of the Franciscans, the "Brothers of the Common Lot." The papers agreed that the Communist Manifesto had gone with Herr Marx to its well-deserved grave after producing nothing.

But the most sensational death was in 1889, in the tragedy of Crown Prince Rudolf, thirty-two, only son of Emperor Franz Josef. When on the cold morning of January 30, Rudolf and his companion, young Baroness Maria Vetsera, were found dead at Mayerling in the imperial hunting lodge, some forty miles from Vienna, the court imposed complete secrecy on those few who knew the truth. The police were banned from the investigation. All evidence and witnesses disappeared. The court's first official communiqué stated that Rudolf had died of apoplexy; the second attributed his death to a heart attack; and the third "confessed" that it was suicide. Dr. Herman von Wiederhoffer, court physician, while preparing Rudolf's body to lie in state, extracted pieces of glass from Rudolf's skull. Talking about the Mayerling tragedy, old Kunzie said to his friends: "Crown Prince Rudolf was the first man in history to succeed in beating himself to death with a champagne bottle."

Among the seventeen versions, one said that Maria Vetsera killed him during a drunken orgy, mutilating her lover sexually, then in a rage Rudolf's butler killed the young baroness.

Other versions held that one of Maria's jealous lovers killed both of them; that the conservative Jesuits killed liberal Rudolf; that Kaiser Wilhelm had engineered the murder; that Alexander III, the new Russian czar, was responsible; that the Habsburg court had liquidated Rudolf because he was too radical, and that Franz Josef had acquiesced in the murder of his own son.

Kossuth's popularity grew higher and higher year by year. In a steady flow, old friends, young journalists, historians, publishers, aristocratic families, delegations of peasants and the new working class, representing the whole of the nation, visited Lajos Kossuth in his Italian exile.

In 1892, the seventy-eight year old Flexi headed the largest delegation to the modest house in Turin to honor the "Great Exile" on his ninetieth birthday.

"I came to greet you," Flexi said to Kossuth, meeting him for the first time, "first of all in the name of my late brother, Dali, if Your Serenity remembers him."

Flexi addressed him as "Your Serenity" because Kossuth had been the regent of Hungary in 1849. But Kossuth had never claimed Metternich's title.

Two years later, Lajos Kossuth died, without again seeing the country he had left on an August night forty-five years before. In his worn-out purse he had preserved the pinch of dust he had picked up on the Danube shore at Orsova before he stepped into the boat for Turkey. His death at ninety-two made headlines throughout the world. "Great men live long," the papers commented: "Talleyrand and Metternich to eighty-six, Czartoryski to ninety-one and Kossuth to ninety-two."

Lajos Kossuth soon established another record no man could outdo. Within a few years after his death, nearly a hundred statues of him had been erected throughout Hungary.

In the following year, 1895, another member of the Dukay family died. Flexi's wife, the former Maria Augusta, Duchess of Schönheim-Altstadt, mother of four, grandmother of nine, after fifty-four years of happy marriage, succumbed in Vienna at seventy-nine.

Early in the spring of 1896, old Flexi, after his usual half-hour trot on the Buda hills in the saddle of his favorite horse,

Alarm, suffered a light heart attack while climbing the two flights of steps to his bedroom. The consulting physicians, headed by Professor Irme Kun, strictly forbade further horseback riding.

2

The beautiful sunset of the century seemed to bear out Metternich's prediction that the nineteenth century would be a very happy one—at least in the inexhaustible genius of French humor. A caricature in a Paris paper showed the too-large family of kings and emperors in the world, all dressed in scarlet. The drawing depicted Queen Victoria, surrounded by her family circle of four sons, five daughters, thirty-one grandchildren, thirty-seven great-grandchildren, all sitting on European thrones or chamberpots. Among them were two great II-s, the fiercely mustached Kaiser Wilhelm II and the melancholy Czar Nicholas II; both were grandsons of Victoria.

The scarlet sunset of the century produced two brilliant spectacles of such oriental pomp they out-did all past pagentries. Both occurred in the summer of 1896.

The first was the coronation of Czar Nicholas II, great grandson of Czar Nicholas I. The purpose of the fabulous and solemn coronation of twenty-year-old Nicholas II was not only to impress the Russian people, but to dazzle the spectators in the "royal boxes" of Europe and the tribunes of world politics. Some saw the spectacle as a polite show of Russia's fist, which had grown fearfully big since the Congress of Vienna.

Grandma Victoria could not attend the St. Petersburg coronation of her beloved grandson, Niki. She was seventy-seven, and the long road from Buckingham Palace to the Winter Palace was too bumpy politically.

Most of the press, all over the world, glowingly pictured the young czar on his accession to the throne as a liberal, if not radical, crusader for world peace. Of course, the praise was not unanimous. There was some criticism in the leftist papers, because of his strong measures to Russianize Finland and Poland, and because of the leniency he had shown toward those involved in the Kishenoff massacre of Jews in Bessarabia.

It was unfortunate, but not the young czar's fault, that he suffered from melancholia. He had lived through typhoid fever at ten, and during his recent Far Eastern trip, had survived a saber cut delivered by a Japanese fanatic. No wonder, as a French correspondent reported, every second guest at the great reception in the Winter Palace was a secret agent.

The second great event was in June, when Hungary celebrated her thousandth birthday, after ten stormy centuries during which many times she had seemed very near to her grave. But now she was more than alive again: she was healthy, happy, independent, standing before another bright millenium, at least in the festive speeches. No one could blame Hungarian wives who, anticipating the effect of the great Millenium, had the night before secretly taken all the money from their husband's purses, in fear that the too patriotic males would give it away to gypsy musicians.

Triumphal arches were erected in every village, decorated with flowers, kerchiefs, bedclothes, bullet-riddled flags, rusty swords, carbines and other relics of the War for Liberty. There was no limit to the exultation of national happiness.

No one could sleep when the sun rose on the great day. The first rays lit the chignon of an oak tree on Svab Mountain. The salvo drowned the song of the orioles, but only for a few seconds. On the top of Svab Mountain still stood the dilapidated "God's Eye" hotel where Baron Dukay-Hedwitz, the young dragoon captain, had arrested Lajos Kossuth in 1837. After the salvo one could taste and smell gunpowder in the cool, clean air, and it brought back the memory of the battlefields.

At six, in the Septemvir Utca palace, old Flexi stepped from his bathroom with a newly trimmed beard and haircut. His two "young" butlers—one over seventy, the other only sixty—had dressed their master in a costume of the Angevin Period, a knee-length *choga*, which took its motif from the capes of wandering Hungarians a thousand years before. The heavy-colored silk was diagonally cut in front and crested with spangles; at the left its hem was split to accommodate the lower half of the Charlemagne sword. When dressed, the old count looked like a majestic Haliaetus Leucocephalus, or Bald Eagle. Balding old Flexi was indeed a human eagle. Even his fingers, yellow from his daily fifty cigarettes, resembled the talons of an eagle.

At seven, one of the butlers announced:

"His excellency Professor Baron Kun."

Seventy-two-year-old Kunzie had been a baron for only one and a half hours. The Millenium brought a shower of decorations, and the official bulletin had arrived at five-thirty this morning. He was the fourth prominent physician of Jewish origin to receive the title baron. Since Flexi's light heart attack the spring before, Kunzie had visited his old friend every morning for a few minutes.

He was surprised to find his patient in gala uniform.

"You are not going to ride in the procession, I hope!" he said to old Flexi.

"Why not? You think there is a Hungarian Millenium every morning? Sit down and share my breakfast," the old man commanded.

"My patients are waiting for me."

"They will live longer if you leave them alone."

The tone between them was the same as usual, but that morning they seemed more solemn and more philosophical.

"I always wondered," said Flexi, "who was right? Richelieu or Lafayette?"

"I think both of them," Kunzie opined. "History is like the rhythm of breathing—one pull, one push. One reaction, one revolution. A peace period pulls in fresh oxygen. Revolutions or war blow out the putrid air."

"I recently read an estimate," Flexi said, "that since the time of Ozymandias, nearly seven billion men have lost their lives on fields of battle."

"Who was Ozymandias?"

"You should know that, Professor. He was the first warlike king mentioned in history."

Professor Baron Kun placed a small bottle on the table, and said:

"In case you don't feel well during the day, take one of these yellow pills."

"I vividly remember a family talk," Flexi continued his topic, "when Father and his friends debated the question—suggested by King Frederick—that instead of war, quarrels between the nations be settled by a pistol duel between the two sovereigns."

"Not a bad idea," Professor Kun declared. "But I hardly believe that Grandma Victoria will fight a duel with her grandson, Kaiser Wilhelm, on the present Cameroon question."

"Well, the pitchfork mustache of the Kaiser is too arrogant," Flexi said. "Still, I strongly believe that mankind feels the need of a long rest, and in the coming centuries there will be no major war."

The English stablemaster entered to say that the horses, Alarm and Falcon, were saddled.

"Why two horses?" Kunzie asked Flexi. "Is someone to accompany you?"

"No. The other saddle will be empty. Sheer sentimentality."

"Dali?"

Flexi nodded.

"That gelding is the great-grandson of the Falcon Dali rode in the Crimean War."

The two remained silent for a few seconds. In such moments memory, brings a man to life as vividly as if he were physically present.

"Dali should have lived to ride next to me in the procession and see Hungary at the peak of her happiness and glory. I am afraid when Dali's deadly pessimism killed him, he had already lost his reason."

"I don't think so," Kunzie shook his gray head. "We discussed the topic of the death of a nation for the first time when we fled toward Turkey, after cremating Andris Zeker. The death of a nation did not mean only Hungary. If a single small nation dies, it is a horrible catastrophe. But if all the small nations die . . ."

"A nation never dies!" Flexi cut in angrily. "Never! Are you saying that today, when a small nation is celebrating . . ."

He could not finish. Kunzie touched his old friend's hand in apology, and tactfully retreated from the topic.

The Millennium procession was scheduled to start in Buda at ten in the morning, but at sunrise the crowd began to gather. There were men in white petticoats and high boots and broad hats, with silver buttons on their waistcoats; women in velvet bodices and gaily colored kerchiefs; simple, kindly faced women; pretty girls with alluring red lips, which emphasized

406

the whiteness of their teeth. Soldiers in skin-tight breeches with oak leaves on their caps shouted patriotic slogans to policemen and obscenities to the girls; young and old paraded in their Sunday best. The buildings, too, were gaily dressed, wearing banners and flags like medals on their chests. Every hotel was overcrowded, the cafés overflowed to the pavements; the gypsy music rose and fell at each street corner. It was the thousandth birthday of a nation.

English dukes came to see the 1100 noble horses of the 1100 noblemen who came from every county to swear allegiance to the King and his Crown in the national celebration. The nobles who were to ride in the procession wore the garb of their ancestors, while their noble horses wore harnesses of silver and turquoise. The brocades and silk tights, fur-trimmed coats and velvet tunics would have been too theatrical and fantastic had it not been a courtly pageant, proper in every detail. The fairy princes were real princes; the huge jewels real jewels; the fur the same that, a few months, years, or decades before had covered a running wolf or bear, hunted by the very men who now wore the skins.

The nobles passed in dazzling, glittering groups, each proud and fierce-eyed, like living portraits of old masters. Among them, in the saddle of Alarm, rode the tallest and proudest nobleman of all . . . the eighty-two year old Count Antal Dukay *de genere* Ordony.

Old Flexi looked about him at a sea of brocades, silks and velvets, a sea of a hundred upon a hundred thousand exalted spectators, everyone shouting or weeping in ecstacies of joy and pride. He heard around him the music, the shouting, the singing, and he said to himself:

"This is what Dali called 'the death of a nation!' "

He waved his jewelled cap to the cheering crowd and those who recognized him shouted:

"Long live Count Antal! Long live Uncle Flexi!"

In the courtyard of the royal palace, 1100 noblemen on 1100 noble horses passed in review before the tribunes of foreign diplomats, high dignitaries of the church, state and army, and representatives of the world press, which Gladstone had called a new world power.

Everyone rose when Franz Josef stepped to the balcony of the palace. The Empress Elisabeth appeared in deep black. She had worn black ever since the death of her only son, Crown Prince Rudolf, in Mayerling.

When the procession passed before the balcony, Franz Josef stood and saluted. Amid the frantic shouts of Long live the king! amid the blare of military bands, the ringing of bells, the thunder of big guns, the figure of Franz Josef standing on the balcony seemed to grow heroic, and everyone viewed him as a momumental ruler. Everybody except a few foreign journalists, among them Robert Davis from the *New York Sun,* who jotted in his notebook: "The unkingly, sixty-six-year-old, 5'6" little emperor, in his padded and tightly-laced General's uniform, wearing smug side-whiskers, looked like a retired Austrian Police Inspector, with fond memories of famous murder cases and an advanced stomach ulcer."

After the review, the procession passed through Buda and over the Chain Bridge toward the parliament on the left shore of the Danube. The sky was blue, the sun warm. Soft June breezes waved the flags and stirred the leaves in the hillside gardens of that prominence on which Buda stands, above centuries and floods. The breeze rippled the Danube, so that it flashed like a thousand hiliographs. The sun shone on the uniforms, making them even brighter. The jewels glittered and the sword blades of the attendant cavalry reflected the dazzling colors. But for Flexi the sun was too strong. He felt an alarming weakness, first in his legs and thighs, then in his hand, which had difficulty in holding the reigns firmly. Falcon, pacing riderless next to Alarm, grew nervous from the loud music and frantically shouting crowd.

Professor Baron Kun, who had followed the ceremony from its start, fought his way through the throngs of pedestrians to keep pace with the slowly moving procession. He did not take his eyes off his old friend, Dali's twin brother, although the crowd pressed him to the buildings, sometimes with such force that the sleeves of his black redingote became white from lime.

"Good morning, Professor!" Flexi shouted to him from the saddle.

He waved his cap again to the cheering people. But a few

minutes later he felt dizzy, as if he were drunk. He had the strange feeling that the crowd was whirling around, especially when he passed a group of university students singing the national anthem *Isten áldd meg a magyart* . . . "God bless the Magyar . . . Bring him joy and wealth . . . He has been punished already . . . For the past and future as well . . ."

The strong young voices singing the old song brought a happy sob from Flexi with each melancholy line. He still felt dizzy, and now the buildings were distorted, too. The small renaissance palaces peered at him, assuming human faces. Balconies were mustaches, doorways were opened mouths, windows, eyes. The irregular blackened roofs were hats, with flags for feathers. The buildings, like the crowd, seemed to be laughing, singing and swaying in uneven cadence.

Then old Flexi felt a sharp pain in his heart. He held the reigns of the dancing Falcon in his left hand and, with his right, reached into the deep pocket of the knee-length *choga,* his fingers desperately searching for the little bottle of yellow pills.

The pocket was empty. Now he vividly remembered leaving the medicine on the round table next to a blue glass plate. Realizing that the absence of the pills left him a victim to his malady, he felt that life had turned its back on him, and the cold sweat of panic glistened on his forehead.

Some twenty paces distant, Professor Baron Kun, elbowing his way through the throng, suddenly cried: "Oh, Lord!" as if seeing a tiler on a tower stumble and pitch down a steep, slippery roof.

"Let me pass! . . . I am a doctor! . . . Let me through!" he pleaded as he fought his way in the singing crowd.

Now, not only Falcon's but Alarm's saddle was empty. The slender legs of the other horses in the procession gracefully and cautiously stepped past the old man who lay on the cobblestones. Falcon, whose reins slipped out of the old man's hand, ran so wildly that women and children screamed as he broke through the line of fleeing spectators.

The procession halted for a few seconds. Riders jumped out of their saddles; in the sudden tumult a lady leaned down and pressed her perfumed handkerchief upon the old man's bleeding skull. The students, without interrupting their hymn singing, made way for those who carried the body, tenderly holding the arms and the legs in their lemon-yellow buskins. The long, straight sword, sheathed in blue velvet, with silver chains through the hilt, reached to the ground, and it danced and clattered as the carriers went toward the next arch and entered the gothic Matthias Church, the coronation cathedral.

The morning Mass was over, and the church was empty. Only a clerk was there, putting out the last high candles on the altar with his long stick. He was so absorbed that he did not even notice when some ten persons entered and silently laid the old count on the cool marble floor. Someone placed a velvet cushion under his head.

Face upward he lay in the dim light of the cathedral under the high gothic arches—the scene of so many coronations.

Professor Kun knelt and felt his pulse. Tensly they watched the old count's bluish lips, and the dilated eyes which seemed to be looking far away beyond the vaults of the cathedral. Professor Kun released the wrist and tenderly placed the hand on the marble floor. He stood up slowly, took a gold watch from the pocket of his dove-gray waistcoat, and solemnly announced:

"Eleven o'clock and fifty-seven minutes."

Meanwhile Falcon, with a policeman's bullet in his neck, had reached the eastern suburbs, galloping at full speed. When, with pricked-up ears, he hurtled over a railway crossing gate, it seemed that a scarlet silk kerchief was draped around his delicate neck. But it was only the glittering blood from his wound.

As the stirrup leathers hanging from the empty saddle rhythmically flapped and clattered, the great-grandson of Dali's horse seemed to fly on strange wings, as if he were a *táltos,* the magic steed of ancient Magyar folklore who fluently spoke every human language on earth.

The ringing of the bells, the ecstatic cheers, the blare of the military bands, the roar of the cannon, and the gay gypsy music gradually faded behind the *táltos* and his invisible rider, as he disappeared on the hazy June horizon with no roofs, no animals, no man in sight.

3

At the christening party of the Dukay twins, Metternich said that the nineteenth century was born October 1, 1814, at ten o'clock in the morning, when the Congress of Vienna opened for the reconstruction of Europe. According to this statement, the century should have died on October 1, 1914.

Metternich was mistaken by 60 days, 9 hours and 23 minutes. It was 7:23 P.M. on August 1, 1914, when the German Ambassador, Count Frédèric de Pourtales, left the large baroque room of Serghei Dimitrievich Sazanoff, Minister of Foreign Affairs of Imperial Russia. Pourtales' visit had been extremely brief.

When the German ambassador arrived, Nordic sunshine was pouring on the huge building of Glany Shtab at the left of the Winter Palace. "Strange, strange was that summer night, an Angry Angel beat her drum in Heaven," wrote Ady, the poet. When the door of Sazanoff's room opened, Pourtales, in a very nervous state of mind, hurried to Sazanoff. Without even greeting the Russian minister, he immediately asked him whether the Russian government was willing to give a favorable answer to Germany's ultimatum, delivered the night before.

"No," said Sazanoff, and shaking his head, he repeated: "No."

Deadly pale, Pourtales reached into his pocket.

"In that case I am authorized by my government . . ."

His voice broke. He did not finish.

Pourtales was not a Prussian. In the seventeenth century his ancient Protestant French family had emigrated to Frederick the Great's Germany. Now, as Kaiser Wilhelm's ambassador, Pourtales gave Sazanoff a sheet of paper with a trembling hand. It was Germany's declaration of war on Russia.

Then Pourtales staggered to the window, leaned to the sill and burst into tears.

The stocky and much younger Sazanoff supported the nearly sixty-year-old Pourtales, whose wrinkled face was shiny with tears.

Sazanoff wrote later in his memoirs about that last moment of the century:

"We silently embraced each other before he left the room."

411